Twisted Strands

Born in Gainsborough, Lincolnshire, Margaret Dickinson moved to the coast at the age of seven and so began her love for the sea and the Lincolnshire landscape.

Her ambition to be a writer began early and she had her first novel published at the age of twenty-five. This was followed by sixteen further titles, including *Plough the Furrow*, *Sow the Seed* and *Reap the Harvest*, which make up her Lincolnshire Fleethaven trilogy. *Twisted Strands* continues the story begun in Margaret Dickinson's most recent novel, *Tangled Threads*.

Margaret Dickinson is married with two grown-up daughters.

www.margaret-dickinson.co.uk

Margaret Dickinson

Twisted Strands

PAN BOOKS

First published 2003 by Pan Books
and simultaneously by Macmillan
an imprint of Pan Macmillan Ltd
Pan Macmillan, 20 New Wharf Road, London N1 9RR
Basingstoke and Oxford
Associated companies throughout the world
www.panmacmillan.com

ISBN 0 330 49050 8

5 7 9 8 6 4

A CIP catalogue record for this book is available from
the British Library.

Typeset by SetSystems Ltd, Saffron Walden, Essex
Printed and bound in Great Britain by
Mackays of Chatham plc, Chatham, Kent

With great affection and deep admiration
this book is dedicated to my uncle, Brian Copley,
who enlisted in 1914 at the age of sixteen in
the 8th Battalion Sherwood Foresters,
(Nottinghamshire and Derbyshire Regiment)
and served throughout the war.

Thankfully, he survived the trenches to live a long
and happy life and it has been a privilege to
share his memories and experiences through his
personal diaries of the time.

Acknowledgements

The area to the west of Grantham around Barrowby and Casthorpe, the village of Ruddington and, of course, Nottingham are once more the places of inspiration for the settings in this novel, although the story and all the characters are entirely fictitious. The siting of a factory and warehouse on Canal Street in Nottingham and the homes of all the characters within the city are also my own invention.

I am deeply grateful to Jack Smirfitt and all his colleagues at the Ruddington Framework Knitters' Museum for valuable information and advice. I also wish to thank Peter Mee, a former twisthand in the lace industry, who so kindly and generously shared his knowledge and experience with me.

My grateful thanks to all the staff of Skegness Library for their interest, encouragement and wonderful help with all my bizarre questions!

My love and thanks as always to my family and friends for their unfailing support.

One

Spring 1914

'I'll run away.'

The young girl, at that fledgling stage between child and young woman – gawky and awkward – stood in the middle of the yard watching her grandmother calmly peg out the washing on the line. The older woman was taking no notice of her and Bridie believed she didn't even care.

The girl promised not classic beauty, but an appeal that would be captivating rather than enslaving. Her lively spirit would attract friendship, loyalty, even love, but perhaps not idolatry or blind worship. But at this moment the twelve-year-old showed little of the adult she would become. Her face was an ominous cloud, her mouth a sultry pout. Her deep blue eyes, fringed with black lashes, flashed with bitterness and resentment and she flicked back her long, thick black plait in a gesture of impatience. Involuntarily her hands tightened into fists at her sides. She moved nearer to her grandmother. Thrusting her head forwards, she muttered through clenched teeth, 'I mean it. I will run away.'

'Oh aye,' Mary Carpenter was still hardly listening. She didn't even glance towards the girl, but bent and picked up the end of a wet sheet. 'And where would you run to?'

1

The reply came promptly. 'To me auntie Eveleen's.'

'Your auntie's too busy to be looking after a trouble-some child like you.'

'I am not a child. I'm twelve. I've been working for seven months.' Her mouth twisted in distaste. 'And I hate it.'

Now Bridie felt her grandmother's glance. 'You're just like your father,' Mary said, but the words were an accusation not a compliment.

The girl bit down hard on her lower lip to stop it trembling, angry at herself that, not for the first time, the mere mention of her father could bring her close to tears; did, in the privacy of her room. It was strange that reference to her mother, who had died at her birth, did not have such a deep effect upon her. Maybe it was because her mother had not been able to help leaving her, whereas her father had done so out of choice. He had disappeared before her birth, refusing to marry her mother and deserting her even before their child had been born. As far as Bridie knew, he didn't know to this day whether he had a son or a daughter. Perhaps he did not even know of Rebecca's death. And worse still, to the child's vulnerable mind, he quite obviously did not care. Not once had he come back from the sea to meet her. Though he had sent home brief letters and cards spasmodically over the years, he had never even asked about her. As far as her father, Jimmy Hardcastle, was concerned, Bridie might as well not exist.

Now her chin rose defiantly. 'All right, I am like him. 'Cos he ran away didn't he? Well, I'm going to do the same, so there.'

Mockingly Mary asked, 'What? Are you going to run away to sea then?'

'I might.'

Pointing to the empty washing basket, Mary said, 'Now stop all this nonsense, child. Take that back to the wash-house, then come in and have your breakfast.'

The girl did not move. Mary sighed. 'It's high time you were about your work. Josh'll be needing your help. And besides,' she added, and now there was a gleam in her eyes as if she knew she was playing her trump card, 'who would look after your injured creatures? What do you think would happen to them if you weren't here? Josh hasn't time to be fussing with wild birds and rabbits. He's enough to do with our own livestock.'

Mary turned and marched back into the farmhouse, disapproval in the set of her shoulders. At fifty-four Mary Carpenter still had the slim figure of a woman half her age, though her hair, drawn back from her face into a neat bun at the nape of her neck, was now more grey than the rich brown it had once been. She wore a white apron over her long black skirt and a crisp, white cotton blouse.

Resentfully Bridie watched her go. It was the only thing that Mary could have said that would touch her; the only thing that could keep her here. The best part of her work on the farm – the part she really enjoyed – was caring for sick or injured animals. Bridie compressed her mouth and frowned. She took a step and then another and picked up the basket. She could not bring herself to leave the blackbird with an injured wing nestling in the hayloft or the wild rabbit with a broken hind leg in a hutch in the yard. She would let the little things go once they were well again, but for now they needed her. Her frown deepened; her grandmother knew that too.

Josh might look after them if she pleaded with him, but Bridie knew, even at her tender age, that once she was gone Mary would have her way. Bridie believed that Josh was fond of her, even though he was only her step-grandfather and therefore no blood relation to her. But in any confrontation between herself and her grandmother, Josh, although he tried to keep the peace, would always take Mary's part in the end.

Bridie was not so sure of her grandmother's affection. She had lived with Mary and Josh since babyhood and knew no other home, but as she had grown older she had begun to feel that she was here on sufferance rather than because she was truly wanted.

Suddenly her heart lightened. There was one person who loved her.

Andrew. Andrew loved her. If her grandmother didn't want her and her aunt Eveleen had no time for her, then she would go to Andrew. She would even take her menagerie with her. Andrew lived in a little cottage and, though she had never seen it, she was sure he must have a garden. Surely there would be room enough for her wounded creatures.

Her mind made up, she picked up the basket and skipped towards the wash-house.

He would be here as usual on Sunday and she would make him take her home with him. Back to the little village of Flawford, near Nottingham, where he lived. There would be plenty of room in his little cottage, for she knew he lived alone.

Yes, Andrew would take her home with him. Bridie could get Andrew Burns to do anything she wanted.

Two

For the rest of the day Bridie skipped through her work about the farm. She milked the cows in the cowhouse, singing at the top of her voice. In the dairy she churned the butter and she was still scurrying to and fro as she laid the table for their supper, whilst Mary and Josh sat on opposite sides of the hearth in front of the kitchen range. Josh warmed his feet on the fender and sighed contentedly. His huge frame filled the Windsor chair and the firelight glowed on his fat, red cheeks. His large nose dominated his face, but his kind eyes shone with love every time they glanced across the hearth towards his wife.

'Well, I'm pleased to see you've changed your tune, miss,' Mary remarked. 'Your mood changes with the wind.'

From behind his newspaper, Josh winked at Bridie and the girl hid her smile. Even though he adored her, Josh was not blind to Mary's little foibles. And if Bridie resembled anyone in her family, she knew it was her grandmother. Mary's own mood swings were like a weathervane. And then the words were springing from Bridie's lips before she could stop them, 'I must take after you then, Gran.'

Mary's head snapped up and her eyes widened. She half rose from her chair. 'You saucy little madam . . .'

Josh crumpled his newspaper and now even he was

frowning. 'Now, Bridie, don't cheek your gran. There's a good girl.'

'Sorry, Gran,' Bridie said airily, with no real note of apology and as she hurried back into the scullery, she was smiling. Soon, she was thinking, I won't be here to be cheeky to anyone. Soon I'll be living with Andrew in his little cottage.

It was an idyllic picture, but one that was purely in her mind's eye for she had never visited Flawford. She imagined that he lived in a tiny cottage, similar to the one down the lane where her friend, Micky Morton, lived with his parents. Micky was lucky, Bridie thought, and her mouth pouted involuntarily. He had been born only a few months after her, but his parents were married and he had grandparents, too, who lived nearby.

A cosy, whitewashed cottage, Bridie dreamed. That was where Andrew would live. With ivy climbing up the wall and a path leading up to a front door framed with roses. Tiny leaded-paned windows would sparkle in the sunshine from her polishing and a tantalizing smell of her baking would greet him as he came home each evening from his work as a framework knitter in the nearby workshop. Oh, how she longed to be grown up so that she could be Mrs Andrew Burns.

It was all she had ever wanted; to be married to Andrew. For as long as she could remember, whenever he had visited, she had rushed to meet him, her arms wide. He would catch her and swing her round and round, their shared laughter echoing around the farmyard. Then, setting her on the ground, he would kiss her forehead and press whatever little gift he had brought for her this time into her hands.

And his gifts were not always little. On her twelfth birthday he had presented her with an exquisite shawl he had knitted on his machine especially for her.

'I had to be careful the old man didn't catch me,' Andrew had laughed. 'But I did it in me own time, so there's not a lot he could say.'

Remembering, the smile faded from Bridie's mouth.

The 'old man' Andrew had referred to was Bridie's maternal grandfather. Someone else whom she had never met. Josh had explained it to her, so carefully, so gently. Perhaps that was why she loved Josh, for he, not her grandmother, nor her aunt Eveleen, nor even Andrew, had taken the trouble to explain the past to her. For that reason, Josh was the only one she would regret leaving.

'It's all a long time ago now, love,' Josh had said as they walked alongside the beck together, taking the cows back to the field after milking, her small hand tucked into his large one. 'And although it's not your fault, none of it – I'm afraid it does affect you. Quite unfairly,' Josh said firmly as he glanced down at her. He took a deep breath and seemed to brace his shoulders. 'Before your gran married me, she was married to the man who was your grandfather, Walter Hardcastle. But you knew that, didn't you?'

Bridie nodded. As they walked, she glanced down at the bubbling water. It was somewhere along here that her grandfather, Walter, had been found, face down in the water having suffered a heart attack. That much she knew, for she saw his grave every Sunday when her gran laid fresh flowers on it. Her gaze lifted to Bernby church standing on the hill in the distance beyond the beck. That was where he was buried.

'After he died so suddenly, the family had to leave Pear Tree Farm,' Josh went on in his kindly, rumbling tones. 'They went to Flawford, to your gran's family.'

'Where is Flawford?'

'It's a village just south of Nottingham,' Josh continued. 'They went to live with your gran's brother, Harry Singleton and . . .'

Bridie remembered interrupting him again at this point in her piping voice. 'Singleton? But that's my name. Why's he got the same name as me?'

The big man at her side had mopped his brow. 'Because your mother, Rebecca, was his daughter and – and . . .' He faltered over the delicate matter. 'You see, mi duck, your mam and dad weren't married, so you've got her surname.'

Bridie had been silent then, digesting the information, trying to work it out in her young mind. Then she said slowly, 'But my dad was Gran's son. I did know that much. So – so were him and my mam cousins?'

'Yes,' Josh said. 'First cousins.'

Again, she was silent. Then, in a voice so quiet that the man at her side had to strain to hear her words, she said, 'And he left her, didn't he? He left us both. He ran away to sea.'

'He was only young, love. No more than a boy, really.'

'Did you know him?'

'Briefly, when he worked in the factory in Nottingham for a short time. It was where I worked then.'

'I thought you said they went to Flawford?'

Josh smiled down at her. 'Oh dear, I'm not very good at this sort of thing. I'm not explaining it very well, am I, mi duck?'

In answer, Bridie smiled up at him, her cheeks dimpling prettily. She gave a little skip, her long black plait swinging. 'Go on,' she encouraged. 'Tell me what happened. Tell me why I've never met me grandfather Singleton.' For a moment there was hurt in her eyes. 'Doesn't he want to meet me?' Then she put her head on one side and eyed Josh speculatively. With a maturity far beyond her years, she asked shrewdly, 'Or is it me gran who won't let *me* see *him*?'

'I don't think so, love, though I have to admit she never sees him herself either.' He licked his thick lips. 'Harry's a hard man. An unforgiving man and he threw your poor mam out of his house when he found out she was expecting a child. In fact, he threw the whole family out, young Jimmy – your dad – and even your gran and Auntie Eveleen too. They all went to Nottingham to find work and that's how I met them.'

'My dad was with them then?'

Josh nodded. 'He didn't stay long, though. He wasn't much of a worker. Couldn't – or wouldn't – get the hang of operating a lace machine.' Suddenly Josh let out a loud guffaw of laughter that startled Bridie. 'Your aunt Evie would have made a better twisthand than him – if she'd had the physical strength, of course. Mind you,' he added reflectively, 'she was a strong lass in those days, having worked on the farm here.'

'Auntie Evie? Did she work in your factory too?'

Josh was still chuckling. 'It wasn't my factory, love. I only worked there. The factory belonged – still does – to Mr Brinsley Stokes and his son, Richard.'

'Uncle Richard?'

Josh nodded. 'Yes, he met your auntie Evie and fell in love with her.' He looked down at her as he added, his voice almost reverent, 'And I met your gran and fell in love with her. So some good came out of it all, didn't it?'

Bridie nodded, unable to speak. Perhaps it had. For them. But what about her? Her father had deserted them, her mother had died and, although she had her gran and Josh, Auntie Evie and Uncle Richard, her grandfather Singleton hated her so much that he never wanted even to meet her.

She drew in a deep, shuddering breath, trying to shut out the hurt and humiliation. There was really only one thing that mattered to her. Or rather, one person.

'What about Andrew?' she asked, trying to still the tremble in her voice.

'Andrew? What do you mean, "What about Andrew"? Sorry, I don't follow. He works for your grandfather and lives in one of his cottages. I thought you knew that. I reckon he was probably born there. I think his dad and mam worked for Harry an' all. He grew up alongside Rebecca, see? And he was very good to all the family when they were in trouble. And, of course, he's your godfather.'

'But he's – he's not related to me, is he?' She held her breath, willing him to make the reply she wanted to hear.

'No, he's not. He's not a blood relative, if that's what you mean. Though . . .' Josh had seemed about to say more, but stopped abruptly.

They had continued to walk along the bank, in silence now. She asked no more questions and only when they approached the gate into the farmyard did she say with a quaint, adult courtesy, 'Thank you for telling me, Grandpa Josh.'

On Sunday, dressed in the shawl he had given her, Bridie waited by the farmyard gate for Andrew to appear at the end of the rough cart track leading to Pear

Tree Farm. Then she saw him, wobbling dangerously on his bicycle as he negotiated the deep, muddy ruts. Picking up her skirts, she ran to meet him.

'Andrew, Andrew.'

The man's smile seemed to stretch from ear to ear when he saw her and he put his feet on the ground to bring the bicycle to a halt. Jumping off, he laid it on the ground and opened his arms to her. Laughing delightedly, Bridie ran into them and was lifted off her feet and swung round and round until she was dizzy.

As he set her down again, Andrew pretended to be out of breath. He put his hand on his chest and panted, 'You're getting far too big for such unladylike behaviour.' But the twinkle in his hazel eyes and the laughter lines that crinkled mischievously around them belied his words. He picked up his bicycle and, with one arm draped across her shoulders, they walked towards the farmyard.

'Aren't you going to ask me what I've brought you?'

Bridie smiled up at him as, her mouth twitching, she said with pretended primness, 'She that expecteth nothing shall surely receive.'

Andrew laughed loudly, startling the hens scratching in the yard, so that they squawked and ran mindlessly about in fright. 'You sound just like old Harry. Him and his preaching.'

'And Gran says you spoil me,' she smiled coyly up at him, knowing that he would never stop doing so.

'Well, if I can't spoil my favourite god-daughter, who can I, I'd like to know?'

Now she laughed aloud too, the sound bouncing on the breeze. 'You! I'm your *only* god-daughter.'

'There you are then. You're bound to be me favourite, aren't you?'

Bridie stopped suddenly and put her hand on his arm. 'Andrew, I want to ask you something. I was going to leave it till later, but . . .'

'Well, if you're going to ask me to marry you, the answer's "yes".'

'Good,' she said promptly, 'because when I'm older that's exactly what I'm going to do.'

'Eh?' For a moment, Andrew looked startled but, as Bridie rushed on, the look of surprise was replaced by one of genuine alarm as he heard her out.

'I want to come back to Flawford with you. I could be your housekeeper. I know you live alone and . . . and . . .'

'Hey, hey, steady on, love.' Andrew actually pulled away from her and held up his hand, palm outwards, as if to fend off her mad scheme. 'What's brought all this on?' He leant closer and said, trying to be stern though he always found it difficult where Bridie was concerned, 'Have you been falling out with your gran again?'

Bridie pouted. 'Not really, but I told her I'd run away and all she could say was that I was like me dad.' Passionately she cried, 'She doesn't care what I do or where I go. I said I'd go to Auntie Evie's, but she said she wouldn't want me either. But you do, don't you?'

He glanced away, unable to meet her eyes now and Bridie felt a chill run through her veins. She frowned and bit down on her lower lip to stop it trembling as she muttered, 'You don't either, do you?'

'It wouldn't be right, you living with me. A young girl with an old bachelor like me. Your gran wouldn't approve.'

Bridie began to protest. 'You're not old. You're . . .' Then she paused and frowned. Suddenly she realized that she had never really stopped to think what age

Andrew must be. He had always been just 'Andrew', whom she had idolized all her life.

'And then there's your grandfather,' Andrew was saying. 'Old Harry.'

Bridie pulled away from him. Pouting, she said, 'You're like all the rest. You don't care about me.'

Andrew grasped her arm so tightly that Bridie winced. 'Don't say that, Bridie. You know I care about you more than anyone else in the world. Don't *ever* say that about me.'

'Then why can't I come and live with you? And then, when I'm older, we can be married.'

She felt his grasp loosen and, as his hand fell away, he groaned deeply. 'Bridie, that's always been just a joke – a bit of fun – between us. I'm far too old for you. I'm almost twenty years older than you. You should marry someone of your own age, not an old feller like me.'

'You've never believed me, have you? Everyone's always laughed at me when I've said I'm going to marry you when I grow up.'

'Bridie, love, from what I'm told, all little girls say they're going to marry the man closest to them. Some even say their dad, or their brother—'

'No, no, that's not allowed.' Bridie was shaking her head vehemently.

'I know it isn't,' Andrew said quickly. 'What I mean is, they say that before they understand the – the ... well, about life.'

She stared at him. 'I don't know what you mean.'

Andrew ran his hand through his brown hair. 'It's not for me to explain things to you, love. That's for your gran to do.'

'Oh, *that*! I know all about *that*.' Suddenly she seemed much older than her twelve years. 'You don't grow up on a farm without knowing what goes on. When the boar visits and—'

'Stop, stop!' Andrew put up his hands once more. 'You'll have me blushing.'

She grinned at him now and he put his arm about her shoulders again. Their easy friendship restored, they walked towards the house. 'When you're older you'll have an army of young suitors beating a path to your door and you'll forget all about wanting to marry me.'

She said nothing, but promised herself: Oh no, I won't. I won't ever stop loving you, Andrew Burns.

Three

Bridie led Andrew into the farmhouse by the back door, through the scullery and into the kitchen. Her grandmother was placing a huge piece of roast beef on the table in front of Josh, who wielded the carving knife against the steel with rhythmic movements to sharpen it.

'Hello, Andrew, come and sit down. Did you have a good journey?' Mary fussed around him, pulling out a chair for him at the table as she invited him to join their meal. Her tone sharpened noticeably as she turned to Bridie. 'Go and drain the vegetables in the scullery, girl. There are two tureens ready. Look sharp.'

Mary turned to the black-leaded range. A roaring fire heated the oven, where all their meals were cooked. On the opposite side was a tank for water, heated by the same fire and ladled out of the lid in the top. A kettle sat on the hob near the glowing coals, singing gently.

Bridie hurried between scullery and kitchen, carrying the tureens laden with steaming vegetables: potatoes, fresh spring cabbage and sliced runner beans preserved in salt from the previous growing season, washed thoroughly now and boiled, to enjoy through the winter.

Bridie loved Sunday dinner, especially when Andrew came. She would pull her chair close to his and listen as the grown-ups talked. Josh would tell him, in detail, all about the work that had been done about the small farm since his last visit. Today he had a piece of news.

'Stephen Dunsmore is selling off bits of the estate. Rumour ses it's to pay his gambling debts. Anyway,' he went on, beaming with pride at Mary, 'We've bought another field alongside the beck. We can increase our herd now.'

'More cows to milk,' Bridie said and cast her eyes to the ceiling.

'No, I – I mean, we . . .' He glanced at Mary in apology, but she only smiled fondly at him. Josh continued. 'We thought we'd buy beef cattle. Breed, you know?'

Bridie felt a thrill of excitement. 'We'd have baby calves?'

Josh nodded and Bridie clapped her hands.

'I thought you were set on leaving, miss,' Mary remarked drily and Bridie squirmed in her seat. For a moment the pull of more animals to care for was strong.

Puzzled, Josh glanced from one to the other. 'What's this?'

'Oh, nothing,' Mary said quickly, 'Only Bridie getting on her high horse and making idle threats when things don't suit her.'

Bridie opened her mouth to argue that her threats were anything but idle, but Andrew was shaking his head in wonderment. 'You're a marvel, Josh.' He smiled. 'How you've taken to the country life. If I didn't know you were a townie born and bred, I'd believe you'd never lived anywhere but here in the whole of your life.'

Josh chuckled and his jowls wobbled. 'There's a lot to be said for city life, but I always had a yen to be in the country.' He laughed again. 'Strange, isn't it? Eve-leen and I seemed to have swapped places. She's taken to the city life.'

'That's because Richard's there,' Andrew said softly and there was an unmistakable note of longing in his tone. 'She's with the one she loves, isn't she?'

'True enough,' Josh said and touched Mary's hand across the table. 'And I'm with the woman I love.'

'Oh, Josh, you old softie.' Mary smiled and tapped his hand as if in gentle admonishment. But even the young girl could see from the pink tinge suffusing her grandmother's cheeks that age was no barrier to love. Bridie watched the interplay, feeling, as she always did at such moments, excluded. She leant against Andrew and smiled coyly up at him. 'Perhaps you'd like to come and live in the country too. Would you?'

'Oho, not me. There's not much I don't know about framework knitting. Trouble is – it's *all* I know. ' He pulled a comical face. 'And besides, I'm frightened of cows.'

Around the table, they joined in his laughter.

'So,' Bridie went on, 'tell us what's been happening to you this week.'

The guarded look that always seemed to come into his eyes when she asked about his home life was there again. 'Oh, just work as usual. You know.'

'No, I don't know,' Bridie burst out. 'I don't know because I've never been allowed to visit you. I don't know where you live and work and—'

'Bridie,' Josh spoke sternly. 'That's enough. I won't have you upsetting your grandmother.'

'But—'

'I said, that's enough!'

Colour suffused the girl's face and she bit her lip as

she flashed a defiant look at Josh, but she said no more. Beneath the table, Andrew squeezed her hand warningly.

For several moments, the meal continued in silence, the only sounds the singing kettle on the hob, the settling of coals in the range's grate and the clatter of cutlery against plates.

At last Mary laid her knife and fork carefully together and leant back in her chair and sighed. 'I suppose I ought to ask you how my mother is, Andrew. And – and my brother?'

Bridie gasped and glanced towards Josh. Even he hadn't told her that Mary's own mother was still alive. And this was a most unusual event. Mary never asked about her family in Flawford and now Bridie was very much afraid that Josh was going to blame her for having raised the subject.

Immediately Josh was reaching out again to take Mary's hand. 'Now, my dear,' he began, 'don't go upsetting yourself.'

Mary smiled at him. 'It's all right. I'm not upset. It's high time I at least enquired after them, even if I can't bring myself to go and see them ever again.'

Before Andrew could answer, Bridie, unable to restrain herself any longer, burst out. 'Your *mother*? You mean to say that I've got a *great*-grandmother and you never even told me? I thought there was only me grandfather.'

For a moment Mary looked shamefaced as her eyes met Bridie's accusing stare. The older woman's glance dropped away, but she nodded.

Andrew cleared his throat awkwardly and said, 'She's quite well. She doesn't get out much now, though. Her legs are bad.'

Mary smiled wryly. 'Not even across the road to the chapel on a Sunday? That won't please Harry.'

18

Andrew laughed. 'She still has to attend chapel. Both services on a Sunday. He sees to that. He pushes her across the road in a bath chair.'

The tension in the room eased a little as Mary smiled too. Then she murmured, 'I'm glad she's all right. It wasn't really her fault, though she could have supported poor Rebecca a little more. No . . .' Her voice hardened as she went on. 'No, it's Harry I blame.'

Andrew folded his arms, leant on the table and said quietly, 'It's him, if anyone, that's not so well these days. His eyesight is beginning to bother him, I think, although he will never admit it.'

'Huh!' Mary almost snorted. 'That's Harry.'

Again there was silence, until Mary, moving with a suddenness that made the others jump, got to her feet and began to stack the plates. 'Well, this won't get the table cleared and the pudding served. Look sharp, Bridie. Stir yourself.'

The subject was closed and even later, when Bridie tried to draw Andrew out some more, he was evasive. 'Look, love, it's up to your gran or Josh to talk to you about it all. It's really nothing to do with me.' And though she tried to wheedle more information out of him, Andrew pressed his lips together and refused to say anything.

'All right, then,' Bridie said, for once capitulating prettily. She tucked her arm through his. 'Let's go and look at the piglets. Bonnie has just had a litter of seven. And I'll show you the blackbird in the hayloft and the little rabbit in the hutch. I'll have to bring them with me when I come to live with you,' she informed him solemnly. But Andrew only smiled and said nothing.

The day ended happily with Bridie standing at the gate, waving goodbye as Andrew pedalled away on his bicycle.

Josh came to stand beside her. 'He's a good lad, that,' he murmured, watching the wobbling figure disappear into the gloom of evening. 'Goodness knows what time he'll get back to Flawford. To think he comes nearly every week just to see you.'

The thought gave Bridie a warm glow, but she said gallantly, 'He comes to see you and Gran as well.'

Josh chuckled and agreed. 'Of course, he does, love, but I don't think it'd be so often if you weren't here.' He put his arm about her shoulders. 'Come on, time you were in bed else you'll have your gran after you.'

'Just mind what you're doing, girl,' Mary snapped the following morning as Bridie turned the handle of the mangle. 'You'll have my fingers trapped if you're so erratic. For goodness sake, turn it steadily. Haven't I shown you often enough? Your mind's not on your job. That's your trouble. Daydreaming again, I'll be bound.' She clicked her tongue against her teeth in a gesture of impatience. 'I don't know what I'm going to do with you. You'll be the death of me, one of these days.'

'Oh, turn it yourself then,' Bridie let go of the handle and began to move away, but Mary lunged towards her and caught her arm in an iron grip.

'Oh no, you don't get away with it that easily. You'll stay here and do as you're told.'

Bridie twisted around to face her. 'No, I won't. I won't stay here another minute. You don't want me. You never have. I'm just some stupid girl's bastard who you've had to bring up.'

'Bridie!' Mary's grasp slackened in shock and Bridie pulled herself free.

'I'm going to live with Andrew. He wants me. He

loves me. Whatever you say, I know he loves me, even if no-one else does.'

'We all know that,' Mary gestured impatiently. 'Of course he does. You're the spitting image of your mother and she was the love of his life.'

Bridie felt as if the breath had been knocked from her body. The pain was physical. 'What – did – you – say?' she managed to gasp at last.

'I said, of course Andrew loves you because you remind him of Rebecca.'

There was a huge lump in her throat and tears prickled behind her eyelids, but Bridie was determined that her grandmother should not see her cry. She turned and staggered from the wash-house, her legs like jelly beneath her. In the fresh air, she pulled in deep, gulping breaths and strength flowed back into her. Though she heard her grandmother calling her name, Bridie picked up her skirts and ran out of the yard and into the field, down to the beck, splashing through it without even taking off her boots and stockings. Then, heart pounding, she ran up the slope towards the covert on the brow of the hill and disappeared into the shadowy coolness beneath the trees.

Breathless, she flung herself to the ground and sobbed. She'd stay here for ever, she vowed. She'd never go back home. She'd starve to death first and when they found her body they'd all be sorry.

Four

Pear Tree Farm lay amidst farmland to the west of Bernby, a small village on a hill just outside the Lincoln-shire town of Grantham. Further west lay the Vale of Belvoir and in the distance, against the setting sun, were the ramparts of Belvoir Castle. Beyond that was the road to Flawford and the city of Nottingham.

Micky Morton found Bridie late in the day. She was asleep in the den they had built as children in the depths of the woodland known as Bernby Covert. The trees covered the hilltop behind the farm and overhung the lane leading up the slope past Fairfield House, the Dunsmores' mansion, and on towards the village.

'Your gran's on the rampage,' he said as he squeezed himself into the hide they had constructed of branches. 'And Mr Carpenter is tearing his hair out.' He paused and then tried to lighten his news by adding, 'What bit he's got left.'

Bridie sat with her arms wrapped around her knees drawn up to her chest. She had been here the whole day and now she was cold and hungry. At first she had cried and cried until she had fallen asleep, exhausted. Now her tears were all cried out and she was filled with a deep sadness that was an ache in the pit of her stomach.

'What's up, then?' Micky asked, blunt as ever and coming straight to the point.

'Nothing.'

'It dun't look like it,' he remarked drily. 'There's not a scrap of work been done about the place according to Mr C. They've been looking for you all day. Mind you, I could have saved 'em the trouble, but he didn't come down to me grandad's place until teatime.'

Micky Morton's grandparents, Bill and Dorothy, lived a short distance down the lane from Pear Tree Farm at Furze Farm. Just beyond that, in a small cottage, Micky lived with his parents, Ted and Alice. Micky paused and she saw him straining through the shadows to look at her. 'I knew where you'd be.'

'No, you didn't.'

'I've found you, ain't I?'

Bridie was silent.

'Your gran said you'd threatened to run away.'

Again, she said nothing, but tears that she thought were dried out prickled again as self-pity overwhelmed her. Now she had nowhere to run to. No-one wanted her. No-one loved her.

'Come on,' Micky said, standing up and grasping her arm. Though he was a few months younger than she was, Micky had been working on the farm ever since the age of seven during out-of-school hours. Now he had just passed his twelfth birthday, he was doing a man's work on the Dunsmore estate, where both his grandfather and his father worked. Indeed, Micky's whole family lived in dwellings tied to their employment. 'I'd better get you home before Mr Carpenter fetches PC Wilkins from Bernby.'

Reluctantly, knowing she faced even more trouble when she arrived home, Bridie allowed him to lead her from the den and out of the woods. They walked down the hill and paddled through the beck.

'There's Mr C now,' Micky said and Bridie looked up to see Josh hurrying towards them.

'Oh, Bridie love. Thank God you're safe.' He was reaching out to her, clasping her to his bulk in an awkward but genuinely fond embrace. 'Come on, let's get you home and into the warm. Have you been there all day? You must be starving.' He turned to Micky. 'Thanks, lad. I wish I'd asked you earlier. You could have saved us all a lot of worry.'

'S'all right, Mr Carpenter. See you, Bridie.' Pushing his hands into the pockets of his trousers, Micky sauntered away and was soon lost to their sight in the gathering dusk, though for some time afterwards they could still hear him whistling.

'She's a wilful little tyke who deserves a good hiding.'

Mary's tirade started the moment Josh opened the back door and ushered a reluctant Bridie into the kitchen.

'Now, now, Mary love. That would do no good. Bridie, be a good girl. Go upstairs and change your clothes. I'll get some hot soup ready for when you come down. Go on now,' he said, giving her a gentle push.

As she climbed the steep stairs, she heard their voices; her grandmother's raised in shrill anger, Josh's calm and rational.

'Fancy her saying no-one loves her. The very idea. Haven't we looked after her all these years? I didn't want another bairn to bring up, not at my age. And that's all the thanks I get. Well, if that's how she feels, she can go.'

'You don't mean that, Mary.'

'Oh, don't I? Isn't she the reason my Jimmy ran

away? And it's because of her he's never been back home in all these years.'

'I rather think it was Jimmy's fault that an innocent child who didn't ask to be born was brought into the world at all.'

'That's right.' Mary's voice was becoming hysterical now. 'That's right. Blame my Jimmy. You never liked him. It was always Eveleen with you, wasn't it? She couldn't do a thing wrong in your eyes, could she? And it's the same now with Bridie.'

In her bedroom, Bridie could still hear the sound of their quarrel but not what was being said. She groaned aloud, sorry now that she had catapulted her grandmother into one of her moods. But more than that she was sorry to have brought trouble upon the kindly Josh.

Still shivering from the cold of the woods, Bridie stripped off her clothes, washing herself all over with cold water from the ewer on her dressing table. Then she pulled on her warmest garments and crept downstairs. She listened a moment at the door at the bottom, which led back into the kitchen. Hearing no raised voices, indeed no sound of voices at all, she opened the door and stepped into the room.

Mary was seated in her chair by the range, her head bent over her pillow lace whilst Josh stirred the soup in a heavy black saucepan over the fire. It looked like an ordinary, calm and peaceful domestic scene, but Bridie could feel the tension in the air. Her grandmother had now retreated into a world of stony silence, her lips pressed together in disapproval whilst her nimble figures twisted the bobbins over and over to form the gossamer lace.

Josh glanced up and saw Bridie standing uncertainly in the doorway. 'There you are, love. Now come and sit down at the table, drink this and then away to bed with you for a good night's sleep.'

She did as he bade and whilst she sipped the soup he sat with her at the table. He leant towards her and spoke in a low tone. 'Now, Bridie, what you did today was wrong. You worried us both very much. But if you say you're sorry to your gran and promise never to do such a thing again, we'll say no more about it.'

Bridie looked up at him, looked into the ugly, but kindly face, and knew that his expression of concern was genuine. She held his gaze steadily and was able to say with far more truthfulness than she could do to her grandmother, 'I am sorry I worried you. Truly I am, but . . .' The next words were difficult to say, for as much as she had been hurt by Mary's thoughtless words, Bridie did not want to wound Josh, who had never once shown her anything but loving kindness. She took a deep breath and hurried on. 'I don't want to be a burden any longer to you and Gran. Maybe it would be better if I went away. Perhaps to – to Nottingham. Into service or . . . or something.' Her words faltered and faded as she saw the bleak look in Josh's eyes and, despite her desire not to hurt him, she saw at once that she had done so.

He dropped his gaze, looking down at his callused hand lying on the snowy tablecloth. His tone was heavy as he said, 'I presume you overheard what your Gran said?' He raised his eyes and caught Bridie's nod. 'She didn't mean it, love.' Then he half twisted in the chair and added, 'Tell her you didn't mean it, Mary.'

Her busy fingers suddenly idle, Mary raised her head slowly. For a long moment, grandmother and grand-daughter stared at each other. The young girl's eyes pleaded for understanding, for a denial of the older woman's earlier words, but in Mary's eyes there was still anger and resentment. Mary's glance flickered briefly towards Josh as he said gently, 'Come now, Mary, love.'

Her grandmother sighed. 'Of course I didn't mean it, but . . .' she added, her tone still firm, 'she must learn not to be so wilful.'

Bridie saw the warning look still in her grandmother's eyes, but Josh seemed satisfied. The matter, for him at least, was at an end. 'There now.' He patted Bridie's hand and his round face shone. 'There now. We'll forget all about it. Off you go up to bed, love. Sleep tight.'

Normally Bridie retorted with 'And watch the bugs don't bite', but tonight she only smiled weakly and stood up. Josh rose too and held out his arms to her. She laid her cheek on his huge chest and he patted her fondly.

'There, there,' he murmured, close to her ear. 'It'll be all right.'

For a moment Bridie pressed herself against his comforting bulk, but in her heart she knew that nothing would be quite the same again. As she climbed the stairs once more to her bedroom, Bridie promised herself: I will go to Nottingham. I can get a job there. Maybe Auntie Eveleen will let me work at Uncle Richard's factory, even if she doesn't want me living with them. At the thought she felt another stab of anguish, but, defying the hurt, she vowed: I'll stand on my own two feet.

I'll show the lot of them.

Five

When she heard the front door open and Richard call out her name, Eveleen wiped the tears from her eyes, blew her nose and tried to plaster a smile on her face.

'I'm in here,' she called, praying that he would not see the telltale signs of her distress. That morning she had discovered yet again that she was not pregnant. She wasn't sure how many disappointments she could take and she knew that Richard felt each false hope as keenly as she did.

She smoothed unruly tendrils of her rich brown hair back into place and, as the door opened, she turned towards it and smiled bravely. 'You're home early. Lovely.' She went towards him, her arms outstretched. Her husband kissed her gently and then held her at arm's length.

'Oh, my darling. Again?'

She bit her lip, but could not stop tears welling. She nodded and was enfolded in his embrace. 'Don't worry, sweetheart,' Richard said, as he always did. 'One day, it'll happen. You're only young.'

'I'm thirty,' Eveleen said dolefully.

'What an old lady! Shall I buy you a walking stick or a bath chair.' His smile crinkled his eyes and lit up his handsome face. She smiled up at him, loving him more than ever, if that were possible, for the way he cajoled her out of her depression.

But today he was serious. He took her in his arms and held her close, murmuring against her ear, 'Evie, even if we are never to be blessed with children of our own, I'd still rather be married to you than anyone else in the whole world. Just remember that.'

'But your father wants an heir.' Her words were muffled against his shoulder. 'I know he does. And you do too, if you're honest.'

Carefully Richard said, 'It would be nice to have someone to pass on the Stokes's empire to. But it's not the end of the world. And there's always Bridie. She's your niece.'

'But she's no blood relation to your family. And – and she's a girl.'

Richard released her and laughed aloud, throwing back his dark head. 'I can't believe you said that. You of all people, who champion the cause of women better that anyone else I know by proving that you can run that huge warehouse single-handedly.' More seriously he added, 'Perhaps that's the trouble. Maybe you're doing too much.'

'Oh, Richard. I can't sit around doing nothing. We have servants galore to do the housework. What would I do with myself all day?'

'Sit on a cushion and sew a fine seam,' he teased.

Eveleen pulled a face. 'I'd sooner be sewing fine seams along with the girls in the inspection room. That's where I belong.'

'And chasing over half the city rounding up your homeworkers,' he admonished gently, tapping the tip of her nose with his forefinger.

She smiled wryly and was forced to acquiesce. But then her thoughts came back to her niece. 'Did you mean it about Bridie? I know you've always been fond of her, but to make her your heir. That's a huge step. And would your parents agree?'

Richard shrugged. 'She's still very young and she may not want it.'

Eveleen looked askance at him, as if she could not believe anyone could turn down such an opportunity. Richard spread his hands. 'She may not like city life, darling. She's happy in the country.'

Eveleen nodded. 'Yes, yes, she is. I don't think she'd ever want to leave the farm.'

'You don't really mean you're going to run away?'

Micky was appalled when Bridie confided her secret to him. 'Yes, I am, and don't you dare tell a soul, Micky Morton, else I'll cut out your tongue and feed it to the pigs.'

'You'd have to catch me first,' he grinned, but then his face sobered. 'Ya'll upset everybody if you do that, y'know.'

'And who's "everybody"?' Bridie asked scathingly. 'Me gran? I don't think so. I told you what she'd said, didn't I?'

'She didn't mean it. All parents say things they don't mean when they're angry.'

'She's not my "parent". That's the whole trouble. She felt obliged to bring me up just because her son got his cousin pregnant and then left her.'

'What about Josh, then?'

Bridie was silent, pulling at the grass on the bank of the beck where they were sitting, dangling their feet in the rushing water. 'He's the only one who might care a bit,' she agreed gruffly.

'I'd care, an' all,' Micky declared stoutly. 'You're my best mate. Even if you are a girl.'

Despite her unhappiness, Bridie gave him a playful shove. They were silent for a while until Micky asked, 'Where will you go?'

She glanced at him slyly. 'Shan't tell you. You might tell them.'

'I wouldn't.'

'You did last time.' Now she glared at him fully, accusingly.

He wriggled awkwardly. 'Well, yeah. I know I did, but that was different.'

'How?'

''Cos I didn't know what was going on. I mean, you could have fallen and been lying hurt somewhere.' He gestured towards the stream in front of them and needed to say no more. They were both remembering the story about her grandfather, Walter Hardcastle, being found dead, face down, in the water somewhere near this very spot.

'Well, I wasn't,' Bridie muttered.

'No,' Micky said carefully, 'but I didn't know that, did I? Not at the time. It'd be different if I knew you were safe but didn't *want* to be found.'

Bridie's eyes widened in surprise. 'Would it really? You mean you'd help me?'

Micky nodded, but added, 'I don't want you to go, but if it's what you really want, then, yes, I'd help you.'

Bridie gave him her most engaging smile. 'Right, then. Just be ready for whatever happens. As soon as I get the chance, I'm going, but I don't know how or when or even where I'll go. I just know that one of these days, I will go.'

'Well, afore you do,' Micky was grinning cheekily, 'there's one of our hens me dad'd like you to look after. The others have set on it.'

At once the image of a chicken with all its feathers pulled out around its tail, its skin red and sore from the vicious beaks of the other birds, came into her mind. Crudely Micky confirmed her fears. 'Its arse is pecked red-raw.'

She was silent a moment and then she saw his grin. 'You!' she flared and punched his shoulder. 'Your dad doesn't need me to look after his hen. He can do that for himself. You're just trying to keep me here.'

Micky's grin widened and he shrugged. 'It was worth a try.'

'Oh, you!' she said again, but she was laughing with him now.

Then, for a moment, Micky was very serious. 'You ought to go to someone, at least to start with,' he added hastily as she glared at him.

'I can look after mesen.'

'I know, I know,' he added hastily, 'but you are only twelve. I know you look older, being tall, but still . . . You ought to go to someone,' he ended firmly. 'What about Andrew?'

'No!' Her tone was harsh, causing the young boy to raise his eyebrows.

'You fallen out with him?' he asked bluntly.

'No,' she whispered. She knew he would hear the hurt in her voice, but thankfully he did not pursue it.

'Your auntie Evie and uncle Richard, then. He's a nice chap. He might be a bit posh, owning a lace factory an' all that. But he ain't a bit stuck up, is he?'

'No,' Bridie agreed, 'but they haven't any children of their own.'

'Why?'

'Dunno. Maybe . . .' She swallowed the lump in her throat, remembering what her grandmother had said. 'Maybe they don't want troublesome children.'

'Oh.' Micky looked puzzled. That was something he could not understand. To the country boy with three younger siblings, it seemed that married couples always had children. Nature was all around them and that was part of it. Confident that there must be some other reason, Micky said, 'Well, I'd give your auntie and uncle a try, if I was you.'

Six

As Eveleen walked towards the Reckitt and Stokes lace factory and warehouse, built side by side on Canal Street, she was aware of the admiring glances she attracted. Her luxurious curly brown hair was piled high in the fashion of the time and on top her wide-brimmed hat was perched at a jaunty angle. The tight-fitting jacket and the long straight skirt accentuated her slim, shapely figure. The costume was an emerald green with a white, frilled-neck blouse beneath it.

'Morning, ma'am,' one of the men greeted her as she climbed the stairs to the top floor of the warehouse. She smiled in acknowledgement, 'Morning, Joe.'

As she opened the door into the inspection and mending room she felt the familiar thrill of pride and she paused a moment to enjoy the scene. The large room, light and airy, was filled with the muted chatter of twenty women and girls, each with a bale of lace spread over their laps and spilling onto the floor as they meticulously mended any flaws and runs in the fabric. It was what Eveleen herself had done when she first arrived in Nottingham, desperate for work. She moved down the edge of the room, nodding and smiling at the girls, her eagle eye on their work as she passed. As she neared the end of the room, she raised her head to smile at the young woman who was the inspection room's supervisor.

'Morning, Helen.'

Helen Binkley rose from her seat and came towards her, stretching out her hands in greeting and bending forward to kiss Eveleen's cheek.

The two women had been firm friends since the day Eveleen had come to work here and it had given her enormous pleasure to promote Helen, quite justifiably for she was an excellent and trustworthy worker, to the post of supervisor when the previous woman had left.

Eveleen drew off her gloves and sat down at her own desk alongside Helen's. 'I've been thinking,' she said, coming to a sudden, impulsive decision, but keeping her voice low so that they would not be overheard. 'Would you be willing to take on more responsibility?'

Helen's bright eyes twinkled cheekily at her. 'Depends.'

Catching her meaning, Eveleen smiled and said playfully, 'Of course we would think of a fancy title to suit your new status.'

She paused, deliberately teasing Helen, who laughed merrily knowing full well she was being led on. 'A fancy title doesn't pay the rent, Evie.'

They laughed together. 'Of course, there would be a pay rise for you too.'

'Ah well, now you're talking. What exactly would all this extra work involve?'

Eveleen's eyes clouded. 'I think I might be overdoing it. If I'm honest, I do get very tired by the end of each week and perhaps . . .' The two friends stared at each other and Helen, understanding at once, said softly, 'You think it could be stopping you conceiving?'

Helen was one of the only two women in whom Eveleen had confided her great sorrow at not being able to give Richard the heir she knew he wanted. Despite his constant loving reassurance, Eveleen knew that, deep down, he longed for children. And his father, Brinsley Stokes, made no secret of the fact. 'When are you going to make me a grandfather?' he had asked regularly during the first years of their marriage. But now, after ten years, even he had stopped asking.

In answer to Helen's delicate question, Eveleen nodded and pressed her lips together to prevent them quivering. The latest disappointment, only this morning, was still fresh in her mind.

'Have you talked about this to your mother?'

Eveleen pulled a face. 'My mother's not the sort of person I can confide in. She's so wrapped up in her life with Josh.'

'What about Win, then?'

Win Martin, Eveleen's only other confidante, had been the very first person Eveleen had encountered on her arrival in the city. Win had not only advised her about obtaining employment, but had also found a house for Eveleen, her mother, brother and her pregnant cousin, Rebecca. Living in the same street for several months, Win had been a tower of strength to the young Eveleen, who, through the tragic circumstances of her father's sudden death, had found herself responsible for her family. Win was also the one to whom all the inhabitants of Foundry Yard turned in times of trouble. Birth or death or illness, Win Martin was ready to help.

'Not recently,' Eveleen answered Helen, 'but I'm seeing her later this morning. I might have a talk with her then.'

'I think you should,' Helen said, forthright as ever. 'What Win Martin doesn't know about babies isn't worth knowing.'

There was a silence between them until Helen prompted, 'So what would you want me to do?'

'Well, I wondered if you'd take over the management of all the middlewomen. It means a lot of walking, visiting them in their homes.'

Throughout the city women were employed as homeworkers for the lace industry. In each area a middlewoman collected the lace from the factory and distributed the work to the homeworkers living nearby. Eveleen had taken it upon herself to be the one to visit the middlewomen who worked for Reckitt and Stokes regularly and to help them with any problems they might have.

Helen beamed. 'I wouldn't mind that. It'd be a nice change from being cooped up in here all day.' Her eyes twinkled merrily. 'And all the walking'd keep me slim. But what about this place?'

'I'd still want you to be overall supervisor of the inspection room, but perhaps we could promote someone to be your deputy when you were out. Can you recommend anyone?'

Helen's thoughtful glance roamed over the heads of the women and girls in her charge. 'Well, there's one or two who might be all right. Do you mind if I think about it for a day or two?'

'Of course not. There's no immediate hurry. It's not as if,' she added sorrowfully, 'I am already pregnant and have been advised to rest.'

Helen reached out and touched her hand. 'Don't worry, Evie. There's plenty of time.'

But Eveleen, at thirty, felt the years were rushing by and though she smiled at her friend, the smile could not quite chase away the worry in her dark brown eyes.

*

Later that morning Eveleen walked to Foundry Yard and passed the door where she had lived when they first arrived in Nottingham, with a pregnant Rebecca fleeing from the wrath of her father, an unrepentant Jimmy and a depressed and difficult Mary. If it hadn't been for the help and friendship of the woman she was about to visit, Win Martin, Eveleen seriously doubted she would have survived that time. As she drew near Win's home she saw a cluster of women outside the door. She felt a moment's stab of fear. Was something wrong in the Martin household? Then she almost laughed aloud at her own foolishness as she realized what time it was. Win was a middlewoman for Reckitt and Stokes. She collected the lace from the factory and distributed it to all the women homeworkers in her area. And this was the time of day when all the homeworkers arrived on her doorstep to receive their day's allocation.

'Don't want her giving you more 'n me,' they would joke to each other.

They needn't have worried. Win was strict but fair, dealing out three dozen parts to each woman to take home and strip. The lace was manufactured in long strips joined by threads, which were then drawn out by the homeworkers to separate the lengths. The women then 'scalloped' the lace where it needed neatening and wound the finished lengths onto cards. This operation was known as 'jennying'. They would bring the lace back to Win's terraced house by eight o'clock the following morning, after they – and sometimes other members of their families too, even children – had often worked well into the night. Over the years Win had built up a group of women workers who were conscientious and meticulous.

There was a strange, friendly rivalry between the

homeworkers. Yet, if one of their number could not complete the required amount of finished yardage because of dirty or damaged work, the other women would contribute a few pennies each to make up her pay knowing that the favour would be returned.

Each morning Win returned the finished lace to the factory on her handcart and collected a new batch and the whole routine started again.

'Morning, Mrs Stokes.' The murmur ran amongst them as they parted to allow Eveleen to approach the door.

She smiled and nodded, recognizing familiar faces. 'Is Win home yet?'

'She's just sorting it out, then we'll be on our way.'

At that moment the door opened and Win Martin beckoned the first woman to step inside. Eveleen waited until the last one had hurried away down the street, a bundle of lace in her arms, before she stepped forward.

'Evie, I didn't see you standing there. Come in, come in. The kettle's singing. I always have a cuppa when they've all gone. Eh, fair wears me out, it does.'

'Oh dear.' Eveleen stepped into Win's kitchen. 'And I've come to ask you if you can take on more.' She pulled off her gloves and sat down without needing to be asked.

Win eyed her shrewdly. 'Summat wrong, love?' Then her face brightened. 'Don't tell me you're . . .?'

Quickly Eveleen shook her head. 'No, no. I'm not. But that is the reason I'm here. I've been thinking that perhaps I'm doing too much. I mean . . .' she faltered, blushing slightly. 'Do you think that could – could stop me conceiving?'

Win made the tea and set a cup in front of Eveleen before she sat down opposite. 'I've got to be honest with you, Evie, I've never heard of that being the case.' She gave a wry laugh. 'It's never stopped any of the women round here falling, yet they work as hard as any I know. Meaning no offence, love.'

'None taken, Win,' Eveleen murmured and sighed heavily. 'I suppose I'm just clutching at straws now.'

'But that doesn't mean to say it couldn't be true in your case. We're all different, love, and it's worth a try.'

'Anything's worth a try,' Eveleen said bitterly. 'I'll soon be too old. Oh, Win, I do so want to have a child. A son for Richard.'

'Aye, I know, I know. Life's unfair, in't it? There's me with six of 'em and though I love 'em all, I wouldn't say they was planned, if you know what I mean.'

The two women smiled at each other. Win reached across and patted Eveleen's hand. 'Don't give up hope yet awhile. One thing I have heard tell is that if you worry too much about it, get too desperate, like, then that can stop it happening.'

'Really?'

Win nodded. 'So just you put it out of your mind and enjoy yourself a bit more. And whatever it is you want me to do, the answer's "yes". I can manage it. Our Elsie'll help me.' Win was referring to one of her daughters.

'Elsie?' Eveleen asked in surprise. 'But I thought she'd just had a baby.' Everyone, it seemed to Eveleen, could have children but her.

'Oh, she has,' Win replied airily. 'But it's high time she was back on her feet and working again.'

'You're a hard woman, Win Martin.' The two women laughed together, both knowing that the exact opposite was in fact the truth.

Win's tone was gentle as she said, 'You take it a bit

easier, love. Get out and about with that handsome husband of yours and let nature take its course.'

'Darling? Darling, where are you?'

It was Richard's voice calling from the hallway. Eveleen hurried from the bedroom and leant over the banister.

Looking down, she asked, 'What is it? Is something wrong?'

He was smiling up at her and beckoning. 'Come down, I've a surprise for you. Come on, Evie.' He was as excited as a little boy.

Laughing, Eveleen ran lightly down the stairs. 'What is it?'

'You'll see.' He took her hand and led her into the morning room.

Eveleen gasped and her eyes widened. Lying across a chair was a warm coat with a fur collar and alongside it a hat with a long scarf.

'Put it on,' Richard said, picking up the coat and holding it out for her to slip her arms into.

'It isn't my birthday.'

Richard could not stop smiling. 'Ah, but there's a very good reason. That's the second part of my surprise.'

'You do spoil me,' she murmured, believing that he had arranged all this just to take her mind off her disappointment. 'It's lovely,' she said, running her hands down the soft fabric, whilst Richard fastened the buttons for her just as if she were a child.

'Now the hat.' Carefully he placed it on her head and then wrapped the long silk scarf across the crown of the hat and tied it under her chin. 'Wait there,' he instructed and hurried out of the room, returning moments later dressed in a long coat and a cap, with a warm scarf wrapped around his neck.

He took her arm and led her from the room, out of the front door and down the steep steps to the street. Directly outside their house stood a motor car.

'There!' Richard was triumphant. 'What do you think of that?'

For a moment, Eveleen was mystified and then realization dawned. 'You've bought a motor car!' Now, like a child herself, she clapped her hands. 'Oh, Richard, how wonderful!'

'It's a Model T Ford,' Richard said proudly. 'Come on, let's go for a ride.'

They giggled like two schoolchildren playing truant as he handed her up into the front seat.

'Are you sure you know how to drive it?'

'Oh yes, I've been taking lessons. And I've got my licence.' He reached up and kissed her on the mouth, not caring that they were in full view of the street. 'Do you think I'd risk endangering my lovely wife?'

It took several turns of the starting handle before the engine burst into life. Eveleen clutched at the side of the vehicle as the whole frame shuddered beneath her. But she was laughing, loving every minute.

Richard climbed in beside her. 'Hold on,' he shouted above the noise. 'Here we go.'

The sight of a motor car was not unusual in the streets of Nottingham, but once they left the built-up area and were bowling along the country lanes, they were amused by the stir they created.

Workers in the fields paused to watch their progress. Women came to the doors of the houses and cottages, wiping their hands on their aprons, to gawk at the noisy contraption. Children ran alongside the vehicle, shouting and laughing. 'Give us a ride, mester?'

It was a warm, spring day, the trees just sprouting into leaf. Bright dandelions scattered the grass verges and daffodils danced in cottage gardens.

Above the noisy engine, Richard shouted. 'Shall we go to Bernby and show your mother and Josh? And we'll take Bridie for a ride. She'd like that.'

Preoccupied, Eveleen nodded. Richard glanced at her, amused. 'Don't tell me. You want to have a try at driving?'

Eveleen grinned at him. 'How did you guess?'

Neither of them had any doubt about her ability to master the technique. Eveleen was a quick learner and she loved any kind of machinery. As a young girl she had learned to operate a framework-knitting machine under the tuition of her uncle, Harry Singleton. Later, in Nottingham, she had by devious means learned the basic skills of a twisthand on the huge lace machines in the Reckitt and Stokes's factory.

It had been at a time when Eveleen was desperate to earn enough money to keep her family together. Thanks to the kindly Win and Fred Martin they had a roof over their heads and work for both her and her brother, Jimmy as an apprentice twisthand in the factory and Eveleen in the inspection room. But then Eveleen had put pressure on her brother to do the decent thing and marry his cousin, Rebecca, who was carrying his child. Jimmy had no intention of being tied down and had even been cruel enough to suggest that the child was not his. He had run away to sea, leaving Eveleen as the sole breadwinner on a woman's meagre wage.

At that time Eveleen and her brother had been

remarkably alike, so much so that people often mistook them for twins. They had the same dark brown eyes, the same well-shaped nose, which on Eveleen was maybe just a fraction too large for real beauty. Their mouths were wide and generous and usually stretched in ready laughter. They even had the same rich brown hair colour, so when Jimmy had disappeared Eveleen had cut her own long tresses, dressed in his clothes and taken his place at the machine. She had been unlucky to be discovered, for she had the makings of a good worker; as good as any man it was said of her later. She could have been sacked for such a deception but Josh, as factory manager, had safeguarded her job in the inspection room.

Now she and Richard could laugh about the incident, which had gone down in the folklore of Reckitt and Stokes, but back then it had been one of the worst times in Eveleen's life.

Now she tucked her arm through Richard's and pleaded winningly, 'Go on. Let me have a go.'

'Maybe. When I've got a little more used to it myself.'

And with that, for the moment, Eveleen had to be content.

Seven

Hens scattered, squawking in alarm, even the curly coat pig shambled away, grunting noisily, as they drove into the yard at Pear Tree Farm. At once Bridie was beside them, jumping up and down in excitement. 'Take me for a ride. Please, *please*, Uncle Richard.'

Mary appeared in the back door of the farmhouse and came towards them. 'Richard, how lovely.' She went to him and held up her face for him to kiss her cheek. Bridie, hanging onto his arm, hopped from one foot to the other. 'We'll drive past the Dunsmores' big house. Even *they* haven't got a motor car.'

Laughing, Richard gently freed himself from Bridie's clinging hands and moved towards the side of the motor to help Eveleen alight. Close to her, Eveleen saw the look of concern cross his face at Bridie's innocent mention of the name Dunsmore. But as she put her hand into Richard's and stepped down, she said brightly, though with a hint of sarcasm not lost on her husband, '*What* a good idea, Bridie. Mam, how are you?'

She kissed Mary's cheek and then turned to see Josh lumbering towards them, his arms outstretched in welcome. 'Eh up, mi duck.'

Eveleen smiled warmly and put her arms as far round his girth as she could reach and kissed his weathered cheek. 'How are you, Josh?'

'Fine, fine,' he said as he always did but, drawing

back a little, Eveleen looked into his face. His answer had been a little too swift and there had been tension in his tone.

'You sure?' she asked softly, thinking that perhaps there was trouble between him and Mary. Her mother had always been a difficult person to live alongside with her temperamental mood swings. But it was unusual for Mary to quarrel with the man in her life. In Mary Carpenter's world, men were the superior beings and it was a woman's place to care for them, cosset them and pander to their every need. It had been so for as long as Eveleen could remember. Firstly with her own father and her brother, Jimmy, who could do no wrong in Mary's eyes. Now it was the same with Josh.

But today Eveleen could feel that something was wrong and as her mother's voice rose shrilly behind her, she knew the answer. 'Bridie, stop behaving like a child and leave Richard alone.'

Eveleen turned to see Mary grasping the girl's arm and physically dragging her away. 'Get back to the dairy and finish your work.'

For one awful moment, Eveleen thought Bridie was going to lash out at Mary. The girl's face was like thunder, her eyes glinting dangerously. Eveleen held her breath and only released it when she saw Bridie pull herself from Mary's grip, turn and march towards the dairy, her head held high in defiance.

Though the incident was not funny, Eveleen had a job to hide a wry smile. It was the way she would have acted at the same age.

Richard, too, had felt the atmosphere for he called after Bridie, 'When you've finished your work, love, we'll take you for a spin.'

'Don't encourage her, Richard. I don't know what's the matter with her these last few days,' Mary grumbled. 'Threatening to run away.'

'What?' Eveleen was startled.

'Oh yes,' Mary waved her hands airily. 'That's her answer to everything when she can't get her own way. She'd get a good hiding and told to be grateful she has a home if I had my way, but Josh is too soft with her. And as for Andrew when he comes, well, he treats her as if the sun shines out of her.' Then, suddenly, Mary smiled and she put her arm through Richard's and walked with him towards the house. 'But never mind that wilful little tyke. I've a batch of scones just out of the oven spread with jam and fresh cream.'

Richard glanced back over his shoulder and pulled a comical face of resignation. Eveleen nodded, but stayed where she was. As soon as they were out of earshot, she turned to Josh. 'Now, tell me. What has been going on?'

Josh ran his hand worriedly over his balding pate. His closed his eyes for a second, sighed and shook his head. 'Oh, Evie, I'm out of me depth, mi duck. They just seem to be clashing all the time. It's becoming a battle of wills.'

Eveleen put her hand through his arm and together they walked into the field and down towards the beck.

'I was like that at her age. Mam and me had some right old battles, I can tell you, with my poor dad in the middle of it all and Jimmy smirking on the sidelines and fuelling the fires whenever he could.'

'Aye. You were always a good lass and loyal to your brother, but he wasn't always the same to you, was he?'

'No,' Eveleen replied shortly and then deliberately brought the conversation back to Bridie, her immediate concern. She didn't want to think about Jimmy just now. 'Has something caused this bother between Mam and Bridie?'

Josh shook his head helplessly. 'Not that I know of, but then I'm not around them all the time. I don't know everything that passes between them, but I can feel something's not right.'

'Mm, so can I and I've only been here a few minutes.'

'She ran off the other day and hid in the woods. It wasn't until I went down to the Mortons and asked young Micky if he knew where she might be that she was found.'

'And you don't know why she did that?'

'It seemed to start from last Sunday when Andrew visited. They were talking about Flawford. Yer mam and Andrew, I mean. Mary asked after her own mother and Bridie got very indignant. It seems she hadn't realized that she had a great-grandmother still alive.'

'Ah,' Eveleen said, understanding at once. There was a pause and then she prompted, 'Was that all it was?'

Josh frowned. 'I think so and yet I can't see why that was enough to make her run off the next day, even if she was upset at not being told. Can you?'

They had reached the bank of the stream and stood watching the clear water babbling over rocks and boulders. They were silent for a few minutes, each thinking their own thoughts, then Eveleen said slowly, 'It's maybe only because she's growing up. She's almost thirteen and I can well remember thinking that because I was a working girl and earning a wage, I was a grown-up.' She sighed. 'It's a difficult age and Mam never was very good at understanding. Especially girls,' she added wryly.

'Your mother's a wonderful woman,' Josh declared stoutly.

'I know.' Eveleen squeezed his arm. 'And you make her so very happy. Nevertheless there's a "but" in there, isn't there, Josh?'

The big man sighed, but could not deny her words. 'I think Bridie could have overheard us talking.' He bit his lip, hesitant to be disloyal to his wife, yet Eveleen ought to know. 'Maybe she got the idea Mary has had her here on sufferance. But . . .' he added swiftly, leaping to Mary's defence, 'she didn't mean it that way. I know she didn't. Mary loves the child. We both do.'

Eveleen patted his hand. 'I know you do. I'm sure it's all a storm in a teacup. Bridie can be a bit wilful, I expect. Come on, let's go back and have some of those delicious scones of Mam's.'

Later Eveleen and Richard took Bridie for the promised jaunt in the new motor car, but above the noise of the engine talk was impossible and besides, Eveleen comforted herself, the child seemed happy enough now.

As they chugged along the lane, Bridie bounced up and down excitedly in the back seat, waving regally to anyone they passed and squealing with laughter when they passed an open-mouthed Micky Morton.

'Go up the hill, Uncle Richard. Past Fairfield House.'

Richard, with a brief glance at Eveleen, turned the motor to the left and up the lane towards where Fairfield House, the home of the Dunsmores, stood on the left-hand side.

Years ago all the land around had belonged to the Dunsmore estate. Eveleen's grandfather, Ben Hardcastle had worked for the Dunsmores and had lived in the tied dwelling of Pear Tree Farm. Walter, Ben's son and Eveleen's father, had worked for the estate all his life, yet only days after his death the family had been turned out of their home and had been obliged to find refuge with Mary's estranged family in Flawford.

It had been an unhappy time for the Hardcastle family. Eveleen, young and in love with Stephen Dunsmore and believing that he returned her love, was bitterly hurt by the young man's callous rejection of her and her family. It had been years before Richard's tender devotion had driven away the demons that haunted her because of it.

But Bridie knew none of this. Pear Tree Farm and the few acres surrounding it now belonged to Josh and Mary Carpenter. The young girl, innocent of the hurts of the past, had no cause to think any worse of the Dunsmore family than that they were the 'posh folks who lived at the big house'. All she knew was that her friend, Micky, and all the Morton family worked on the estate, their homes owned and their lives ruled by Stephen Dunsmore.

And so she was oblivious to Richard's anxious glances towards his wife, of Eveleen's hands, resting in her lap, clenching involuntarily. All Bridie wanted was to ride past the big, wrought-iron gates and show off Uncle Richard's fancy new motor car.

Richard took the car up the steep hill beneath the overhanging branches of Bernby Covert. At the top of the hill, he turned the car and they hurtled down again, Bridie shouting with delight. The tension left Eveleen's face and she clutched at her hat and laughed aloud too. But as they approached the gate to Fairfield House again, a horse cantered out, the rider unprepared for a horseless carriage rocketing down the hill towards him. Richard operated the brakes. The car slithered and shook and the horse whinnied and reared and then leapt over the hedge into the field opposite the driveway and galloped away, terrified by the noisy monstrosity. Half-way across the field, the rider was unseated and fell heavily to the ground where he lay motionless.

The car came to a shuddering halt and Richard cut the engine. At once Bridie was climbing out of the back seat. 'That was Mr Stephen. He might be hurt.'

'Bridie—' Eveleen began, but at once Richard put his hand on hers. Quietly he said, 'We must see if the fellow's hurt, my darling. But Bridie and I will go. You stay here.'

Already Bridie was running to the gate into the field a little further down the lane. Richard followed her, his long legs loping easily over the ground. Eveleen remained motionless in the car, her heart pounding, afraid to even look across the field towards where Stephen Dunsmore lay.

Eight

When Richard reached the prone figure, Bridie was already squatting beside him. 'Mr Stephen. It's me, Bridie. Are you hurt? Shall we fetch help from the house?'

To Richard's immense relief the man on the ground groaned loudly, rolled over and sat up slowly. He felt his head and then carefully all over his body. Richard stood watching. He had not even spoken to the man, leaving Bridie to play nursemaid.

'Can you stand up, Mr Stephen? Lean on me.'

The man looked up at Richard. 'What the hell do you think you were doing driving that monstrosity about the countryside like a maniac?'

'I'm sorry,' Richard said curtly, 'but you came out of that entrance without looking.'

'I don't expect to have to look on my own property.'

'I believe the lane is a public highway,' Richard said evenly.

Now the man was scrambling to his feet, hanging so heavily on Bridie's outstretched hand that he almost pulled the girl over. 'Is it, by God? We'll see about that.'

Once Stephen was on his feet, Bridie retrieved his riding hat and whip, lying a few feet away on the ground, and silently handed them to him.

Stephen, his fair hair blowing in the wind, took it

and glanced at her. His blue eyes sparked and his face was red with anger. 'Thanks,' he said curtly. 'Oh, it's you. The Carpenters' little bastard granddaughter, eh?' His lip curled and he turned towards Richard, staring at him. 'And I see who you are now.' His glance went beyond the two of them towards the motor standing in the lane.

He smiled maliciously. 'And the lovely Mrs Stokes, no less.' He pulled on his riding hat and slapped his whip against his leg. 'Well now, perhaps we'll say no more about it if you'll allow me to greet your delightful wife, whom I remember so *very* well.'

Puzzled, Bridie glanced between the two men. For a brief moment she thought Richard was going to punch Stephen in the face. She saw that his hands were clenched and he seemed to be having difficulty in keeping them firmly by his side.

'I don't think that would be a very good idea,' he said tightly. 'I'm relieved you're not hurt and I apologize that I was the cause of your horse being startled. But now we'll bid you good day.'

'Not so fast,' Stephen said through thin lips and he strode away towards Eveleen.

'Damnation take the fellow!' Richard muttered and hurried after him, Bridie running alongside to keep up.

As they reached the motor, Bridie saw Stephen doff his hat, bow in an exaggerated manner and say with heavy sarcasm, 'Well, well, well. Mrs Stokes. And how *are* you, my dear?'

Bridie glanced towards her aunt. Eveleen's cheeks were flaming, but her eyes were so cold and hard that Bridie gasped aloud. Eveleen's mouth was tight and she stared straight ahead, not even glancing at the man standing beside the vehicle. When she spoke, the tone of her voice matched her expression. 'I'm extremely well, thank you, Stephen.'

Richard lifted Bridie into the back seat and then moved to the front of the motor to swing the starting handle. As the engine burst into life and Richard climbed into the driving seat, Stephen moved back a pace and raised his hat once again, sarcasm in every movement.

As they drove home, no-one spoke, but even at her young age, Bridie could feel the tension between the two adults in the front seats.

'I'm just glad he wasn't injured,' Richard said. 'Or we might have been facing a lawsuit.'

Eveleen gave a very unladylike derisive snort and muttered, 'Knowing him of old, you still might be.'

'Oh, darling, please don't let him upset you. Not now.' They were standing alone together in the yard back at Pear Tree Farm. Richard put his arms around her. 'It's all a long time ago and . . .'

Eveleen was stiff, unyielding in his embrace. 'Richard, he . . .' Then suddenly the tension went out of her and she sagged against him. 'Oh, I suppose you're right.' She looked up at him and then, standing on tiptoe, kissed his cheek. 'What would I do without you?' she whispered.

Watching the tender scene from the scullery window, Bridie felt very envious and, suddenly, so very lonely.

'Where has the dratted child got to?' Mary was angry.

'Maybe she's gone to round up the cows for evening milking,' Josh said calmly.

'And when did she ever do anything useful of her own accord?' his wife snapped back.

Eveleen and Richard were ready to leave, but Bridie was missing. No-one had seen her since their return to the farm after their drive.

'She'll be hiding in the woods again. Well, she can stay there all night as far as I'm concerned.'

'Oh, Mam,' Eveleen said at once. 'You can't do that. It might be April, but the nights are still cold.'

'Your mam's only threatening,' Josh said. 'She wouldn't really want that.'

'Wouldn't I?' Mary muttered morosely.

Josh looked helplessly at Eveleen and Richard for a moment. A look that said: See what I mean?

'Do you want us to stay and help look for her?' Richard asked.

'No, no,' Josh tried to smile. 'We'll find her. If she doesn't turn up soon, I'll get young Micky to look for her.' His smile broadened. 'He seems to know all her hiding places.'

'It's ages since I saw the Morton family,' Eveleen said. 'We really must come and spend a day here and visit them. Anyway, we must get back now.' She kissed her mother and Josh and then the four of them went out into the yard. Mary and Josh stood watching as Richard started the car and, with everyone waving, drove out of the yard and up the rough cart track towards the lane.

Above the noise, he shouted, 'I don't like leaving whilst Bridie's missing. I hope she's all right.'

Eveleen tucked her arm through his. 'Josh will find her,' she said confidently and then, changing the subject, she smiled winningly at him. 'Now, before we reach the main Nottingham road, are you going to let me have a little drive?'

Richard gave an exaggerated sigh as if he were the epitome of a henpecked husband. 'Oh, very well then. I just hope the local bobby doesn't catch us. You're supposed to have a licence.'

He brought the vehicle to a halt and they changed seats. He gave clear and detailed instructions, yet the motor car still spluttered and bucked under Eveleen's efforts. But worse still, she could not immediately get the hang of steering and the vehicle veered wildly first to the right and then to the left, criss-crossing the narrow lane and bouncing over the deep, muddy ruts on the grass verge. Then they felt the vehicle begin to slide sideways into a shallow ditch. The motor car came to rest at a lurching angle, its nearside wheels firmly embedded in the water.

Richard hung onto the side to prevent himself being flung from the vehicle, whilst Eveleen could not help letting out a cry of alarm.

And from the back seat, under a rug, came an echoing squeal of fright.

Nine

As the engine noise petered out, Richard and Eveleen stared at each other and then slowly they turned together to look at the figure now sitting bolt upright on the back seat, startled and dishevelled but otherwise, like them, mercifully unhurt.

Their faces were a picture of surprise as they both said together. 'Bridie!' whilst the girl stared back belligerently.

'What on earth are you doing?' Eveleen asked.

'Running away,' the girl said promptly. 'To Nottingham.'

'You mean you want to come and live with us?' Richard asked.

The girl's chin rose defiantly. 'No, 'cos I don't suppose you want me either.'

Richard and Eveleen exchanged a swift glance then Eveleen asked, 'Whatever do you mean?'

Bridie bit hard on her lower lip, but not before the two adults had seen its sudden tremble. Richard reached over the back of the seat and touched her hand. 'What is it, love? You can tell us.'

Now tears filled the girl's eyes as she blurted out, 'I'm just some girl's bastard that nobody wants. Even Mr Stephen called me that, didn't he?'

'He *what*?' Eveleen cried and Richard's mouth tightened angrily.

'Yes, he did. Forgive me, Bridie, but in the heat of the moment I didn't really think about what he was saying. I wish now I *had* punched him on the nose.'

Even amidst her tears Bridie gave a hiccuping laugh. 'I wish you had too, Uncle Richard.' Then she sighed and said, 'But he's not the only one. It's what they called me at school.'

Eveleen gasped. 'Oh, how cruel!'

'Well, no-one's going to call you it ever again, if I can help it,' Richard said firmly. 'But now I want you to tell us exactly why you want to run away from your gran and Josh.'

Bridie plucked at the edge of the rug and avoided the concerned look on both their faces. 'It – it's not, Josh, so much as – as . . .' she mumbled, hesitant to speak ill of Mary to her daughter, but Eveleen was quick to understand and to end the sentence for the girl by saying wryly, 'My mother.'

Richard probed further, but gently. 'Is it something that's just happened?'

'Well – sort of.'

They waited, oblivious now of the time or even of their predicament, whilst the motor car's wheels settled even deeper into the ditch.

'She was telling me off. Nothing much, just that I hadn't fed the hens and that I was always running off to play with Micky and not doing my work.' She looked up at Eveleen. 'You know.'

Eveleen nodded and said softly, 'Yes, I know.'

'And then I said I'd run away and she said where to and I said I'd go to you.' Again there was silence, until Bridie blurted out, 'And she said you were too busy to be looking after a troublesome child like me.'

'Oh, darling.' Eveleen laughed, trying to make the

sensitive girl understand. 'That's just your gran's way. She's always been a bit – well – sharp.'

Richard was watching Bridie's face and said softly, 'There's more than that, isn't there, love?'

Bridie blinked but then nodded. 'It – it was about Andrew. You see, I thought if you and Uncle Richard didn't want me, then Andrew would. I was sure Andrew loved me . . .' Her voice, thick with disappointment, faded away.

'He does love you, Bridie. We all know that. *You* know that.'

'Yes.' The girl was leaning towards them now, almost shouting at them in her anguish. 'But *why* does he love me?'

The two adults stared at her, completely mystified. Then Richard gave an awkward laugh. 'You're getting a bit deep for me now, Bridie. You might well ask why anyone loves another.'

The girl shook her head vehemently. 'No, no. You don't understand. *He only loves me because I'm the daughter of the love of his life.* He doesn't love me for *me*.' She jabbed her forefinger into her chest with such ferocity that it hurt.

'Who on earth told you a thing like that?' Eveleen said, angry and disgusted at the person who could have been so unfeeling.

Bridie hung her head and plucked at the edge of the rug again, shredding the fabric between her restless fingers. 'Gran,' she muttered.

Eveleen groaned and closed her eyes for a moment. 'I might have known,' she murmured.

'Look,' Richard said, thinking quickly and leaning over the back seat to take Bridie's cold hand in his, 'we can't sort all this out sitting here and we've got to get

59

help from someone to pull this contraption out of the ditch or we're never going to get home tonight. But I want you to promise me something, Bridie.'

The girl looked up at him trustingly. 'What?'

'If you will go back home now and be a good girl, Eveleen and I will say nothing about this to anyone.' As Bridie opened her mouth to protest, Richard went on firmly, 'And we'll let a week or two elapse and then we'll ask your gran to let you come and have a holiday with us in Nottingham. We'll have time to talk about this and to reassure you,' he squeezed her hand comfortingly, 'that we all love you because you're *you* and not because of whose daughter you are.'

Bridie smiled tremulously, but was still not convinced.

'And now,' Eveleen said brightly, 'because your auntie Eveleen has been so very naughty, we really must get help. It'll be getting dark soon.'

Richard laughed aloud and said, 'No-one's hurt, that's all that matters. Including our stowaway. Now,' he went on, 'who do you know with a big, strong carthorse?'

Bridie stood up and began to scramble out of the motor. 'Micky's dad. I'll run and fetch him.' And before either of them could stop her, she was running up the lane. 'Wait there,' she called back. 'I'll fetch Mr Ted.'

'As if we're going anywhere,' Richard remarked ruefully, as he climbed out and stood in the lane looking at his beautiful new motor car, tilted forlornly in the ditch. 'Really I ought to put you across my knee.' He arched his black eyebrows wickedly at his wife. 'If I didn't think you might enjoy it.'

'Really, Richard,' Eveleen admonished, but she was

smiling playfully. 'Fancy saying such a thing.' She stood up and held out her arms to him. 'Darling, I am sorry.'

'You're forgiven,' he said, lifting her out and setting her down on the road. Then he slid down the grass slope and tried to examine the motor.

'Do you think it's damaged?' Eveleen asked anxiously.

'As far as I can see, no.' Richard climbed back up towards her. 'Luckily the ditch is only very shallow and so the workings beneath the car haven't touched the bank. It's still actually resting on its wheels as far as I can make out. So, hopefully, not a lot of harm done.'

Eveleen gave a sigh of relief. 'Thank goodness.'

At that moment they heard the sound of clopping hooves coming down the lane and turned to see Bridie running ahead of a man leading a huge shire horse towards them. Walking beside him was a young boy about Bridie's age.

'It's Ted.' Eveleen clapped her hands. 'And that must be his son, Micky. Oh, it's ages since I last saw them.'

Richard smiled at his wife indulgently and, as she hurried towards them, her hands outstretched, he murmured wryly, 'Ah well, it's an ill wind that blows nobody any good.'

The motor had been pulled easily back onto the road and Richard, after a better inspection, declared that he thought no serious damage had been done. 'Mind you, if a wheel falls off between here and Nottingham, I'll know who to blame.'

He held out his hand to Ted Morton. 'Thank you so much for your help.'

'Glad to be of service, Mr Richard,' Ted said. Then he glanced at Eveleen and winked. 'But you don't have to cause an accident to get to see me, Evie. Come and visit me and Alice soon, won't you? And me mam and dad are always asking after you.'

Ted and Eveleen had grown up together and their fathers, living and working on the same farm estate, had been good friends. As a youth, Ted had flirted with her, but Eveleen had always managed to answer his saucy comments with good-humoured banter.

She laughed now. 'I see you haven't changed, Ted Morton. But we will come and see you all. I promise.'

As they lay together in bed that night, their arms about each other, Eveleen said, 'I don't know whatever possessed my mother to say such a thing to poor Bridie. Mind you,' she added bitterly, 'I ought to know.'

'I can hardly believe she would say such a thing.'

'Oh, she would. Believe me.'

'I've never seen that side of your mother.'

'You wouldn't. You're a man.'

'I don't understand.'

'My mother dotes on men of all ages. She's no time for girls.' Eveleen's sigh came from deep inside. 'If we had been lucky enough to have a son, she would have been besotted with him. But a girl? No.'

Richard's arms tightened about her. 'Don't say that in the past tense, my darling. There's plenty of time.'

'Is there? I'm the wrong side of thirty now.'

In the darkness, he kissed her forehead. 'Remind me to order you that bath chair.'

Eveleen dug him in the ribs.

'Ouch!'

'Serves you right.' She paused and then added seriously, 'But I did take to heart what you said the other day. I've made plans to cut down my workload a little. I'm giving Helen more responsibility.'

'I'm glad. It might help her too.'

They were silent, each thinking about Eveleen's friend. Shortly after their own marriage, Helen had begun walking out with a young man who worked in the factory. She had been ecstatically happy and they had been planning to be married, when the young man had been taken ill. Consumption had been diagnosed and the last sight Helen had had of him had been waving to him through the window of the hospital, where no visitors were allowed.

He had died during the week they had planned to be married.

'She went through a dreadful time,' Eveleen murmured, 'but just lately she's begun to look a little happier. I think she might have met someone else. She's not saying much, not even to me, but I can't blame her for that. She must feel rather afraid to love again.'

'Like someone else I know, though for a very different reason.'

Now Richard was kissing her mouth and all talk was stopped, except his murmured words of love.

Ten

'Mam, we've been thinking. We'd like Bridie to come and stay with us for a holiday.'

They were visiting one Sunday and Eveleen broached the subject as she helped her mother to wash up after dinner.

Mary crashed a plate down on the draining board and glanced over her shoulder. 'So that's what the little madam's been up to, is it?'

Eveleen kept her expression as innocent looking as she could manage. 'I don't know what you mean.'

'Oh, I think you do. She's been telling you how badly I treat her, no doubt making it far worse than it is. She needs a firm hand, Eveleen. She's a wild, disobedient little tyke and Josh won't discipline her, so I have to.'

Mary dried her hands on a towel and turned to face Eveleen. 'He treats her very much like your father, my poor Walter, used to treat you. You girls wrap these men round your little fingers and they can't see any wrong in you. Look at all that business with Stephen Dunsmore. If you had only listened to me, you'd have saved yourself and all of us a lot of heartache. And maybe,' she wagged her forefinger in Eveleen's face, 'just maybe your father would still be alive to this day.'

Eveleen had fought hard through the years to come to terms with her mother's accusation, but even now the words were like a knife in her heart.

'It was all your fault we were turned out of our home and had to go to Flawford and look where that led. Rebecca setting her cap at Jimmy and getting herself pregnant just to trap him. I don't blame him for running away to sea. I would have done the same if I'd been in his shoes, but it doesn't stop me missing him every day of my life. And I've you to thank for that.'

'Mam,' Eveleen said, trying hard to hold onto her patience, 'do you have to rake up the past and throw it at me every time we come home?'

'Only because, if Bridie comes to live with you, she'll copy some of your bad ways. She's better staying here with me where I can keep her in line.'

'I didn't say anything about her coming to live with us. I just said for a holiday.'

'Oh aye. But once she's there, she'll wheedle her way round you. And Richard, because he's every bit as soft with her as Josh is. She's desperate to get away from me. She even suggested going to Andrew's. I soon put a stop to that.'

Yes, I know you did, Eveleen thought resentfully, and in a very cruel way. But she held her tongue. Old as she was now, answering her mother back would still serve no purpose. She finished drying the dishes and pulled down the sleeves of her blouse. She wished that she had left it to Richard to speak to her mother. She was sure that he would have won Mary over.

By the time Josh, Richard and Bridie returned from their walk around the farm, Eveleen and her mother were barely speaking to each other. The two women were sitting in silence on either side of the fire in Mary's best parlour, a room only used on Sundays and special occasions. Richard came to the hearth and stood between them, rubbing his hands and holding them out towards the blaze, for the May day was unusually cold, a blustery wind blowing and rain threatening.

'All settled, then?' he asked, glancing from one to the other.

Eveleen shook her head. 'My mother doesn't trust me to look after her.'

Mary turned to Bridie standing near the table. 'Go upstairs, child. This is not for your ears.'

'But, Gran—' the girl began.

'Do as I say,' Mary snapped. The girl glowered and clamped her jaws together to silence any protest. She turned and wrenched open the door leading into the small hallway. No-one in the room spoke as they listened to her stamping her way up the stairs and slamming the door of her bedroom.

Josh ran his hand across his forehead and Eveleen and Richard exchanged a glance.

Frowning slightly, Richard pulled out a chair from beneath the table and placed it carefully next to Mary.

'And you needn't start your wheedling, either,' Mary said, but now her tone was playful and the look she cast up at him, coy.

Richard smiled at her. 'Just tell me,' he asked in his soft, deep tones, 'why you think we can't look after her properly.'

'I didn't say you.' Mary sniffed. 'I said her.' She nodded across the hearth at her daughter.

Behind them, Josh gave a sigh and lowered his bulk into a chair near the table, as if resigning himself to a long, wrangling argument. Then all at once, he stood up again. 'Evie, you come with me, mi duck. We'll leave your mam and Richard to talk.' When Eveleen seemed to hesitate, he added firmly, 'Come on.'

He took her coat down from the peg behind the back door and held it for her, whilst she slipped her arms in.

As Josh held open the back door for her, Eveleen overheard her mother, with a different, much gentler tone, say, 'I realize you must think I'm too harsh with Bridie, but I'm responsible for her. I know what can happen to young girls. Believe me. And sometimes, Richard, I am so afraid for her . . .'

'The rain's still holding off,' Josh said, interrupting Eveleen's eavesdropping. 'We'll walk to the beck.'

They walked in silence through the farmyard, hens scattering at their approach, through the gate and into the neighbouring field, which led down to the stream. It wasn't until they were standing on the bank, Eveleen's arm tucked through Josh's, and watching the rushing water that Eveleen said quietly, 'It was about here I found him.'

Josh nodded. 'Aye, I know, lass, I know.'

'She still blames me for his death, you know. She says that the worry over my involvement with Stephen Dunsmore caused his death.'

'That's nonsense.'

'I know. His family had some sort of weakness of the heart. His own father had died in much the same way. But you won't convince my mother of that.'

'When I first got to know you and your family,' Josh said. 'I knew things were – well – difficult between you and your mother, but at the time Mary and I married I thought it would get easier.'

'It did. Much easier.'

'Is it my fault do you think? Is she not happy with me now?'

'Oh, Josh, she's wonderfully happy with you. Don't

ever think that. This has absolutely nothing to do with you. What I mean is, it's not your fault in any way.' She sighed. 'It's me. Or rather, it's because Bridie is growing up and Mam has the same concerns about her as she once had about me.'

Josh digested her words and then nodded. 'I see what you mean.' He pulled a comical face and added, 'I think.'

Eveleen glanced at him. Carefully she said, 'And then there's her own unhappiness she suffered as a young girl.'

She was treading very tentatively, anxious not to divulge secrets that her mother had not shared with Josh. But he nodded and said quietly, 'Yes, she told me all about that, even before we were married.' He turned his head and smiled at Eveleen now. 'She was so afraid it would make a difference to me.'

Eveleen squeezed his arm. He was such a good, kind man and he loved Mary unconditionally. Eveleen believed that, whatever Mary might have done in her youth, it would have made no difference to the man standing beside her, just as it never had to her own father.

'Her family treated her so cruelly,' Eveleen said with compassion. 'There's no wonder the scars are still there.'

'It's a shame, though,' Josh reflected sadly, 'that the past is still blighting the present.'

Now he patted her hand as it rested on his arm. 'Mind you don't let that happen. Don't let Stephen Dunsmore's cruel desertion of you spoil your happiness with Richard.'

Eveleen's eyes clouded. 'I thought I was completely over the hurt, but when I saw him again the other week – you know, when our motor frightened his horse – I have to admit, though only to you, Josh, that it opened the wound again.'

Josh was firm as he said, 'Well, you really shouldn't let it. Richard adores you. He'll never hurt you.'

They walked back to the house and found Richard ready to leave, but it wasn't until they were in the car and heading home that he admitted, 'I didn't get any further with her than you did, darling. But we won't give up. It's time that poor child saw another side to life.'

From an upstairs window, Bridie, biting hard on her lower lip to stem tears that threatened, watched them leave.

Both Richard and Eveleen had come to her bedroom to say goodbye to her. They had hugged her and promised that somehow they would persuade her gran to change her mind.

But, as she watched them go, Bridie did not believe their promises. She felt betrayed and deserted by everyone around her.

Eleven

It took Richard three more visits to Pear Tree Farm and until almost the end of June to persuade Mary to allow Bridie to visit Nottingham.

'And only a week, mind. I want her back here next Sunday without fail. There'll be our haymaking soon. She'll be needed and Ted Morton says there'll be work for her on the estate. I don't want her getting used to a life of idleness.'

'Oh, she won't be idle,' Richard promised, winking at Bridie. 'We've got such a lot of things planned. She'll not have a minute to call her own.'

Mollified a little, Mary sniffed. 'I'm pleased to hear it.' Then she glanced at him shrewdly. 'But I don't expect it's honest hard work you've got planned for her, is it? Just a lot of gallivanting.'

What intrigued Bridie more than anything was the way her aunt and Richard lived.

'Who's the man who opened the door?' she whispered when she first stepped into the house.

'That's Smithers,' Eveleen said, leading the way into the morning room and crossing to the fireplace to pull on a bell cord.

Only moments later a young girl, not much older

than Bridie but dressed in the smart afternoon uniform of a parlourmaid, entered the room.

'Emily, would you bring tea for us, please?'

The girl bobbed a curtsy and left, but not before the two young girls had eyed each other.

'You've got a maid too?'

Eveleen laughed, 'Yes, darling. And a cook and a kitchenmaid, but that's all.'

'All!' Bridie exclaimed.

'A lot of people would have about twice as many. Smithers doubles as a butler and as Uncle Richard's valet, and Emily is a housemaid in the mornings and parlourmaid in the afternoon. And she acts as my personal maid too.'

Bridie pulled a face. 'And I thought I worked hard on the farm.'

'Richard is very fair to his employees both at home and at the factory,' her aunt explained as they sat down together to wait for the tea to arrive. 'And I would say your work is harder. You have to be out in all weathers and work even longer hours than our servants do.'

Bridie giggled. 'I can't get used to it. You having servants.'

Eveleen smiled and leant forward conspiratorially. 'It took me a long time to get used to it, too. In fact, I don't think I am even now. I'm always doing things for myself that Emily says should be her job.' She straightened up as the door opened. 'Ah, here she is with the tea.'

Fascinated, Bridie watched as the young girl set the tray on the low table near Eveleen.

'Thank you, Emily. I'll pour.'

The girl bobbed again. 'Very good, ma'am.'

'And would you take some tea to Mr Stokes? I think he's gone to his study.'

As the door closed behind her, Bridie said, 'Won't Uncle Richard have tea with us?'

'No, love. He's got some paperwork to do, but he'll join us for dinner naturally.'

Naturally, Bridie thought. None of this was 'natural' to her. She glanced at the clock on the mantelpiece. If she'd been at home now, she'd be setting the table for tea and then going outside into the yard to help Josh milk their six cows instead of sitting here in this elegant room, sipping tea out of delicate bone-china cups and nibbling at dainty fancy cakes.

'Won't I see him till tomorrow dinnertime, then?' she asked.

For a moment, Eveleen looked puzzled and then smiled. 'Oh, I'm sorry. I was forgetting. We have dinner in the evening. Lunch is our midday meal.'

'Oh,' Bridie said, realizing that she had a lot to learn about life in the city.

'Your bath's ready, miss.' Emily had woken her on her first morning at eight o'clock.

Bright light streamed through the curtains, which the girl had opened and, startled, Bridie jumped out of bed. 'Oh, whatever time is it? I'm late.' Then realizing where she was, she laughed. 'I forgot.'

'Your bath's ready, miss,' the maid repeated and added, 'And breakfast is served in the dining room at nine o'clock.'

'Bath?'

'Yes, miss. The bathroom's just outside your door, to the left.'

'Oh. Thank you.'

Bath night to Bridie was on a Friday in a tin bath on the pegged hearthrug in front of the kitchen fire, her gran pouring in hot water from the range whilst Josh was banished to the front room until she had finished. Now, it seemed, she was expected to bathe each morning.

When the maid had gone, Bridie tiptoed a little nervously into the bathroom and gasped. Shiny, patterned wallpaper covered the walls and on the floor was black-and-white chequered linoleum. A huge cast-iron bath with clawed feet, half full of steaming water, was against one wall and near the opposite wall was a marble-topped, tile-backed washstand with a bowl and water jug. This too was full of hot water. Soap and sponge lay in matching dishes and a brand-new hog's hair toothbrush had been laid out for Bridie's use. White, lace-edged towels hung on a rail and soaps and perfumes lined a shelf. Bridie had never seen anything like this in her life, but sinking into the gloriously hot water, she thought: I could get used to this.

Her aunt's home was so very different from the farm where both she and Bridie had been brought up. This was a town house in an elegant street of tall, terraced houses. It had an entrance hall with rooms on either side. What did Auntie Evie call them? Bridie wrinkled her nose, trying to recall. The morning room, the drawing room, and then there was the dining room and Uncle Richard's study too. And somewhere, at the back, there must be the kitchen and scullery and maybe a servants' sitting room. Upstairs there were four bedrooms, the bathroom she was in at this moment and then up another flight of stairs, were the servants' bedrooms.

What would her gran think to all this? Bridie

thought, as she began to soap herself all over, relishing the luxury.

How lucky Aunt Eveleen was to be married to a man like Uncle Richard. But then, the girl thought: I'd be quite happy to live in a tiny cottage with a tin bath on the hearth once a week, if only Andrew really loved me.

They did indeed do a lot of gallivanting. Eveleen took her round the city shops, buying her niece a dark blue dress with a white, lace-trimmed smock to wear over it, a coat and beret-type hat.

'Now, you really look a grown-up young lady,' Richard said as the girl paraded before him that evening. She didn't really, Bridie thought, for the style was still childish, but she had not liked to seem ungrateful for her aunt's generosity.

'Tomorrow,' Richard was saying, 'I'll take you on the river. And the following day I'll take you on a tour of the factory, that's if you'd like to see it. Then on your last night here, we'll take you out to dine in a smart restaurant and then to the theatre.'

Bridie clapped her hands. 'Oh, I'd love to see where you work.' Hurriedly, she added, 'Where you both work. Then when I'm back home I can picture you at home and at work too. I can imagine what you're doing.'

Eveleen and Richard exchanged a glance. Her words had a sad and lonely ring to them.

Twelve

'Do you know, Richard, it's a joy to see her delight in everything,' Eveleen told him as they sat across the breakfast table before Bridie appeared on her last morning with them. 'I've just heard her singing in the bath.'

'Mmm,' Richard said absently, not looking up from his newspaper.

'Darling, did you hear what I said?'

He lowered his paper and smiled at her, but she was quick to see that a worried frown did not quite leave his face.

'What is it, dear? You haven't minded having her here, have you?'

Now he laughed and, for a moment, the anxiety fled his face. 'Oh, my darling, of course not. She's an enchanting child. I've loved having her here,' he assured her, but now the apprehensive look came back as he prodded the newspaper with his forefinger. 'No, no, it's something here in the paper. It's looking increasingly as if we're going to be plunged into trouble in Europe. It might even lead to war.'

Eveleen blinked. 'War!' Wrapped up in her own little world of life with Richard, her work at the warehouse and overseeing all the homeworkers, Eveleen took little interest in news, politics and world affairs. Richard's prophecy was a profound shock to her. 'Who with, for goodness sake?'

'It's a bit complicated . . .'

'Too difficult for my little woman's mind to understand?' Eveleen bridled.

'No, no, darling. I can't understand why we need to be involved myself, but it sounds as if we might be. Archduke Franz Ferdinand, the heir to the Austro-Hungarian throne, has been assassinated in Sarajevo. He was shot by a Bosnian nationalist – a nineteen-year-old student.'

'Nineteen!' Eveleen was appalled. 'What on earth does a nineteen-year-old know about politics?'

Richard sighed. 'I'm very much afraid, my love, that at that age they think they know it all. It says here the archduke's wife flung herself across her husband and was killed too. She died instantly, he a little while later. You know,' Richard continued grimly, 'it reads as if it was a carefully planned plot. Earlier, they'd had a bomb thrown at their car, but had escaped injury then.'

'But why? What's he done? Why should someone want to kill him?'

'It seems,' Richard said slowly, scanning the printed page, 'it's something to do with the oppression of the Serbian people.'

Eveleen waved her hand, 'You're right, I admit it. It is too complicated for me to understand. Why should that involve Britain in a war? It's nothing to do with us.' When Richard did not answer, she pressed, 'Is it?'

'I suppose, put simply, if there's trouble in Europe we'll be involved, firstly in trying to keep the peace, but if that fails . . .'

'Oh, Richard, no,' Eveleen's eyes were wide with fear and she covered her mouth with trembling fingers.

At that moment they heard Bridie's footsteps outside the door.

'Don't say anything in front of Bridie. We don't want to spoil her first visit to us,' Richard said hurriedly.

With a supreme effort, they both turned to greet the girl with wide smiles.

'You've spoilt everything.' Bridie, in floods of tears, stamped her foot.

'Don't you take that tone with me, my girl, or I won't let you go again,' Mary snapped. 'Anyone would think you're not pleased to be home.'

'I'm not.' The rash words were out of her mouth before she could stop them. Horrorstruck, she stared at her grandmother.

'Well!' For a moment even Mary was lost for words.

'Gran, I didn't mean it.' Bridie rushed to her, trying to put her arms about the older woman's waist, but Mary pushed her away. 'I'm sorry. Truly, I am. I didn't mean it. It's just that I've had such a lovely time and – now you're finding fault with the clothes Aunt Eveleen's bought me and – and everything we've done.' She hung her head and muttered, 'And it just spoils it all.'

'You're the only thing that's been spoilt, my girl. Well, whether you like it or not, you are back home and here you're going to stay. Now, if you want to show me you're really sorry, you'd better get some work done.'

Gone in an instant were all the cosseting, the being waited on by Emily, having her bed made, her clothes laid out and her bath made ready. No more luxuriating in scented water and lying between fresh smelling sheets.

Bridie was home and back to reality with a bump.

*

The troubles in Europe dominated the conversation over the next few weeks.

'It's all a lot of nonsense,' Mary declared emphatically. 'Why do we have to get involved in trouble that's happened thousands of miles away?'

Josh, with a greater understanding of political matters, sighed. 'Well, as I see it – of course, I might be wrong—'

'Oh, I'm sure you're not,' Mary patted his shoulder as she passed by his chair. 'You men are so clever over such matters, but I still don't see why Britain has to become involved.'

She sat down at the table and leant her chin on her hand, smiling at him coyly, 'Explain it to me.'

Watching, Bridie smothered her amusement. Her gran was openly flirting with Josh, playing up to his vanity.

'We'll get involved because if we don't and a full-scale war breaks out, we could soon be next in line. We'll try to keep the peace.'

Mary smiled and said smoothly, 'I see.'

Josh eyed her over the top of his newspaper. 'Mary Carpenter,' he said, feigning severity, 'I do believe you're teasing me.'

She laughed, stood up and planted a kiss on the bald patch on the top of his head. 'Of course, I'm teasing you, Josh. What do any of us poor mortals know about politics and foreign parts? Why, I've never been further than a day trip to the seaside and I don't intend to either.'

'To the seaside? You've been to the seaside, Gran?' Bridie's face brightened. 'How did you get there?'

'On the train from Grantham.'

Bridie clapped her hands. 'On a train! I've never been

on a train. Oh, can we go? I've never seen the sea. Can we?'

'We could go on August bank holiday Monday,' Josh said. 'There'll be day trips on, I dare say.'

'Oh no.' Mary put up her hands. 'This child's done enough gallivanting for the time being. High time she settled down now.'

'But we could all go. The three of us,' Bridie said eagerly and even Josh looked at Mary hopefully.

'Oh aye,' her grandmother rounded on the girl. 'And who would do the milking and feed the livestock, might I ask?'

Bridie's face fell. Even though she had no personal experience, she realized that a day trip would take just that, the full day from early morning to late evening and the animals needed looking after during that time.

Crestfallen, she sighed. 'Yes, Gran,' she said, feigning meekness. She rose from the breakfast table and began to clear away the dirty dishes into the scullery, biting her lip to stop the tears of disappointment. She was not even heartened by Josh's helpless shrug, as if he too would have enjoyed a day at the sea.

As she went about her daily chores with an outward show of obedience, Bridie's heart hardened and her resolve to escape this life of drudgery grew stronger.

Thirteen

'You there, Bridie?' It was Micky's voice in the yard.

'In here,' she called from the dairy. She stopped churning as he appeared in the doorway. Wiping her sweating forehead, she went towards him. 'Isn't it hot? Too hot for the butter to come. It's taking me hours.'

'Here, I'll give it a go for you.' Micky grinned, showing white, even teeth against his tanned skin. His fair, straight hair flopped across his forehead and his blue eyes sparkled with merriment.

Out of breath from her labours, Bridie leant against the doorframe. 'I won't say no, 'cos I'm out on me feet.'

Micky took the handle and turned it steadily, whilst Bridie mopped her face, the back of her neck and her hands with a piece of old towelling. Above the rattling of the churn, Micky shouted, 'There's a day trip from the village to the seaside on Monday. You know, the bank holiday?'

Bridie nodded without looking at him. Instead she concentrated on carefully wiping each finger.

'Me mam and dad and us kids are going on it. Even me grandma's coming. Grandad's staying to feed the livestock, but we're all off. Why don't you come with us? We're going on the train from Grantham.'

'Gran won't let me.'

Micky stopped churning briefly. 'What?'

'I said, Gran won't let me.'

'How do you know?'

'Because I've asked her. She's says I've had enough holidays at me auntie Evie's.'

'Oh.' Micky's disappointment was obvious. 'That's a pity. I reckon we could've had a good time at the seaside. You an' me.'

'Yes,' Bridie said, her tone flat. 'We could.' She sighed and moved towards him. 'I'd better get on with this.'

'I'll do it,' Micky said, and began to turn the handle again, muttering, 'What an owd beezum your gran can be at times.'

Bridie managed a thin smile, but the misery in her heart deepened.

She tried once again at breakfast time the next morning, relating to Josh and her grandmother what Micky had told her.

'Why not let the lass go with the Mortons, Mary love?' Even Josh was pleading her case now. 'They'll look after her.'

'Huh! You think so? You don't know what Ted was like as a youngster. His son'll be just the same. After anything in skirts.'

'Mary, they're twelve years old, not seventeen. What on earth do you think they're going to get up to on a day trip to the sea with half the village with them?'

'She's not going and that's final,' Mary said firmly and added as a wily excuse, 'besides, Andrew's coming. You won't want to miss seeing Andrew, will you?'

On the Monday morning of the bank holiday, Bridie was up before dawn. As the rising sun cast its first fingers of light across the misty landscape and the sky to the east was streaked with pink and a glorious apricot colour, Bridie climbed the five-barred gate at the end of the yard and sat on top of it. Straight down the rough cart track and then the lane beyond was Furze Farm, where Bill and Dorothy Morton, Micky's grandparents, lived. Beyond that, about half a mile further down the lane, was the cottage where Micky lived.

There were sounds reaching her ears now, through the silence of the early morning; voices raised in excited anticipation of the day ahead. She saw the shadowy figures of Micky and his family walking up the lane towards Furze Farm, where they disappeared into the yard. A few moments later she heard the rattling of cartwheels and saw the farm cart come out of the gate and turn into the lane, coming towards her. When it reached the place where the cart track to her own home came straight ahead and the lane turned to their right on its way towards Bernby village and then on to Grantham, Bridie saw Ted pull the cart to a halt. He raised his hand and waved. 'You coming with us, love?'

'No, Mr Morton,' she shouted, her voice echoing eerily in the still morning. 'Have a good time, all of you.'

The two younger children were already squabbling in the back of the cart, with their mother trying vainly to calm their excitement. Bridie forced herself to smile and to wave. 'Bring me back a shell from the beach,' she called as Ted slapped the reins and the cart set off once more.

She watched them until they turned another corner and were out of sight. Straining her ears she could still just hear their voices as the cart went up the hill past Fairfield House and on to Bernby.

Bridie sat there staring into the distance as the sun rose behind her, feeling as if everyone had deserted her.

Andrew arrived mid-morning and Bridie went to meet him, but this time she did not run towards him, flinging herself at him so that he lifted her up and swung her round.

He put his arm round her shoulders and kissed her cheek, then stood back from her a little and looked down at her. 'What have I done?'

She could see the concern in his face, his eyes anxious. Suddenly she felt guilty. He knew nothing of what her grandmother had said. He had not changed. All right, his love for her wasn't what she had thought it to be – hoped it to be. But, if she was fair, that was hardly his fault. She decided to tell the truth, but not the whole truth.

She smiled at him. 'Gran says I'm too big now to be lifted up like a little girl. I should start acting more like a young lady. She's going to let me put my hair up when I'm thirteen in September.' She demonstrated, picking up her long, thick black plait and winding it in a circle around her crown.

All at once there was a haunted look in Andrew's hazel eyes and when he spoke, his voice was cracked with emotion. He reached out and touched her cheek tenderly. 'Oh, Bridie. That was how your mam used to wear her hair sometimes. You look so like her.'

He couldn't possibly know how his words hurt her.

Fourteen

'Oh no!'

On the Tuesday morning Richard was standing in the hallway, the morning paper open in his hands, as Eveleen came down the stairs.

'What is it?'

Slowly he raised his eyes and his voice was hoarse as he said, 'We've declared war on Germany.'

'Germany? Why Germany?' Eveleen asked.

'Mm?' Richard was only half listening, his concentration once more on the newspaper.

'I said, why Germany? I thought all the trouble started in Sarajevo when the Archduke was assassinated at the end of June.'

'It did,' Richard said grimly, turning a page of the newspaper. 'But it reads here as if that was just the spark that ignited a conflagration that was waiting to happen. Austria was bound to retaliate and they declared war on Serbia last week.' He sighed. 'The delicate balance of power that existed between all the nations trying to keep the peace has just gone horribly wrong.'

'But what's that got to do with Germany and us?'

'Germany's allied itself with Austria.'

'But – but our royal family's related to the Kaiser.'

Richard sighed. 'So's the Tsar. He's his cousin, but it hasn't stopped the Kaiser declaring war on Russia.

Family ties don't seem to matter when it comes to political issues. And now it seems as if the Kaiser has taken offence at Britain's attempts to mediate. Germany declared war on France a couple of days ago and now, because they've marched into Belgium, we've declared war on Germany.'

Eveleen's eyes widened in alarm as the dreadful truth began to sink in. 'All those countries involved already?'

Richard nodded.

'So what will it mean for us?' She put her hand on his sleeve. 'You won't have to go, will you?'

Richard's tone was sober as he said carefully, 'I won't be *made* to go, not at first, no. Lord Kitchener has been appointed Secretary for War and he's calling for volunteers.'

Eveleen gasped and her hand fluttered to cover her mouth. She knew him so well, knew what his words meant. 'You mean – you mean you *want* to go? You want to volunteer?'

His dark eyes regarded her soberly. Quietly he said, 'I shall think about it very seriously, my love. But I promise I won't do anything without talking it over with you first.'

She put her arms around him and laid her cheek against his chest and heard the steady beat of his heart. 'I won't let you go,' she murmured. 'I swear I won't let you go.'

Richard stroked her hair, but he made no answer.

'Well, thank the good Lord you're too old to go.' Mary slammed a tureen down on the table. 'What on earth is our government thinking of? Getting us involved in a stupid war that's none of our making.'

Josh was sitting by the range, devouring the newspaper.

'Oh, put that paper down, Josh, and come and get your dinner.'

Bridie was moving silently between the scullery and the kitchen table. She was anxious. She had listened to all the talk of war and she was suddenly very afraid. Micky had come to the farm that morning full, not of the trip to the seaside and bearing her a gift – he'd even forgotten to bring her a shell – but of the impending war.

'By heck!' Micky had said, thumping his fist against the palm of his other hand. 'I wish I was a bit older. I'd be off.' His eyes were shining. 'Me dad's talking about going. Lots of the young fellers from round here are going already. They're off to Grantham or Nottingham today to volunteer.'

'What do you want to go and get yourself killed for?' Bridie had asked him bluntly.

'Killed?' he scoffed. 'Who said anything about getting killed? I'd just like to go and fight for me country.'

'And isn't that what happens in a war?' Bridie asked quietly. 'Don't people kill each other?'

'Well, I suppose a few get killed,' the young boy admitted, but then he added proudly, 'but mostly you get mentioned in dispatches and the King pins a medal on your chest. Besides,' he added saucily, 'if I get wounded, you could be a nurse and look after me.' His grin widened. 'I'd like that.'

Bridie had said no more, but now, seated across the dinner table from her grandmother and Josh, she felt the fear rise in her throat.

'Who will have to go? Will Micky?'

'No, no, love,' Josh smiled at her, though the anxiety

did not quite leave his eyes. 'He's far too young. I don't expect it will last very long. A few weeks at the most.'

In a small voice she said, 'Micky said his dad's talking of going.'

'Ted?' Mary, in the act of spooning vegetables onto a plate, stared at Bridie. 'Well, now I've heard everything. Mind you, I suppose I shouldn't be surprised. He was a right tearaway when he was young. It's just the sort of thing he would do.'

'It's a very courageous thing to do,' Josh said, pouring gravy over his food. 'To volunteer to fight for one's country. If I was a few years younger—'

'Thank God you're not, then,' Mary said tartly. Glancing at Bridie, she said, 'Eat your dinner, child, and let's have no more talk of war.'

But Bridie was staring at Josh, her eyes large with fear now as she calculated quickly. Her voice trembled as she said, 'If Micky's dad's the right age to go, then — then so is Andrew.'

Now the three of them stared at each other. Josh nodded soberly, 'She's right, y'know. And Richard too. He's from the sort of family that would be one of the first to volunteer. See it as their duty to defend their country.' He reached out and covered Mary's hand with his large one. 'And you do realize, love, who might very well be caught up in this, don't you?'

She frowned thoughtfully, 'Well, any of the young fellers. Even Stephen Dunsmore, I suppose.'

'I was thinking more of someone who is already in the services.'

'I don't know who you—' she began and then she dropped her knife and fork onto her plate with a clatter. Her hands flew to her face as she stared, wide eyed, at Josh. 'Oh no! No!'

Slowly Josh nodded.

'Who?' Bridie asked urgently, her frightened glance darting from one to the other. 'Who do you mean?'

Now both of them turned to look at her.

'My Jimmy,' Mary whispered hoarsely. 'He's at sea. In the Royal Navy.'

Bridie gasped. 'My dad? You mean my dad?'

Sadly Mary nodded, whilst she gripped Josh's hand so fiercely that her knuckles showed white.

When Richard drove the motor car into the factory, the yard was crowded with workmen. Even some of the women were there instead of in the warehouse at their work.

'What on earth's going on?' Richard exclaimed.

'We'll soon find out,' Eveleen said grimly. 'There's Mr Porter pushing his way through to reach us.'

They climbed out of the motor and waited until Bob Porter, the general manager of the factory – the position that had once belonged to Josh Carpenter – reached them.

'Thank goodness you've come, Mr Richard. I can't get 'em to start work. It's all this talk of war. It's got the young fellers that excited. I reckon half of 'em are off to volunteer this minute.'

Richard nodded. 'I'll speak to them,' he said and pushed his way through the throng to reach some steps where he could stand above the crowd. Eveleen and Bob Porter followed in his wake.

It was a few minutes before he could make himself heard above the hubbub and gain their attention. 'I know that all of you will be anxious to answer the call of your country, but I would ask you to continue your work until we hear more news—'

'Oh aye, thinking it'll hit your pocket, Mr Richard? That all you can think about?'

Richard regarded the man steadily. 'It'll hit us all, Jake, and not only our pockets. All I can say to you now is that, when the right time comes, those of you who wish to volunteer will go with my blessing. And whilst none of us knows what the uncertain future holds for us, if the company of Reckitt and Stokes still exists at the end of it all, your job will be here for you when you come back.'

There were mutterings amongst the crowd. 'He can't say fairer than that, Jake,' one voice, raised above the rest, said. 'Yer've got to admit that.'

Jake Morrison, one of the younger twisthands, had the grace to look ashamed.

'And in the meantime,' Richard was still speaking, 'while you are away, the company will do its best to look after the welfare of your families.'

The comments grew louder at their employer's generous offer. Only Bob Porter, standing beside Eveleen, muttered, 'I 'ope he knows just what he's offering.'

But Eveleen was smiling, her eyes bright with tears of pride as she gazed at the tall, handsome and authoritative man who was her husband.

As the men filed into the factory, Richard stepped down and came towards her. 'Evie, go and talk to the women in the warehouse, will you? Try to reassure them that if their menfolk are bent on enlisting, we will continue to employ them. The women, I mean.' He smiled wryly. 'But just warn them that they might have to do other jobs to keep the factory going.'

Even in this dark moment of uncertainty, Eveleen laughed, relieved even for a brief moment to be able to say with light-hearted teasing, 'You don't mean you'd have women helping to work the machines?'

Richard smiled and touched her cheek and said softly, 'It's been done before, hasn't it?' He sighed and now he was very serious. 'And it might very well come to it, Evie, before we're through with this.'

Fifteen

Eveleen's task proved far harder than Richard's. She was faced with a clamour of fear, even tears from some of the women.

'My dad was killed in the Boer War. I know what war really means. If they go to war, we'll never see any of them again.'

'That's right. My uncle was killed in that lot, an' all. I don't want my young man to go.'

But there were several voices raised in patriotism. 'Well, I don't want to be married to a coward. I'd be right proud to see my Bert in uniform. If he goes, I'll wave him off with a flag just to show him how much I love him and how proud me and the kids are of him.'

The hubbub grew louder and the arguments flew back and forth. Rather than try to stop it, Eveleen let the women have their say.

Joining Helen at the end of the room, she said, 'Let them get it off their chests, then they might settle down to work.' She glanced at her friend. 'Are you all right, Helen? You look very white.'

The young woman nodded but her voice quavered as she said, 'I – I just don't want Leslie to do anything daft like volunteering, that's all.'

Eveleen smiled. 'Leslie? And who,' she asked pointedly, 'is Leslie, might I ask?'

Helen's cheeks turned a faint pink. 'Leslie Holmes. He works in one of the machine shops with Luke Manning.'

Eveleen nodded. She knew Luke Manning well and now she remembered having seen a tall, serious-looking young man working alongside him.

Helen continued hesitantly, her blush deepening. 'We – we've been walking out together. About two months.'

'And you never told me?' Eveleen pretended mock indignation.

Helen shrugged. 'After what happened before, I suppose I was a bit frightened to say much about it. In case, well, you know?'

Eveleen nodded and put her arm about Helen's waist. 'I know, love, I know,' she said huskily.

In the last few weeks she had observed the change in her friend. Helen was a pretty young woman with fair hair, a small nose and, usually, a laughing mouth. She had always been Eveleen's staunch ally, but since the untimely death of her fiancé, the once bright, vivacious Helen had been subdued, the grief haunting her. Lately, however, the mischievous sparkle had come back into her blue eyes and Eveleen had secretly crossed her fingers that the cause of it was some nice young man.

But now the bleak fear was back as Helen said softly, 'It's just the sort of thing Leslie'll do. I just know he will.'

As Eveleen hugged her friend, trying to offer what comfort she could, she was nevertheless thinking: Yes, and it's what Richard will do too.

*

Andrew arrived at the farm the following Sunday.

'I'm volunteering,' he told them proudly. 'I'm off to fight for my country.'

The colour drained from Bridie's face as she flung herself against him and wrapped her arms around him as if she would physically hold him there. 'No, no. I don't want you to go. You don't have to. I know you don't. Josh said you wouldn't have to go.'

Andrew was startled by her passionate outcry and even more surprised when her grandmother made no effort to restrain her. Instead Mary said, 'The child's right, Andrew. What on earth do you want to go for?' She glanced at Bridie. 'She's not got many of us in the way of family, poor kid. You're family to her. As good as.'

Bridie lifted her head and stared at her. They were the kindest words she'd heard spoken about herself by her grandmother for a long time, indeed if not ever.

'I feel I have to,' Andrew said. 'I want to. I want to get away from Flawford. I've lived and worked in that same little yard all me life. I want to see something of the world.'

'And you think going to war is a good way to see the world, do you?' Mary countered.

'I want to do something with my life. Something worthwhile.'

'Oh aye.' Mary was not going to give in. 'Throw it away, more like.'

'Well, wouldn't it be a worthwhile cause? In the defence of one's homeland?'

'No, no, *no*!' Bridie shouted and clung to him all the tighter. 'I won't let you go. I won't. I won't!'

'Now, now, love . . .' It was Josh who prised her clinging arms from Andrew. 'Let's sit down and talk about this quite calmly. You've got to respect a fellow's wishes. If Andrew feels it's his duty to go—'

'Duty! Pah!' Mary was vehement. 'It'll be our Jimmy's duty, I'd agree with you there. Though I wish it wasn't so. But he joined up, signed on or whatever they call it, into the Royal Navy and I daresay when you do that part of your pledge is to answer your country's call if need be. But why you?' She flung out her hand towards Andrew. 'Why civilians?'

'They're asking for volunteers,' Andrew said. 'There's several of us going from the yard.'

'What's going to happen to my brother's workshops then, if you young fellers all go rushing off to the war? Have you stopped to think of that, eh?'

'Well.' Andrew shrugged evasively. It was obvious that he had not. 'There'll be enough older men left. I expect the work'll drop off anyway.'

'That's just where you're wrong. What's wanted might alter a bit, but you all make knitted garments, don't you? Don't you think there's going to be a heck of a lot of garments needed to clothe an army?'

Andrew blinked. 'I hadn't looked at it that way.'

'No,' Mary said shortly. 'You wouldn't. You'd be better off staying put and helping the war by making the clothing that's bound to be needed.'

'There you are, you see,' Bridie said triumphantly. 'You don't need to go. You can be much more useful here.' She put her arm through his and gazed up at him imploringly. 'Do say you won't go. Please, Andrew.'

'I don't suppose,' Josh said thoughtfully, 'there'll be much call for lace if the war lasts for long. I wonder how it will affect Reckitt and Stokes?'

'Aye,' Mary said. 'I can't see soldiers wanting lace trimmings on their long johns.'

No-one even smiled at her effort to lighten the talk and there was silence as everyone's thoughts turned to Richard and Eveleen.

At that very moment a family conference was also being held in the Stokes's household. Richard and Eveleen were at the home of Richard's parents for Sunday lunch.

Brinsley Stokes sat at the head of the table. At fifty-five he was an older edition of his son, Richard. Looking at her father-in-law, Eveleen could almost see what her husband would look like in twenty years' time. He was tall and still slim, though his once black hair was now liberally peppered with white. His features were still remarkably clear-cut; a long, straight nose and a firm jaw. There were wrinkles around his eyes, but they were laughter lines rather than the signs of ageing. He was capable of looking quite stern, as he was doing at this moment, but his dark brown eyes were always kindly and full of concern.

His voice was deep and, when he spoke now, not quite steady. 'You must do what you feel is right, my boy, but like Eveleen I wish you'd give the matter a lot more thought before rushing in headlong on a wave of patriotism, praiseworthy though it no doubt is.'

Eveleen's glance went from her father-in-law to her husband, her eyes wide with fear, but for once she bit back the words on the tip of her tongue. Now that she knew Brinsley was on her side, she was sure Richard would listen to his parents, for whilst his mother had not yet voiced an opinion, Eveleen was sure she would discourage Richard's madcap proposal. What mother would gladly wave her only son off to war?

Sophia sat at the opposite end of the table, a serene,

sophisticated woman in her early fifties. Her hair was dressed in an immaculate, smooth chignon and her flawless face showed few signs of ageing. Her figure was slim, kept so by a rigid diet. She ran her household with the same discipline. She was the perfect hostess and the perfect wife and mother of successful businessmen, although she took no part in the life of the factory and, indeed, displayed little interest in the workings of the place that gave her a very comfortable lifestyle. But although Richard's mother was always friendly and kindly disposed towards her, Eveleen felt she was somehow distant, a little aloof perhaps. But surely, Eveleen thought, this time Sophia would intervene. This time she would have some feelings on the matter.

Sophia did, but to Eveleen's amazement they were not what she had imagined or what she had hoped for.

'My dear, Richard must be allowed to decide for himself without influence from any of us.' Her calm glance included Eveleen. 'As he says, the factory can manage very well without him. You are there to oversee everything and Eveleen,' her smile was warm as she included her daughter-in-law, 'if I understand it, has the warehouse running like clockwork.'

Richard smiled and, for a moment, his brown eyes twinkled with their usual mischief. 'What you mean, Mother, is that I am not really needed here at all.'

'I didn't quite say that, dear,' Sophia inclined her head towards him. 'What I should have said, perhaps, is that I admire your courage. It is laudable and I would be so proud to see you in an officer's uniform.'

Unable to hold back any longer, Eveleen sprang to her feet, pushing back her chair with a violent movement so that for a moment it tottered, threatening to crash to the floor.

'Proud to read his name in the lists of casualties? Proud to tend his grave?'

Richard, on the opposite side of the table, rose too. 'Evie, darling, please—'

Now she rounded on him. 'Don't "Evie darling" me. You don't care about me, about any of us, if you insist on this crazy notion.' Her voice softened a little as she turned to look down the table towards Brinsley. 'I know I've disappointed you not being able to present you with a grandson, an heir for you, but—'

'Eveleen . . .' Suddenly Richard's tone was firm. 'This is hardly the time or the place.'

'But,' Eveleen continued, disregarding his rebuke. 'I'm hardly going to have the chance now, if he gets himself killed, am I?'

Brinsley looked up at her, his dark eyes filled with the same sadness and hopelessness that she knew were mirrored in her own. They stared at each other for a long moment, so much of what had happened between their families surfacing in both their minds. They shared secrets from the past, in which, though fully aware of them, neither Richard nor his mother were involved. For a brief moment, it was as if Brinsley and Eveleen were alone together in the room, the other two forgotten.

Poignantly, Eveleen said softly, 'I won't have any more chances.'

Brinsley knew all about lost chances.

But now Sophia spoke, dragging them back to the present drama and pushing their unhappy memories into the background. The present was every bit as bleak as the distant past had been.

'My dears, Richard will be an officer. He won't be where the danger is. You'll see,' Sophia said, standing up and bringing the conversation, as far as she wished to be concerned in it, to a close. 'He'll make us all so proud of him, I know he will.' She moved down the table and kissed Richard's cheek fondly, before turning and making her way to the door out of the dining room. 'Besides,' she added, waving her hand airily, 'they say it's not going to last for long. He'll be home by Christmas.'

As the door closed behind her, the three people left in the room regarded each other gravely.

Sixteen

The four people at Pear Tree Farm looked at each other with equally solemn faces.

'So you're really set on it, then?' Mary broke the silence at last.

'I'm sorry, but yes, I am,' Andrew said quietly. There was apology in his eyes, but a steadfast determination in his tone. Nothing and no-one could change his mind.

'You don't love me,' Bridie cried passionately and now the tears were coursing down her face. 'Gran said you didn't and she was right.'

'I never said any such thing!'

'What?'

'Bridie, mi duck . . .'

The three of them spoke at once, Mary with indignation, Andrew with confusion and Josh with concern, trying to pour oil on what he could see would be very troubled waters any minute now.

Casting resentful glances at all three of them, Bridie muttered, 'You wouldn't go if you did.'

Andrew reached out and took her hand and even when she tried to pull free he held it firmly. 'You are the most important person in the world to me, you know that.'

She wanted to tell him, wanted to blurt out what her grandmother had said, that he only loved her because she reminded him of the great love of his life, but the

99

words would not come. If he was going away, she could not let them part in anger, with misunderstanding between them. And, even at her tender age, she was mature enough to know that if she told him he would deny it. He would say he loved her for herself. But she realized now that she was no more than a child in his eyes. A dear, beloved child, of that she had no doubt, for whatever reason – but only a child.

Bridie swallowed the bitterness and knew suddenly it was time to behave more like an adult than a silly little girl. She would be thirteen next month.

Time to grow up, Bridie Singleton, she told herself, echoing the very words that her grandmother had said to her so often. And if this war lasted any time at all, things were going to be very different for everyone.

Andrew visited again on the last Sunday in August.

'Now just you be ready next Saturday.'

Impishly Bridie said, 'Next Saturday? Why? What's happening?'

Andrew tweaked her nose. 'Don't tell me you've forgotten it's your thirteenth birthday?'

Bridie could keep up the pretence no longer. She grinned. 'I can't wait,' she confided. 'Gran's shown me how to put my hair up and I've been practising all week.'

Andrew's face softened. 'We'll go into Grantham to have your birthday photograph taken.'

Every year on the Saturday nearest to her birthday Andrew had insisted that she should have her photograph taken in a proper photographer's studio. This year her birthday actually fell on the Saturday. 'And I should like to buy you something really special, especially as . . .' He stopped, cleared his throat and changed the subject, but Bridie guessed that he had been going to say, 'Especially as I shall be going away soon.' Instead, he continued, 'Do you think your gran would let me buy you a smart hat to go with your new hairstyle?'

'You can ask her.' She laughed. 'She's more likely to say "yes" if it's you doing the asking.'

'I will,' Andrew promised.

About mid-afternoon, they heard the sound of Richard's motor car pulling into the yard.

'Andrew.' Eveleen crossed the yard to greet him affectionately. 'It's far too long since we've seen you.' She drew back and studied him. 'You look well . . .' she began and then she saw the look in his eyes, the look that was on the faces of so many men these days. A cross between excited anticipation and dread of the unknown. 'Oh no,' she breathed. 'You're going too, aren't you?'

Mary, hearing her words, said, 'You don't mean to tell me Richard's been daft enough to volunteer an' all?'

Eveleen grimaced. 'Not yet, but he seems set on doing so.'

'But what about the business – the factory?'

Eveleen shrugged. 'He's leaving his father and me to manage everything.'

'Brinsley.' Mary spoke the name softly and, in spite of herself, she smiled. A look of understanding passed between her and Eveleen as Mary moved to her side and asked in a low voice, 'Is he well? How does he look? Have you seen him lately?'

Eveleen took her mother's arm and drew her a little apart from the rest. 'We had lunch at their house last week. He's fine.' She smiled impishly at her mother. 'As handsome as ever. Almost as good looking as his son.'

They bent their heads together, laughing softly. But their laughter soon died as they turned back to the others.

All afternoon the talk was of the war and how it would affect them, so directly now that their menfolk were to be involved.

'Mam, I was wondering. Would you allow Bridie to come to live with me for a while?' Eveleen asked her mother when they were alone in the scullery washing up the tea things. Bridie and Josh were doing the evening milking and Richard and Andrew were sitting by the fire which burned winter and summer, planning their uncertain future. 'I would love to have her. She could be a big help to me if Richard does go.'

Mary looked at her sharply. 'Is this suggestion because you think she's not happy here? Because you think her and me don't get on?'

'No, Mam, it isn't,' Eveleen said, pushing away the thought that deep down there was some truth in Mary's surmise. 'To be honest, I'm dreading Richard going away. I shall miss him so and I'd really be glad of the child's company.'

Mary was silent, plunging her hands deep into the washing-up suds as she pondered. 'Just so long as you remember, Eveleen, that she won't be a child for much longer. She's at that awkward age and it'll get worse before it gets better. I well remember your own "awkward age",' she added pointedly and Eveleen smiled wryly.

'I will look after her, Mam, but I thought she could work in the inspection room. She's a neat little needlewoman.'

'She's good at bobbin lace,' Mary remarked and added pensively, 'it's in the blood, isn't it, from both sides.'

There was silence for a moment until Eveleen asked tentatively, 'Does Andrew ever mention your mam and Uncle Harry?'

Mary emptied the washing-up bowl and dried her hands before she answered. 'I asked him not long ago. I think they're reasonably well in health, but lonely.'

'Do they still live in their own separate cottages?'

'I think so, but I think they both have lodgers who are employed in Harry's workshops, so they're not exactly alone.'

'Just lonely,' Eveleen murmured. Then as an afterthought she asked, 'How old is your mother now, Mam?'

Mary wrinkled her forehead. 'About seventy-five or six, I think. Andrew did say,' she went on, 'that Harry's having trouble with his eyesight.'

'Really? But he can't be that old, surely?'

'He's a couple of years older than me. He'll be fifty-six this year. But that job, sitting squinting at rows and rows of fine knitting all day. It's bad for the eyesight.'

They put away the plates and dishes and when the scullery was tidy Eveleen said, 'Well, what do you think about Bridie, then?'

Mary nodded. 'I'll talk to Josh, but yes, I think we'll have to let her go.' She smiled. 'I'll miss the naughty little tyke, but don't tell her I said so.'

Eveleen said nothing, but she was thinking: If only my mam would do exactly that, would tell the child how much they'll miss her, maybe poor Bridie would not feel so unloved and unwanted. She had no doubt that Josh would voice it, but, coming from her gran, it would mean so much more to Bridie.

*

'Now, which is it to be? The photograph first or lunch in the best place we can find?'

'The photograph,' Bridie decided. 'Can I have it taken in my new hat?'

'Of course you can.' Andrew smiled at her fondly and then added with regret, 'I wish you'd let me buy the whole outfit for you.'

Having gained Mary's permission to buy Bridie a new hat, Andrew had tried to go further. A smart costume, the sort worn by girls of sixteen or so, had caught his eye in the shop. 'Try that on, Bridie.'

Bridie pulled a face. 'I don't think Gran would let me wear that. It's a bit old for me.' In her determination to act in a more grown-up manner, Bridie had decided that the best way to start was by acquiescing to her grandmother's wishes. Perhaps she would even be able to persuade Mary to trust her a little more.

'The young lady's quite right,' the thin-faced, middle-aged shop assistant agreed. She smiled, showing large teeth that dominated her face. She turned to Bridie. 'You have a very generous father, miss, but—'

Bridie frowned. 'He's not my father,' she said swiftly.

The woman tried to purse her lips, though the action was difficult for her over the large teeth. She glanced disapprovingly from one to the other and they could guess the thoughts spinning around her mind.

Andrew looked uncomfortable. 'I'm her godfather,' he said gruffly.

'I see,' the woman said stiffly. She sniffed and went on, 'Well, it's still most unsuitable for a young girl. How old are you, miss?'

'Thirteen today.'

'Quite. I'm sure your mother wouldn't allow you to

104

wear that sort of costume until you were at least sixteen. Besides, you would need to wear,' she coughed discreetly and added, 'a certain undergarment to show the apparel to its best advantage.'

Bridie grinned mischievously, seizing her chance to embarrass the woman. 'Oh, a corset, you mean.' Then she capitulated with charm. Beside her, she heard Andrew trying to stifle his laughter. 'I'm sure you're right. Perhaps in a year or so's time. But I could, don't you think,' she went on, eager to have the woman on her side now, 'have a nice straw boater?'

The woman nodded, her disapproval melting a little at the prospect of a sale. 'I have just the thing, miss.' She hurried away, returning a moment later with a straw boater decorated with a ribbon. 'If the gentleman agrees, we can supply you with different coloured ribbons so that you can change them to match the colour of your coat or dress or whatever you are wearing. It will still be a most appropriate hat when you are a little older, miss.'

'What a good idea.' Bridie smiled, perching the boater on the top of her head.

'If you'll permit me . . .?' the woman murmured. Gently she moved the hat forwards a little so that it rested against the roll of plaited hair at the back of the girl's head and tilted, almost provocatively, over her forehead. Bridie peeped out mischievously from beneath its brim to see Andrew smiling down at her.

He cleared his throat and his voice was not quite steady as he said, 'You look adorable, Bridie.'

Neither of them noticed the look of disapproval return to the shop assistant's face.

*

Andrew insisted on having several photographs of Bridie, but she could not persuade him to have his taken.

'But I'd like one of you,' she pleaded. 'Won't you have one taken with me? Please?'

But Andrew was adamant. 'No. It wouldn't – look right.'

Bridie pursed her lips, knowing that the woman in the shop had caused this. 'Then what about one on your own? If you really are going to join up, I would so like a photograph.'

'One in your uniform would be nice for the young lady,' the photographer suggested. He was far more tactful than the woman in the shop had been. He smiled understandingly. 'I'm going myself. I got my papers yesterday. I've to report next week. These,' he indicated the camera and the plates he was taking of Bridie, 'will be the last photographs I take.'

Bridie stared at him and then swallowed hard at the poignancy of his words. Huskily she said, 'Until it's all over and you come back.'

The young man looked at her gratefully, but then shrugged. 'I hope you're right, miss, but who knows, eh?' He cleared his throat and added more briskly, 'There'll be a chance for you to get your photograph taken, sir, when you've got your uniform.' He grinned now. 'My mam won't let me go unless I promise to send her one.'

Bridie held Andrew's gaze. 'Will you promise to get one done and send it to me?'

Slowly Andrew nodded.

Seventeen

Shortly after her birthday, Bridie came to live with Eveleen in Nottingham. They all knew that very soon both Richard and Andrew would volunteer. They could not be dissuaded by anyone.

The Prime Minister, Herbert Asquith, had called for another half million men to sign up for the army. Recruiting posters, with Lord Kitchener pointing his finger outwards and exhorting Britons to 'Join Your Country's Army!', were appearing everywhere. And now, the papers said, almost as many men were joining the army in a day as were normally recruited in a year.

For the moment, the news from across the Channel was hopeful. In the first decisive battle on the Western Front, the Allies had driven the enemy back and removed the threat to Paris. British losses had been heavy, but one of the generals had remarked that they had not been 'excessive in view of the magnitude of the great fight'.

Eveleen almost ripped the newspaper to shreds when she read it. To her mind, even one casualty was one too many. As she was about to throw down the paper in disgust another item caught her attention and she picked it up again.

'First Shots Are Fired in War at Sea' the headlines screamed at her. Her hand flew to her mouth and she found she was holding her breath as she read on. Enemy submarines had sunk three British cruisers off the Netherlands. Hundreds had survived and had been picked up by another cruiser, only to be torpedoed again and cast back into the sea.

'Oh, Jimmy,' Eveleen whispered. 'I hope you're safe. God keep you safe too.' She closed her eyes and sent up a silent entreaty that her mother had not seen the newspaper. Even if they rarely heard from him, and despite what had happened in the past, Eveleen still cared about her brother and she knew that he was never far from her mother's thoughts. But she realized that the odds were stacked heavily against every one of the menfolk in her life coming safely home and the thought was like the cold hand of death clutching her heart.

Bridie said her goodbyes to Micky and his family, to her gran and to Josh, who had hugged her tightly.

'Don't forget, mi duck, we're always here for you. This is your home and always will be.'

Mary gave her a list of commandments, almost like Moses with his tablets of stone, Bridie thought impishly, trying to keep a straight face.

'Now don't you be getting into bad company. And don't go getting involved with soldiers. They'll be all over the city. You look a lot older than you are and you'll be attractive to the wrong sort of feller. Specially when they're going to war and not knowing if they're going to come back. They'll say all sorts of things to make you – well – do things you shouldn't.'

Bridie resisted the temptation to ask innocently: What things, Gran? She knew that Mary would see through her. Bridie hadn't grown up on a farm without understanding the facts of life from an early age. Instead she said meekly, 'Yes, Gran.'

The blackbird in the loft was long gone and the

injured rabbit had been released back into the wild some weeks earlier. Now there was nothing to keep her at Pear Tree Farm and, despite her gnawing fear over Andrew – and Richard and all the others who were planning to go – she was thrilled that her aunt wanted her.

Over the next few weeks Eveleen and Bridie found themselves so busy that they scarcely had time to mope. Eveleen was becoming more involved with the running of the factory, as well as overseeing the warehouse. Each morning she and her father-in-law met to discuss the immediate future of Reckitt and Stokes, but Richard refused to join them.

'Won't you help us, Richard?' Eveleen begged. 'We need to know what you want us to do.'

'I don't know what's going to happen over the next few months, years even. I'm not going to be here . . .'

Eveleen gasped in alarm. 'Oh, don't say that.'

Richard shrugged. 'My darling, none of us know how long this war is going to last. We have to face facts. Besides, I have things to see to before I enlist. I have to see our solicitor . . .' His voice trailed away and he said no more, but Eveleen shuddered inwardly. She guessed he intended to make a will. To her, it felt as if he was tempting fate.

'You know,' Brinsley Stokes said at their first meeting, 'we're going to have to train women to take the place of some of the men in the factory.' He glanced sideways at her, his smile teasing her gently.

Eveleen laughed, knowing he was remembering the time she had dressed up as a boy to take her brother's place alongside Luke Manning.

'Well,' she said coyly, feeling suddenly more light-hearted. Plunging herself into work and all its present problems gave her less time to think and consequently less time to worry herself sick. 'I think it's been proved that it's possible for a woman to work in the machine shop.'

They laughed together, remembering.

'They won't be able to become fully fledged twist-hands. You do know that, don't you? Some of the work required would be far too demanding physically. It's very heavy. But women could certainly do all sorts of jobs that assist the twisthands. Winding bobbins, threading and stripping.'

'What's stripping?'

'It's the last twenty yards on a bobbin that can't be used. It has to be stripped off by hand.'

'Oh, I remember now. Yes, Luke used to have me doing that.'

'We'll need to talk to the men who are left first. What I suggest is that we put a young woman with each of the old hands – the ones who aren't likely to volunteer or even to be conscripted, if it should come to that.'

Already, Eveleen thought with an inward sigh, another reminder. The war could never be far away from any of their thoughts.

Brinsley was continuing. 'I say "young women" because I think they'll be quicker to learn than the older ones, although, of course,' he wrinkled his brow, 'younger women may have more in the way of family commitments. What do you think, Eveleen?'

She thought a moment before saying carefully, 'If we pick single women first, then the young married women who have no children. If their husbands have gone to the Front, they're – they're not likely to have children now, are they?' There was a catch in her voice. Her statement so poignantly applied to herself.

Brinsley glanced at her and then his gaze dropped away. 'No, my dear,' he said softly and she knew he understood her feelings.

Eveleen continued determinedly. 'There are one or two I could recommend to you immediately from the inspection room and we could recruit young girls just out of school to take their place. I'll go and see Win Martin. She'll probably know of some.'

Brinsley nodded. 'How's young Bridie shaping up?'

Eveleen smiled. 'She loves it. She's the youngest there and of course all the women are making a huge fuss of her.'

'Good, good.' Brinsley stood up. 'Now we'll take a walk through the machine shop and see what gaps all this volunteering is going to leave us. There are several all planning to enlist along with Richard. By doing so they all hope to stay together. Did you know?'

Eveleen, unable to speak for the lump in her throat, merely nodded.

'We need to talk to Bob Porter about our plans to bring women into the factory,' Brinsley shouted above the noise as they were walking together down the aisles between the rows of machines. Every so often a machine stood idle, its operator already gone to war. As they moved into the office overlooking the machine shop, Eveleen said, 'He'll not like it. He's one of the old school. He'll say it'll cause more trouble than it's worth.' She smiled wryly. 'I could wish it was Josh still in charge at this moment. Bob Porter's not an easy man at the best of times.'

Brinsley helped himself to Bob Porter's chair and sighed as he sat down. 'I know. But we've got to try at least. Go and find him, my dear, would you?'

Eveleen half-turned and then glanced back at her father-in-law. 'Are you all right? You look very tired.'

Brinsley passed a weary hand across his forehead. He looked suddenly much older than his fifty-five years. 'I'm not sleeping too well,' he admitted. 'I'd begun to take it easy, to hand over the reins, as it were, to Richard, but now . . .'

He left the sentence unfinished, but Eveleen understood. He was going to have to work far harder than he had done in recent years and, coupled with the worry over his son and indeed his concern for all the young men he had employed who were now volunteering, the extra burden would take its toll.

Eveleen knew just how he felt. Already she was experiencing sleepless nights and extra responsibility was being thrust upon her too. But she was young and fit and determined to cope. Besides, by throwing herself into work she could put aside, even if only for a few hours, her anxiety over Richard.

A rush of affection for Brinsley, who had been involved with her family even before she was born, made her move to his side and offer, 'Will you let me take some of the weight off your shoulders? I mean, if women are coming into the factory, then maybe it would be better if Bob Porter and I worked together more.'

Brinsley shook his head and sighed. 'You're a sweet girl to offer, but you're doing enough already. It wouldn't be fair to expect you to do any more. You still have to cope with overseeing the warehouse and all the homeworkers.'

Eveleen sat down opposite him and leant on the desk. 'But I have Helen at the warehouse. She's more than capable of taking on more responsibility there. And I've already asked Win Martin to do the same. You see . . .'

She hesitated to reveal what was a very private matter between Richard and herself, but now she would have to do so. She took a deep breath and went on. 'You see, before this war started I'd been planning to do a lot less myself.' She looked him straight in the eyes now as she said softly, 'You must know how desperately I want to give Richard a son.'

Brinsley nodded.

'Well, we wondered if I was doing too much and that was – well . . .' she stammered to a halt. It was not the sort of thing that was talked about in polite circles and certainly not between a young woman and her father-in-law. But Brinsley came to her rescue. He smiled sadly and said, 'And you were planning to take life a little easier and see what happened, eh?'

Eveleen nodded and sudden tears filled her eyes. 'But now he's going away.' Then she brushed such a show of weakness aside impatiently and added firmly, 'I shall *need* to work. Harder than ever.'

Brinsley nodded slowly and said heavily, 'Maybe I do too. It gives you too much time to think if you're not busy, doesn't it.'

Eveleen nodded, then added, 'But you mustn't do so much that you become ill.'

'Nor you, my dear.'

She smiled again and said, accentuating the Lincoln-shire dialect she had never quite lost, said, 'Oh, I'm tough as owd boots, mester.'

They regarded each other across the table, under-standing one another's feelings implicitly.

'We'll work at it together then, Eveleen. It's what I'd like more than anything.'

'That's settled then,' Eveleen said as she rose. 'Now

I'll go and find Bob Porter.' She pulled a wry expression. 'I think he's going to take more persuading than anyone.'

'I ain't 'aving troublesome women in my machine shop and that's final.' Bob Porter was adamant. 'It's not that I've anything against women. They're all right. In their place. But that's not in a factory.'

'But, Bob, we've lost several men already and more are going each day.' Brinsley spread his hands with a gesture of inevitability. 'How do you think we're going to run the factory without using women?'

'There's young lads we can get and older men. Women's all right in the warehouse, I grant you. And working at home.' Bob jabbed his forefinger at the floor. 'But not here.'

Brinsley and Eveleen exchanged a look before he got to his feet. Drawing himself to his full height, he said with authority, 'Well, I'm sorry, Bob, but that's the way it's going to have to be. Now, Mrs Stokes will work with you. In fact, she will be responsible for the women workers, if that's how you feel.'

Bob Porter's face was like thunder and Eveleen sighed inwardly. Tight-lipped, Bob said, 'Whatever you say, sir.' He turned on his heel and marched out of the office.

'Oh dear,' Brinsley said with a thin smile. 'I think we've upset him.'

Despite her qualms, Eveleen forced herself to say brightly, 'Don't worry. I'll handle him.'

With a chuckle that chased away some of the anxiety from his face, Brinsley said, 'I don't doubt it for a minute, my dear.'

*

When Brinsley had left for the day, Eveleen faced Bob Porter in his office. 'Now, Bob, let's sit down and talk this matter out calmly.'

His head thrust forward belligerently and malevolence sparked in his eyes. 'Ain't nothing to talk about, missis. The boss has given me 'is orders and that's it.'

'No, Bob, it isn't. You're a very important part of the running of this factory. You know that. We're not trying to antagonize you or usurp your authority. It's just . . .' she sighed and for a moment her shoulders sagged. 'Oh, Bob, it's all sorts of things.'

The man stared at her. 'I don't understand.'

'Sit down, Bob, and let's talk. Please.'

The man made to sit in the visitor's chair in his office, but Eveleen gestured to the chair behind his desk where Brinsley had sat, the chair that was rightly Bob Porter's. 'No, no. This is your office, Bob. Not mine.'

The man gave an ungracious grunt, though he sat down in the chair. 'I thought you was tekin' over.'

Eveleen stood in front of the desk, looking down on him. She had invited him to sit down deliberately, but she remained standing. It gave her a feeling of advantage. 'We seem to have got off to a bad start.'

'Ain't no good start as far as I'm concerned, if you're bringing women in here.' He nodded through the glass partition separating his small office from the machine shop, a mournful look on his face as if all that he held most dear was about to be swept away.

'What is it you have against women, Bob?'

'Nowt. Just that to me a woman's place is in the home, looking after her family. Mebbe doing a bit of drawing at home. And it's all right young unmarried lasses working in the warehouse, I suppose, but . . .'

Eveleen's patience was being severely tested and

before she could prevent herself, she had snapped, 'Oh, very magnanimous of you.'

Bob, a stocky, balding man, leapt to his feet with surprising agility. 'Don't you play the high 'n mighty with me, missis. I remember where you came from. Off the streets.' His tone implied much more than that Eveleen and her family had once been homeless. 'And if it hadn't been for Mr Richard marrying you,' he wagged a grimy forefinger in her face, 'you'd still 'ave been there.'

Eveleen, her eyes flashing with anger, glared at him, their faces only inches apart, so close that she could feel the waft of his stale breath. 'But he did marry me,' she said pointedly. 'And right now it's me who could have you put out on the street.'

She drew back and willed herself to calmness, but her tone was icy as she said, 'Now, Bob, you have two choices. You can either work with me on this or you can leave right now.'

'Oh aye, reckon you could run this factory single-handed, do you?'

'No,' she said levelly, knowing that for the moment she had the upper hand. 'But there are plenty of men out there,' she waved her hand through the office window, 'who've worked here long enough and could take over your job tomorrow without batting an eyelid.'

A look of doubt crossed the man's face. 'Think so? It's not as easy as it looks.' His words were defiant, but she could see that his confidence was shaken. One word from Eveleen to her father-in-law and the factory manager knew he could be out on his ear. And without the words needing to be spoken, Bob knew that the man who had once held his position was now Eveleen's stepfather. No doubt Bob would think that Eveleen only had to ask and Josh Carpenter would come to her aid.

He was not a man to cave in too quickly, but she knew she had rattled his confidence. Defiant to the last, Bob said, 'Mebbe it's time I picked up mi scissors and hook and walked down the road, eh?'

'And where exactly would you walk to, Bob? You know as well as I do that all the factories are facing the same difficulties as we are.'

'Mebbe, but they aren't bringing women in,' he said scathingly.

'I think you'll find,' Eveleen said quietly, 'that, in time, they'll do just that. They'll have to if they want to survive.'

There was a long silence between them until at last Bob sat down in his chair again, leant back and linked his fingers across the paunch that drinking five pints every night in the pub on the corner of his street had caused. 'So,' he said sarcastically, 'what's this grand plan then?'

Eighteen

Bridie didn't think she had ever been so happy in her life. At least that would have been the case but for the ever-present worry over the war and all its consequences.

On her first morning Eveleen had taken her up to the inspection room on the top floor of the warehouse building and left her in Helen's care.

'You must remember to call her Miss Binkley when you're at work,' Eveleen had warned her. 'Not Auntie Helen.'

Bridie had nodded, speechless with excitement. Her hair was plaited, as always, but now it was wound around her crown and pinned in position. Her aunt had also bought a plain white blouse and a long black skirt for her to wear for work. Gone, now, was the frilled white smock of childhood. As they entered the workroom, Bridie could see that all the girls and women were similarly dressed. Only Helen, as the supervisor, wore a smart, close-fitting plum-coloured costume with a white, ruffle-necked silk blouse beneath it.

When Eveleen left, Helen said, 'Now, I'll put you with Mrs Hyde. She looks after all the newcomers.'

The woman was large and rotund, her grey hair scraped into a bun at the nape of her neck. But her round, florid face beamed a welcome. 'Come and sit by me. We'll soon show yer what's what.'

In spite of her nervousness at facing a roomful of chattering women, all of whom were eyeing her curiously, Bridie smiled. Mrs Hyde's way of talking was just like Josh's and immediately Bridie warmed to her.

It was not long before she had heard Mrs Hyde's life history. 'I've got seven kids and they're all terrors, the lot of 'em. But I wouldn't be without 'em for the world.'

'How old are they?' Bridie was wide-eyed and envious of a large family with brothers and sisters.

'Mi eldest daughter, Janie, she's eighteen. That's 'er over there. And next to her is Kathleen. She's seventeen. Then there's Bertie, sixteen. Joyce is fourteen. She's over there.' The woman twisted slightly in her seat and jabbed her sewing needle in the air towards a thin, mousy-haired girl stooping over her work. Mrs Hyde leant towards Bridie and lowered her voice. 'She's not ever so strong, bless her. Had scarlet fever as a bairn and 'as never been right since. Still, she's a good little worker and Mrs Stokes and Miss Binkley are very understanding if she has to 'ave a day off now and then. Then Christopher's nearly twelve, Lillian's ten and Connie's eight. They're still at school, o' course, but Christopher's going to start in the factory when he leaves.'

'How lucky they all are, to be part of such a lovely, big family.'

'You got brothers and sisters?' the kindly woman asked.

Bridie shook her head. 'No, there's only me. Me mam died having me.'

'Aw, that's a shame, luvvie.'

About her father, Bridie volunteered nothing.

*

At the end of September Richard and Andrew volunteered together with three more young men from Singleton's Yard in Flawford and seven volunteers from the Reckitt and Stokes's factory, one of whom was Leslie Holmes, Helen's young man.

'We've all enlisted in the Sherwood Foresters and we have to report to Newark next Friday,' Richard told Eveleen when he returned home. 'We'll be in the same regiment, even the same company, I think. Don't worry, I'll look after them all.'

'But who's going to look after you?'

'We'll watch out for each other,' he tried to reassure her, but she was not so easily convinced. 'We won't be going to France for ages yet. We'll have all sorts of training – a lot of drill, I expect – and all sorts of courses to go on.' He tickled her chin with his forefinger. 'Let's make the most of this last week. We'll all have a lovely day at the Goose Fair on Thursday, the day before we leave.'

Eveleen smiled thinly. Only a week and he would be gone.

On the Wednesday evening Richard, Eveleen and even Bridie and Andrew were invited to dinner at the home of Richard's parents. The atmosphere was strained. Andrew was uncomfortable in his best suit and starched collar and Bridie was nervous at being in such grand surroundings as the Stokes's elegant home. She dropped her knife on the floor and, when she bent to pick it up, her head collided with the manservant's, who had also bent down to retrieve it for her. Bridie was scarlet with embarrassment, even though Richard smiled at her understandingly.

'I don't know why you have to join the ranks, Richard,' Sophia was saying, angry and disappointed that she would not be able to boast to her elegant friends. 'You'd be so much safer as an officer too apart from, well . . .' She paused, realizing that her comments were a little out of place in the present company. Bridie, forgetting her own discomfort, glanced across the table at Andrew. But he sat silently, his eyes downcast, and she knew he was feeling every bit as awkward and out of place as she was. The thought comforted her. She glanced to the end of the table towards their hostess, admiring the elegant, sophisticated Sophia Stokes. She is very beautiful but she's cold, the girl thought with an astuteness beyond her years. Mr Brinsley's nice – he's like Uncle Richard – but she's only bothered about whether or not her son is going to be an officer.

In answer to his mother's remark, Richard only smiled. 'I'd much rather be with friends, Mother.'

At the end of the meal, as they moved from the dining room to the drawing room, the gentlemen accompanying the ladies instead of staying at the table to smoke and drink port, Andrew drew Eveleen to one side. 'I have something to ask you,' he said quietly.

'Of course I'll look after Bridie,' Eveleen said at once. 'You don't need to ask.'

He smiled, though his eyes were troubled with a hint of the apprehension that all those who had volunteered must be feeling. 'I know you will. It wasn't that. Eveleen, when I filled in the papers, I put you as my next of kin. I hope you don't mind?'

'Of course, I don't mind, but isn't there anyone else?'

Andrew shook his head. 'I have no family and I didn't want to put Mr Singleton's name. I – I'm not sure he would let you know – let Bridie know – if anything happened to me.'

Eveleen clutched at his arm. 'Nothing's going to

happen to you. To any of you.' She sounded so determined that Andrew could almost believe that the very strength of her will would make it so. 'It'll all be over in a few weeks and you'll be home again.'

There was a silence between them for a moment before he went on, 'And I've arranged for part of my pay – and that . . .' She wasn't sure what the 'and that' meant, but she said nothing. 'To come to you. Will you see that Bridie gets it? Put it in a bank account or something for when she comes of age.'

'Oh, Andrew,' Eveleen said unsteadily. He seemed to have thought of everything. But, even yet, he hadn't finished. And again he was thinking of others before himself. 'One thing more – and this is the most difficult to ask.' He bit his lip, as if still uncertain whether to make this particular request.

'Go on,' Eveleen prompted gently.

'Could you – will you – go to Flawford now and then to see that they're all right there?' He squeezed her hand tightly, emphasizing the need for his request – a request he knew would cause Eveleen a great deal of soul-searching and courage. He rushed on. 'I don't know what's going to happen there once I've gone.'

She forbore, at this final moment, to say in harsh accusation: Then why are you going? Instead she said huskily, 'Of course I will. I'll make sure they're all right.'

As the evening ended, much to the relief of both Bridie and Andrew, Richard said, 'So, are we all going to the Goose Fair tomorrow?'

'Oh, my dear,' Sophia said languidly, 'count me out. I can't bear all those crowds. Your father has promised to take me to Derby to see an old friend. Her son left for the Front last week. He's been in the army for several years. He's a regular.' She paused and added pointedly, 'Of course, he's an officer.'

Richard turned to Andrew. 'So, it's just the four of us, is it? You'll come, won't you, Andrew?'

Andrew shook his head apologetically, but before he could speak Bridie burst out, 'Oh Andrew, I've never been to the Goose Fair. You must come.'

'Bridie, love, I'd like nothing better. Believe me. But I must go home to see how things are. There's so many of us gone from what is only a small workshop anyway that . . .'

'You care more about them and your work than you do about me,' Bridie burst out petulantly. She was suddenly the little girl again.

Andrew regarded her helplessly. 'That's not true, but I just have to go home.'

'Can't you go the day after?'

Andrew shook his head sorrowfully. 'We leave at midday on Friday. There wouldn't be time. I'm sorry, Bridie.'

'What about you, Evie? You'll come with us, won't you?' Richard asked.

Eveleen glanced helplessly between her husband and her father-in-law. 'I – I don't think I can. I shall have to stay at the factory. One of us ought to be there. There'll be so many leaving the next day and so much to see to. I'm sorry, Richard.'

The first three girls brought in as auxiliary workers to help the twisthands had started that morning and Eveleen dared not leave them to the tender mercies of a very disgruntled Bob Porter. The reaction of the other male workers had been mixed.

'Mek a nice change, I reckon, seeing pretty lasses

about the place instead of your ugly mug,' Jake Morrison chafed a workmate. But when the girls had arrived dressed in long overalls and their hair tucked out of sight beneath a frilled cap, his face had fallen.

'Well, they do look a sight,' he had sniffed and turned back to his own machine.

'They've got to be sensibly dressed,' Luke Manning had pointed out. 'We can't have their hair or part of their dress getting caught in the machinery, can we?' He had walked over to where the three young women were standing with Eveleen. 'I'll tek one of 'em, Eveleen.'

Years before, Luke had been the one to try to train Jimmy and, unknowingly at the time, also Eveleen. He had never seen the need to change his attitude towards her just because she had married Richard Stokes.

Eveleen smiled at him. 'Thank you, Luke. What about the other two?' she asked. 'Who do you suggest for them?'

Luke glanced about him. 'Arthur for one, and Jake for the other.'

Eveleen frowned. 'Arthur, I agree, but I'm not sure about Jake.' It had been Jake who had raised a protest at the start of the war, suggesting that Richard's motives were less than altruistic.

Luke laughed. 'He's a bit of a loudmouth, but he's all right. And I'll keep me eye on the lasses.'

'Thanks, Luke,' Eveleen said, thankful to have at least one of the old hands on her side. Luke would be like a father to them, but even so Eveleen had wanted to be on hand whilst the new arrivals settled in.

'I'm really sorry, Richard,' she said again.

Richard regarded her gravely, 'So am I, Eveleen. So am I.'

Nineteen

'So, Bridie, it's just you and me, is it?'

Bridie nodded. 'Andrew can't come. He – he has to go home to see how things are at Flawford.'

Richard raised his left eyebrow sardonically. 'Seems they're smitten with the same bug.'

'Pardon?' Bridie was puzzled.

'Work's more important to them. Never mind, my dear. We'll have a lovely day. Just the two of us. How about it?' Bridie nodded and giggled as he crooked his arm with a gesture of gallantry. 'Your escort awaits, m'lady.'

They walked along, Richard shortening his long stride to match Bridie's steps. He was wearing, not his uniform as she had hoped, but a grey worsted suit, gloves and a trilby hat with a black band. He wore grey spats over black leather shoes and he carried a cane.

'You look awfully smart, Uncle Richard.'

He glanced down at her, his eyes wrinkling as he smiled. 'So do you. I like the boater.' Bridie was wearing the straw hat that Andrew had bought her, today trimmed with red, white and blue ribbons to show her patriotism.

'Why's it called the Goose Fair?' she asked.

As they walked, joining the throng all heading towards Market Place, Richard explained. 'Nottingham

Goose Fair has been famous for centuries. There's not much you can't buy there – even a wife!'

'A wife?' Bridie looked up at him.

'Not now, of course,' Richard chuckled. 'But they say that in the old days men used to auction their wives. I always thought it a bit dubious anyway. I mean, if a man had a good wife, why would he want to sell her?'

'I read a book about a man selling his wife to a sailor. He was drunk at the time, I think.'

'I expect most of them were. Farmers from neighbouring counties and even beyond used to walk here, driving their geese and covering about ten miles a day.'

'You mean the geese had to walk?' Bridie, tender-hearted as ever, asked. When Richard nodded, she murmured, 'Poor things.'

'They used to fatten them up in the cornfields after harvest.'

Bridie nodded. Even now, back home on the Dunsmore estate, geese were allowed on the stubble left in the fields after harvest. She laughed. 'They're like gleaners.'

'That's right,' Richard agreed and went on, 'but to prepare them for their long walk, the farmers would drive them over alternate patches of wet tar and sand to give them a sort of sole for their webbed feet.'

'How clever. So that's how the fair got its name?'

'Something like that. And, of course, it's very famous for cheese too, but there's a livestock market and a horse fair. They come from miles away. Some of the horses are wild and unbroken. And there's every kind of thing you can think of on sale.' He glanced down at her. 'I hope you've brought your purse.'

Bridie shook her head and grinned. 'It wasn't worth bringing, Uncle Richard. There's not much in it.'

'Don't tell me your aunt isn't paying you much?' he said, pretending to be scandalized.

Bridie laughed. 'I get what the other workers of my age get, but before I came here I didn't get much from Gran. I had to work for me keep, she said.'

'Did she indeed?' she heard Richard murmur, but then her attention was taken by the scene unfolding before her eyes.

They were nearing Market Place and already they could hear the sound of music from fairground organs. All around them, people seemed to quicken their pace, eager to be caught up in the excitement.

Forgetting, for a brief moment, her intention to be more grown-up and ladylike, Bridie gave a little skip and pulled on Richard's arm. 'Come on,' she urged. Together they were caught up in the flow of humanity moving towards the fun.

Bridie could not remember ever in her life enjoying herself quite so much. For a few hours they both forgot about the war. All around them, it seemed as if everyone was determined to do the same. Laughter and chatter filled the air, squeals of delicious fear from girls on the roundabouts and swings and the raucous shouts from young men who, already, had imbibed a little too freely.

'Now, what do you want to see next?' Richard asked.

'Everything!' Bridie flung her arms wide as if trying to embrace it all.

Richard smiled indulgently. 'Right then. We'll start with the menagerie. I know how you love animals.'

They made their way to the area always reserved for the largest menagerie. There were rows of large wagons. One side of each wagon was enclosed with iron bars, over which shutters were fastened when travelling. Now they were open for the public to view the animals. Lions and tigers, sea lions and seals and a very clever chimpanzee that kept the crowd enthralled with his antics.

On a patch of grass an elephant and two camels were giving rides to small children, but Bridie shook her head when Richard offered to pay for her. 'No, I'd sooner watch.' But when a man invited her to nurse a tiny, baby monkey, Bridie held out her hands eagerly. The little creature clung to her and when she tried to give it back it grabbed at the ribbons on her hat, threatening to pull it from her head. Laughing, she gently disentangled herself.

'You'm got a way with 'im, missy,' the man said. 'Like to keep 'im, would you?'

'I'd love to,' she said, 'but it's not possible. Besides . . .' She looked at the man shrewdly. 'Isn't he too young to leave his mother?'

'Ain't got no muvver,' the man said. 'Reared by hand, this little 'un.'

'Well,' Bridie said firmly, handing back the baby monkey. 'I think he needs a little more rearing before you sell him.'

They had not moved more than a few paces before Bridie saw the man offering the tiny creature to another couple with a young boy.

Bridie turned and, dodging through the throng, hurried back towards the man, ignoring Richard's warning. 'Bridie, leave it, love . . .'

'You can't sell him yet.' Bridie faced the man hotly. 'He's too young. It's cruel.'

'Now look 'ere, miss . . .' The man's weather-beaten face was suddenly fearsome. 'Don't meddle in matters you know nowt about.'

'But I do know. I live on a farm. I know when an animal is big enough to be weaned.'

'Clever little bugger, ain't yer?' the man sneered.

'That's enough.' Richard's quiet but authoritative voice spoke behind her. 'The girl's right. You shouldn't be trying to sell it yet.'

'He's older 'n he looks. Small breed, they are.' The man was trying to bluster his way out of trouble now.

'I'll pay you not to sell him . . .' Bridie began, but Richard touched her arm and bent to whisper in her ear. 'It wouldn't do any good, love. He'd only sell him again once our backs are turned.'

Looking at the rough clothes and the greedy eyes of the owner, Bridie could believe it.

'Can I have him, Dad?' The young boy beside them now had the monkey on his shoulder and was stroking it gently, the monkey clutching his finger, its bright, beady eyes round and large in its tiny face.

'Well, I don't know, son. What do you reckon, Martha?' The man turned to his wife, who, much to Bridie's surprised relief, smiled. 'If the man tells us how to look after him. Like this lass 'ere ses, he does look ever so little.' She turned to Bridie, 'But we'd look after him. I can promise you that. I had a monkey when I was a bairn, so I know a bit about them.'

Bridie smiled and nodded, but would not leave until she had witnessed the transaction taking place and the monkey borne away by the delighted boy.

Richard put his arm about her shoulders. 'Come, I think I'd better get you away from these animals before you want to buy them all.' But he was laughing as he said it.

Bridie slipped her hand through his arm again. 'Sorry, Uncle Richard. I know I get carried away when I think an animal's not being treated properly.'

Richard squeezed her hand to his side. 'Don't apologize,

Bridie love. If there were more people with your caring ways, the world would be a better place.'

His words brought a flush to her cheeks and a warm glow to her heart.

'Now,' Richard went on. 'First of all, I'll buy you a toffee apple. I used to love those when I was your age.'

To Bridie's amazement, Richard bought two and they walked around, licking and biting the toffee until they came to the tang of the apple beneath the sweet coating.

'You look so funny,' she laughed. 'Eating a toffee apple dressed in your posh clothes.'

Richard grinned down at her. 'Today, Bridie, I don't care. My mother's not here to scold.'

Bridie smiled impishly. 'Nor's my gran.'

'Come on . . .' He grabbed her hand and almost pulled her along in his eagerness. 'Let's go on the gallopers.'

They rode side by side on the brightly painted horses. Up and down and round and round until Bridie felt dizzy. But she loved it, laughing out loud as she held onto her hat.

'Now we'll go on the gondolas,' Richard said as they climbed down unsteadily from the roundabout. 'You'll think you're in Venice.'

After that, they stood for a moment, looking about them. They heard the raucous shouts of a showman outside a boxing booth.

'I think we'll give that a miss, if you don't mind, Bridie. I don't particularly want to see two men fighting. Not today.'

Bridie shuddered inwardly, understanding at once. Very soon Richard would be fighting in earnest. This day was for enjoyment, for revisiting childhood. Today he didn't want to be reminded of the battles to come.

Instead, Richard tried to win a coconut for her but,

despite three attempts, he could not knock one from its stand. 'I never was very good at it,' he apologized. 'It seems I'm still not.'

'Never mind, Uncle Richard.' Bridie tucked her hand in his arm and led him towards the ornate frontage of the bioscope with its gold-painted pillars and archways. 'Can we go in here? I've never seen moving pictures.'

They stepped into the darkness of the huge tent and took their places in the rows of seating facing the white screen. When the show began there were gasps of surprise from the audience. Bridie was enthralled by the flickering images, her gaze fixed on the screen, but she was aware that from time to time Richard glanced at her as if he was enjoying watching her pleasure as much as the show itself.

At the end, they emerged from the darkness and blinked as they looked about them. The light was already fading as the day drew towards night. Market Place was still busy, but now the majority of the people were youngsters, out to enjoy the evening. Young men waved tickling sticks, targeting the pretty girls. Bolder ones stole kisses, vying with their friends to be the one to kiss the most girls. And the girls, giggling together, threw confetti at each other and then at the boys to capture their attention.

Bridie watched them, wishing she were older and able to join in the fun.

'I think it's time we went home,' Richard said, though she could hear the reluctance in his tone too. 'Your aunt will be waiting dinner for us.'

Only one incident marred a perfect day.

As they were leaving, a woman was walking amongst the crowd handing out white feathers to any young man not dressed in uniform.

She approached Richard and, standing before him, her glance raked him up and down. Her lip curled disdainfully and she held out a white feather. 'You may be a little older than some of them here.' She spoke in modulated tones and Bridie noticed she was well dressed. 'But you're young enough.'

Richard's only answer was to raise his hat politely and give a little bow. Then he turned and walked away, leaving the woman staring after him, the feather still in her gloved hand. Bridie scurried to catch up with him.

'What was all that about? What is she doing handing out feathers?'

'A white feather, Bridie,' Richard said tightly, 'is a symbol presented to a man deemed a coward. She is suggesting that any man who has not taken the King's shilling is such a person.'

He was walking so quickly now, marching along angrily, that Bridie had to run to keep up with him. 'I don't understand. How can she possibly think . . .?'

Richard stopped abruptly and turned to face her. 'It wouldn't have happened if I'd been in uniform. Women like her are taking it upon themselves to present white feathers to anyone they think is young enough to volunteer.'

'But you have.'

'She doesn't know that.'

'Then I'll make sure she does,' Bridie said promptly and turned at once to hurry back to the woman.

Richard caught her arm, the anger gone from his tone now. 'No, leave it, love. It doesn't matter.'

'Of course it matters,' Bridie retorted hotly. 'I won't have anyone thinking you a coward, Uncle Richard, because you're not.'

'Oh, my lovely Bridie.' He laughed. 'I think I should

take you with me to the Front. You'd have the enemy routed in no time.' Then, more seriously, he said, 'No, leave it, my dear. It really doesn't matter. She's not important. And one more thing, Bridie.'

She looked up at him.

'Please, don't tell anyone else about this. Promise.'

'All right then, but I wish you'd let me set her right.' Bridie cast a frown back through the crowd to where she could still see the woman handing out the insulting feathers, then, reluctantly, she followed her uncle.

Twenty

'Darling, I'm so sorry I couldn't get away to come with you today,' Eveleen apologized as the three of them sat down to a late dinner. She had not arrived home until gone seven that evening.

'It's quite all right,' Richard said tersely, but his tone told her that it was anything but all right. 'What was so important to keep you at work until this time?'

Briefly Eveleen explained about her problems with Bob Porter. 'And I'm worried about your father. I know he's not old, but suddenly he seems very weary.'

Richard glanced at her in concern, his earlier chagrin forgotten. 'Is he ill? Ought he to see a doctor?'

'I don't know. Surely your mother would persuade him to do that.'

Richard glanced at her out of the corner of his eyes. Drily he said, 'I doubt my mother would notice anything was wrong unless he collapsed in front of her and interrupted one of her social gatherings.'

Eveleen gasped. 'Richard! That's the first time I've ever heard you criticize your mother.'

Richard shrugged and then his tone softened. 'I've always admired my mother. I still do. There have been certain things in my father's life before he met her, as you well know, that she has been very understanding about. I thought, at the time, that understanding came from a loving nature. But since I've known you . . .' His disappointment forgotten for a moment, Richard's eyes caressed her, his glance roaming over her face as if he would commit her every feature to a memory that he could carry with him always. 'Since I've known you, known your warmth, your concern for others . . .' His smile became a little wry. 'Even when they don't really deserve it. I've begun to wonder if my mother really *cares* about anyone except herself and her place in the eyes of her fancy friends.'

'Oh, darling, I'm sure she does. It's just . . .' Eveleen hesitated and then smiled. 'It's just she's come from a different background to me. She's sophisticated and elegant and – and serene. I'm from working-class stock. I was nothing until you married me, as Bob Porter was quick to remind me.'

'What?'

Eveleen tried to shrug it off, realizing too late that she had said too much. 'I told you, we had a bit of a set-to.'

'I didn't realize he'd insulted you. What exactly did he say?'

'It was nothing, honestly.'

'Eveleen.' Richard's tone was sharp and adamant.

Sighing, she recounted the conversation, adding, 'But I can handle it.'

'I'll speak to him . . .'

'No!' Now Eveleen was firm. 'Leave it. Please. You'll only make matters worse. I've got to be able to handle things while – while you're away.'

They stared at each other, until Richard capitulated, saying slowly, 'Perhaps I've been wrong to get caught up in this war.'

Eveleen could not bring herself to contradict him. She could not lie, not even to save his feelings. Instead, all she could say was, 'It's done now and we have to make the best of it.'

There was an awkward silence before Richard said, 'Aren't you even going to ask if we had a nice day?'

'What? Oh, I'm sorry.' The worried frown scarcely left her face as she tried to smile. There was silence and then she added, 'Well, did you?'

'It was wonderful,' Bridie said in a small voice, joining in the conversation for the first time. Her tone belied her statement. She was sitting between them, halfway down the table, pushing the food around her plate, hardly taking a mouthful. She had listened to the interchange between her aunt and uncle and had felt the tension between them. Then what was really distressing her came tumbling out as she raised tormented eyes to Richard. 'But – but now it's over and you're going away tomorrow. You and Andrew and – and . . .' Her voice died and her head drooped.

Richard reached out and covered her hand with his. 'I know, love. I know. But we'll soon be back. I'm sure we'll get leave.'

'But you'll be going to France. How will you come back from there?'

He smiled. 'They'll have it all organized somehow, I expect.' He was trying to reassure her, to give her hope, yet even the young girl could see that he wasn't sure himself of what he was saying.

Eveleen sat silently. It should be me asking my husband these questions, she thought guiltily. And it should have been me with him today. On his last day. She smiled at Richard, promising herself that later, in their bedroom, she would make it up to him. But first there were matters that must be discussed. 'Darling, I must talk to you after dinner. The factory . . .'

Richard stood up, his own meal hardly touched. 'I'm sorry, Eveleen, but I must go to see Mother and Father to say goodbye. Don't wait up.' His voice was tight and it was only when he looked at Bridie that he smiled. 'Goodnight, my dear, and thank you for a lovely day. I shall treasure the memory of it.'

He turned and left the room whilst Eveleen stared after him in dismay.

Weary though she was with the day's dramas at the factory, she was determined to stay awake until Richard came home, but when he returned after midnight Eveleen was fast asleep.

Eveleen woke with a start. The half-light of dawn filtered through the curtains, but the city was already awake. From the street she could hear sounds: the clip-clop of horses' hooves, the rattle of cartwheels and carriages. Even the sound of a noisy motor car, which sometimes still brought people rushing to their windows. The house, which Richard had bought just after their marriage, was in a street of tall, terraced houses, fashionable yet still not too far from the city centre or the factory.

She turned her head cautiously, anxious not to disturb Richard, but found that he was lying next to her, wide awake, his hands behind his head, and staring up at the ceiling.

She cuddled close to him and put her arm across him. 'Darling, I am sorry about yesterday. Forgive me?'

She heard his sigh and then his arms were about her and there was a sweet desperation in his kiss. Their love-making was tender, yet tinged with the poignant sadness of finality.

Later, as they were dressing, she asked, 'What time does your train leave?'

'Noon.'

'I'll just have to go into the factory first thing, but I'll be back in good time.'

The disappointment showed clearly on his face. 'I thought we might spend the morning together.'

Eveleen felt torn in two. 'I'm sorry, but I must go in.'

'I realize there must be a lot of adjustments to make, with several leaving today, but surely Bob Porter is quite capable of doing that.'

'Well, yes,' she said carefully. 'But I know he doesn't like me being more involved with the running of the factory now . . .' her voice faltered. 'Now you're going.'

'I'll come with you, then. Maybe I should have a word with him.'

'No,' Eveleen said sharply. 'No. It'll undermine my authority. I've got to win it on my own.'

Richard shrugged and all he said was, 'Very well.'

'But I'll be at the station. I'll be there to see you off. I promise.'

'Miss Binkley, please may I have a little extra time at dinner? I'm going to the station to see Uncle Richard and Andrew off.'

'There's no need. Your aunt will be there and you had yesterday off to go to the fair.'

'But they might be going away soon. Right away. To France.'

Helen's face was bleak. 'I know that only too well, Bridie. My – friend will be on the same train. But I can't leave and neither can many of the girls and women in this room who have relatives leaving today.' She waved her hand to encompass the other workers. 'Don't you think we'd all like to go? I'm sorry, Bridie, but you cannot be treated any different from anyone else.'

Bridie bit her lip but, as she took her place beside Mrs Hyde and picked up her work, her mind was scheming. I will go, she promised silently. She's not going to stop me. Bridie knew she was courting trouble, but she didn't care. She had to see Andrew off. She just had to. And Uncle Richard too, of course.

All morning Bridie was in a fever of excitement, watching the crawling hands on the clock. It earned her a sharp reprimand from the usually even-tempered Helen.

'What's got into you, Bridie? That run you've mended looks as if you've used a knitting needle. You must do it again and I don't want to be able to see where the mend is when you've done it.'

'Yes, Auntie . . . Miss Binkley,' she said hastily. 'Sorry.'

Helen moved away down the room, weaving her way amongst the workers, glancing at their work, checking and rechecking that all was as it should be. Bridie bent her head over her work. Tears filled her eyes.

'Here, let me do it.' At her side, Mrs Hyde whispered, 'Come on, 'and it over. You do this 'un of mine. It's only a little run.'

By the time Helen turned round at the end of the room and began to walk back towards them, the kindly woman and the young girl had exchanged their pieces of work.

'What the eye doesn't see, the heart doesn't grieve over,' Mrs Hyde murmured softly and gave Bridie a huge wink.

*

The railway station platform was seething with soldiers, with volunteers still in civilian clothes and with all their wives and loved ones seeing them off. At one end of the platform a brass band played military music. Banners and flags were waving and children ran about excitedly, unchecked by the adults, who were far too caught up in the drama of the moment to bother.

Brinsley and Sophia Stokes stood with Richard, an awkward constraint between them, whilst Bridie clung to Andrew as if she would physically prevent him from climbing aboard the train. If her strength had been enough, she would have done so.

Above the sound of the brass band playing, the cheering and calls of farewell and the hiss of steam from the engine, she shouted, 'You will write to me, won't you? I'll write every week and send you parcels. Mrs Martin says we're allowed to. Auntie Evie says Mrs Martin's getting a ladies' committee together to organize knitting things for the soldiers. I'm going to join it. I'll send you some lovely warm socks.'

Andrew hugged her hard and tried to smile, but there was a catch in his voice as he said, 'I can't wait to wear them.' He drew back a little and held her away from him, looking down into her upturned face. 'Listen, Bridie, I want you to do something for me. Something very important.'

She nodded earnestly.

Andrew glanced about him. 'I'd hoped Eveleen would be here to see us off, but it doesn't look as if she's going to make it.'

A few feet away Richard's anxious glance scanned the seething mass, his hopes fading with every second that Eveleen did not appear.

'She'll be here. I know she will. She wouldn't

miss Uncle Richard going. Or you,' Bridie added hastily.

'Well, you're here,' Andrew said softly and hugged her again, murmuring in her ear, 'my little Bridie.'

Her heart swelled with love for him, blotting out for a brief moment her terrible fear for his safety. 'What is it you want me to do?'

'Remind Eveleen to go to Flawford to see her grandmother. I have asked her and she promised to see that they're all right. I'm not sure what's going to happen there once I've gone.' For a moment his face was bleak with regret. 'I almost wish I hadn't volunteered now. They need looking after. Her uncle – your grandfather – too, though . . .' A small smile played at the corner of his mouth. 'He'd be the last to admit it.'

'I'll tell her,' Bridie promised. 'But she'll get here in time for you to tell her yourself. I know she will.'

But when the whistle blew and there was a mad scramble to board the train Eveleen had still not appeared.

Bridie hugged Andrew and then Richard. 'Can't they wait? She'll be here. She must have got held up.'

'Oh yes, she's got held up all right. Eveleen's got far more important things to do now that she's running the factory single-handed.'

Young as she was, Richard's bitterness was not lost on Bridie. 'Oh, Uncle Richard, she . . .' The final whistle drowned her words of excuse.

Richard kissed his mother's cheek, shook his father's hand and then turned back to Bridie, giving her a bear hug that almost lifted her off her feet.

'Take care of yourself, my little Bridie,' he whispered in her ear. 'And don't eat too many toffee apples while I'm away.'

He set her down, turned and pushed his way through the crowd. And although she watched him until he disappeared into the carriage, he did not look back. The guard walked down the platform, slamming the doors. Soldiers hung from the windows, waving and shouting. Bridie pushed her way to the edge of the platform, reaching up to touch Andrew's hand one last time. 'Take care, oh, do take care. Both of you. Come back safely.'

All along the length of the train, the same words were being echoed.

'Come back safely.'

As the train drew slowly out of the station, Bridie heard a cry close behind her and turned to see Eveleen pushing her way through the crowd, her desperate gaze on the moving train.

'Oh no, no!' she gasped as the train gathered speed. Standing on tiptoe, she waved wildly.

'He'll not see you,' Bridie said harshly. 'He was looking for you until the very last moment.'

'I couldn't get away and then the streets are so busy . . .'

'Yes,' Bridie said, twisting the knife even more, 'that's what Uncle Richard said. He said you'd far more important things to do now.'

She turned and began to follow the throng moving out of the station, leaving a forlorn and guilty Eveleen on the edge of the platform staring after the disappearing train.

Twenty-One

Brinsley and Sophia were waiting near the station entrance. 'Bridie, my dear, over here.' She heard his deep voice calling her. 'Where's Eveleen?'

'Watching the train. She was too late to say goodbye.'

'Oh dear,' Brinsley said. 'Never mind, they'll soon be home on leave, I expect before . . .' He cleared his throat and gruffly changed the subject. 'Go and fetch your auntie and I'll take you both for a spot of lunch. I don't know about you, but I'm hungry.'

Bridie opened her mouth to protest. She would be in enough trouble already for having disobeyed Helen. Then she sighed. So what would another hour matter? She retraced her steps, to find Eveleen still standing on the edge of the platform watching the train receding into a tiny speck. She did not move, not even when the train was gone from her sight.

Bridie, her anger dissolved by the look of anguish on her aunt's face, touched her arm. 'Come on, Auntie Evie. Mr Stokes is going to take us for lunch.'

'I couldn't eat a thing,' Eveleen murmured.

'Nor me,' Bridie said. 'But Mr Stokes is right. We ought to try.'

Brinsley found a table in the restaurant of a local hotel. 'Now, we'll sit here in the window,' he said, holding the chair for his wife. 'We've a good view.'

But the scene outside the window was only a further

143

reminder. Would-be soldiers marched in ranks along the street, heading for the station to catch yet another train, whilst the pavements were lined with well-wishers cheering them on.

The food was wonderful, but Eveleen and Bridie only picked at it. Sophia seemed unperturbed at having just waved her only son off to war and Eveleen found herself thinking that her mother-in-law's serene exterior went much deeper than the schooled outward appearance of a well-bred lady. She remembered Richard's words at dinner the previous evening. Perhaps he was right. Perhaps Sophia Stokes didn't really care. But there was no mistaking Brinsley's feelings. Whilst he tried to be jovial, tried to keep their spirits buoyant, Eveleen could see the anxiety in his eyes.

'Now,' he said, when the meal was finished and the coffee served, 'we need to have a board meeting.'

Eveleen looked startled. 'A board meeting? But that's only you and Mrs Stokes now that that – that Richard's gone.' Was every sentence, everything they planned going to remind her?

'That's true. Since the only Reckitt left in the business died five years ago, the company has belonged entirely to our family.' He glanced at Sophia and his smile broadened as he addressed Eveleen. 'That's why, my dear, we want you to join the board of directors.'

'Me?' Eveleen was startled. 'But – but I don't know a thing about – about being a director. I'm – I'm . . .' She smiled wryly. 'I'm a worker, not a boss.'

'You underestimate yourself, Eveleen. You have run that workroom and all the homeworkers most successfully. And you've already become involved with the factory side. So, what do you say, my dear?'

'Well . . .' she said doubtfully and glanced at her mother-in-law. It was important to her that she had Sophia's support.

'We've discussed it at length – the two of us. And we talked it over with Richard last evening,' Sophia said in her soft, modulated tones. She patted Eveleen's hand. 'He, of course, was all for it.'

'In that case, I can hardly refuse, but I haven't the faintest idea what happens at a board meeting or what will be expected of me.'

Brinsley chuckled. 'You'll soon find out.'

Helen Binkley was angry. Very angry.

'You had no right to disobey me,' she said in a voice loud enough for half the workroom to hear her. 'You deliberately took time off without my permission. In fact, I forbade it.'

Red in the face, Bridie stood before her.

'It was very unfair on everyone else. I suppose, because you are Mrs Stokes's niece, you thought you could get away with it. Well, you can't. I shall have to speak to her about this. I have every right to dismiss you.'

Bridie raised her chin defiantly, her hands clenched by her sides. 'It'd've made no difference. It had nothing to do with her being my aunt. I'd've gone anyway.'

'Well!' Helen was robbed of coherent speech. 'I've never heard the like.'

'Now, now.' Mrs Hyde had heaved herself up from her chair and was coming towards them. 'Don't be too hard on the lass, Helen.'

Few people now called Helen by her Christian name

since her promotion to supervisor in the inspection room, but Mrs Hyde had worked there far longer than Helen had.

'She's only young and she wanted to see her family off. You can't blame her for that, when all's done and said.' Then the woman added bluntly, 'None of us know who's going to come back.'

There was a ripple around the room and the colour drained from Helen's face. 'You don't need to remind us, Mrs Hyde,' she said stiffly, her voice breaking. 'But there are several here who would dearly have loved to have been on the station platform today. Including me,' she ended bitterly.

'Aye well,' Mrs Hyde's tone was gentler. 'You're right there.' She turned to look down at Bridie. 'You were wrong to disobey Miss Binkley. But me and the others,' she gestured with a nod of her head towards the other women in the room, 'aren't going to hold it against you.' Then she added firmly, 'Not this time. From now on, you be a good lass and do what Miss Binkley says, eh?'

Bridie nodded and looked at Helen, who seemed to be struggling inwardly. At last she said, 'You're a very lucky girl to have such kind friends to stick up for you. Now, go and sit down and we'll say no more about it.'

But Bridie was determined to have the last word. 'I'm sorry I disobeyed you, but I'm not sorry I went to the station to see them off. There was only Mr and Mrs Stokes to see Uncle Richard off. And Andrew had no-one else but me.'

Helen stared at her in amazement. 'Whatever do you mean? Surely Eveleen was there?'

Bridie shook her head. 'No. She came, but she got there just too late. The train had gone.'

She turned away, leaving a shocked Helen gazing after her.

Eveleen was beside herself with remorse. She even thought of taking the next train and trying to follow Richard. She knew they were going to Newark, but where after that she had no idea. With a stab of guilt, she realized that she had not listened. She might never see him again and she had not even said a last goodbye. Her heart beat rapidly with fear each time she thought about it – he might never come back. She had been so resentful against him for volunteering in the first place, and then wrapped up in the problems at the factory, that she had let him go without a loving word. Even the memory of their love-making on that last morning was now spoilt because she had not said a proper farewell.

On her way to see her confidante and friend Win Martin, Eveleen walked along the street, her head held high, her back straight, determined that no-one should see the ache in her heart. She was dressed in a navy costume with a long, hobble skirt, with three buttons hiding a discreet slit to allow easier walking. The tunic-style coat was knee length with a broad waistband and a velvet collar. The feather in the small matching hat rippled in the breeze as she walked. Beneath it Eveleen's wild, unruly hair had been tamed into fashionable curls and waves, swept up into a chignon at the back of her head. Her outward appearance was that of a confident, fashionable woman of the town, but beneath lay insecurity and a terrible dread.

As she turned into Foundry Yard, the sight of the terraced house where she and her family had once lived brought the memories flooding back and she was again reminded of her brother. Only days earlier she had seen in the newspaper that the enemy were now laying mines indiscriminately in the North Sea, so that not only British warships fell victim but innocent fishing vessels and neutral ships too. Jimmy was in as much danger as the soldiers at the Front.

As she passed down the street to knock on Win's door, she knew that many of the women scrubbing their doorsteps, shaking their mats or returning from the market with heavy shopping were hiding the same anxieties she harboured.

Win answered the door quickly, flinging it open. 'Oh, Evie, it's you.' For the first time that Eveleen could remember, there was no welcoming smile on Win's face, even though she gestured for Eveleen to step inside.

'What is it, Win? What's wrong?' she asked at once. 'Because I can see there's something.'

Win pulled a face. 'It's our Elsie's husband. He's only gone and volunteered. Leaving our Elsie just as she's had the bairn, an' all.'

Eveleen groaned. 'Oh no! When did that happen?'

'He went same day as your man. Silly bugger went to a recruiting rally somewhere a couple of weeks ago and lots of the young fellers got swept up in all the patriotic nonsense.' She sniffed and added wryly, 'And some of the not-so-young fellers, an' all. One of 'em being our Elsie's Sid.' The fact that Win had resorted to swearing bore testament to the depth of her feelings.

'Win, I'm so sorry. What about your own sons?' Eveleen had hoped to confide in Win about her own guilt at missing waving goodbye to Richard, but Win had far deeper worries of her own. Now was not the time. The woman lifted her shoulders in a helpless shrug. 'They haven't gone yet, but I reckon they will.

It's spreading like wildfire amongst the young fellers. If you don't go, you're thought to be a coward. And if conscription comes in . . .' She left the rest of the sentence hanging in the air.

Win and Fred Martin's family were all grown up now, but as Win always said, 'They never stop being your bairns, do they?' And now she had sons-in-law to worry about too.

'What's going to happen, Win?' Eveleen whispered fearfully. 'How will it all end?'

But for once the woman who had helped Eveleen so much, who had always seemed to the younger woman to be a rock of common sense and optimism, could offer no word of comfort.

Twenty-Two

'That girl you've put with Jake, he's tearing his hair out. She's useless,' Bob Porter greeted her one morning.

'What? Oh, yes, right. I'll go and see.'

She found the girl, Gladys, in tears and Jake shaking his fist at her.

'What on earth is going on?'

'Just get 'er out of here, missis,' Jake roared above the clatter. 'She's forever tekin' the day off and when she is here, she's bloody useless.'

'Jake, please come to the office at the end of your shift and we'll sort it out then. We can't talk here,' Eveleen suggested, trying to keep her voice calm and her temper in check. 'Gladys, you'd better come with me now. You're in no fit state to work anyway.'

'That's bloody women for you,' Jake said, casting a vitriolic glance at the weeping girl. 'Turn the water taps on to get 'emselves out of trouble.'

Eveleen glared at him but said no more – for the moment. She would have plenty to say later, she thought grimly, as she put her arm about the girl's waist and led her away.

'Now,' Eveleen said, in the relative quiet of a room along the passage, well away from the machine shop and from Bob Porter's office. Eveleen had turned this into her office at the factory. 'Tell me your side.'

'I've been trying me best, ma'am, but he's that impatient.'

'Would you rather be put on another job?'

The girl nodded tearfully. 'I thought I liked machines. Y'know, they've always fascinated me.'

Eveleen nodded. She shared the same enthusiasm for machinery. But there, it seemed, the similarity between herself and Gladys ended. Whilst Eveleen had been a quick and deft learner, Gladys was not. 'But I just can't get the hang of the bobbin winding, missis, and the minute he starts shouting an' swearing at me . . .' The girl dissolved into easy tears once more.

Eveleen was thoughtful, staring at the girl yet not seeing her. An idea was forming in her mind. Gladys's performance in the machine shop had done the cause of bringing women into the factory no service at all. Sadly the girl had just proved right the men who were against the idea.

Now, Eveleen was thinking, if a woman were able to prove herself capable as an auxiliary worker, then perhaps the men's attitude would change.

'Don't worry any more, Gladys,' Eveleen said, 'I'll find work for you in the inspection room. See me in the morning. I'll have worked something out by then.'

'Oh, thank you, ma'am. Thank you very much.' Gladys stood up. 'I – I am sorry I've failed you, ma'am. I did so want to help with the war effort . . .' Her voice trailed away.

Eveleen stood up, more energy in her movement than there had been since Richard had left. 'You will be, Gladys, so think no more about it. Whatever job anyone does in these difficult times is helping indirectly, even if it doesn't feel like it.'

The girl smiled thinly, obviously wanting to believe what Eveleen said.

'Run along home now.' She patted the girl on the shoulder and walked with her to the factory entrance. There they parted and Eveleen, a spring in her step, ran up the stairs leading to the top floor of the warehouse.

'Do you know, Helen,' she greeted her friend, 'I've just had the most marvellous idea. Now, can you keep a secret?'

Jake presented himself at her office a few minutes after the end of his shift. Bob Porter was with him.

'Come in and sit down.' Eveleen smiled, hardly able to keep her face straight. The more she thought about her plan, the better she liked it, but she had no intention of telling either of the two men sitting opposite her.

'Now, Jake, Gladys herself has admitted that she cannot do the work, so I have found a place for her in the inspection room and I have also got a replacement for her with you.'

Jake groaned. 'I don't want another like her, missis. I'm sorry I offered to take one now.'

'I'd have thought you'd have learnt your lesson, Mrs Stokes, if you don't mind my sayin' so,' Bob Porter said.

Eveleen smiled. Hugging her secret to her, she was able to answer them serenely. 'As it happens, Bob, I do mind. Not all the girls and women we try out in the machine shop are going to be satisfactory. I know that. But that doesn't mean to say that none of them can do the work. I am sure there are plenty of girls who are capable of becoming skilled workers. It's just a case of finding them.'

'Well, that's where we don't agree, ma'am. I don't

reckon there's a female that's capable. I know they're only going to do the sort of labouring jobs, but even so they have to be quick and handy at it. The twisthands will rely on them. But if you reckon you can find one, Mrs Stokes,' he hooked his thumbs through his braces and rocked on his heels, 'then you can prove me wrong.'

Eveleen merely smiled and said nothing, but inside she was thinking: Oh, I'll prove you wrong, Bob Porter. You just wait and see.

After dinner that evening Bridie followed her aunt to Richard's study and stood in the doorway. 'Auntie Evie, Andrew asked me to tell you something. When they were leaving, he sent you a message. He said he'd asked you to go to Flawford to see the old folks. He's worried how they're going to manage without him.'

Eveleen was rifling through papers on the desk and made no reply.

'Auntie Evie, did you hear what I said?'

'Yes, dear,' Eveleen said absently. 'We'll go soon. One Sunday, perhaps. Now.' She shuffled the papers together, turned from the desk and held out her hand. 'I want you to come upstairs with me. I have something to show you.'

'What is it?' Bridie was intrigued in spite of herself. Eveleen's eyes were gleaming.

'You'll see. And I can't wait to see Bob Porter's face in the morning.'

Twenty-Three

At the start of the early morning shift the following day, Eveleen walked down the aisle between the machines. She was dressed in a coat-like overall, buttoned at the front, with a wide belt. A frilled cap covered her hair and she wore no jewellery except her wedding ring.

She arrived by Jake's machine and waited for him to turn and see her. She did not step into the twisthand's alley, the space that ran along in front of his machine. This was his domain and even Brinsley Stokes himself would not dream of going into the area until he had a nod from the man in charge of the machine.

Eveleen stood a moment, fascinated as always by the rhythmic motion of wheels and cogs, levers and bars, all working in harmony to twist thousands of fine threads into intricate and delicate patterns. She marvelled again as the finished length of lace came clanking slowly out of the machine.

As Jake turned, she saw the smirk on his face. 'So you're the new . . .' he began and then she saw his jaw drop as he recognized her. 'Mrs Stokes? You?'

'Yes. Me. You, Jake, are going to teach me all there is to know about bobbin winding, changing the bobbins, stripping and how to look after the machine when you want a few minutes' break.' Her smile widened. 'And anything else I'm capable of doing to help you. I had an

154

excellent teacher years ago, Jake, so mind you're as good as Luke Manning.'

'But – but . . .' the young man blustered, 'it ain't right. I mean, what will Mr Porter say?'

'You heard what he said last night, Jake. That if I prove to him a woman can do the job as well as a man, then he'll have to change his mind.' She smiled winningly at him. 'So, Jake, who better to prove him wrong than me?'

'I'll be a laughing stock amongst me mates, missis,' Jake grumbled.

Eveleen put her head on one side and said quietly, 'Would another penny a rack whilst you're training me, and others, help you to deal with your workmates' teasing?'

A rack was the measure of cloth by which the twist-hands were paid. On average they received sixpence a rack and could produce four racks an hour.

'What about mi butty?' Jake was quick to ask, referring to the twisthand who operated this same machine on the alternate shift.

'If he agrees to train someone else on his shift, then yes, he'd be paid the same,' Eveleen agreed. 'I propose to pay any man who undertakes to train women workers – properly, mind – the same.'

Jake's face cleared and for the first time he smiled. 'Right you are then, missis. Now, we'd better get started else we'll have the foreman after us.'

'You can't do it, Mrs Stokes. We'll have a strike on our hands.'

At the end of her first shift Eveleen took off her overall and cap, smoothed her hair and put on her costume jacket as she faced Bob Porter's red and angry face across her desk. Immediately she became the employer, no longer the employee.

'Are you referring to me working as an auxiliary or to the extra money I mean to pay those who undertake to train women?' Eveleen found it difficult to hide her smile as she remembered again the look on Bob Porter's face as he had walked through the machine shop that morning and seen her at Jake's side. Like Jake, he had not recognized her immediately, but when he had, his face was a picture; one that Eveleen would never forget.

'Both. You'll have the rest of the men up in arms.'

'Who is the union man in the factory? I'll talk to him.'

'Charlie Allen, but he'll do as I say. He took over from me when I took Josh Carpenter's place.'

Her mouth tight, Eveleen said, 'I see.' It seemed that despite being promoted to a management position, Bob Porter had not left behind his strong union affiliation. 'Right then. Sit down, Bob, and we'll get this matter sorted out here and now.'

'There's nowt to sort out, missis. It won't work and that's all there is to it.'

'Why? Just tell me why.'

'Women can't work machines. They haven't got the right kind of brain. They're mothers. That's what nature intended.'

He couldn't know how much his words wounded her. Eveleen swallowed hard and managed not to let the hurt show in her expression.

'I'm not suggesting that they can become twisthands,' she snapped. 'Few women would be physically strong enough, I know that. But your remark about the inability to learn is insulting. Besides, single women, at least, surely ought to have the right to earn their own living.'

Bob's lip curled. 'Oh aye, until they catch a feller to provide for 'em.'

Pointedly she glared at him. 'Sadly there may not be many left for them to catch.' She regarded him steadily. Bob Porter was a very bitter man. She could hear it in his tone, but she had no idea what had caused his seeming resentment against all women.

'Are you married, Bob?' she asked suddenly.

His head jerked up. 'What's that got to do with it?'

'Nothing,' she said mildly. 'I just wondered.'

He gave a grunt and there was a silence between them before he said morosely, 'I was, but she upped and left. Ran off with another feller.'

'I'm sorry.' There was no doubting the sincerity in Eveleen's voice, even Bob Porter could hear it. 'Betrayal is very hurtful.'

Bob stared at her. 'I shouldn't think you can begin to know what it feels like, missis. I don't reckon Mr Richard would ever . . .'

Eveleen shook her head, 'Oh no.' Her voice broke a little at the mention of his name. 'No, Mr Richard is a wonderful husband, but before I knew him, when I was very young, there was someone who hurt me very badly. I was naive and foolish.' Suddenly the memory of warm summer days and the excitement of her clandestine meetings with Stephen Dunsmore in Bernby Covert was so strong that she could almost hear the rustle of the leaves above them and feel his arms about her . . .

She drew in a sharp breath, hating herself for even thinking about Stephen when her beloved husband might, at this very moment, be facing death.

'I'm very sorry, Bob, truly. But you shouldn't let it

colour your whole view of women. We – we're not all like that.'

Now he sat down heavily in the chair on the opposite side of the desk and for a moment the fight seemed to drain out of him. It was as if her genuine sympathy had actually touched him for a brief moment. 'Aye,' he said. 'Aye, well, mebbe you're right, but I still don't reckon women's place is in a factory. They should be at home looking after their husbands and bairns.'

'We're only going to employ single women or married women with no children whose husbands have gone to war.'

'Oh aye.' Bob was disbelieving. 'That's what you say now, but it'll be the thin end of the wedge. As time goes on, you'll say . . .' He mimicked a woman's voice, high-pitched and whining. 'There's Mrs So-an'-So. Her husband's been killed and she's three bairns to support. Can't we find her a job?'

Eveleen laughed and was honest enough to admit, 'You may well be right, Bob. I can't deny it.' Then her expression sobered and she sighed. 'Bob, if this war goes on for any length of time, there's going to be a real shortage of men. More and more are going to go. There's talk already of bringing in conscription.'

A look of fear crossed the man's face. 'What age?' he asked sharply.

'Men between nineteen and thirty-five. I think I read somewhere that was likely to be the age range.'

Bob Porter relaxed visibly. 'Thank God I'm forty, then,' he said with a tinge of humour though the sentiment was heartfelt.

Eveleen could not resist the opportunity to say, 'It depends how desperate they get, Bob.'

He grunted and then realized that she was teasing him and had the grace to smile. He heaved himself to his feet. 'Well, missis, I can't support you in this. I never will, but you're the boss and since Mr Brinsley is on your side an' all, there's not a lot I can do about it, is there?' He stood above her, looking down at her. 'But I wish you'd stop this nonsense with Jake. You're making me look a fool in front of the fellers.'

Eveleen pursed her mouth and shook her head. 'I'm sorry, Bob, but I mean to carry on. I've something to prove. And not just to you. Oh, I admit when I first thought about it, it was just to prove you wrong, but now I've actually started I can see that I'm proving it to everyone. You, the other men, and even the women themselves.' She stood up and faced him. 'The only person who's going to look a fool, Bob, if I can't do it, is me.'

A fleeting expression crossed his face that said: And I hope you can't. But it was masked in an instant and instead he growled, 'Well, I still reckon you're stacking up a lot of trouble for yourself. That's all.'

Then he turned and left the room.

'I do wish you'd discussed it with me first, Eveleen. You've been very impulsive, my dear. I know your motives are admirable, but it's not really the place for a director of the company, is it?'

To Eveleen's disappointment, Brinsley disapproved of her action. He was sitting behind the desk in her office, his brow creased in a worried frown.

'I'm sorry, but don't you see, if I can prove that a woman can do the work . . .' She broke off suddenly.

Brinsley had put his hand to his chest and his face was distorted with pain. Eveleen hurried round the desk to him.

'Oh, what is it? What's the matter?'

'It's nothing. Just – just a little indigestion. That's all.'

'I'll get Fred Martin to take you home. You must rest.'

Whilst Eveleen now drove Richard's motor car, Fred Martin, Win's husband, had learnt to drive too and often ran errands for Eveleen, using the motor for the company, including driving Brinsley to and from the factory.

'I can't. If you're set on this madcap scheme, then I shall have to take on the administrative work.'

'No.' Eveleen spoke harshly. She was suddenly very frightened that Brinsley could be suffering a heart attack. Was this how her own poor father had died in the beck? Had he been suddenly overcome with dreadful pain and there had been no-one there to help him?

'I'm getting Fred to drive you home and sending a message to the doctor to come at once.'

'Don't fuss, my dear. It's only indigestion . . .'

'Well, the doctor will tell us,' Eveleen argued. 'But you're not to worry any more about the factory. Leave it to me. I'll cope.'

She would not allow it to be said that her actions had caused Brinsley to be unwell. She refused to carry that guilt too.

'Come along, let's get you home,' she said firmly and it was indicative of how ill he must be feeling that Brinsley did not argue.

Twenty-Four

As the days turned into weeks and Christmas came and went, the nation realized that the war was not going to be over in a few months. In January a new threat came from the air. A Zeppelin, a huge, bulbous monstrosity making a terrifying burring sound, dropped bombs on the Norfolk towns of Great Yarmouth and King's Lynn, killing civilians.

By March even the government was making urgent appeals for the women of Britain to serve their country by doing vital jobs, so releasing men for fighting. Now Eveleen felt vindicated. Surely not even Bob Porter could argue with the government.

Leave for Richard and Andrew was promised and then cancelled as the war intensified, but letters came regularly from them.

We are still all together, Richard wrote. *And everyone is fine. Sid is with us too. That was a stroke of luck, wasn't it? The whole brigade had a big inspection the other day by a general, no less!*

Eveleen and Bridie wrote every week. Eveleen, after working all day at the factory, often sat writing far into the night, sometimes falling asleep in Richard's study, her arms spread across his desk.

Brinsley had had no reoccurrence of the chest pains and the doctor had merely suggested more rest. Now Brinsley only came to the factory two or three times a week and never stayed very long. He did not even offer to attend to the paperwork. Eveleen had the uncomfortable feeling that, because he had not fully approved of her action in working in the machine shop, her father-in-law was tacitly refusing to help her.

Eveleen said nothing in her letters to Richard about her problems at home. Grimly determined, she soldiered on alone, learning the hard way. She felt as if she had been thrown bodily into a fast-flowing river and had to learn how to swim in order to survive. Daily she was forced to bite back sharp retorts in answer to Bob's scathing remarks. She needed him. She needed to draw on his knowledge as factory manager.

Reluctantly Eveleen had to admit that she could not manage without Bob Porter. And because of that she would have to put up with whatever he said or did.

At least, for the time being.

In April the news came of a desperate battle being waged near the town of Ypres. At the same time a new and terrible weapon was being launched by the enemy on the Western Front. An insidious, silent, greenish-yellow vapour drifted across from the enemy lines and crept into the Allied trenches. Without proper masks, the soldiers, choking and half-blinded, could only hold wet cloths to their faces as an inadequate protection against the chlorine gas.

On one of the occasions, all too rare nowadays, when she visited Win Martin in Foundry Yard, Eveleen felt weariness overwhelm her. 'Where is it all going to end, Win?' she asked her old friend.

'I don't know.' Win's cheerful smile was missing these days and there were dark shadows of worry beneath her eyes. 'Our Elsie's bairn's sick. He's wheezy. You know?' She tapped her own chest. 'It's the damp in these houses.' Win glanced around her own cosy home. The back-to-back houses in the narrow streets and yards of Narrow Marsh had not all had the loving care spent on them that Fred Martin and his wife had lavished upon theirs.

'I like it here,' Win said. 'I wouldn't think of leaving. I like the folks, but not everyone's as lucky as us.'

'Not everyone's as hardworking as you and Fred.'

'Aye well, that's as maybe. Our Elsie's Sid was all set to do up their place, but then he went and got caught up in the war.'

'How is he? Richard told me in one of his letters that Sid's in their company too. Have you heard from him?'

Win shook her head. 'He's not much of a letter writer, our Sid.'

Eveleen was appalled. 'You mean – you mean that Elsie doesn't hear from him?'

'Just now and then. He fills in one of them cards. Y'know, puts a tick to show he's well and then just signs his name at the bottom.'

How awful, Eveleen was thinking. She couldn't bear to think of life without Richard's reassuring letters.

'Can we go to Flawford this Sunday?'

'What? Oh, I'll have to see. Don't worry me now. I have these orders to look through.'

It was late and Bridie had been about to go to bed when she put her head round the door of Richard's study to see her aunt sorting through a mound of paperwork on the desk.

'The number of orders coming in is dropping off

alarmingly. One after another of our outlets seems to be closing.' Eveleen sighed, as Bridie stepped into the room and stood beside her. 'I suppose it's to be expected. Our exports have virtually stopped. At this rate there won't be a factory for the men to come back to after it's all over.'

Bridie wrinkled her forehead. 'I had wondered why there seemed to be less work coming to the inspection room, though at the moment there seems to be enough to keep most of us busy.'

'If things don't pick up soon I shall have to lay workers off.' Eveleen gave a humourless laugh. 'Mind you, Bob Porter will no doubt be pleased if we find we don't need women workers after all.'

'You'll need them for a while,' Bridie said in a small voice. 'There are six more men leaving on Friday.'

Eveleen looked up sharply. 'How did you know that? I didn't know.'

'Mrs Hyde told us today. Her sixteen-year-old son is one of them. He only started in the machine shop a fortnight ago, yet now he's going.'

'Sixteen! They can't go at sixteen, can they?'

Bridie shrugged. 'Mrs Hyde said them recruiting people aren't asking too closely what their age is. They just tek 'em anyway.'

Eveleen looked sorrowful for a moment at the thought of the brave young man volunteering. 'Sixteen,' she murmured again and shook her head at the sheer waste of it all.

'Could I have a word with you, Mrs Stokes?'

As Eveleen walked out of the machine shop towards

her office at the end of another shift, Jane Morgan, the trainee with Luke Manning, caught up with her.

Eveleen closed her eyes for a moment and groaned inwardly. Surely not another problem? She was so desperately tired. All she wanted to do was to go home and sleep the clock round. But she couldn't. She had vowed to prove that women could be as good as the male twisthands, but no-one else had all the administrative work of running the factory to attend to out of shift hours.

'Of course,' she replied to Jane. 'Come into the office.'

Once the door was shut, Jane, smiling broadly, said, 'Mr Manning reckons I'm ready to work with another twisthand as his assistant while he trains another lass.'

'Oh, Jane, that's really good news.' She smiled back at the girl. 'You've just beaten me to it. Jake said only today that there's not a lot more he can teach me.'

The girl put her head on one side and regarded Eveleen steadily. 'Will you be carrying on work, missis?'

Eveleen laughed and shook her head. 'No, Jane. I've plenty of other work I need to catch up on. I only did it to prove a point, but it seems you have done it for me. Mind you, I shall stay the course, just for the satisfaction of showing Bob Porter that not one, but two women have done it. However, we'll be putting you with someone else very soon. There are several of the young fellers gone and it's left some of the skilled twisthands very short-handed. I'll sort out the details with Mr Porter.' Her heart sank a little at the prospect, but then her resolve hardened. She was still the boss and he would have to do as she instructed.

'Will I get more pay, missis?'

Eveleen wrinkled her brow. 'I haven't had time to give it much thought, Jane, to be honest. But I don't see why not.'

'But it'll be less than a man'd get doing the same job, won't it?' There was resentment in her tone.

Slowly Eveleen said, 'You have got a point there.' Then, a little too impulsively, she said, 'Yes, I agree. If you can cope on your own and do all the work that's expected of you, then, yes, you should be on the same wage as a man in the same position would be.'

Jane beamed. 'Thank you, missis. I knew you'd be fair.'

'You can't do that. Put a woman on the same wage as a man?' Bob Porter, when he heard of Eveleen's latest promise, was incensed. 'We'll have a riot, let alone 'em downing tools.'

'Whyever not? If she does exactly the same work as a man.'

Bob's lip curled. 'Oh aye. And what happens when there's something heavy to lift?' Once more he mimicked a weak female. 'Oh, can you help me? I can't lift that.'

'I said,' Eveleen repeated slowly, 'if she does the same work as a man would do. And that's *exactly* what I mean.'

Bob shook his head. 'It won't work. I tell you, it won't work.'

He turned on his heel and left the office. Eveleen stared after him with the uncomfortable feeling that Bob Porter intended to see that her proposal had no chance of working.

*

'Well, missis, I don't reckon there's much more I can teach yer. You could work alongside any twisthand now, like Miss Morgan.' Jake nodded across the aisle to where Jane was winding bobbins. The girl did not see them watching her, her gaze was intent upon her work.

Eveleen laughed and held out her hand. 'Thank you for everything, Jake. You've been an excellent teacher.'

The young man grinned. 'As good as Luke Manning?'

'Oh, every bit as good,' Eveleen said, her eyes twinkling mischievously. She had done it, her heart was singing. She had proved herself capable and, better still, so had Jane Morgan.

What argument could Bob Porter possibly have now?

Eveleen found out the following morning. When she arrived at the factory, a little later than usual now that she was no longer to work a shift at the machine, she found the factory strangely silent. Jane was the only one working, loading huge reels of yarn onto a barrow.

'What's happened?' Eveleen asked her. 'Where is everyone?'

Jane pointed. 'Out the back. In the yard. Mr Allen's called a union meeting.'

'Has he indeed?'

Tight-lipped, Eveleen marched out of the back entrance to the factory and paused to take in the scene.

But it was Bob Porter who was standing on a box addressing the men thronging around him.

'He's gone off to war without a thought for his employees leaving an old man and a woman in charge. And you all know where *she* came from,' he sneered. 'She was nowt but a worker in the inspection room.' His voice changed, became placating. Eveleen grudgingly admired his clever oratory. 'I've done me best for you all, but the place is falling apart. We aren't getting the orders in now. There'll be no work for anybody soon, if it carries on.'

Unobserved, Eveleen crept closer.

'And then she brings women in. I tell you, she'll be trying to train 'em as twisthands next. Trying to work our machines.'

'Well, the missis could do it, an' all . . .' To Eveleen's surprise, it was Jake who raised his voice in protest. 'If she was strong enough.' He laughed and those around him joined in. 'And it's not like me to admit that, but I've gotta be fair. Mrs Stokes is a worker.'

When the noise died down, Luke Manning, too, spoke up. 'Jane Morgan's done well an' all. She's a good lass.'

'But don't you realize?' Bob leant towards them to emphasize his point. 'They're tekin' men's jobs, men's livelihoods.'

There was whispering amongst his listeners until Luke asked, 'How come? No-one's been laid off, even though the amount of work has slackened off a bit. They've only taken on women to replace the young fellers who've volunteered.'

'I tell you, you –' Bob jabbed his finger towards Luke and glanced at Jake too – 'are training women to take men's jobs.' He nodded sagely. 'Women are cheap labour. They don't get a man's wages.'

'That's not right.' Luke shook his head. 'Miss Morgan said that she's to be paid the same rate as a lad doing the same work.'

The grumbling grew louder.

'And is that fair?' Bob countered at once. 'To give a *woman* equal pay to a man?' He jabbed his finger towards them all now. 'It's taking away a man's pride.

The man's a breadwinner for his family. Always has been. Always will be.' Bob dropped his voice and the crowd fell silent. 'And another thing. Do you really think that these women are going to give up their places, earning their own money, when the war's over and all the men come home?'

The muttering rose once more in belligerent anger and, as Eveleen pushed her way to the front, fists were shaken at her and voices raised.

'Listen. Listen to me, please.'

'Let her speak,' Luke shouted above the rest. 'Let's at least hear what she's got to say.'

When the noise had abated, Bob Porter stepped off the box and, with a sarcastic gesture, invited her to step onto it. Eveleen found her knees were trembling. As she faced the hostile crowd, for a moment she could not speak. Then, taking a deep breath, she said, 'Mr Porter is quite right.' She paused as a murmur of surprise rippled amongst the men. 'Orders are falling off and, yes, if it continues there won't be enough work for everyone.'

Now they faced her silently with stony expressions.

Eveleen spoke quietly now, knowing she held their attention. 'But there are six more men leaving us on Friday and –' She glanced around at them all, at the faces before her she knew so well. Working amongst them over the past weeks, she knew each and every one of them personally. And, best of all, they knew her. Perhaps these workers knew more about her now than Bob Porter did.

She had worked with them, eaten with them, laughed with them. And she had mourned with them when the news from the Front was bad and a former workmate was reported killed. Gradually, without realizing it themselves, they had begun to treat her as one of their own.

Eveleen had proved herself one of them.

'– there will be more going each week until we are left with those too old to go and young boys, barely trained.' She paused again and, now, no-one spoke.

'You all heard what Mr Richard said before he left. When you come back, after it's all over, your jobs will be here waiting for you. And if – if Mr Richard does not come back, I swear to you now that I will honour his promise.' She lowered her voice and said quietly, but with sincerity. 'A woman will never, ever, take a man's job. Not in this factory. The women themselves know that. They have been employed on that basis. And, yes, I have agreed the same rate of pay for women as long as they do exactly the same work as you men.'

She paused for a few moments whilst the men talked amongst themselves, then she raised her voice. 'Now, it's up to you. If you decide to strike in protest,' she shrugged her shoulders, 'then I can't stop you, but I must warn you that there is less and less work coming in. Because of the war many of our overseas outlets are closed to us now. And if we cease to operate, what work there is will go to other factories in the city.' She paused significantly and then added, 'I'll leave it to you to decide.'

Further explanation was unnecessary. The men knew full well that if Reckitt and Stokes's trade went elsewhere, even for a short time, in these difficult circumstances the factory would never recover. They would never win back lost trade.

Eveleen stepped down from the box and without another glance at anyone she marched back into the building and went at once to her office, intending to work on orders and invoices. But she could not concentrate and paced the floor restlessly until, after half an hour, the door was thrown open and Bob Porter stood there.

For a moment they stared at each other, he, red in the face with anger, she, her eyes wide with the unspoken question.

'Well, missis, I hope you're satisfied.' His voice was tight with resentment. 'You've won. You've beaten me in front of me own workers and made a right fool out of me. They've believed you, the silly buggers.' He shook his head in wonderment. 'By heck, but I've got to hand it to you, missis. You're clever. But one day you'll come unstuck, and don't expect me to be there to pick up the pieces 'cos I'm giving you me notice here and now and—'

Eveleen shook her head. 'Oh no, you're not, Bob Porter. This factory needs you. The men need you. I need you. I might have proved a point over training to be a twisthand and I might have won, as you put it, today. But I can't run the factory. You know that very well.'

His face twisted into a sneer. 'Well, get your precious Josh Carpenter back then.'

Eveleen shook her head. 'No, Bob.' She drew in a deep breath and knew she had to lie deliberately. 'I don't want Josh back.'

What she wouldn't have given at this moment to have Josh walk through the door with his cheery, 'Eh up, mi duck,' and to know that the factory was once more in his safe hands.

Bob shook his head. 'Nobody makes a fool out of me, missis. I'm going and I'm going this minute. There's plenty of other jobs in this city and, even if there aren't, the army'll take me.'

He turned and pulled the door to behind him with a slam of finality.

With trembling fingers, Eveleen reached for the chair and sat down as her legs gave way beneath her, the full weight of responsibility pressing down upon her.

Twenty-Five

Bridie held out a letter to Eveleen.

'Andrew's still asking if we've been to Flawford. He's very worried about them. You promised we could go just after Christmas and I've kept asking you and asking you. And now it's April already and we still haven't been.'

'Does he really think I've time to go traipsing over there when I've everything to look after here, now that Mr Stokes isn't well and Bob Porter's walked out on me too?'

'It is your grandmother and your uncle.'

'I don't need reminding,' Eveleen snapped. 'But why should I concern myself with people who turned us out when we desperately needed help? A man who turned his back on his own daughter and has made no effort in over thirteen years to meet his granddaughter?'

Bridie looked down at the letter in her hand, at Andrew's sprawling writing. She folded it carefully to put it away in her treasure box, yet knowing it would be brought out time and again to be read and reread just like the others she had received from him. His letters kept him close to her, told her he was still alive, still surviving.

She looked up at her aunt. 'If you haven't time to go –' the accusation in her voice was ill-concealed – 'then I'll go.'

Eveleen stared at her for a moment and then gave a wry, humourless laugh. 'Good luck to you then. You'll certainly need it.' She relented a little to say, 'I'll get Fred to take you.'

Then she sighed. 'The people we really ought to visit are your gran and Josh. We haven't been for ages. I tell you what,' her face was suddenly brighter, 'we'll go on Sunday and we'll talk to your gran about Flawford.'

'She'll try to stop me going, if you do,' Bridie said morosely. 'I don't think we ought to tell her.'

'Oh no, you keep the child away from them. I won't have her going anywhere near them, not after the way they treated me. All of us, if it comes to that.'

Bridie had been right. Mary would not hear of the girl visiting their estranged family in Flawford.

'I only let Andrew visit us here because he knew the situation and respected it. He never spoke about them unless I asked and I trusted him not to go home tittle-tattling to them about what was going on here. Oh no, Eveleen, you're not to let her go.'

Bridie glowered at her aunt, as if to say, I told you so.

As ever, it was Josh who brought a calming influence to the discussion over the dinner table. 'Would you agree to her going if I went with her?'

Mary glanced at him. 'You? Why should you want to go?'

'Well, from what the lass says about his letters, Andrew seems very worried about them.'

'Then he shouldn't have gone off playing the hero, should he? He should have stayed and shouldered his responsibilities.'

'They aren't really Andrew's responsibility, though, are they?' Bridie said quietly. 'They're not his relatives.'

'Aye, an' he's the lucky one they're not,' Mary said sharply. 'And don't you start giving your opinions about things you know nothing about, miss. We'll decide whether you go or not and I say you don't.'

Across the table Eveleen smiled at her mother, 'Well, for once, Mam, you and I are in agreement.'

Bridie kept her gaze lowered so that no-one would see the spark of defiance leap into her eyes. The more they told her she should not visit her grandfather and great-grandmother, the more determined she was to do so. As the conversation around her turned to other matters, a plan began to form in Bridie's mind. She said nothing and listened with only half an ear as Eveleen said, 'Josh, I need your advice. The orders for dress lace are falling. We had another order cancelled last week and now I have several bales of finished lace stored in the warehouse and no buyers. Maybe I'll find a use for it somewhere, but it's the future I'm worried about.'

Josh was thoughtful for a moment. 'You say there's still a demand for curtaining?'

Eveleen nodded. 'Goodness knows why, but yes, there is.' She stared at him, puzzled. 'But we have Levers machines, not curtaining machines.'

Josh smiled. 'Then get some.'

Eveleen was surprised. 'But you don't have both sorts in one factory, do you?'

'Not usually, no, but these are unusual times. And, from what I hear . . .' He grinned sheepishly. 'Oh, I still know what's going on even if I do live out here in the countryside. From what I hear, there are lace factories closing every month because of the war. Now, there'll be machines going cheap. Talk to Mr Stokes, mi duck.

He'll see the sense of it. He's a clever businessman. He'll not want to see his factory go to the wall because of a war.'

'But where would we put them? You don't mean get rid of the Levers?''

'Lord, no. You'll want them again when all this lot's over. But I bet there's still plenty of unused space in the factory just being used as a dumping ground at present. There was when I was there and I don't expect it's changed. Get it cleared out and you'll be able to have a new machine shop.'

Eveleen thought of the clutter filling an area right next to the existing machine shop. She put her arms around him. 'Oh, Josh. Thank you. You're so clever.'

'Haven't I always said so,' Mary put in proudly. 'But don't start asking him to come back to Nottingham, 'cos I need him here.'

Eveleen and Josh exchanged a fond glance, as Eveleen said with feigned meekness, 'I wouldn't dream of asking, Mam,' even though that very idea had been her first thought the day that Bob Porter had walked out.

As she drove home, Eveleen said, 'I'll take you home, Bridie, but I must go and see Mr Stokes right away about this. It's such a good idea of Josh's, but I must talk to my father-in-law about it. I don't know why I didn't think of it myself. You'll be all right, won't you?'

'I'll be fine,' Bridie murmured, her mind busy with her own plans.

For a time, Brinsley was thoughtful when Eveleen told him of Josh's suggestion. Then, as she watched him, the spark of interest that seemed to have been missing for some time was rekindled in his eyes.

'That's a capital idea, Eveleen. I'll get on to it first thing in the morning.' His face sobered. 'One of my old friends has just been forced to close his small curtain-making factory. He may be only too pleased to sell his machines.'

Whilst she was delighted that Brinsley was once more becoming enthusiastically involved, she had a confession to make. Swiftly, the words tumbling out, she told him of the recent events, culminating in Bob Porter's resignation.

As she fell silent, Brinsley grunted, 'Stupid fellow!' He glanced at her and smiled. 'Don't blame yourself, my dear. He's always been a volatile type. To my knowledge that's the third time he's picked up his scissors and hook and walked out.' His smile widened. 'But he always walks back in sooner or later. Mind you, perhaps this time the factory will run better without his disruptive influence.' Brinsley cleared his throat and added, 'I have to admit, Eveleen, that you were right to have women trained. And by doing it yourself you blazed the way. I apologize for having doubted you.'

Swift to forgive, Eveleen hugged him impulsively. 'Oh, you don't know how happy that makes me. Thank you. I thought I'd made you angry with me.'

Brinsley chuckled and patted her shoulder. 'My dear, dear girl, I could never be angry with you for long. Let's just hope that there's enough demand for curtaining to justify the purchase of the new machinery.'

They both recognized that there was still a risk. Trade for curtaining might fall off too and then what?

As Eveleen drove home, she felt happier that her father-in-law was once more taking an active interest in the business. But even he could not take away the ever-present worry.

Could they keep the Reckitt and Stokes factory going until Richard came home? And what if . . .? Determinedly, Eveleen kept her mind from even dwelling on that awful possibility.

Somehow she must keep his factory working. It was a talisman. If Reckitt and Stokes survived then Richard would too.

Eveleen clung to that belief.

On the following Saturday, when Bridie should have gone into work for the morning, she feigned severe stomach cramps.

'Maybe I should call the doctor,' Eveleen said worriedly, standing by Bridie's bed whilst the girl writhed and moaned and clutched her stomach.

'No, no, I'll be all right.'

'But you've not had anything like this before. I've never known you be ill. Not so much as a cold.'

'Oh, I have. I often get these sort of cramps, you know, every month. But they've never been as bad as this.'

Eveleen nodded understandingly. 'I suppose it's your age,' she murmured. 'But if they go on, we'll have to see the doctor.'

'They'll soon go. They usually do,' Bridie said and then, taking a risk, she added, 'I'll try and come into work later.'

As she had hoped, Eveleen said at once, 'No, no, there's no need. I'll explain to Helen. After all, you'd be finishing at one o'clock anyway.'

As she left the bedroom, Eveleen turned at the door. 'I'll send Emily up with a tray.'

'Thank you, Auntie Evie, but I really don't feel like eating at the moment.'

'Well, ring for her if you change your mind. 'Bye now. I'll see you later.'

Bridie lay perfectly still, her heart beating rapidly, listening. When she heard the front door close and her aunt's footsteps tapping down the street, she flung back the bedcovers and leapt out. Dressing quickly, she crept down the stairs and let herself out of the front door, running swiftly to the place where she could catch the early omnibus to Flawford.

She was on her way to meet her grandfather and great-grandmother for the first time.

Bridie stepped down from the omnibus and looked about her. She had no idea where her family lived. All she knew was that their name was the same as hers: Singleton.

Children were playing cricket on a patch of land in the centre of the village. Bridie presumed it was the village green, though there was no grass. A woman, large and round and homely looking, stepped awkwardly off the omnibus behind Bridie, struggling to carry bulging shopping baskets.

'Let me help you,' Bridie offered.

'Aw thanks. A bit of help's worth a lot of pity, they say.'

'Where are you going? I'll help you carry them.'

'I don't want to take you out of your way,' the woman said. Now she was looking directly at Bridie, frowning slightly, her head on one side in contemplation.

Bridie grinned. 'Trouble is, I don't know which is my way. Maybe you can help me.'

Slowly the woman said, 'Aye, I reckon I can. You're poor Rebecca Singleton's lass, aren't you?'

Bridie's mouth fell open in a startled gasp. 'How – how do you know?'

''Cos, mi little lass, you're the spittin' image of her. I knew Rebecca all her life. She were a quiet, docile little thing.' Bridie felt the woman's scrutiny again as she added, 'You've a bit more of the devilment in your eyes than she had. 'Spect you get that from that rascal of a father of yours. It was the worst day's work Mary ever did, bringing her family back here.' The woman shook her head sadly. 'Poor Rebecca. If it hadn't been for him, she'd have been happily married to Andrew Burns with a brood of bairns around her now.' The woman smiled down at Bridie. 'I shouldn't be tellin' you all this. T'ain't your fault, though, what went on in the past, is it?'

Bridie grimaced, smiling ruefully as she did so. She had warmed immediately to this outspoken woman. 'I suppose not. But I seem to get the blame.'

They walked along side by side for a few moments, then Bridie picked up on something the woman had said. 'You must know my gran then.'

'I know 'em all. The whole family. I've lived in this village all me life. But you mean Mary?'

'Yes.'

'Me an' Mary were best pals when we was young. Cut me to the quick when she ran off without a word to anyone.'

Bridie stopped walking, staring at the woman in surprise. 'My gran? Ran off?'

The woman stopped too and turned back to face her. 'Oh aye. Didn't you know?'

Bridie shook her head.

'Ah.' The woman appeared to be struggling with her inner self. Whether to impart a juicy morsel of gossip or whether she should hold her counsel. Her better nature won and she shook her head. 'They ain't told you then. Well, t'aint my place. You'd best ask yer family. Talking of which,' she went on briskly, resuming her walking, 'I'd best take you to Singleton's Yard. I'm not sure what sort of a reception you'll get, mi little lass. Specially from *'im.*'

'Who's "him"?'

'Harry Singleton. Your grandfather. Heartless beggar. Turning 'is own daughter out just 'cos she made a mistake that a lot on us have. 'Im an' all his chapel ranting, yet he couldn't be forgiving to 'is own. Hard man, he is, as you'll find out. Yer mam were just a lass who fell in love, that's all.' The woman sniffed. 'Pity it was with a wrong 'un. But there you are, that's life. Here's my little place.' They had arrived outside a row of cottages and the woman pushed open a white-painted gate and walked up the path. 'I'll just put me shopping down . . .' She paused and then asked, 'Would you like a cuppa?'

'Yes, please,' Bridie said thankfully. Feigning illness, she had had nothing to eat or drink that morning. She followed the woman into a neat and homely kitchen.

'Sit yer down and I'll soon mek us a cup.'

'I don't know your name.'

The woman laughed. 'No more you do. My name's Gracie Turner. Sit down, love, mek yourself at home. Now, what's your name then? I know who you are. It's as plain as the nose on yer face, *who* you are. But what d'they call you?'

'Bridie. Bridie Singleton.'

'Bridie, eh?' Gracie smiled knowingly. 'After the old woman.'

Bridie sat down at the scrubbed kitchen table. 'Is that my great-grandmother?'

'Aye, that's her. Bridget Singleton. Poor thing, not much of a life she's 'ad.' As she bustled about her kitchen making tea, Gracie chattered.

'Why do you say that?' Bridie asked curiously, her mouth watering as Gracie put a plate of buttered scones on the table. Her fingers itched to take one, but she held back out of politeness.

'Go on, lass, tek one.' Gracie laughed. 'I can see you're hungry. You were on the early bus, weren't you? I stayed in town overnight. Me eldest daughter's married and lives there and I was minding the bairns for her last night. Did me shopping yesterday.' She gestured towards the baskets. 'But what my old man's going to say when he sees that little lot, I don't know.'

She laughed as she said it and Bridie knew that, whoever her husband was, he wasn't going to say very much.

'Come from Nottingham, have you?'

Bridie nodded. 'I'm staying with my auntie Eveleen.'

Gracie placed the teapot on the table and sat down opposite her with an exclamation of delight. 'Eveleen. Ah, now there was a lovely lass. She didn't 'alf go through it, poor love. What with Mary moaning and groaning all the time and that brother of hers . . .' She cast a shrewd glance at Bridie and added apologetically, 'But I shouldn't call him names. He is your dad, after all.'

'You can say what you like about him, Mrs Turner,' Bridie said tartly, reaching for another scone. 'I've yet to meet him.'

Now the woman's mouth dropped open as she stared at Bridie. 'Wha . . .? You mean to say, you've never . . .? He's never . . .?'

Bridie shook her head. 'I've not been told very much about my family, Mrs Turner. In fact,' she smiled warmly at the woman, 'you've told me more about them in the last ten minutes than I've known the whole of me life. But I did know that me dad ran away to sea before I was born *and* . . .' she added with a trace of resentment, 'before he married my mother. That's why I'm called Singleton and not Hardcastle.'

Gracie was contrite. 'I'm sorry, mi little lass, if I've opened my big mouth and let it run away with itself.'

'Please, don't apologize. It's high time I knew about my family, but it all seems to be such a big secret, especially with my gran. Mary, I mean,' she added to make it clear about whom she was talking.

'I'd best say no more, 'specially not on that subject.' Gracie clamped her lips together to stop them uttering any more gossip. 'Drink up and I'll show you the way to Singleton's Yard, but I'll not come in with yer, if yer don't mind. I'm not exactly Harry Singleton's favourite person.' She smiled ruefully. 'Bit too free with me tongue. I'm likely to give him a piece of me mind when I see him and I wouldn't want you to get off on the wrong foot with him because of me.' The woman dropped her voice, but Bridie's sharp ears picked up her words. 'That'll happen without any help from me.'

Twenty-Six

They were standing at the end of a narrow street.

'This is Ranters' Row,' Gracie said, smiling. 'That's what us locals call it, but its proper name is Chapel Row. It's a dead end as you can see and your grandad's place is up there on the left-hand side.' The woman placed her hand on Bridie's shoulder. 'Good luck.' She turned to go and then glanced back. 'If you need any 'elp, you know where I live.'

'Thank you, Mrs Turner.'

Bridie took a deep breath and walked up the street, coming to a halt in front of a solid green gate. To her left was a long brick wall with windows and a door in the centre. Bridie pushed open the gate and stepped inside.

She was standing in one corner of a rectangular-shaped enclosure. To her left was a line of cottages, the back wall of which was obviously the one facing the street. Now she could see the front doors of the three homes facing the yard. The street side of the building had looked austere, but on this side a huge tree climbed the walls, straddling the whole frontage. Curiously she looked about her. A brick path ran in front of the cottages and halfway along it was a pump. From this, another path ran the length of the yard, branching off to the buildings on each side and at the far end. There were patches of garden on either side of the path, but the ground was neglected, growing wild and any plants were choked with weeds.

There was no-one about, the place seemed deserted, but then she became aware of the noise of machinery. Bridie stared up at the two-storey buildings. These were obviously not homes. On each floor there was one window, with tiny square panes, running the full length of the wall. Bridie smiled, knowing at once what these were.

These buildings were her grandfather's workshops. The windows were just like the ones in the back streets of Nottingham, where lacemakers and framework knitters worked in their own homes.

This was where Andrew worked. She glanced back towards the cottages, wondering which one was his home. Suddenly she felt close to him and tears started in her eyes. She had longed to see his home and, although she was here at last, he was not. Impatiently she brushed away her sentimental thoughts and approached one of the buildings. Inside, she climbed the steep stone steps to the upper floor, the clatter of machinery coming closer and closer.

At the top, she was standing in a long room. The machines, twenty or so, were set close together with the operators sitting back to back, and in a row down the side of the room beneath the long window. Only three machines were in use, two operated by older men and one by a young boy about Bridie's age. Against the opposite wall, too, there were machines, even though the light would not be so good there. These stood idle.

No-one had noticed her arrival; they had not heard her above the clatter so, for some time, Bridie stood watching the rhythmic operation of the framework knitters, trying to work out which of the two men was her grandfather.

As if feeling her gaze, the young lad looked up and grinned cheekily at her. Bridie smiled back, but the boy did not get up and come over to her. Instead, he shrugged and gestured towards the man sitting directly behind him. Then he pulled a grimace and drew his hand across his throat, intimating to Bridie what he thought the man would do to him if he left his work.

Bridie nodded, understanding. For a moment, she stood unobserved, watching the man. He was a big man, but his broad shoulders were stooped with the long years spent at his machine. He had a bushy white beard and moustache, which completely hid his mouth, and his heavy eyebrows met across the bridge of his large nose. He wore thick spectacles, but even with their aid he leant forward, peering at the rows of knitting as if he had trouble seeing them. She moved forward into his line of vision, hoping he would see her, but his whole attention was on his work.

After a few moments the young lad slid off his seat, tapped the man on his shoulder and gestured towards Bridie. The man looked up, squinting towards her. Without even pausing in his operation of the machine, he gestured with a swift, angry movement of his head that she should leave. The boy lifted his shoulders in a shrug then stepped nearer to her, putting his mouth close to her ear to shout, 'He'll not stop till dinnertime. You'd better go.'

But now the man did leave his work. He stepped towards them, his arm raised, and dealt the young lad a blow across the side of the head that sent him reeling halfway across the room. 'Get back to your work, you idle beggar. And you,' he thundered, turning to

Bridie, 'be off with you. And don't come here to see him again.'

For a moment, she thought the man might hit her too, but she stood her ground and faced him squarely. Now two machines were stopped, only the one worked by the other older man still making a noise, and Bridie could make herself heard. 'It's not him I've come to see.' Taking a chance that this was the right man, for he seemed to be the one in authority, she added, 'It's you.'

'What d'you want?'

She was aware of the boy's curiosity and even the other man, though still working, kept glancing at her.

Well, they'd all know sooner or later, she thought, so she lifted her chin and said boldly, 'I reckon you're me grandad.'

She saw the man start and then he leant closer, squinting at her. Suddenly he gripped her shoulder and hustled her towards the top of the stairs, almost pushing her down them in front of him, but keeping hold of her shoulder with such a strong grip that his fingers dug into her.

Out in the yard, he spun her round to face him. 'Now, I don't know who you are or what you're after, but I don't want to see you round here again. That clear?'

Bridie stared at him. Then, quite calmly, she gripped his wrist, trying to release his grasp on her. 'Let go,' she said firmly. 'You're hurting me.'

'I'll hurt you, you little tyke.' It was the same name, the same tone that her grandmother, Mary, had used so often that Bridie almost laughed aloud. But the moment was far from funny.

'That's a nice way to greet your granddaughter, I must say.'

The man released her suddenly as if the touch of her was burning his hand. 'I haven't got a granddaughter.'

'Yes, you have.' For a brief moment, Bridie wondered if she had picked the wrong man in the workshop. Maybe the bent, wizened little old man on the other machine was Harry Singleton. But some instinct told her she had made the correct choice.

She lifted her chin higher, staring boldly up at him. 'You had a daughter, Rebecca, didn't you?'

He was about to deny it, even opened his mouth to refute it, but the words never came. Suddenly the huge shoulders sagged and he put out his hand to the nearby wall to steady himself.

'She's dead.'

'I know that,' Bridie said, her tone gentler, 'but I'm her daughter, Bridie. I've lived with me gran, Mary. She's your sister, isn't she?'

He nodded dully, but still he kept his gaze averted.

'She'd never let me come to see you.'

He gave a harsh, humourless laugh. 'Well, that doesn't surprise me.'

'She said you wouldn't want to see me.'

Now he was silent and to her, desperate to hear his denial, it was instead confirmation.

'Even Andrew wouldn't let me come.' There was a catch in her voice.

Now the man met her gaze, but he was still frowning. 'Andrew? Andrew Burns? What's he got to do with it?'

'He's my godfather. He used to come most Sundays to the farm to see me.'

'Well! Well, I never.' Harry – for now she was sure it was her grandfather – seemed genuinely surprised, but he was still not pleased. 'And how long has this been going on?'

Bridie shrugged. 'As long as I can remember.'

'He never said.' There was accusation in his tone.

'It was in his free time. You don't own him.'

'Mebbe not. But I employed him. I gave him his living. And I own the cottage he lives in.' He jerked his thumb over his shoulder. 'I could sack him and turn him out of his home, if I had a mind. Just like that.' He snapped his finger and thumb together. His voice dropped to a deep, aggrieved rumble. 'In fact, I might just do that. His place is standing empty now the silly young beggar's volunteered. Rushed off with all the rest of 'em into the Good Lord only knows what.'

'Which is his cottage?' Bridie asked, craning her neck to look beyond the huge frame of the man standing in front of her.

'What's it to you? Don't think you can go meddling in there.'

'Andrew wouldn't mind.'

'*I* don't know who you are. You could be anybody, for all I know.'

'Yes, you do,' Bridie insisted. 'I'm Rebecca's daughter. I even look like her. Andrew said.'

'I can't see the likeness myself.'

'That's because you can't see very well now, can you?'

'Who told you that?' he barked, his resentment surfacing again swiftly.

'I don't need anyone to tell me. I watched you at work. I was stood there for ages before you saw me.'

'Can't hear anything above the noise.'

'Mebbe not. But you were squinting at the knitting as it came off the machine. And there was a flaw in it you didn't notice.'

'Cheeky little baggage, aren't you? You're not like

189

my . . .' he began, almost tricked into acknowledging that at least it was a possibility that she was his granddaughter. As if to counter his moment of weakness, he made an angry gesture with his right arm. 'Be off with you. And don't come here again.'

Bridie regarded him steadily. Far from being frightened of him or fazed by his anger, she felt sorry for him. It was obvious his once thriving business was struggling. Only three to carry on the work; an old man, a young boy and a man who could hardly see now. It was obvious Harry Singleton needed help. But he was too stubborn to seek it.

She would go – for now – but first there was someone else Bridie wanted to see. With a quiet dignity that belied her tender years, she said, 'I'm going nowhere, Grandfather, until I've seen my great-grandmother.'

Twenty-Seven

Bridie let herself into the end cottage in the row. She stood a moment until her eyes became accustomed to the gloom. Then she glanced around the room, cluttered with possessions accumulated over the years. Everywhere was covered with a film of dust. There was no fire in the grate in the range, only ashes not yet cleaned out. The range itself was dull and neglected. She tiptoed through into the scullery to find unwashed post and bits of mouldering food. There was a stale smell about the place too. In the far corner of the scullery was the staircase and Bridie climbed it, calling out as she went.

'Are you there, Great-Gran?' She didn't know what else to call the old lady who lived here. The full title – great-grandmother – was such a mouthful, but she didn't want to appear in the old lady's bedroom unannounced and startle her.

A querulous voice came from the larger of the two bedrooms on the first landing. 'Who's that? Is that you, Lil?'

Bridie pushed open the door. The old lady was lying in the double, metal-framed bed against a mound of greyish-looking pillows. Her white hair stuck up in unkempt tufts and her thin face was a network of lines and wrinkles. Her bony, purple-veined hands plucked at the covers and her voice was frail as she quavered, 'Who are you?'

Bridie moved to the side of the bed and began to say, 'Don't be frightened, I'm . . .' but the old woman clutched at the covers until her knuckles were white and shrieked, 'Rebecca!'

Bridie stopped and gasped in surprise as they stared at each other. Both were startled but the old lady had a look of sheer terror in her eyes.

Bridie reached out towards her. 'I'm Rebecca's daughter, Bridie.'

'Bridie?' she quavered. Then she moaned and closed her eyes. 'Oh, dear Lord. She's come for me. It's my time. Rebecca's come for me.'

'Great-Gran,' Bridie said firmly. 'Please listen to me. I'm Bridie. I'm Rebecca's daughter. But I know I look a bit like Rebecca.'

The old lady seemed to be recovering her senses a little after the first shock. She opened her eyes and stared at her. 'Bridie? Your name's Bridie too?'

'My name is Bridie,' the girl said mystified. 'But what do you mean "too"?'

'That's my name, Bridget, but me da always called me Bridie.'

The young girl beamed. 'Then obviously I'm called after you.'

'After me? Why?'

The poor old thing confined to her bed was obviously confused. Patiently Bridie explained. 'Because I'm your great-granddaughter.'

The old lady blinked, trying to focus her watery eyes on the figure standing at the end of her bed. 'My . . .' She began and then lapsed into silence, lost in thought and trying to catch hold of vague, ephemeral memories. Then she let out a long sigh and fell back against the pillows.

'Bridie. Now I remember. Eveleen came with a little baby, Rebecca's baby, and said they were going to call her after me.'

'That's right,' Bridie said eagerly. Perhaps the old lady was not so senile after all. Perhaps all she needed was a little tender loving care.

'Brought the baby back here to be christened in the chapel across the road. But Harry didn't go. Harry wouldn't even go to the poor little mite's christening.'

That 'poor little mite' was me, Bridie was thinking. But she said nothing, allowing the frail old lady to come to the truth in her own time.

Bridie moved closer to the bed. 'I can't stay much longer today, but . . .'

Bridget's bony hands were reaching out. 'Don't go. Stay and talk to me. Nobody comes to talk to me now.' The voice was pitiful. 'Please, don't leave me.'

'Great-gran, I have to go.' Bridie gave a nervous laugh. 'My Aunt Eveleen's going to skin me alive as it is for coming. She doesn't know I'm here.'

'Eveleen.' The old lady said the name as if it had not been spoken aloud for years. 'Ah yes, Eveleen. I always liked Eveleen. Strong, she was. Braver than all the rest of us put together.'

Questions tumbled around Bridie's mind. There was so much she would like to ask, so much that her great-grandmother must know. Instead, anxious that the old lady should not be upset any more, she said, 'I'll make us both a cup of tea before I go.'

'Aye, I could do with one.' Her voice was stronger now, laced with resentment. 'That Lil should have been in this morning but she hasn't been near.'

'Who's Lil?' Bridie asked.

Bridget tossed her head. 'Lives in the cottage facing

193

the street. She's supposed to clean for us. Make our meals an' that, but half the time Harry has to do it when he's finished work.' She sniffed. 'Still, there's no-one else to do it, so I s'pect we'll have to put up with 'er doing it when she feels like it.'

Several minutes later, Bridie helped her great-grand-mother to sit up in the bed, plumping the pillows behind her. 'Now, here's your tea. Don't spill it.'

'You'd make a good nurse,' Bridget said, slurping her tea thirstily.

'Does my grandfather live here with you?' Bridie asked as she perched on the end of the bed to drink hers.

'No. He lives in the cottage at the other end.'

Bridie ran her tongue over lips that were suddenly dry. 'So – so Andrew lives in the cottage next door? Between the two of you?'

The old woman squinted at her. 'That's right. But he's not here. He's gone to the war.'

Bridie nodded. 'I know.'

There was silence between them as they drank their tea until Bridie said, 'I can't stay much longer. I must get the omnibus back to Nottingham. Will my grand-father be finishing work soon?'

The old lady gave a wry laugh. 'What? Him? No. Works all day and 'alf the night now.'

'Really?' Bridie was surprised. From what her aunt had told her, work at the factory was falling off. So why . . .? Her great-grandmother's next words gave her the answer.

'He's pulled out the place with work, and no-one to do it now all the young fellers have gone off to the war.'

'I don't understand. Where's all the work coming from? Auntie Evie says the Reckitt and Stokes's factory is going through a bad time. No-one wants lace in wartime.'

'Well, no, they won't. But what your uncle makes is knitted garments. Fine underwear – long johns, vests, socks. And all the officers' families round here are climbing over themselves to have well-made garments for their boys. We're getting orders from Nottingham and even other places, now word's spreading. And when Queen Mary appealed to the Empire to knit three hundred thousand pairs of socks for the troops, well, Harry nearly had a heart attack.'

Bridie placed the empty cups on the tea tray and bent to kiss the old lady's wizened cheeks. 'I must go now, Great-Gran. I have to go back and face my aunt. But, whatever she says, I will come back.' She glanced around at the neglected room and thought of the state of the rooms downstairs. 'You need me far more than she does,' Bridie murmured.

As she passed Andrew's cottage on her way out, Bridie peered through the windows. She could see little of the dim interior, but she laid her hand against the door and whispered, 'I'll be back. I promise I'll be back.'

'Emily, how is Miss Bridie?' Eveleen asked as soon as she stepped over the threshold that evening at six o'clock. Although it was a Saturday and the workforce usually finished at lunchtime, nevertheless Eveleen had remained at the factory.

Brinsley had visited that morning and, feeling much better than he had of late, had involved Eveleen in lengthy discussions on the seriousness of the current state of the order book. He had insisted on touring the machine shops and talking to the men and women now working the lace machines. He had even climbed to the top floor of the warehouse to visit the inspection room and speak to Helen. Then he had stopped at each floor on the way down.

When their tour was over, he had insisted that Eveleen should go to lunch with him in the city. By the time they had finished, it was three o'clock and Eveleen still had paperwork to complete at the factory before going home.

'I haven't seen her all day, ma'am,' the girl replied now, taking Eveleen's coat and hat. 'Dinner will be ready in half an hour, Cook says.'

'Thank you,' Eveleen said absently, but her mind was still on her niece. 'Is she still in her room? Haven't you been to see if she wanted anything?'

'You said to leave her and she would ring, ma'am.'

Eveleen clicked her tongue against her teeth in agitation. 'I know I did, but – all day! Surely you thought to go and check that she was all right?' When the young girl looked crestfallen, Eveleen said, 'Oh, never mind. I'll see for myself.'

She ran lightly up the stairs and, opening the door quietly in case Bridie was asleep, tiptoed into the bedroom. The bed was unmade but empty and, further along the landing, the bathroom showed signs that Bridie had washed hurriedly. On closer inspection, Eveleen found that the girl's clothes, including her outdoor hat and coat, were also missing.

Downstairs she rang for the young maid. 'She seems to have gone out. Are you sure you heard nothing?'

'No, ma'am. Mind you, I've been down in the kitchen for a lot of the day, so I wouldn't have heard her going out of the front door.'

'And you haven't looked in her bedroom all day?'

The girl shook her head, easy tears starting in her eyes. 'I'm sorry, ma'am, if I should have . . .'

'No, no,' Eveleen held up her hands. 'It's not your fault, Emily.' More to herself now than to the maid, Eveleen murmured, 'But I wonder where she can have gone.'

'Maybe she felt a little better and went to work?' Emily tried to suggest helpfully.

Eveleen shook her head. 'No, I'd have seen her.'

'Maybe she's gone shopping.'

Eveleen wrinkled her brow. 'It's possible, I suppose. But she's never been into the city on her own before.'

'Would she go home, I mean back to the farm, to see her gran?'

Eveleen stared at Emily. 'No,' she said slowly. 'No, I don't think she'd go there. But now you've made me think, I know exactly where she has gone.'

Emily still looked puzzled. 'Where, ma'am?'

'Never mind,' Eveleen said, her mouth tight, 'but just wait until the little madam gets back home.'

Twenty-Eight

'You deliberately disobeyed me.'

An hour later, Bridie was facing an angry Eveleen. 'I'm sorry you're cross with me, Auntie Evie, but I'm not sorry I went.'

Eveleen gasped and her eyes widened in surprise at the audacity of her young niece. But as the girl went on, her anger died to be replaced by her own guilt.

'Andrew was right, Auntie. They do need help badly.' Swiftly she explained all that she had seen in Singleton's Yard. 'My grandfather doesn't want us there. Doesn't seem to want anyone, but poor Great-Gran, she needs looking after, Auntie Evie. She'll die, else.'

'Oh, I think that's being a bit melodramatic, Bridie.'

The girl shook her head vehemently. 'No, it isn't. I called at Mrs Turner's on the way back to catch the omnibus and . . .'

'Mrs Turner?' Eveleen searched her mind for the memory of the large, bustling woman who had been her mother's childhood friend. 'Gracie Turner,' she murmured.

'That's her,' Bridie went on. 'Well, when I told her that Great-Gran thought I was someone called Lil coming up the stairs, Mrs Turner said there was no wonder they were in a state. She said that this Lil is a right – ' she hesitated, trying to remember the unfamiliar word – 'a right slattern.'

Despite her growing anxiety, Eveleen had to smile, but it soon faded as Bridie stepped nearer her and put a hand on her arm. 'Auntie Evie, I am sorry I disobeyed you, but they do need help. Both of them. My grandad can hardly see, and the poor old lady, I don't think she can get out of bed without help. And,' she added pointedly, 'there's no one to help her.' Looking into the girl's dark blue eyes, Eveleen could read her genuine distress.

She patted Bridie's hand, 'It's all right. You're forgiven.' She pulled a comical face of contrition. 'It's me who should be saying sorry. It's me who should have gone.' She was ashamed to think that it had been a thirteen-year-old girl who had undertaken what should have been an older person's responsibility. 'But I didn't think we'd be welcome there.'

'Oh, we're not,' Bridie said airily. 'But that's not the point, is it? They need help, both of them, even if they won't admit it. And,' she grinned impishly at her aunt, 'whether they like it or not, they're going to get it.'

'Oh, Bridie.' Eveleen opened her arms to the girl. 'Give me a hug.'

They stood together holding each other close, drawing comfort from each other, united in their loneliness, in missing the menfolk they adored.

'Come,' Eveleen said at last, taking Bridie's hand. 'Let's go and have the dinner that's Cook's been holding back for an hour and discuss what we're going to do.'

'Do you think we should go to the farm and talk it over with your gran?' Eveleen said as they reached the pudding course.

'I've only ever heard her ask Andrew about them

199

once or twice.' Bridie's voice hardened. 'Do you really think she's bothered?'

Eveleen sighed. 'She harbours such a lot of bitterness about things that have happened in the past.'

'What things?'

Eveleen regarded her steadily. 'I can't really tell you. Not just now, anyway. Maybe one day.'

'About my mother and me, you mean?'

'That's part of it,' Eveleen said carefully.

Sharply inquisitive, Bridie said, 'But not all of it?'

Eveleen shook her head. 'Oh no. Not all of it. Not by a long way.'

For a moment they were both quiet, lost in their own thoughts, before Bridie dropped a bombshell into the silence. 'Why don't I go and live there and look after them?'

Eveleen's spoon clattered into her dish. 'I don't think that's a very good idea. Your gran wouldn't like it.'

'Gran's got nothing to do with it,' Bridie said, once more sounding very much older than her years. 'We've just decided that she's probably not that bothered.'

'I don't think we ought to say that . . .' Eveleen began, but Bridie interrupted impatiently, 'Well, you know what I mean.'

'But I need you here,' Eveleen protested.

Gently Bridie said, 'No, you don't, Auntie Evie. Not really. There's dozens of young girls in Nottingham who'd leap at the chance to work in Reckitt and Stokes's warehouse. You don't really need me.'

'But I want you here, Bridie,' Eveleen insisted. 'You said yourself your grandfather doesn't want you there. Doesn't want any of us.'

Bridie laughed, her blue eyes glinting with a sudden steely resolve. 'I know, but they need me, Auntie Evie.

There's a big difference, isn't there, between being wanted and needed. For a long time I didn't think anyone wanted or needed me.'

'That's not true, Bridie . . .' Eveleen began to protest.

'I know. I know that now.' The young girl, who was growing up so fast, almost before Eveleen's eyes, said gently, 'Gran and Josh must have wanted to keep me as a baby, because they needn't have. And Andrew . . .' Her voice wavered slightly as she thought about him soon to be in a foreign, dangerous land. 'I know he does love me. In his own way.'

'We all do, Bridie,' Eveleen said softly.

The girl nodded and then, with words that tore at Eveleen's heart, she said simply, 'But for the first time in my life someone really *needs* me.'

'If you're really sure, then . . .' Eveleen began.

'I am. There's no-one to look after Great-Gran. Grandfather is working all hours, even though his sight is bad. There's only him, one other old chap and a young lad in the workshops. They can't cope with all the work that's coming in.' She laughed as she repeated the old lady's words. 'They're pulled out the place.'

'What?' Eveleen was suddenly alert. 'What work?'

'It seems everyone's after their knitted undergarments to send to the men at the Front. You know?'

Eveleen stared at her and slowly shook her head. 'No, I don't know. Explain it to me slowly.'

Bridie repeated all that her great-grandmother had told her. 'Funny, isn't it?' she added. 'You've got too many workers and not enough work and he's got more . . .' Her voice faltered as she stared back at her aunt. Slowly her own mind began to realize what was going on in Eveleen's. 'He's got more work than he can cope with.'

'Exactly!' Eveleen sprang to her feet and held her arms wide. 'My darling Bridie. I think you've just brought home another answer to help save your Uncle Richard's factory.'

'But – but you can't make those things on lace machines, can you?'

'No, of course not. But we can send workers out to Flawford or bring the work into the city. There must be a lot of frames standing idle now since their operators have gone to war. Maybe we could even bring some into the factory. We're already making plans to turn over to curtain-making machines and with knitting machines too . . .' Eveleen clapped her hands in delight. 'Richard's factory will survive. Oh, Bridie, I know it will.'

The strain of the past few weeks was lifted and Eveleen, despite the ever-present worry over all the men at war, looked happier than she had done for months.

Bridie smiled and asked impishly, 'So I'm forgiven, then, for going to Flawford?'

Eveleen laughed. 'Oh yes, Bridie, you're forgiven.'

They hugged one another and danced around the room. They came to a breathless halt and leant against each other.

'There's just one thing,' Eveleen panted. 'We'll have to tell them at Pear Tree Farm. I need Josh's advice about all this now.'

Bridie pulled a face. 'Oh, all right then. But Gran'll be mad I've been to see them. And she'll try to stop me going back there. I know she will.'

'You'll do no such thing.'

Mary was adamant and she turned to Josh for his

support. 'You'll back me in this, won't you, Josh?' She whirled back to face Eveleen and Bridie and wagged her forefinger at them. 'I knew it would cause trouble, her coming to live with you. You haven't time nor, to my mind, the inclination,' she added, derisively, 'to be keeping your eye on her properly. I told you, she's a wilful little tyke who needs a firm hand. Well.' Now she turned her attention directly to Bridie. 'Well, you'll be feeling the back of mine, if you're not careful.'

Bridie glanced at Eveleen and saw her mouth tighten and saw too, Josh glancing helplessly from one to the other of them. He was caught up in a quarrel, rooted in the distant past, that was none of his making.

Bridie forced herself to keep calm. Reasoned argument might convince her grandmother as no childish pouting and stamping of feet ever would. 'Gran,' she said quietly, but with an adult firmness that Mary had not heard before, 'if you'd only seen them, you'd understand why I must go back and care for them. You wouldn't leave animals in that state.'

'Have you been?' Mary glared accusingly at Eveleen. 'Have you seen for yourself because I wouldn't believe a word she's saying? I think it's all—'

'No, Mam,' Eveleen cut in. 'But I mean to take her there anyway, when she goes, so I shall see for myself.' She glanced swiftly at Bridie, who, despite her resolution to keep calm, had opened her mouth to protest, 'Not that I don't believe you, Bridie, I promise you. But I want to know that you're going to be all right. That you'll be able to cope there on your own.'

Bridie closed her mouth, smiled and nodded, 'I'll cope, Auntie Eveleen. If I can't,' her smile widened to a mischievous grin. 'I'll call in reinforcements. I'll fetch Mrs Turner.'

'Gracie Turner?' Mary picked up the name. 'Oh, I might have known she'd be sticking her nose in where it's not wanted.' She glowered at them all, including Josh. 'But it seems as if it's all decided. I don't really know why you've come here to ask me.'

'Maybe we shouldn't have, but you're still Bridie's guardian and—'

'Then I say she's not to go,' Mary snapped.

Only just managing now to hold onto her temper, Bridie asked, 'Why, Gran? Just explain to me why you don't want me to go.'

There was an awkward silence in the room, a tension between the three adults that the girl could not understand.

'Because – because . . .' Mary was hesitant, her glance roving round the room as if unable to meet the steady gaze of her granddaughter and as if she was searching for a plausible excuse. Bridie had the distinct feeling that she was not hearing the whole truth. Not from any of them. Mary jumped up suddenly, galvanized into action. 'Do what you like then, but don't come running back to me when they treat you badly.' She nodded. 'You'll soon be back. You'll not stand it there five minutes.' And she added sagely, 'I know them. And you.' She turned to Eveleen again. 'You'd better go there every week while she's there to see what's going on.'

'It's probable I shall be going there quite a lot, Mam. That's the other thing I wanted to talk to you about. Well, to Josh really.'

Swiftly she explained all the circumstances, the lack of work in the city and the abundance of orders at Singleton's Yard. 'Do you think we can do it, Josh? Turn our workforce to making clothes for the troops?'

'I think, mi duck,' he said slowly, 'that it's the only

way you're going to survive the war. But will your uncle agree?'

Before Eveleen could answer, Mary butted in. 'Huh! You're asking if Harry will agree to making money? You might well ask if the sun will rise tomorrow morning.'

The tension between them eased and Eveleen and Bridie left soon afterwards, Josh giving Bridie a firm hug.

'Ne'er mind what yer gran says, mi duck. If you've got trouble, you come back here. You know yer gran. Her bark's worse than her bite.'

Bridie smiled up at him. 'I know,' she said softly to the big man alone. 'And I know *you*.'

There was no need for further words between them; their understanding was mutual.

As Eveleen drove the motor car back towards Nottingham, she breathed a sigh of relief. 'That went better than I expected.'

'Better!' Bridie exclaimed in surprise.

'Oh yes. Believe me, she could have stopped you going. She is your legal guardian and there's not a thing I could have done about it.'

'Oh.' Bridie was thoughtful for a moment before she asked, 'Then why didn't she?'

Eveleen frowned. 'I don't really know, Bridie. Maybe, deep down, she does want someone to look after them. But she won't go herself. Never in a million years.'

'Why? What happened to make her so bitter?'

'Don't ask me, love. It's not my place to tell you. Maybe when you're older . . .' was all her aunt would say and with that, for the moment, the girl had to be content.

Twenty-Nine

'Oh, it's you. I might have known you'd be behind sending her here.'

On the following Sunday morning, Eveleen and Bridie knocked on the door of the first cottage in the row in Singleton's Yard. Now they stood facing Harry Singleton as he squinted at them, peering into first one face and then the other.

'May we come in, Uncle?' Eveleen asked, stepping across the threshold before he had time to refuse.

'Seems like you're in,' he grunted, turned and shuffled back towards his chair by the range, feeling his way past the furniture.

Eveleen bit her lip as she watched him. He was a changed man from the last time she had seen him thirteen years before. She glanced around the room, which had once been so neat and shining. Now papers, clothes, bits and bobs cluttered every surface. The white tablecloth, looking as if it hadn't been removed between meals for a week, was stained with spills.

Eveleen sat down in the chair opposite him. 'Uncle Harry, Bridie has come to stay here a while to look after you and Gran.'

'We don't need anyone.'

Eveleen smiled, though a little sadly. Not quite all the fiery independence had gone.

'Gran needs some help, even if you don't.'

'She's got Lil Fairbrother . . .' He jerked his thumb over his shoulder, indicating the adjacent cottage, the one facing the street. 'She looks after her.'

'She's not doing a very good job of it,' Eveleen said bluntly and beside her Bridie felt a shaft of admiration for her aunt.

He grunted. 'It'll do for us.' Then he roused himself, seeming to summon up some of his old strength, some of the vigour that Eveleen remembered so well. 'I don't want you or her here. You brought trouble on this family. Aye, you and your mother before you.' He flung out his arm towards Bridie. 'Born in sin, she was, thanks to you and your precious family. And I lost my lovely Rebecca because of it. I don't forget, Eveleen, and I don't forgive.'

'I'm very sorry to hear you say that, Uncle. I thought perhaps by now, you could find it in your heart not to bear a grudge against an innocent girl. It was none of her doing, now was it?'

'It was your brother who took my girl down. Shamed her and – and . . .' For a brief moment the big man's voice trembled. 'And caused her death. But for him, she'd have still been here to care for me and her grandmother.'

Indeed she would, Eveleen thought bitterly. An unhappy spinster tied to a life of drudgery. But she gave nothing of her own thoughts away. Instead she said, with as much gentleness as she could muster, 'But now her daughter is here instead.'

'Well, we don't want her.' It was his last vestige of fight, for now he lay back in his chair and covered his eyes with his hand.

Eveleen leant across and touched his knee gently and,

using the very words that Bridie herself had used, said, 'Maybe not, but you do need her, Uncle Harry.'

'Now it's come to it, I don't like leaving you here.'

Later, standing beside the motor car in the narrow street, Eveleen looked down at the slight figure of the girl in front of her. She looked so young and yet, suddenly, there was an air of inner strength about her. A determination that now had nothing to do with wilfulness. There was a sense of purpose in her eyes and a firm resolution to the set of her jaw. Bridie was a girl with a mission.

At the thought, Eveleen smiled inwardly. How ironic, in view of Harry Singleton's devotion to the chapel, that that was the phrase that should spring to her mind.

As she hugged Bridie, she said, 'Are you sure the money I've given you will be enough? By the look of it, you'll need to restock the pantry.'

'It'll be fine till you come again.' She laughed. 'I shall enjoy playing at being a housewife.'

'There won't be much "play" about it, love. But don't forget, if you have any problems, let me know at once. Promise?'

'I will, Auntie Evie, and thank you for everything.'

Eveleen held her close. 'It's me who should be thanking you.'

As she drove home alone, Eveleen was already missing Bridie's lively company. When she opened the door and stepped into the house, even the knowledge that below stairs there were servants did not drive out the feeling of emptiness and loneliness. She dined alone in the immaculate, yet soulless, dining room and vowed that in future she would eat on a tray in her cosy sitting room, instead of placed at one end of the long polished table staring at the empty chairs. Richard's, and now Bridie's too.

Work, she promised herself as she got into the huge bed, work was her salvation. There was plenty to organize, much to do and tomorrow she would talk to Brinsley. She lay down and, as she always did, she put out her hand to touch the pillow where Richard's head should be and, like that, she fell asleep.

Bridie lay down on the rug in front of her great-grandmother's range and pulled a moth-eaten blanket from the spare bedroom over her. She had lit a fire in the range and now the downstairs front room was warm, even though the mustiness of neglect had not yet been driven out. She would sleep here for her first night, for the spare bed upstairs was damp. Tomorrow she would lug the mattress down to air before she would consider sleeping on it.

Upstairs the old lady now lay between fresh sheets, warmed earlier in the day in front of the fire. A fire now also burned in the grate in her bedroom and Bridie had spooned hot soup into the toothless mouth.

She had seen nothing of her grandfather since the moment Eveleen had left. Bridget, and the sorry state she was lying in, were the girl's first concern. At least her grandfather was mobile. He was capable of climbing the stairs to his bed and of getting himself some sort of a meal, meagre though it might be.

Tomorrow, Bridie promised silently as sleep claimed her, I'll sort him out too.

The following morning the girl was awake early, stoking up the fire in the range and preparing a breakfast tray for her great-grandmother. There was little food in the house and Bridie suspected the same would be true of her grandfather's home. When she had made the old lady comfortable and given her her breakfast, Bridie saw her uncle making his unsteady way to the workshop. Once she knew he was safely at his framework knitting machine, she felt she could investigate.

First she toured the small cottage where Bridget lived. The front door opened directly into the living room and beyond that was the scullery, out of which steep stairs led to the first-floor landing, where there were two bedrooms. From that floor there was a ladder to an attic bedroom, which bore signs of once having been occupied, no doubt by male lodgers who worked for her grandfather. Then, leaving her great-grandmother's home, Bridie walked along the path and, holding her breath, tried the door of the cottage at the opposite end of the row. This was her grandfather's house and the place where her own mother had once lived. The layout was much the same as Bridget's home, but the opposite way round. Bridie had been right about one thing: there was little food in the pantry. Her heart thumping, she climbed the stairs, peeping into the main bedroom and the smaller one on the first floor. She swallowed hard as she looked at the single bed, still neatly made. Had this been where Rebecca had slept? Then she climbed the ladder to the attic room. Here an iron bedstead with a mouldy mattress still stood in the room and the floor was littered with old toys and books and the junk of many years. Bridie picked up an old school slate and ran her fingers over it. There was even a tiny piece of white chalk. These must have belonged to her mother and the girl felt a strange affinity with the long-dead woman. She was touching something that Rebecca had once held. Her fingers were now resting in the same place that her mother's had once done. Somehow, here in the place where her mother had lived, Rebecca was almost a living, breathing presence. Suddenly, for the first time in the whole of her life, Bridie felt close to the woman who had borne her and she wanted, desperately, to know much more about her. Reverently she fingered the other toys. She must have been a very special person, Bridie thought, to have earned Andrew's undying devotion. He had never married, never, so far as Bridie knew, even looked at another woman.

If only, she thought, brushing away an unbidden tear, he would love me in the same way.

She stood up, promising herself that when time allowed she would clean this attic room and set Rebecca's belongings out as she would have liked. She would wash the lace-trimmed runner on the dressing table and the patchwork quilt folded at the end of the bed. She would clean and tidy this room and keep it as a lasting memorial to the child, the girl and the woman who had perhaps once slept here.

Downstairs again, Bridie stepped out into the yard and looked about her. Investigating the other buildings, she found that at the end of the building on the right-hand side there was a wash-house, with a copper, rinsing tub, dolly pegs, posser and a mangle.

'I'll soon have that going,' she murmured, closing the door for the moment. She walked between the two workshops on either side, hearing the clatter of the machinery coming from the upper floor of the one to her left. It seemed to be the only one now where any work was being done, for when she peeped into the other workshops she saw the lines of idle frames. Auntie Evie will soon have those busy, Bridie thought to herself, smiling, if I know her. The buildings across the end of the yard housed communal lavatories for the workers as well as for the residents of the cottages, a coal store and an empty pigsty, where the smell of the one-time occupants still lingered.

Bridie turned and walked back towards the cottages, coming to a stop in front of the door of the centre dwelling. Her hand trembled as she touched the doorknob and turned it. To her surprise, it opened and, holding her breath, Bridie stepped into Andrew's home.

Thirty

Bridie moved around the living room in Andrew's home.

Although a thin layer of dust lay everywhere, everything was painfully neat and tidy. Bridie sat in his chair by the range and let her eyes roam around the room, drinking in the sight of his belongings. Her glance came to the mantelpiece above the range and she rose to look closely at the photographs there. Her eyes widened and she gasped.

Each, in its own silver frame, was a photograph of her, one for every year of her life from babyhood to the age of twelve. Tears filled her eyes and the images before her blurred.

'Oh, Andrew, Andrew,' she whispered brokenly.

Then she moved to the roll-top desk in the corner and lifted the unlocked lid. Yet more photographs of her were laid out in neat bundles. There were a few envelopes or letters tied up with ribbon and, before she even touched them, she knew that they were what she had sent or given him. Christmas cards and birthday cards that she had made for him from the time he had given her a box of paints. Bridie wrinkled her brow, trying to recall how old she had been. Five was it, or six? There was even the letter she had sent to him when he had been ill and unable to visit the farm for a few weeks. Her childish scrawl evoked the memory of that time and how she had missed seeing him so dreadfully, yet again forbidden by her grandmother from visiting him at his home.

She wandered through to the scullery, where the pots and pans were neatly stacked, poignantly awaiting a need for their use. Then she climbed the stairs and stepped into the main bedroom. Here again everything was so heartbreakingly neat and tidy. On the small table beside his bed stood a larger copy of the last photograph on the mantelpiece downstairs, the one taken on her twelfth birthday.

'But there should be another one,' she said aloud. 'We had one taken in Grantham when I was thirteen, just before they left . . .' And then she understood.

That photograph was missing because he had taken it with him to war.

In May, the sinking of the *Lusitania* brought America down firmly on the side of Britain and her Allies. At the end of the month, Richard wrote that he had had an inoculation that day – *Not very pleasant.*

Because the months had passed and Richard, Andrew and the others had not been sent overseas, Eveleen – and Bridie too – had begun to hope that they would never go. But now it sounded as if they were being prepared. A month later his letter contained news that made Eveleen's heart leap in fear.

> *Three hundred and fifty men have been warned for draft, some from our company – Sid is one of them. Andrew and I did our best to get on the draft, but no go. So we have to kick our heels and wait! We are going to musketry school in Luton on a machine-gun course instead. I don't know if we'll get leave before we go*

overseas. We do get the odd thirty-six-hour pass, but it isn't long enough to get home.

'Can you believe it?' Eveleen exclaimed to Bridie on one of her weekend visits to Flawford. 'Richard talks as if they can't wait to get over there.'

Bridie was solemn-faced. 'I suppose they feel that's what they've volunteered for.'

Eveleen glanced at her. Bridie seemed to have grown taller during the last few weeks. She was still only thirteen, but now seemed so much older. The war had taken away her childhood, bringing her worries and possibly grief that no young girl ought to know. She was frowning now as she went on. 'I don't know if I ought to say this . . .'

'Go on,' Eveleen prompted gently.

'Well, I didn't want Andrew or Richard or any of them to go, but – but now they have, I do feel ever so proud of them. And yesterday I saw more volunteers marching along the village main street. Some of them didn't look much older than me. They looked so brave, all going off to war. I – I couldn't help joining in the cheering, even though part of me still wanted to run up to them and tell them not to go.'

There were tears in Eveleen's eyes as she held out her arms to the girl. 'Oh, Bridie, I know exactly what you mean. I feel just the same. All mixed up inside.'

'But they're still here in this country, aren't they? Andrew and Richard.' Bridie was determined to be optimistic. 'Maybe it will soon be over and they won't even have to go to the Front.'

'Maybe,' Eveleen murmured, but said no more. She read the papers each day and they gave not even a glimmer of such a hope.

Further Zeppelin raids on the east coast of Britain had killed twenty-four people.

'It's getting a bit too close for comfort,' Mary muttered and Josh, who seemed to have his head buried in a newspaper most of the time, said, 'The government are denying that they're going to bring in conscription, but they passed the National Registration Bill. I reckon that's the start of it.'

At the beginning of August Eveleen received the letter from Richard that she had been dreading. As she read the words, she gave a little gasp and, with trembling fingers, felt her way to a chair to sit down.

We've been warned for draft and will probably be leaving in a few days. Oh, and I've been appointed Lance Corporal, so Mother should be pleased . . .

Eveleen closed her eyes and groaned aloud, wishing in the same moment that Bridie was here with her and yet glad that she was not. Eveleen's mind raced. Perhaps they wouldn't go. Perhaps word would come that hostilities had ceased and they wouldn't be needed. But she knew it was a vain hope.

The letter slipped from her lap and fell to the floor as Eveleen covered her face with her hands and wept.

Richard's next letter came from France.

Reveille 4 a.m. We struck camp on the 10th August, marched twenty-one miles in full overseas kit to Watford – very hot day. Now we know what all that training was for! Pitched camp for a few days and then caught the train to Southampton, embarking on a paddle steamer at 5.30 p.m. on the 18th. Arrived Le Havre at midnight, where we stayed till noon the next day and then went up the Seine to Rouen. It was a good journey. You wouldn't believe that not that many miles

away there's a war going on. We're in a rest camp near
Rouen, so we've had a look at the cathedral and even
went up the spire! We are to be on guard at the docks.
Don't worry – most of us are still together. Andrew and
Leslie are fine, but we've had no news of Sid . . .

It was only a week later that Eveleen had to write to
Richard to tell him that Sid had been wounded very
badly in the leg and had arrived back in England. She
paused, her pen hovering above the paper. Elsie is lucky,
she thought, at least Sid is still alive and she will have
her husband back with her. But the words remained
unwritten.

The following week there was no letter from Richard,
nor one from Andrew to Bridie. Eveleen's anxiety grew,
but she tried to suppress it by throwing herself into her
work. She arrived at the factory earlier each morning
and left later every evening. But even there the war and
its tragedies were never very far away.

Luke Manning, who seemed to have stepped, unoffi-
cially at present, into Bob Porter's shoes met Eveleen at
the entrance to the factory one morning. 'You'd best get
to the warehouse, Eveleen. There's trouble in the inspection room.'

'Trouble?' Eveleen said, her brow puckering.
'Where's Helen?'

'Seems she's the cause of it.'

'Helen?' Now Eveleen was shocked. She turned and
then looked back briefly and nodded towards the factory. 'Everything all right?'

Luke smiled. 'Don't you worry. We're right as nine-
pence now he's gone.'

Her eyes widened. 'You mean Bob?'

Luke nodded grimly. 'He was a troublemaker. He

should never have been promoted into Josh Carpenter's job. We're best without him. Only trouble is there's not going to be much work for any of us soon, is there?'

Eveleen smiled now. 'I want to talk to you later, Luke. I've got some ideas about what we can do. But now I'd better get to the inspection room.'

Eveleen smiled as she hurried towards the warehouse. It had come as a pleasant surprise that Luke, and perhaps the rest too, were pleased to see the back of Bob Porter. There was nothing to stop her recruiting more women if only she could find the work for them. But now, she hoped, she had the answer in her uncle's yard.

Every day more and more men were volunteering and the workforce at Reckitt and Stokes – indeed at all the workplaces throughout the city – was being rapidly depleted. And now Eveleen had official approval for employing women. The government had appealed for women to serve their country by signing on for war work. Perhaps the making of lace could not be classed in that category, but the manufacture of clothes for the troops certainly would.

Eveleen climbed the flights of stairs to the top floor, breathless when she arrived in the inspection room. The women were all crowded at the far end of the room and no work was being done. The lengths of fabric lay strewn about the floor, as if work had started that morning only to be cast aside.

As Eveleen approached the huddle of women, they became aware of her presence, nudging each other as they spotted her. They fell silent until the only noise left was the sound of uncontrollable weeping. Then they stepped back, parting to make way for Eveleen until she saw the cause of the women's concern and the reason they had deserted their work.

Helen was sitting on the floor rocking backwards and forwards, her arms wrapped around herself, her face wet with tears. Mrs Hyde knelt beside her, her arm about the young woman's shoulders. As Eveleen knelt down too, she and Mrs Hyde exchanged a helpless look.

'Her young man's parents have had a telegram, Mrs Stokes.'

There was no need for Mrs Hyde to say any more.

Eveleen took the distraught Helen home with her. Since the death of both her parents Helen had lived on her own, but this was no time for the young woman to be alone.

Eveleen tried to comfort her, but there was nothing she could say or do that would bring Leslie back. With the first death to touch their lives so closely, Eveleen's terror for Richard, and for Andrew too, increased.

For the first time, she was truly glad Bridie was safely in Flawford.

'He could still be alive,' Eveleen tried to give Helen a vestige of hope to cling to when at last she heard the exact words of the telegram. 'It only says, "missing, *presumed* killed".'

Helen raised her face, swollen and blotchy from the tears she had shed, yet at this moment there was an almost pitying look on her face. 'Evie, they can't find half the bodies. They're blown to bits by the shells. Sometimes they don't find anything, not even their tags.'

Eveleen shuddered and said nothing. There was nothing she could say.

Helen's weeping had stopped now, as if she had cried and cried until there were no more tears to shed.

'There'll be no grave even, just his name recorded somewhere. In a book, maybe, or on a monument. Along with thousands of others, he'll just be a name. Nothing more.'

'Helen, don't say that.' Eveleen squeezed her hand. 'He'll always be so much more to everyone who knew him, especially to you.'

'I seem to lose everyone I love, Evie, don't I? First Ronald, now Leslie. Even both my parents. They were only in their sixties. It's too soon, Evie. I lose everyone far too soon.'

Again, there was nothing Eveleen could say. She could only put her arms about the grieving young woman, hold her close and wonder how long it would be before she too would be mourning her loss.

And Bridie? What about Bridie? How would the poor child cope if word came that Andrew had been killed?

At that moment Bridie had more pressing matters on her mind. Although Andrew was never far from her thoughts, indeed living here in Flawford she felt closer to him than ever before, but her every waking moment was taken with caring for her great-grandmother. At least she was making headway with her. Now the old lady had regular and nourishing meals, her clothes were washed and the house was warm and comfortable.

But Bridie was getting nowhere with her grandfather. He refused resolutely to acknowledge her presence. Although he made no effort now to send her away from Bridget's house, he made it clear he wanted nothing to do with her. He closed and locked the door of his cottage whilst he worked. If he passed her in the yard, he turned his head away.

'Great-Gran, why doesn't he want me here?' Bridie settled herself on the end of the old lady's bed.

Now that she was well cared for Bridget's mind had improved and, whilst she still occasionally absent-mindedly called her great-granddaughter Rebecca, she was almost back to what must have been her normal self.

'It goes back a long way, lass,' Bridget said. 'None of it's your fault, yet you're taking the brunt of his bitterness.' She closed her eyes and sighed. 'And there's nothing I can do about it. Maybe once I could have stood up to him, but I'm too old and too tired now.'

Bridie reached out and patted the wrinkled hand. 'I don't expect you to fight my battles,' she said and smiled mischievously. 'I'll fight me own.'

Bridget smiled at her. 'You've a lot of your auntie Eveleen in you, love. She's a fighter.'

'Auntie Evie?' Bridie said in surprise. 'Really?'

'Oh aye. When her father died suddenly, she carried that family. And they caused her a lot of trouble. But I expect you know all that.'

'No, I don't.'

'Then mebbe I should keep my mouth shut.' The old lady gave a toothless grin.

Bridie laughed. 'I was rather hoping you wouldn't, Great-Gran.'

'Oh well, maybe I'll tell you all about it one day. When you're older.'

It was the same answer that her aunt Eveleen always gave her. What were all these family skeletons, the girl wondered, and would anyone ever tell her what they were?

She bit her lip, watching the old lady. 'Just tell me

one thing, Great-Gran. How can I get Grandfather to talk to me?'

Bridget lay with her eyes closed and Bridie thought she had fallen asleep, but then, without opening her eyes, the old lady said, 'You could try attending the chapel services on a Sunday.'

Thirty-One

On the following Sunday Bridie walked across the road to the chapel and stepped inside. She saw her grandfather sitting in the front pew, his head bowed in prayer. The congregation now consisted mainly of women, old men and young boys. There were only one or two younger men of volunteering age and they looked wary and ill at ease as if, at any moment, they expected to be challenged as to why they were not in uniform. Perhaps they're expecting to be handed a white feather, Bridie thought, remembering the look on Richard's face that day at the Goose Fair.

She slipped into the pew beside Harry Singleton, knelt on the hassock, put her hands together and closed her eyes. When she heard his movement beside her, she sat up on the seat but kept her gaze firmly on the lectern, where a huge bible lay open. When the minister came through from the room behind the rostrum, the congregation rose and the service began.

'Well, what did he say?' Bridget was impatient to know what had happened when Bridie returned to the cottage.

'Nothing. I sat next to him. I didn't even look at him. Not once. I didn't speak and nor did he.' Bridie grinned at her. 'Two can play at that game.'

Bridget chuckled. She was sitting up in bed now, a

lace shawl around her shoulders, looking much better and a good deal perkier than when Bridie had first visited three weeks earlier.

'Now . . .' The young girl began to bustle about the bedroom. 'Let's get you looking your best. Auntie Eveleen might come this afternoon.'

'Do you feel like a little drive into countryside, Helen? I ought to visit Flawford today to see how Bridie is coping.'

It's a lot for a young girl, she thought. She was surprised that Bridie hadn't packed her belongings and come back to Nottingham long before now.

'No, no. You go, though, Evie. I don't want to be a burden to you.' Helen's eyes filled yet again with ready tears.

'You're not that and you never could be.' Eveleen put her arm about her. 'But I think you should come with me. I'd be glad of your company. I don't quite know what I'm going to find when I get there.' Then she added persuasively, 'And besides, it's what Leslie would have wanted. He wouldn't have wanted you to shut yourself away from the world. It doesn't mean you're being disloyal or that you'll stop thinking about him.'

'I think about him every moment,' Helen whispered. 'I don't know how I'm going to carry on without him.'

Life certainly had dealt poor Helen a double bitter blow, Eveleen thought, but aloud she said, 'I know, love. But you're going to have to be every bit as brave as he was when he volunteered, when he went into battle . . .' Her voice faltered as she added softly, 'When he laid down his life.'

Helen was lost in thought for a moment. Then she

raised her head, scrubbed away the tears from her face and tried to smile. 'You're right. He was brave, wasn't he?'

Eveleen nodded.

'Then I must be too. Yes, I'll come with you.'

They set off after an early lunch, Eveleen driving the motor car along the city streets and out into the countryside. Helen sat beside her, well wrapped up, for the late summer day already had the smell of autumn in the air. At first, she sat huddled in rugs and shawls staring straight ahead, but as their journey progressed she began to look about her. She glanced up at trees that now and then formed a canopy above their heads as the road passed beneath them. Then she watched cows and sheep in the fields.

Eveleen breathed a sigh of relief. She had been right to persuade Helen to come. Already there was a pink glow in her cheeks, and she was taking an interest in the world around her for the first time since she had received the dreadful news.

As they reached the village, Eveleen slowed the vehicle and stopped outside a row of cottages.

'Is this it?' Helen asked as the noise of the engine died.

'No, but there's someone I want to speak to first, if she's at home. Come on, we'll go and see.'

'Are you sure you want me to come?'

'Of course.'

They climbed out and walked up the narrow garden path towards Gracie Turner's front door.

'Eveleen!' The large woman beamed with delight and flung her arms wide in welcome, as if to embrace them both at once.

Eveleen made the introductions as Gracie ushered

them into her warm, inviting kitchen, which smelled of fresh baking bread.

'That little lass of yours,' Gracie launched straight in without preamble and Eveleen held her breath at what she might be going to hear now, 'is a marvel.' Eveleen heaved a silent sigh of relief as Gracie continued. 'The old lady's looking grand. She's still bedridden, but she's perked up no end.'

'What about my uncle?'

'Oh, him!' Gracie snorted derisively. 'I don't think even Bridie will be able to win him over.' She laughed. 'But do you know what the little minx does?'

The two visitors shook their heads as Gracie's double chin wobbled with laughter. 'She goes to all the chapel services and sits beside him in the family pew. Never looks at him, never even speaks to him, just comes and goes. She's playing him at his own game and he can't say 'owt 'cos she's not doing 'owt wrong, is she?'

Eveleen shook her head wonderingly. This was a new Bridie she was hearing about.

The surprises continued for her when they arrived at Singleton's Yard. As she opened the door of her grandmother's cottage, the smell of roast beef met them.

'Auntie Evie – and Helen too. How lovely. Come in, come in,' Bridie greeted them as if welcoming them into her own home. 'Dinner'll be ready in a minute.'

'Oh, darling, we've eaten. I never thought.' For a moment Bridie's face was crestfallen, then she brightened and smiled impishly. 'Never mind, maybe me grandad would like a plateful. I'll take one along when I've taken Great-Gran's up.'

'I'll do that,' Eveleen said, pulling off her gloves. She turned to Helen, 'Make yourself at home, love. I'll just help Bridie in the scullery.'

Once in the back room, Eveleen hurriedly broke the sad news to the young girl of Helen's loss. Though she did not cry, Bridie's eyes filled with sympathy for Helen and sudden terror.

'Oh, Auntie Evie,' she whispered. 'What about Andrew and Uncle Richard?'

Eveleen squeezed her arm and nodded. 'I know, love, I know. But we must keep our spirits up. Now,' she said in a louder voice, 'which do you want me to do? Take Gran's up to her or beard the lion in his den?'

'You take Great-Gran's,' Bridie said. 'She's been reckoning on you coming. I'll take his lordship's, though I'll probably get it thrown in my face.'

Bridie walked along the path in front of the cottages, carefully carrying a plate heaped with meat, potatoes, carrots and cabbage and a well-risen, nicely browned Yorkshire pudding. She knocked on her grandfather's door, but when there was no answer she opened it and stepped inside. She blinked two or three times before her eyes became accustomed to the gloom. Then she could see her uncle sitting in a chair by the range.

The table in the centre of the small room was bare, showing no sign that he had eaten a Sunday dinner.

'Hello, Grandad,' Bridie greeted him brightly. 'I've brought you some dinner. Auntie Evie and her friend have come, but they've already eaten.'

'Well, you can take it away,' Harry said gruffly. 'And don't call me that.'

'Why not?' the girl said pertly, her head on one side. 'It's what you are.'

'Not by my choice.'

'We can't always have the things we want in life,' Bridie said, placing the plate on the table. 'Can we? Now, where do you keep your knives and forks?'

Harry roused himself, rising to tower over her. 'I thought I told you to take it away.'

Bridie stood still, undaunted, unafraid of his large figure looming above her. She put her hands on her hips and glared up at him. 'Are you going to waste good food? There's nowt wrong with my cooking. Me gran – your sister – taught me.'

'Oh aye? Did she tell you to put poison in anything you served to me?'

Bridie gasped. She was so shocked that for a moment she could think of nothing to say, then she blurted out, 'Are you wrong in the head? Don't talk so daft.'

'Don't you speak to me like that, you cheeky young wench.'

Suddenly Bridie giggled. She put her hand on his arm. 'Oh, Grandad, don't let's quarrel. I wish you'd let me get to know you. I'd love us to . . .'

He snatched his arm away from her as if her touch had burned him.

'I told you not to call me that,' he thundered. 'And get out of my house.' He thrust his face close to hers. 'You're not welcome here.'

Bridie was trembling, but was determined to show no fear, nor let him see how upset she felt. She managed to shrug her shoulders. 'Have it your way, then.' She turned away and pulled open the door, glancing back once to say, 'Eat your dinner afore it gets cold. I'll come back for the plate.'

Later in the afternoon, when she knew her uncle would be at the chapel, Bridie returned to the cottage to fetch the plate.

The untouched meal still lay on the table, where she had left it.

Thirty-Two

'You wouldn't think anyone could be so stubborn, would you?' Bridie said, showing her aunt the cold, congealed meal later.

Eveleen chuckled. 'You ought to keep heating it up and leaving it for him until he does eat it. It's what was done to us as kids if we didn't eat anything.'

'Me gran still does,' Bridie said, with feeling. She was thoughtful. 'No,' she murmured, 'I shan't do that. I'll just keep taking him nice meals. Every day from now on. Until he gives in.'

Eveleen sighed. 'It's up to you, love. But you'll be wasting your time and a lot of good food. He'll never give in.'

Bridie raised her gaze to meet her aunt's eyes, a glint of determination in her own. 'Neither will I, Auntie Evie. Neither will I.'

'Bridie seems to be managing very well,' Helen said, shouting above the noise of the motor as they drove homewards. Helen herself looked better for the outing, but Eveleen did not remark upon it. 'And your grandmother's a character, isn't she?'

Eveleen smiled, thinking of the hour she had spent that afternoon with the old lady, whom she had not seen for over thirteen years.

Bridget had held out her arms to Eveleen when she had entered the bedroom, tears coursing down her wrinkled cheeks. 'My dear girl. How I've missed you. Come and kiss me.'

Eveleen had bent and kissed her cheek and then had hugged her, alarmed to feel the bony thin body. She sat on the bed and took Bridget's hands in hers. 'You need looking after.'

The old lady chuckled with delight. 'Bridie's doing a fine job of that. She's a grand girl.' Bridget put her head on one side and met Eveleen's gaze with bright, beady eyes. 'Reminds me a lot of you.'

'Me?' Eveleen was startled. 'But I thought she was more like Rebecca.'

'Oh, to look at, yes. But she's more spirit than poor Rebecca ever had. She's – what's the word I want?' She thought for a moment and then said triumphantly, 'Feisty! That's it. She's bold as brass, but for all the right reasons. Just like you always were.' She sniffed. 'Pity you didn't get more support from that rascal of a brother of yours. If it hadn't been for him and Rebecca being so foolish, you'd all have still been here.'

'Maybe,' Eveleen said guardedly. 'But Mam would never have settled here for long. She always wanted to go back to Lincolnshire.' And, she was thinking, if we hadn't been forced to go to Nottingham, I wouldn't have met Richard and Mam wouldn't have met Josh. Aloud, she said, 'My only regret is that we haven't been able to see you in all these years.'

The old lady sighed. 'That's partly my own fault, isn't it? I should have been stronger. Stood up to my husband all those years ago over your mother, and then I should have supported Rebecca and you against

230

Harry.' She sighed and added regretfully, 'I'm all talk and no do, that's me.'

'Don't blame yourself. We live in a man's world, or at least,' Eveleen added, prophetically, 'we have until now. I think somehow this dreadful war is going to change all that. You'll never guess what . . .' Skilfully turning the subject away from the old lady's morbid and guilt-ridden reminiscences, Eveleen began to tell her how, because of the war, women were now being employed in the Nottingham factory.

'Who'd have thought it?' Bridget said shaking her head. 'It makes sense, of course, but I can't see Harry ever having women working his frames.'

'He nearly did once,' Eveleen reminded her. 'Remember? He taught me how to operate a framework knitting machine.'

'I do,' Bridget laughed, 'But for goodness sake don't tell Bridie, else she'll be down that path and into the workshops before you can say knife.'

'I'm afraid Grandfather won't even acknowledge her existence,' Eveleen said sorrowfully, 'let alone let him help him in any way.' And she told Bridget about the uneaten dinner.

Bridget gave a very unladylike snort. 'Then he's even more of a fool than I thought he was.'

Eveleen smiled as she stood up, 'Well, I need to talk to him and this time I just might have a proposition to put to him that he can't refuse.'

'Women? Women at my machines? In my workshops? Never. The men wouldn't stand for it.'

Eveleen faced her uncle across the hearth in his

cottage as she said quietly, 'What men, Uncle? From what Bridie tells me, you've hardly anyone left.'

He cast her a furious look, but could not deny the truth. She leant towards him. 'Uncle, it's sound business sense. You've lost nearly all your workforce. I've plenty of women anxious to work – needing to work – and yet little for them to do. If the single girls and young married women without children came out here . . .'

'I don't want a lot of flighty wenches bringing trouble to the village.'

Eveleen sighed. 'It's not very likely, with nearly all the young men gone.'

Harry grunted, but again he could not argue with fact.

'And I'm sure,' Eveleen went on, pressing her point, 'there are plenty of women in the village who wouldn't mind taking in lodgers. As for my end of things, I am hoping to buy some frames for the factory.'

'How do you know you'll have the outlets? Surely the government has got all that sorted.'

'Mr Stokes is handling that side of things. He has the contacts. Knows all the right people. We've already got one contract for five hundred pairs of long johns – just like the ones you've always made here. And socks! Well, it seems they can't get enough of them. I'm hunting out all the Griswold machines I can lay my hands on. The women can work those in their own homes, like they always have.'

A Griswold, a small, hand-operated machine that could be attached to a table, produced a knitted tube. It was ideal for making socks.

'What about my private orders?' Grudgingly, in spite of himself, Harry could not help showing interest. 'The ones the officers' families have ordered for them? I can't let folks down.'

'They'll all be honoured.'

He was silent for a long time until at last he nodded. 'I don't like to see the workshops empty and if it'd be helping the war effort . . .' Eveleen said nothing but knew that Harry was also thinking of lining his own pockets. 'But don't think,' he added gruffly, 'that you can worm your way in here because of this. You can take that girl home with you.'

Eveleen stood up. 'This has nothing to do with Bridie. This is purely business. But as for her leaving, no, Uncle Harry. Bridie is staying.'

The war was now more than a year old, yet, despite her constant worry, it was an exciting time for Eveleen. Plans for the changes at the factory and the involvement of her uncle's workshops were going well. Brinsley was enthusiastic and helpful. He also looked much better. He was enjoying business lunches with his contacts, who could assist with their scheme. There was only one point on which Brinsley disagreed with Eveleen.

'It's a pity you let Bob Porter go. He was a good man,' he said reproachfully. For once Eveleen held her tongue. She had not been sorry to see the man go and, better still, she now had the support of her workers at the factory. They were only too pleased that she had found alternative work for them, as the orders for lace were dwindling with each day. She found several framework knitting machines for sale, many of them owned by men who had worked in their own homes before volunteering. Now, sadly, they would never return to work them again.

'I can't bear to see it standing there,' one widow had told Eveleen. 'Just take it out my way, missis.'

Eveleen had paid the woman generously and, along with several others, had it transported to an unused room in the factory that became known as the knitting workshop.

'There's a couple of our chaps who've had experience on these machines,' Luke told her. 'They're willing to train the rest of us.'

Eveleen smiled. 'Men and women?'

Luke chuckled. 'Oh aye, women an' all. They'll play an important part.'

Each morning Eveleen hurried to the factory and returned late in the evening. But there was one day when a knock on her front door made her take the morning off.

Emily entered Eveleen's bedroom as she was dressing. 'There's a Mrs Martin at the door, ma'am.'

'Win? Here?'

Though they were good friends, Win had rarely visited Eveleen's home and then only at Eveleen's insistence.

'She – she looks ever so upset, ma'am. She's crying.'

'Oh no!' Eveleen breathed. 'I'll come down at once. Please show her into the morning room.'

Only minutes later Eveleen entered the room to find Win pacing the floor, a handkerchief pressed to her lips, her eyes red from weeping.

'It's our Elsie's Sid. He's been sent home from the hospital. He's with her now but, oh, Evie, he's a changed man. He's swearing and carrying on. He – he even hit her the other day when she was holding the babby.'

'Is there anything I can do?'

234

'I've got to get him away from her. He's not bad enough now to be kept in a military hospital and none of the local hospitals will take him either. I'm at me wit's end, Evie. Really I am.'

'What's Fred say?'

Win glanced at her nervously and then looked away. 'I – I daren't tell him everything that's going on, Evie. If he knew . . .'

She needed to say no more. Eveleen knew that Fred would leap to his daughter's defence.

'It's all he's been through. It's just not our Sid. He was a lovely feller before he went away. But now . . .' Win's voice trailed away in defeat.

'I'll try to think of something, Win,' was all Eveleen could promise. She stood up. 'In the meantime, I'll come with you to Elsie's and see for myself.'

Eveleen had not encountered Win's son-in-law before, but she could well imagine that the man she met that morning was a very different personality from the man Elsie had married.

'What d'you want, you interfering busybody?' was his greeting as Win stepped through the door. 'Leave me and mine alone.'

Elsie came into the room from upstairs and Eveleen almost gasped aloud to see her black eye and swollen lip.

'You're coming home with me, m'girl, right now,' Win said at once. 'Leave this brute to fend for 'imself. When your dad hears about this—'

'Oh aye,' Sid cut in nastily. 'Reckon I'm frightened of a feller who's too old to go to the Front.' He prodded his own chest. 'I've faced the Hun, I have. And she . . .'

he caught hold of his wife's arm and twisted it viciously, 'is going nowhere.'

'Ma, I'll be all right, but take the baby for a few days, will you?' Elsie pleaded.

'Aye, you can take that squealing brat and keep it, for all I care,' Sid said.

Half an hour later, Win and Eveleen left the tiny, terraced house, Win carrying her grandson clutched to her breast. The child was crying; a strange, gasping sound that bore no resemblance to the lusty bawling of a healthy infant.

'There, there, my pet. You'll be all right. Your daddy's just poorly. To think how tickled pink he was when the little mite was born. I can hardly believe what's happening now.'

'I'll send for the doctor. That child's ill, Win. Even I know that,' Eveleen added wryly.

'Oh, I can't afford—'

'Don't worry about it.' She put her hand on Win's arm. 'After all you've done for me over the years, it's the very least I can do.'

'Well, for once I'm not going to argue. I can swallow me pride when one of me own's in need. And this little chap is.'

'Yes,' Eveleen agreed. 'And so's his poor father.'

Thirty-Three

Eveleen once again asked Helen to go out with her on the Sunday. This time she intended to visit Pear Tree Farm. Helen took both Eveleen's hands in hers. 'Evie, you've been wonderful. You still are, but if it's all the same to you I think I should go home today. I've got to make the effort some time.'

'No, you haven't. You can stay here as long as you want.'

'I know and I can't thank you enough for having me here. But I'd like to go home, just for the day to start with, and then maybe stay a night or so. See how it goes.' Helen had returned to work very quickly after the dreadful news of Leslie's death, but Eveleen had insisted that her friend stay with her.

'If you're sure.' Eveleen had to agree. It was a sensible idea.

So Eveleen drove out to Bernby alone. The last few weeks had flown by and it was September already. It was a peaceful, warm, late summer day. Only the sound of Eveleen's motor car and birds, frightened into flight by her approach, disturbed the calm. It was hard to believe that only a few hundred miles away across the sea a savage war was being waged. At least, she thought, in this weather the trenches would be dry. Although perhaps the heat was just as uncomfortable with all the equipment and heavy packs the soldiers had to carry.

She passed through the village of Bernby, but as the vehicle emerged from beneath the trees of Bernby Covert overhanging the lane, the engine spluttered and died. The motor car free-wheeled down the hill, coming to rest by the ford across the beck. For a moment Eveleen sat there helplessly, wondering what to do. She had no idea about the internal workings of the car. She clambered down and tried to restart it by swinging the starting handle, but the engine only gave a brief stutter and refused to fire into life.

As she stood in the middle of the lane, biting her lip, she heard the sound of hoofbeats behind her and turned to see Stephen Dunsmore riding towards her.

'Oh no,' she breathed. 'Not him.'

There was nothing she could do, no means of escape. She was obliged to wait whilst Stephen dismounted. As he came towards her, she could not fail to notice his unsteady gait and when he came closer and took her hand, she could smell the alcohol on his breath.

'My dear Eveleen, how lovely you look.' His bold gaze ran appraisingly down the tight-fitting costume she wore. He raised her hand and brushed her fingers with his lips, his gaze holding hers. 'Are you, by any chance,' he asked softly, 'a damsel in distress?'

She pulled her hand away and replied, 'If you mean am I having trouble with the motor, then, yes, I'm afraid I am.' She arched her eyebrows and enquired sarcastically. 'Any good with engines, are you?'

'I'm afraid not,' Stephen drawled, 'But I know someone who is. If you'd care to come to the house . . .' He gestured towards the gateway to Fairfield House, which was only a few yards up the lane, 'Then I'll send for him whilst we – er – wait.'

There was an undercurrent in his tone that suggested so much more.

'I'd be glad of your help,' Eveleen unbent enough to say, 'but I'm quite happy to wait here.'

'Oh, but I insist,' Stephen said, his blue eyes glinting in the way she remembered so well when he was determined to get his own way. Then he turned on the boyish charm. 'Please say "yes", Evie . . .' And then he whispered softly, 'For old times' sake.'

She was in no position to refuse. She needed his help. Or rather, she needed the help of the mechanically minded man he knew. Forcing herself to smile, she put her hand on his arm and said, 'Thank you, Stephen. I'd be obliged for your help.'

They walked together towards the big house, Stephen leading his horse. The front door opened as if by magic at his appearance on the driveway and the sour-faced butler held it open for them to step inside. At once Stephen barked orders, for refreshments for them both and for the man to be sent for to attend to Eveleen's motor car. The manservant closed the front door, bowed in acquiescence and disappeared below stairs.

'Please,' Stephen said smoothly, 'come into the morning room.'

Eveleen felt as if she were a fly being invited into a spider's web.

The room surprised Eveleen. It had an unlived-in feel. It wasn't that it was neglected – far from it. Every surface gleamed. Not a speck of dust could be seen and a fire glowed in the grate. But there was nothing personal lying about that spoke of recent occupation. No book or newspaper being read and laid aside; no embroidery being worked by the lady of the house, Stephen's mother, or perhaps by now his wife.

'Please sit down.' Stephen gestured towards the sofa and went towards a drinks cabinet. 'Tea will be here in a moment. Or perhaps you would prefer something stronger?'

Eveleen shook her head and almost said: What, at eleven-thirty in the morning? But she held her tongue and watched in silence as Stephen splashed a generous measure of whisky into his glass, which was obviously not even his first of the day.

He put his glass on a small table and sat down beside her. 'Well, well, who'd have thought it?' His gaze roamed over her, taking in her appearance from head to toe; the blue tailored suit with an ankle-length skirt and a white lace blouse beneath. Eveleen removed her straw hat and smoothed back her hair into its neat pleat.

'My lovely Eveleen, all grown up,' he murmured and there was no mistaking the tinge of sadness in his tone. 'Are you happy, Evie, or do you still remember the times we had? They were good, weren't they?'

Eveleen returned his gaze steadily. 'I remember them very well, Stephen. But I was young and foolish and had no way of knowing that your intentions were far from honourable.'

Stephen ran his tongue round his lips in a lascivious gesture and made no attempt to deny her accusation. 'You can't blame me for trying. Pity your "honour" was stronger than your love for me.'

For a brief moment Eveleen's voice softened. 'I loved you very much, Stephen.'

He took her hand again and squeezed it gently. Before she could stop him, his lips were on her mouth, gently pleading. 'Oh, Evie,' he whispered against them.

Eveleen closed her eyes and the years fell away. She

was once more the naive young girl who had responded to his kiss and to his sweet words. She could almost hear the birdsong above them in the trees of Bernby Covert, where they had met in secret, and feel the soft grass beneath them. He had been her first love . . .

Her eyes flew open and she pulled away with a startled gasp. Ashamed and angry with herself, she sprang up. 'Don't.'

He too rose and tried to take her hands again, but she backed away from him, holding out her hands, palms outwards to fend him off. 'Don't,' she repeated. It seemed to be all she could say, but he took no notice and reached for her, pulling her roughly into his arms. She struggled, pushing against him, but his mouth found hers, urgent now, no longer gentle.

'You still love me. You know you do,' he muttered, between hard, demanding kisses. She twisted her face away, but he buried his head against her neck, his hand now gripping her breast.

With one almighty heave, she pushed him from her and they stood staring at each other, panting hard; he with longing, she with the sheer effort of resisting him.

'How dare you?' she spat, her eyes blazing. Gone in an instant were any tender memories of him. Now the recollection of his callousness, when she had needed him most, returned.

'You loved me. You've just said so.' His blue eyes were dark with desire.

'That was then,' Eveleen said harshly.

'And now?'

Her voice broke at the thought of Richard. How could she have allowed what had just occurred in this room? 'I'm very much in love with my husband.'

241

'But he's in a faraway land, isn't he, Evie? Fighting for hearth and home. Whilst I,' he came towards her again, holding out his hand in supplication, 'am here.'

'Don't touch me,' she began, but at that moment the door was opened by the butler bringing a tray laid with a silver teapot and bone china cups and saucers.

He set it on the low table in front of the sofa and began to pour. Helplessly Eveleen smoothed her dishevelled hair. Escape now was impossible. The manservant straightened up from his task. 'The boy has gone to fetch young Morton, sir. Will there be anything else?'

'No. Get out,' Stephen snapped. The interruption had come at precisely the wrong moment for him.

Eveleen looked at Stephen as the butler left the room. 'Morton? Is that Ted Morton?'

'No,' Stephen growled. 'His son – whatever they call him.'

'Micky,' Eveleen said. 'But he's younger than Bridie. What does he know about motors?'

Stephen shrugged. 'He works with motors somewhere in Grantham.' He glanced up at her and added testily, 'Oh, do sit down, Evie. I promise not to lunge at you again.'

Eveleen sat down, but this time she chose an armchair so that Stephen could not get close to her.

They drank tea in uncomfortable silence until Eveleen said, 'I thought Micky worked for you?'

'He did. I sacked him.'

'Why?'

For a moment, although Eveleen wondered if her eyes deceived her, Stephen looked ill at ease, almost embarrassed. Gruffly belligerent, he said, 'Can't employ all my workers' offspring. Not enough for them to do.'

Eveleen stared at him. The Dunsmore estate was huge. Then she remembered that a few years back Josh had said something about Stephen selling off parcels of land. Perhaps . . .

She glanced around the room, noticing again the absence of a woman's presence. 'How are your mother and father?'

Stephen shrugged indifferently. 'Hardly see them. They live in London. He's a big noise in the government now. And with this war . . .'

With characteristic bluntness – a trait she had never been able to correct – Eveleen asked, 'So, will you be volunteering?'

'Me?' Stephen laughed. 'What on earth would I do a daft thing like that for?'

Torn between her own anger at Richard leaving her when she had begged him not to and a sense of pride that he had the courage to do just that, she stared at the man before her, seeing him suddenly as he was now. His handsome face was puffy, probably from over-indulgence in drink. Tiny red veins mottled his cheeks and his body, once so trim and firm and lean, had given way to fat. The charm, which had once been boyish and attractive, was now more of a lecherous leer. For a moment she allowed herself to mourn the loss of his fair, Adonis-like, good looks and even had a fleeting regret for the idyllic time of her youth when she had believed herself in love with him and he with her.

Realizing at last what a self-centred man Stephen really was, Eveleen said slowly, 'No, I don't suppose you would.'

*

'Eveleen. How lovely.' Josh came towards her across the yard at Pear Tree Farm. 'We'd've waited dinner if we'd known you were coming today.'

Eveleen climbed down and kissed his plump cheeks in greeting. 'I should have been here in plenty of time, but my motor car broke down.'

Josh glanced at the vehicle and Eveleen laughed sheepishly. 'I ran out of petrol.'

Josh stared for a moment and then laughed too. 'Well, you're here now. Come along in. I'm sure your mother has some food left.'

Whilst she ate they sat at the table with her, plying her with questions about Richard and Andrew, Bridie, and what was happening at Flawford.

'The child has put me to shame,' Mary admitted. 'I really ought to visit, but Harry . . .' She gave a shudder and said no more. There was no need.

Eveleen put out her hand and touched her mother's. 'We understand, Mam. But I think Gran would like to see you.'

'We'll go, Mary. Soon. I'll be with you.'

'Yes, yes,' Mary agreed readily. 'I should go. If anything happens to my mother, I'd regret for the rest of my days that I hadn't gone.'

'I'll come to fetch you and take you in the motor car,' Eveleen offered.

Josh chuckled. 'I'll bring a spare can of petrol.'

'What? What's that?' Mary's sharp ears missed nothing.

'I ran out of petrol in the lane,' Eveleen admitted, her face turning pink. 'Micky Morton found out what the trouble was.' She omitted to tell them about her encounter with Stephen Dunsmore and skilfully turned the conversation away. 'He seems very clever with mechanical things. He tells me he has a job in Grantham.'

Josh nodded. 'Aye. Dunsmore sacked him – reckoned he hadn't enough work to support all the Morton family.'

'It's to be expected,' Mary put in. 'Since Stephen Dunsmore's selling up the estate bit by bit to finance his drinking. And gambling, so they say.'

'The lad's been working in the town the past couple of months,' Josh went on. 'Doing well, so Ted says.'

'He soon found out what was wrong,' Eveleen smiled ruefully. 'Says it's common with lady drivers.'

'I think you're very brave to drive it at all, Eveleen,' Mary said. 'I know I couldn't.'

Picking up on his wife's earlier remark, Josh said, 'We've bought a bit more land off him, Evie. The field on the other side of the beck, right up to where the trees of Bernby Covert start. So now we can get some more beast.'

'It'll make a lot more work for you, won't it, Josh?' Eveleen said worriedly. Although only in their fifties, the pair now no longer had Bridie's youthful vigour.

'I shall just get beef cattle, so's not to cause more dairy work.'

'I've got Micky's younger sister helping in the dairy now. She's a good little lass,' Mary said and murmured, 'But I still miss Bridie.'

'Then I'll take you to see her. How about next weekend?'

Later in the afternoon Eveleen took Mary to Bernby church to lay flowers on Walter Hardcastle's grave.

They stood side by side, looking down at the place where Eveleen's father lay.

'I've been a lucky woman, really,' Mary murmured. 'After – after my bit of trouble, running away from home and that, I was so lucky to meet your father. He was a wonderful man. And now I've got Josh. He's so thoughtful and kind, Evie.'

Eveleen squeezed her mother's arm, but said nothing.

As they turned away and walked back towards the motor car parked near the gate, Mary asked tentatively, 'How is Brinsley? Does he ever ask after me?'

Eveleen smiled. 'Often, Mam. And he's fine now. He wasn't too well a few months back, but now he's very much involved in our new plans.'

'What new plans?'

'I'll tell you more over tea because I want Josh to hear about them too.'

A little later as they sat down to cold ham and tomatoes, Eveleen said, 'You remember me asking your advice, Josh? Well, things are going very well. I've managed to buy several knitting machines and Griswolds. Four boys, too young to volunteer, and three women have already moved out to Flawford and now we have a knitting workshop within the factory.'

'I'm glad. Turning to war work should keep the factory going.' His face sobered. 'I wish there was more I could do to help the war.'

'You are,' Mary declared stoutly. 'You're supplying food.'

'I know, but . . .' Josh shrugged his huge shoulders and spread his hands. 'It doesn't feel like I'm doing much.'

'There is something you could do,' Eveleen said slowly, glancing from one to the other, 'but it would involve both of you and it wouldn't be easy.'

Swiftly she explained about Win's son-in-law.

'Bring him here, love,' Josh beamed delightedly. 'Good country air and Mary's cooking will soon have him right.'

Eveleen glanced at her mother, half expecting Mary to protest, but instead there were tears in her eyes as she reached out and touched her husband's hand. 'There you go again, always thinking of others.'

'You don't mind though, do you, Mary love?'

Mary pressed her lips together as if to trying to prevent more tears flowing. 'No,' she said huskily. 'No. I just hope that perhaps somewhere someone is treating my Jimmy with as much kindness.'

Thirty-Four

It was a merry little party that bowled along the country lanes from Bernby to Flawford the following weekend.

Josh and Mary sat in the back seat, whilst Helen, bravely trying to hide her own sadness, sat beside Eveleen. Mary held onto her hat, giving little squeals of alarm as Eveleen rounded the corners. 'Don't go so fast, Eveleen. You'll tip us over.'

By the time Eveleen turned the motor car into Ranters' Row, Mary was pink cheeked and breathless. 'Oh my!' she gasped, patting her chest. 'You'll give me a heart attack.'

Josh helped her down and Eveleen noticed that she clung to his arm as they went into Singleton's Yard. There was no-one about, but from the workshops came the gratifying noise of busy machinery.

'My goodness!' Eveleen exclaimed. 'Uncle Harry's even got them working on a Sunday.'

Then a joyful shriek made them all jump and Bridie was running towards them along the path in front of the cottages.

'Gran. Grandpa Josh. Oh, how lovely.' She flung herself against them, hugging them rapturously. Tucking her arm through Mary's, she almost dragged her along the path towards the end cottage, chattering delightedly. 'Auntie Evie let me know you were all coming. Dinner's ready and Great-Gran's managed to get downstairs for the first time.' Bridie beamed. 'Especially in your honour.'

Eveleen looked concerned. The last time she had seen Bridget, the old lady had looked too frail even to get out of her bed, let alone manage the steep staircase.

Catching the look, Bridie reassured her. 'Mrs Turner helped me, Auntie Eveleen. Great-Gran's all right.'

'Oh aye,' Mary remarked. 'Gracie Turner'd have to have her neb in.'

'She's been very good,' Bridie countered. She leant closer to her grandmother and dropped her voice to a whisper as they passed by the cottage in the middle of the row. 'Lil – she lives in the cottage behind Andrew's – she was supposed to be looking after Great-Gran, but she wasn't making a very good job of it. Only came in when she felt like it. Anyway, here we are, come on in.'

They clustered into the tiny front room to greet the old lady, who was sitting by the range as if she were holding court. At first the atmosphere was strained and awkward, but once dinner was served on the snowy cloth and they sat around the table the conversation became easier.

At the end of the meal even Mary was obliged to say, 'That was lovely, Bridie. You're a credit to me.'

Everyone laughed, but Bridie said quite seriously, 'Thank you, Gran.' Then she rose from her place and began to pile a plate high with meat and vegetables. She also spooned bread and butter pudding and custard into a bowl. 'I'll just take this along to me grandad.'

Eveleen smiled at her. 'Will he eat it?'

'Shouldn't think so for a minute,' the young girl replied cheerfully. 'He hasn't yet. But I live in hope.'

As the door closed behind her, Bridget shook her

head and said, 'He's a stubborn old fool. That girl takes him a dinner every Sunday, aye, and sometimes in the week. But will he eat it? He'd sooner starve than give in.'

When Bridie returned, Mary, Eveleen and Helen were already clearing away and washing up in the small scullery, whilst Josh sat across the hearth chatting to Bridget.

'Do you mind if I go to chapel?' Bridie said.

Mary turned to look at her in surprise. 'You go to chapel?'

Bridie nodded. 'It's all part of the plan to win me grandad round, but don't tell him I said so.'

'I've no intention of saying anything to him,' Mary replied drily and plunged a dirty plate into the bowl of soapsuds as if she wished it were her brother's head she was dunking.

Bridie grinned and exchanged a knowing glance with her aunt. Then she said, 'You won't go before I get back, will you? Only I don't want to give him the chance to say that I've missed a service,' she giggled, 'because of entertaining.'

'No, no, we'll still be here,' Eveleen assured her. 'Off you go.'

The preacher was one of the 'fire and brimstone' ministers who had given Ranters' Row its local name. He stood on the rostrum and harangued the congregation for their sinful ways. Bridie sat placidly watching his antics, whilst beside her Harry Singleton grew more and more excited, waving his arms and shouting 'Amen' at the end of each sentence the preacher delivered. At the end of the service, Bridie waited by the door whilst

Harry shook the man's hand, pumping it up and down vigorously.

'Grand sermon, Minister,' he said. 'We don't get enough like you these days. All simpering do-gooders, that's what the new breed is now.'

They talked for a few moments more before they both came down the aisle towards her.

She smiled and asked, 'Did you enjoy your dinner, Grandad?'

'I've told you not to call me that,' he growled and made to push past her. 'And you're doing nowt but waste good food.'

The minister paused in front of Bridie and smiled down at her from his great height, his bushy side-burns bristling. 'Is this your granddaughter, Harry?' he boomed, his voice as loud as if he were still addressing the full congregation. He held out his huge hand and gripped hers tightly, making the girl wince. 'I'm very pleased to meet you.'

'She's no granddaughter of mine,' Harry said abruptly. 'I disowned my daughter when she got herself into trouble.'

The minister glanced from one to the other, perplexed for a moment. Then, as realization dawned, a look of disapproval crossed his face. To Bridie's surprise, it was not directed at her but at her grandfather. 'Harry Single-ton – I'm ashamed of you!'

'Wha . . .?' For a brief moment, Harry was discon-certed, but then his mouth tightened and he actually had the temerity to shake his fist at the minister. 'You mind your business, Mr Simmonds, and I'll mind mine.' Leav-ing a shocked minister and an even more surprised Bridie, Harry turned and marched across the street towards his home.

'Well!' The man seemed lost for words and at once Bridie said, 'I am sorry, sir, but my grandad is very bitter about what happened in the past. I don't know everything except that I was born out of wedlock. I think that is the politest way to put it.' She smiled up at him ruefully, then added sadly, 'And my mother died at my birth.'

The big man put his hand on her shoulder. Suddenly all his bluster and fire was gone and his tone was gentle and understanding. 'My dear child, then you should be loved and treasured even more.'

At this stranger's unexpected kindness, tears sprang to her eyes more readily than if he had treated her harshly.

'Thank you,' she murmured, her voice breaking. She dropped her head as she added, 'I wish my grandfather felt the same.'

She felt the minister squeeze her shoulder. He said no more, but she saw him looking thoughtfully across the road in the direction of Harry's home.

'I must go,' Bridie said. 'It's been nice to meet you, sir.'

The man patted her back and his voice boomed with goodwill once again. 'Take heart, my child. I'll see what I can do to help.'

He walked across the road at her side and she left him with his hand raised to knock on her grandfather's door.

Thirty-Five

'Did you hear it?' Mary said as they climbed into the motor car to go home. 'Whatever was all that shouting as we passed Harry's cottage?'

Bridie, standing beside the vehicle, said, 'It's Grandad and the minister. I think they're arguing over me.'

'Over you?' At once Mary was suspicious. '*Now* what have you been up to, girl?'

'Being born, Gran,' Bridie said simply. 'That's all.'

'Eh?' Mary was mystified and even Eveleen looked at her questioningly.

Bridie sighed. 'I think the minister's telling him off for the way he treats me because – because I'm illegitimate.'

Mary sniffed. 'Not before time, but I shouldn't think it'll do any good. He doesn't know Harry like I do.'

There was a flurry of goodbyes and much waving and Eveleen turned the vehicle around and headed down the street. Conversation was difficult between the four of them above the noise of the engine, so it wasn't until they reached Pear Tree Farm and were sitting together having a cup of tea, before Eveleen and Helen made their way back to Nottingham, that the conversation turned again to Bridie.

'Well, I have to say it and you know I'm not given to praising folk . . .' Mary began and her daughter hid her smile, 'but that child is doing very well.'

'She is,' Helen agreed. 'She was a good little worker in the mending room, but even I can see that she's in her element caring for people.'

'You'd certainly think so, Mam, if you'd seen Gran when she first went there. If Bridie hadn't insisted on looking after her, I don't know what would have happened by now.'

'I managed to sneak a look in the workshops whilst Harry was at chapel,' Josh said. 'The new folks you've sent there, Evie, are doing very well by all accounts.' He chuckled as he added, 'Even the women. There was an oldish man teaching a young girl. "What's this?" I said, "Working on a Sunday?" The old feller laughed and said, "Old Harry can turn a blind eye when it suits him."'

'How was the girl shaping up?' Eveleen was anxious to know.

'All right, as far as I could see.'

'It's surprised me that Harry's ever agreed to your plans, especially having girls working there,' Mary said.

'I don't think he had much choice if he wanted his workshops to survive,' Josh said. 'Your mother said his eyesight is poor now, but he won't admit it.'

Mary sniffed. 'If I know my brother, it's more a matter of money. He'll do anything to make a bob or two.' She glanced at Eveleen. 'He let you have a go on a frame when we lived there, didn't he? But that was only because he couldn't bear to see even one frame standing idle.'

Eveleen nodded. 'Yes, and if it hadn't been for the trouble over Rebecca and Jimmy, I think he'd have let me carry on working one.'

'Aye.' Mary was pensive. 'But for them, I reckon we might still have been living there.'

'No, we wouldn't, Mam,' Eveleen countered. 'When we were forced to leave here, I promised I would bring you back one day.' She pulled a wry face. 'Though I have to admit it would have taken me a long time on the wages I earned in the inspection room.'

The four of them laughed together, then Mary said, 'Well, Master Stephen's high 'n' mighty ways haven't done him a lot of good. Josh heard the other day that he's put the estate up for sale – what's left of it. Even Fairfield House is on the market.'

Eveleen digested the news with mixed emotions. It saddened her to think that the once great estate that had supported several families, her father and even her grandfather before him, had been broken up and sold bit by bit because of one spoilt, self-centred and dissolute young man.

'What'll happen to the families who still work for him? What about the Mortons?'

Mary shrugged. 'He'll turn 'em out, I expect, just like he did us, when he's no more use for them.'

'Micky works in Grantham now,' Josh put in. 'And Ted's volunteered. He went the day before yesterday.'

'Oh no, not Ted too.' Eveleen was sorry to hear that her childhood friend had gone. She hadn't even had a chance to say goodbye. Another 'goodbye' unsaid.

'Well,' Mary said, her mouth tight as she rose to clear away the cups and saucers, 'I tell you one person who won't be going. Master Stephen. He's too much of a coward.'

Eveleen stared at her. 'You've changed your tune, Mam,' she said bluntly. 'I thought you didn't hold with the war.'

'No more I do, but if all the fine young men – Richard, Andrew . . .' Her tone softened. 'And somewhere I expect

255

my Jimmy's caught up in it too – why should someone like Stephen Dunsmore escape?'

'I don't think he will for long, love,' Josh said solemnly. 'If it goes on much longer, they'll bring in conscription, then he'll probably have to go.'

Mary's eyes were suddenly fearful. 'You won't, will you?'

Josh smiled, but there was a hint of regret as if, deep down, he would have liked the chance to prove his love for his country. 'No, love. I'm far too old. But – ' his face brightened – 'we'll do our bit here at home.' He turned to Eveleen. 'You bring that poor young feller out here as soon as you like. We'll look after him. What do they call him?'

Eveleen touched his hand. 'Sid Robinson. Thank you, Josh. Win will be so grateful.'

'We've all got to do our bit where we can. Even little Bridie's doing hers, looking after the old lady and her grandfather too, if only he'd let her.'

'He'll never do that,' Mary remarked as she disappeared into the scullery. 'Not till the sun shines both sides the hedge at the same time.'

'We don't need you here. We don't want you here. And you had no right to go snivelling to the minister, telling him of our family's shame.'

Harry's huge, outraged figure seemed to fill Bridget's living room. She sat still and silent, hunched in her chair by the fire, whilst, standing in front of her great-grandmother as if to protect her from his onslaught, Bridie faced him boldly.

'Great-Gran needs me even if you don't.'

'Lil can look after her,' he boomed.

'No, she can't. She's a slattern. Did you even know what this place looked like when I arrived? Did you even care enough to visit your own mother?'

'Don't you dare answer me back, girl—'

'I'm not afraid of you. I can walk out of here whenever I like—'

'That's exactly what I want you to do.'

'But I'm staying. I'm staying to look after me Great-Gran and I'd look after you too, you stubborn old man, if only you'd let me. But no, you're too proud, too – too unforgiving.' She flung her arm out towards the old lady cowering in her chair. 'You'd sooner watch her die than unbend enough to let me help. Well, I'm not going anywhere, so you might as well get used to it.' She took a step closer to the man. 'If you want me gone, you'll have to carry me out bodily.' Suddenly she grinned so saucily, so cheekily, that only the hardest of hearts could have resisted. 'And even then I'll come back.'

But it seemed that Harry Singleton's heart was made of stone. He turned on his heel and left the cottage. Bridie heard a sob behind her and turned to kneel beside the old lady.

She put her arms around her. 'There, there, Great-Gran, don't cry. It'll be all right. This war's got to be over soon and then Andrew and all the others will come home. Everything will be all right then.'

Everything will be all right for all of us, Bridie promised herself silently, if only Andrew comes home safely.

Eveleen drew the motor car to a halt outside her home. As the engine noise died away, Helen said, 'Eveleen, I can't thank you enough. I don't know what I would have done without you these last few weeks. I would never have got through.'

Eveleen covered Helen's hand with her own. 'Nonsense, of course you would.' She smiled gently at her friend. 'Darling Helen, it's your own courage that's carried you through. Leslie would be so proud of you.'

Helen nodded, smiling bravely through unshed tears, but she could not speak. Eveleen patted her hand. 'Come on. Let's go in. It's getting dark.'

'I won't come in, if you don't mind. I'll go home.' She bit her lip as she glanced at Eveleen. 'I've got to face being on my own at night sooner or later.'

'You should have said. I could have dropped you at your home first.'

'It's not far. I'll walk.'

'Well, just come in and have—'

The front door of the house had opened and Emily, holding up her skirt, was running down the steps. She was holding out a yellow envelope and her face showed signs of tears. She was breathless and anxious as she reached them.

'Oh, ma'am. I didn't know what to do. This came this morning. I didn't know where to find you. Oh, ma'am. It's a telegram. From the War Office.'

For a moment, Eveleen was frozen, unable to move, then she reached out and took the thin paper into her hands. She felt Helen slip her arm around her shoulders as, with trembling fingers, Eveleen tore open the telegram.

'Oh no!' Her fingers fluttered to her lips. 'It's Andrew. "Missing in action", it says. Oh, Helen.' She turned to face her friend, her eyes already filling with tears. 'However am I going to tell Bridie?'

Thirty-Six

'I don't believe it, Auntie Eveleen. Andrew's not dead. I'd know it if he was.' She put her hand over her own heart. 'I'd feel it here.'

Eveleen had sent word to Pear Tree Farm of the dreadful news, but she had come again to Flawford the very next day to break the news to her niece herself.

'It only says "missing". They don't know for sure,' Bridie insisted, denying even the thought that she would never see him again.

Eveleen watched her helplessly. How could she tell this young girl that the conditions out there were so terrible that men died, blown to a thousand pieces, so that no recognizable trace was ever found. That soldiers were buried together hurriedly during a lull in the fighting, their identities unknown, their resting place unmarked. Wounded soldiers, sent home from the Front, were telling the truth now about what this war was really like. And talk of it was rife amongst the workers at Reckitt and Stokes.

'Well, yes, that's true,' Eveleen said haltingly, feeling guilty at confirming Bridie's hope. Perhaps it would be kinder, in the long run, to convince her of Andrew's death. The sooner the girl came to terms with it, the better. 'But, darling, I don't think they would send a telegram if there was the slightest chance that—'

Bridie was adamant. 'Yes, they would. Mrs Turner's

259

got a friend in the village. She was telling me. She got a telegram about her son. Just the same as that.' Bridie prodded her finger accusingly at the offending piece of paper. 'And then he turned up alive. He'd been wounded and taken to a field hospital. His identity tag was missing and because he was unconscious they didn't know who he was. So it *does* happen.'

'Yes, of course it does, but . . .' Eveleen bit her lip, coming to a sudden decision, right or wrong. Let the poor child have hope for a while longer. Maybe coming to the truth gradually was the best way for Bridie. Eveleen forced herself to smile, though her own heart was heavy. She could not believe, not for a minute, that Andrew was still alive. Aloud she said, 'Pray God you're right, Bridie.'

She held out her arms and they hugged each other fiercely. When they drew apart, Bridie said quietly, 'If you're not in a rush to get back, perhaps you could sit with Great-Gran for a while. I – I'm going across to the chapel.'

Eveleen nodded, unable to speak for the lump in her throat. She watched the girl leave the cottage, pass by the window, her shoulders hunched, her head down. 'She knows all right,' Eveleen whispered. 'She knows the truth, but she's just refusing to believe it.'

Sadly Eveleen turned and went upstairs to tell Bridget.

'Aw, that's bad news,' the old lady was saying moments later. 'That child worships him.'

'He's been very good to her. Visiting the farm almost every week since she was a baby.'

'I thought as much, though he never said.'

'I suppose he didn't want to cause trouble here. Uncle Harry might have sacked him if he'd known.'

260

Bridget gave a wry laugh. 'I don't think so. Harry's no fool when it comes to money and Andrew was a good worker.'

Eveleen glanced out of the window at the workshops. 'He hasn't many of his own workers left now, has he?' she asked quietly.

Bridget shook her head. 'No, they've all gone. All the good ones, that is.'

Eveleen looked out of the window towards the workshops. Behind one of the long windows she could see the shadowy shape of her uncle.

'I'd better go and tell him about Andrew,' she murmured.

Bridie knelt at the altar rail until her knees hurt, yet she was unaware of the pain. She prayed aloud, talking to God as if he were standing in front of her.

'Please, don't let him be dead. Please let him be alive and come home to me. I love him so much. I don't care if he doesn't love me in the same way, only please let him come home. And Uncle Richard too. He's such a nice, kind man. Please let him be safe.'

Behind her, the door opened and closed again softly. There were tiptoeing footsteps and the squeak of protesting woodwork as someone sat down in one of the pews, but Bridie scarcely noticed.

'Please, stop the war. All the maiming and killing, it can't be what you want. I know it can't. I'll take care of Andrew, even if he's injured. Only let him be alive and I'll look after him for the rest of my life.' Her fingers were so tightly laced together in supplication that they were white, the feeling in them almost gone.

Stiffly, she shifted and became aware of the discomfort

in her legs. She bowed her head and ended her prayers. 'God bless all my family. Gran and Josh and Eveleen. And please, God, spare my great-gran and help me to care for her properly and keep her safe. And God, bless my grandad and help him to know that I'm so sorry I'm a disgrace to his family, but I want to know him. I so want to love him.' Then she repeated the words she had heard the minister intone at the end of his prayers, ending with the customary 'Amen'.

She stood up, bending forward to rub the life back into her limbs before turning to walk down the aisle. She drew breath sharply as she became aware of the motionless figure of Harry Singleton sitting in a pew at the back. But she did not even glance at him. Holding her head proudly, she walked down the aisle and out of the chapel.

She didn't notice that he was watching her every step of the way or see the tears rolling silently down his cheeks.

'Great-Gran! Great-Gran!' Bridie was racing up the stairs, arriving breathless in Bridget's room. But her eyes were shining and the grin on her wide mouth seemed to stretch from ear to ear. 'You're not going to believe this. He's eaten it. I did his favourite, like you told me. Lamb's liver fry and he's eaten it. Every last bit. Look!'

She had even brought the empty dinner plate upstairs to show to the old lady.

Bridget smiled, eyeing the plate and then looking at the girl's face, flushed with triumph.

'Well, well. He was either starving hungry or you've won.'

Bridie nodded. 'We'll see what he does tomorrow.'

But the next day's plate was cleared too and whilst Harry still never came to his mother's cottage, still never spoke to Bridie as she passed him in the yard, he now ate the meals she prepared and left on his table each day.

It was a small, but significant victory.

Bridget improved with each day and, as the weeks passed, she grew stronger and now she was dressing and coming downstairs each day.

'You can wheel me across to the chapel on Sunday, Bridie.' She smiled widely at her great-granddaughter. 'Harry'd like that. It'd be another feather in your cap in his eyes if you got me to a service.'

Bridie put her arms around the old woman's shoulders, knowing that she was making the suggestion more to help her than because she hankered to attend chapel. 'Only if you're sure you're up to it.'

'I'm up to it, love. I haven't felt so well for years.' Her beady eyes, bright in the wizened face, twinkled with merriment. 'Must be having you around.'

They laughed together and Bridie hugged her. 'I'm so glad I came here,' she whispered. 'So glad I've found you.'

'Not half as glad as I am,' Bridget said with feeling. 'I'd have been a goner now if it hadn't been for you.'

'Oh no, Great-Gran, I'm sure—'

'Oh yes, I would,' Bridget said with asperity. 'Lil was happy enough to pocket the money Harry paid her to look after me, but she didn't give a damn. And I was too weak to do anything about it. I shan't have her back in here when you go.'

'Trying to get rid of me, are you?'

'No, love.' The old lady looked pensive. 'But you

don't want to be tied to this place with an old woman and a stubborn old fool of a man. Anyway, I bet Eveleen's missing you even though she never says anything. And your gran, if it comes to that.'

Bridie was thoughtful. Mary's attitude towards her on their visit here had surprised, yet pleased, the young girl. It was the first time her grandmother had shown anything approaching affection towards her.

'But while you are still here –' Bridget's voice dragged her back to the present – 'you can get me to chapel this Sunday.'

There were plenty of willing helpers on the Sunday afternoon when Bridie manoeuvred the cumbersome borrowed bath chair across the road.

'We'll not get that through the door.' Georgie Turner, Gracie's husband, scratched his head thoughtfully. 'Tell you what. Leave it outside here and me and one of the other lads'll help her inside.'

Bridie stifled her giggles at Georgie Turner calling his cronies 'lads'. They were all over fifty if they were a day! But she kept her face straight and said, 'Thank you, Mr Turner.'

'Can you walk, Mrs Singleton?' Georgie now addressed Bridget.

''Course I can,' she began indignantly, but then was obliged to confide, 'but I do need help.'

The minister whom Bridie had met before took the service. At the end he stood by the door, shaking hands with everyone as they left.

'Ah, Harry Singleton's granddaughter, if I'm not mistaken,' he boomed so that those left could not fail to hear. He shook her hand vigorously and then Bridie saw him glance beyond her. 'You come to your senses yet, Harry?'

Harry pushed past them, his face like thunder. 'I told you before,' he muttered, 'you mind your business, Minister. And I'll mind mine.'

Ignoring the man's outstretched hand, Harry strode across the road towards Singleton's Yard. Bridie's heart felt as if it had dropped inside her and she almost groaned aloud. Oh no! She'd been making headway, she thought, even if it was only a very small step, and now the minister had unwittingly spoilt it all.

The next day and in the days that followed Harry did not eat the dinners that Bridie took him.

'Stubborn old fool,' Bridget muttered, whilst the young girl looked sadly at the wasted food and murmured, 'I just wish the minister hadn't said anything.'

September 1915 had brought news of an autumn offensive on the Western Front with combined attacks by the French and the British. The newspapers spoke of victories, but Richard's letter, received later in the month, gave a different picture.

> *We haven't been involved, but we hear that what could have been a successful attack overrunning a village as the enemy weren't expecting our lads, failed in the end because reserves were late arriving and the enemy had sealed off the breach.*

He ended, as always, by sending his love to Bridie. *I hope the poor child hasn't taken the news of Andrew too badly.*

Eveleen had folded his letter thoughtfully. The

trouble was that Bridie had not accepted the news at all. She stubbornly refused to believe it and Eveleen feared that eventually, when the girl was obliged to face facts, her grief would be all the more terrible.

Thirty-Seven

Bridie received a letter from Richard.

> *Today is the first of October and how I wish I was with
> you back home in dear old Nottingham and visiting the
> Goose Fair. I can still taste that toffee apple and hear
> the fairground music, but I expect the fair has been
> cancelled this year. Still, after the war, we'll go again.
> All of us.*

She was acutely aware that he did not add '. . . who
are left.'

Bridie felt guilty not sharing this letter from Richard
with her aunt. Eveleen always brought the letters she
had received from him for Bridie to read. But the girl
felt her uncle's reference to their day spent at the Goose
Fair would revive unhappy and guilty feelings for Eveleen. The next letter she was able to show her.

> *I have had my first experience under shellfire. We had to
> go out on a digging party. We split up into small
> sections with twenty-yard intervals between us.
> Suddenly everyone else dived into the ditches on either
> side of the road. I heard an awful shriek and a terrific
> explosion and I soon made a dive for the ditch too. I
> was told these are five-point-nines and that I'll get to
> know the sound only too well! Now we're getting
> shelled every day on our way back. Perhaps it has*

*something to do with the German 'sausage' overhead –
that's an observation balloon.*

'He's not told me any of that,' Eveleen remarked,
folding Bridie's letter and handing it back to her.

'Perhaps he doesn't want you to worry too much,'
Bridie soothed, wondering whether she should have
shown Eveleen the letter at all. Trying to change the
subject, she said, 'He hasn't mentioned Andrew. Do you
think Uncle Richard thinks he's still alive somewhere
too?'

Now it was Eveleen's turn to feel guilty that she had
not shown her niece the letter in which Richard had
intimated that he had accepted the news of Andrew's
loss. Now Eveleen could think of nothing to say in
answer.

In the following months Richard wrote often to Bridie
and it seemed that he found it easier to write to her
about the conditions at the Front than he did in his
letters to Eveleen.

In November Richard wrote,

*I have been in the trenches for the first time. We left our
billets in platoons at dusk. It was very dark and
strangely quiet. When we left the road we entered a long
trench known as the communication trench. It was in a
dreadful condition; knee deep in water and it was still
raining! I didn't sleep much the first night. It takes a bit
of getting used to when rats as big as cats snuggle under
your armpits in the night to keep warm! We stayed
there for eight days – four days in support and four days
in the front line. The daytime was spent in trench
repairing and the night in sentry duty – two hours on*

*and four off. We all stand at battle positions one hour
before dark and again an hour before dawn. After that
we stand down and get our fires going to boil water and
fry bacon, being careful not to make much smoke or
this brings the shells! We were lucky on our sector – it
was very quiet, though we had to be careful to keep
below the parapet because of snipers. Now we have
been relieved and have gone back to digging.*

Eveleen and Bridie still continued to show each other
the letters they received, but those to Eveleen gave news
only of the times that he was away from the front line.
His letter in December was cheerful.

*We've been relieved by the 7th SF. We had a six-hour
march and were all very tired, but at least we've seen the
last of the trenches and the mud – for a while anyway!
We seem to be moving about a lot just now. At one time
we were billeted in a small château on the banks of the
Lys.*

To Bridie he wrote,

*Feeling rather war torn and my feet are not too good.
I've had a touch of flu and felt very wonky whilst on
guard duty.*

No letter came for over a month and both Eveleen
and Bridie began to feel anxious. His next letter to
Eveleen explained the long silence.

*Haven't been able to write for a while. At the beginning
of January A and C Companies (I'm in A) left for M . . .
in the south.*

The rest of the name had been heavily scored out,
but from what followed, Eveleen guessed the place was
Marseilles.

It took us three days by train to get there and where we were camped had a splendid view of the Château d'If. Don't know why we were taken all that way – maybe the officers know, but they're certainly not telling us. However, a few of us were lucky enough to get passes into the city and docks. Had tea at a restaurant and then went to the pictures. Visited Notre Dame de la Garde – superb view of the gulf and the islands and indeed the whole city. I had to be vaccinated so my arm's a bit painful, but it hasn't stopped me visiting the zoological gardens and the Palais de Longchamps. Then, suddenly, we were on the move again. We marched eight miles back to the station, where we were given a splendid send-off by the locals. Another three days on the train, but travelling through the valley of the Rhône was wonderful . . .

A letter to Bridie admitted,

The thirteen days in the south were great, but it makes coming back to the trenches all the harder. And now it's snowing . . .

'He must know we swap letters,' Bridie remarked, trying to make light of the marked difference between them. 'He's just telling us different news, that's all.'

Again, Eveleen said nothing.

At the beginning of 1916 the House of Commons voted overwhelmingly for military conscription and in February well-off families were urged to dispense with their servants. But Emily – the only one in Eveleen's household who was still young enough to do useful war work – left of her own accord.

'I'm going into munitions, ma'am,' she said as she handed Eveleen her written notice.

'After it's all over, Emily, come back and see me, won't you?'

'Oh yes, ma'am,' the girl smiled, but Eveleen had the distinct feeling that once her maid had tasted life outside domestic service, the girl was unlikely to want to return.

No letters came from Richard throughout February.

'You haven't had a letter, Bridie,' Eveleen asked anxiously, 'and not shown it to me?'

'No. Have you?'

Eveleen bit her lip and shook her head. Then she decided to confess. 'There's been only one letter I haven't shown you. After – after Andrew was posted missing.'

'Why? What did he say?'

'Just – just that he hoped you hadn't taken the news too badly.'

'Oh,' Bridie said quietly. So she had been wrong. Richard did believe that Andrew had been killed.

Eveleen was watching her. 'What about you?'

'What – what do you mean?'

'Are there any letters you haven't shown me?'

Bridie smiled apologetically. 'Only one. The very first he ever wrote to me. He – he talked about us going to the Goose Fair and – and I thought it would upset you.'

Eveleen smiled sadly. 'We've both been trying to protect the other, haven't we?'

Bridie nodded. 'But I promise I've shown you all of them since. And I will in future, whatever's in them.'

Eveleen held out her arms. 'So will I.'

Bridie hugged her aunt and against her shoulder she murmured, 'But I wonder why he hasn't written lately.'

*

At the beginning of March there was a knock on the cottage door in Singleton's Yard.

Bridie opened it to see a tall figure dressed in soldier's uniform standing there. His back was to the light and for a moment she could not see his features. She drew breath sharply and for an instant the name sprang at once to her lips. Andrew! But then she realized he was too tall. Her fleeting disappointment evaporated when she realized the visitor's identity. She gave a delighted squeal and flung herself against him.

'Uncle Richard!' She pulled him into the living room, firing questions at him without giving him a moment to answer. 'Oh, you're home! Is Auntie Eveleen with you? Are you home for good? Is the war over? Great-Gran, this is Uncle Richard. Sit down, sit down. I'll make a cup of tea. Oh, it's wonderful to see you.' And again, she hugged him. Richard put his arms around her and held her so tightly he almost squeezed the breath from her. At last he released her a little, but still stood with his arms about her.

It was Bridie who pulled away and said, 'Come and meet my great-grandmother.'

Richard bent and took the old lady's hand. 'I'm pleased to meet you, Mrs Singleton.' Then he sat down in the chair on the opposite side of the hearth. For a moment Bridie stood biting her lip and looking down at him. There was something different about him. He smiled at her in the gentle way he always had, but the smile did not reach his eyes.

'What is it?' she asked quietly. 'What's happened?'

He looked up at her, puzzled. 'Happened? Er – nothing, as far as I know. Why?'

'Oh, I just wondered. I mean . . .' her voice faltered and she turned, murmuring, 'I'll get the tea.' As she prepared the tray, she glanced through the open door from the scullery. He was talking to the old lady, his head bend slightly to one side in that kindly, solicitous manner he had always had and for a moment Bridie thought she had been mistaken. He was as he had always been, but when she carried the tray through, mashed the tea from the kettle on the hob, poured and handed him a cup, she could see again that there was something different about him.

It was in his eyes. As he talked, there was no change of expression in his eyes. Even when he smiled, it was a merely mechanical stretching of his mouth and not an emotion he was really feeling. His eyes were like those of a dead fish.

She sat down and, at a lull in the conversation, asked again, 'Are you home for good?'

Richard shook his head. 'No, I'm afraid not. Just on leave. I've been very lucky to get back to England. Oh, we get leave in France, but there's never enough time to get all the way home.'

Bridie watched as he sat gazing into the glowing coals in the grate. 'Is it very bad out there, Uncle Richard?'

As he turned his head slowly to look at her, Bridie could have bitten her tongue off for having asked the question. The look in his eyes that had replaced the vacant expression was far worse. Terror, horror, even loss of faith – all were there.

'Don't ask me, Bridie,' he said huskily. 'You don't want to know. Believe me, you really don't. If there is such a place as hell, it couldn't possibly be worse than the trenches in France.'

Thirty-Eight

She took him to the workshops, up the stone steps to meet her grandfather, and was gratified that Harry had the courtesy to shake his hand, although his manner was gruff and unwelcoming.

As they stepped into the yard again, Bridie blurted out, 'He doesn't want me here. He never speaks to me or comes to Great-Gran's cottage.'

Richard put his hand on her shoulder. 'You've done a grand job here, Bridie. Eveleen was telling me, but perhaps now that the old lady's better it's time for you to come back to Nottingham.'

Bridie glanced towards Andrew's home. 'I want to stay here. At least, a while longer. I – I'm waiting for Andrew to come home.'

His fingers tightened on her shoulder. 'Bridie, love, you must come to terms with the facts. Andrew isn't going to come back.'

'How do you know? Did you see him killed? Have you seen his body?'

'No, but he went out with a raiding party at night. When they do that they have to remove all identification marks and badges. Two men didn't come back. Andrew was one of them.'

'What happened?'

Richard shrugged. 'No-one knows. The two of them got separated from the rest and in the dark they just disappeared. Maybe they got taken prisoner, but – but shots were heard, so . . .'

'So,' Bridie took up his sentence, 'it was just presumed that he – and the other feller too – had been killed.'

'It's all we can do, Bridie. We can't go looking for them.'

The girl tried to imagine what a battlefield must be like as, haltingly, Richard tried to explain. There were lines of trenches, he said, on each side protected by barbed wire and a stretch of ground between them called 'no man's land'. Was that where Andrew had gone missing? she wondered. Perhaps he had been lying out there, still alive but needing help.

'Can't you look for them in the daytime?'

'If you so much as put your head above the trench parapet, a sniper will pick you off. We use a kind of makeshift periscope made with mirrors to look across to the enemy lines.'

Despite what they all said, despite even what Richard said, who knew better than anyone, Bridie refused to give up hope. She looked up at him, her eyes afire with determination. As if by the strength of her will, she could make it so, she said, 'He will come back, Uncle Richard. He's not dead. I know he's not.'

The following day Bridie went to see Gracie Turner.

'I've been thinking,' she said, once they were sat at the kitchen table, a cup of tea and freshly baked scones in front of them. 'Maybe I should go back to Nottingham. Auntie Eveleen is so busy at the factory. She works such long hours. Now Emily's left her and Uncle Richard told me that Cook's legs are bad now, maybe I should go back. I can always come back here when Andrew comes home.'

''Course you can, mi little lass. The old lady's a lot better and I can look after her now, if you want me to.'

Bridie beamed. 'That's why I've come to see you. I was hoping you would. I don't want that Lil back in her house.'

It was all settled between them, even that Gracie should cook meals for Harry.

'It needn't be every day,' Bridie said, 'maybe just two or three times a week. Just so's he gets a good meal now and again. You know? That's if he'll eat them!' she added wryly.

'Oh aye, I know all right. He's a fool to himself is Harry Singleton. Always has been. But if them at the chapel told him to jump in the river and drown himself, I reckon he would. He takes after his father. Hard-hearted old bugger, he was. No wonder your poor gran ran away like she did.'

Bridie's eyes widened. 'Me gran? Ran away from home?'

'Oh aye,' Gracie said, filling both cups for a second time and settling down to impart a piece of gossip, completely forgetting that she had once said it was not her place to divulge family secrets. 'She fell in love with a young feller and got herself pregnant. Denounced in front of the whole congregation, she was, by her own family. Well, by her father and her brother, Harry.'

Bridie gasped. 'What do you mean "denounced"?'

Gracie waved her hands vaguely. 'It's a very old custom. Gone long since in most places, but not here.' She nodded her head. 'Old man Singleton, that's your great-grandmother's husband, he believed in all that sort of thing. If anybody did anything wrong, 'specially adultery and what they call fornication . . .' Gracie grinned. 'Doing what comes naturally, that's what I call it. Anyway, they used to haul the culprits up in front of the whole congregation and make 'em confess their sins.'

'They did that to Gran and her – her young man?'

Gracie shook her head. 'They couldn't get hold of him, else they would have done. He was from a well-to-do family in Nottingham. His family sent him away, so poor Mary was left to face the shame alone. Then she ran away and we didn't hear from her again until she and her family – your auntie and your dad too, of course – arrived on Harry's doorstep.'

Bridie was thoughtful, piecing together the rest of the story. That was how her mother, Rebecca, had met Jimmy Hardcastle and had fallen in love with him and become pregnant. And then she too had been cast out by Harry Singleton.

'Who was me gran's young man?' she asked suddenly.

'Oh, well now, I'm not rightly sure.' Gracie was avoiding meeting her direct gaze and Bridie had the distinct impression that the older woman knew far more than she was telling now. Gracie stood up and began to clear away the cups and saucers, bustling about as if to avoid answering any awkward questions. 'I've said too much already,' Bridie heard her murmur. 'Me an' mi big mouth. It'll get me into hot water one of these days.' Raising her voice, Gracie changed the subject. 'Now, it's all settled then. I'll look after your gran and you go back to Nottingham and help your auntie Eveleen.'

'I'm so sorry, Evie. I – I can't.'

They lay in the big bed together, holding each other

close. Richard had not been able to make love to her, even though Eveleen's body yearned to offer him comfort.

'It's all right. It doesn't matter,' she tried to reassure him, yet she knew he would feel his failure as keenly as she did. She kissed him tenderly and whilst he returned her kiss, there was none of the passion, the sudden spark of fire, that had always been between them.

She mourned its loss, but understood. She had not questioned him about the conditions in the trenches, but she too had seen the dreadful look deep in his eyes.

'We'll go out tomorrow. We'll go to the farm.' She had been disappointed because Richard had made no effort to visit the factory, had displayed no interest in it at all or in everything that she was accomplishing. Apart from his trip to visit Bridie in Flawford, he had been nowhere. He had sat in the morning room all day, each day, just staring into the fire.

'A day in the country will do you good.' She kissed his cheek and then pulled out of his arms. 'Try to sleep now.'

She lay beside him staring into the darkness and slept only fitfully herself, disturbed by his restlessness and his mutterings. More than once he shouted out and she held him in her arms as he trembled and buried his face in her neck, his tears wet against her skin.

Eveleen drove the motor car the following morning. At first Richard sat morose and silent beside her, but gradually he began to look about him. The day was cold and sharp, but already there was a feeling of spring in the air. Lambs, without a care in the world, pranced in the fields and snowdrops dappled the grass verges.

As they drew into the yard, Josh came towards them,

his arms stretched wide in welcome. Behind him was Sid, limping towards them but smiling broadly. Wordlessly he shook Richard's hand and then turned to Eveleen as Josh drew Richard away towards the house.

'I can't thank you enough, missis, for bringing me out here. Your mam and dad – ' he was referring to Josh, not knowing that he was Eveleen's stepfather – 'have worked a miracle. It's the countryside. It's so calm and peaceful. It was the noise out there that got to me, missis. The shelling and the gunfire getting nearer and nearer and never knowing when it was going to be your turn. It was living with the constant fear. And we was all afraid, missis, every man jack of us. It didn't stop us doing what we had to do, but anyone who tells you he wasn't afraid is a bloody liar. Beggin' yer pardon, missis.' Eveleen smiled understandingly as Sid went on, 'But I'm fine now, honest. I was only saying yesterday, I'm ready to go back home now. I won't be like I was, missis, I promise. How I could have treated my Elsie like that . . .' He shook his head. 'I don't know. I'm that ashamed.'

Eveleen touched his arm. 'It wasn't your fault. You were ill. But if you really feel well enough, you can come back with us this evening. We'll take you home.'

Sid's face brightened. 'That'd be grand. Not that I'm not happy here, but I want to get back to Elsie.' He pulled an apologetic face. 'I've a lot of making up to do.' He glanced over his shoulder and nodded towards Richard. 'He doesn't look so good himself. Just got leave, has he?'

Eveleen nodded, but could not speak for the lump in her throat.

Mary fussed around Richard until Eveleen felt quite left out. But she smiled to herself – her mother had always been this way. The men in Mary's life were paramount and girls and women of little importance. And perhaps, Eveleen reminded herself, young men of Richard's age were a substitute for the son she never heard from.

After dinner Richard went outside to walk around the smallholding with Josh. Mary, watching them from the scullery window, shook her head sadly. 'Oh, Eveleen, he's a changed man.'

'I know,' Eveleen agreed, but tried to be positive. 'But when the war's over and he comes home then everything will be all right. I'm sure of it. It's just – well – knowing he's got to go back and face it all again. It can't be easy.'

'Has he got to go back? I mean, he volunteered. He's done his bit now. Can't he be – well, I don't know – be released or something?'

Eveleen bit her lip and shook her head. 'No. He joined up and he's there for the duration now.'

'Can't he just – not go back?'

Now Eveleen was vehement. 'No. He'd be shot as a deserter.'

Mary gasped. 'Do they really do that?'

Eveleen nodded. 'Oh yes.'

Soberly they both watched as the two men walked across the yard and into the field.

'Today's been marvellous for him, Mam. For the first time since he came home he's begun to relax.'

'Why not stay a few days then? Till he has to go back?'

'Oh, we can't. I have to get back. The factory . . .'

Mary cast a wry glance at her daughter. 'Surely your husband's welfare comes before the factory,' she said primly.

'Well, yes. But Richard agreed to me becoming a director whilst he's away. I don't want to fail him.'

'You'll be failing him if you drag him back to the city, where he's obviously not quite so at ease. But if you don't want to stay,' there was accusation in her tone, 'then let Richard stay with us for a few days. Bridie's bed is always made up and aired in case she arrives back suddenly.'

Eveleen said, 'If he wants to, of course he can.'

But when the two men returned to the house and the idea was put to them, Richard shook his head sadly. 'I would love to have stayed, but I have to report back the day after tomorrow. We – we sail for France in three days' time.'

'So soon?' Eveleen cried and put her arms about him, steeling herself not to beg him to stay, to desert, as moments ago her mother had suggested.

As the light began to fade, they said goodbye, Sid profuse in his thanks. 'I wish all my mates could have had what you've given me.'

As they were driving home up the hill towards Bernby, Richard glanced up the driveway of Fairfield House. 'Is he still there?'

Carefully Eveleen said, 'I believe so.'

'The place looks neglected.'

'The whole estate is up for sale. Even the house. It seems Stephen has drunk and gambled away the family fortune,' Eveleen explained.

'Oh, so that's it. I thought he might have joined up.'

Eveleen gave a wry laugh. 'I don't think Stephen Dunsmore will go to war willingly.'

His voice was lower now and above the engine noise Eveleen only just caught her husband's words. 'Perhaps he's the sensible one.'

Thirty-Nine

'Do you know,' Eveleen was telling her father-in-law three days later, as they walked around the factory together, 'Sid is so much better. We brought him back on Sunday evening. It was like a miracle to see the change in him. Even Richard managed to relax a little, although he was only there a few hours.'

'Yes, Richard did mention it when he came to say goodbye before he left. I expect it was the peace and quiet. They say that on the south coast you can hear the gunfire from France. Imagine what it must be like to be there.'

Brinsley and Eveleen exchanged a sober look.

'I suppose,' she said thoughtfully, 'that, even though Sid was back home, somehow it's never completely quiet in the city, is it? Not even at night. Perhaps that's why he couldn't recover here.'

'Not like in the country,' Brinsley agreed. He was silent for a moment and then asked, 'Have you seen the wounded around the city? Those that are so badly injured they'll never go back to the war?'

Eveleen nodded and bit her lip to stop it trembling. 'Yes,' she said at last. 'It – it's frightening, isn't it?'

'One of our former employees came to see me yesterday. He's lost an arm and can't find work. Of course, he can't go back to his previous job as a twisthand.

282

Even he knows that. But I'm trying to find something for him to do. Any suggestions?'

'There might be something in the warehouse. I'll see what I can do.'

Brinsley nodded his thanks. 'Of course, what would do him good is a spell in the countryside.'

They both spoke at once. 'What we ought to do—' 'Couldn't we—?'

They laughed and then Brinsley continued. 'What we ought to do is buy a property somewhere in the countryside for the soldiers to go when they're discharged on medical grounds. A place to convalesce where they can heal physically and mentally. Perhaps they could even learn new skills that would help them to find employment of some kind. I'm a wealthy man, Eveleen. I'd like to do something like that. I'd feel I was doing my bit to help with the war.' He glanced at her and then looked away, adding softly, 'It – it would help me to think I was keeping Richard safe.'

Impulsively Eveleen reached out for his hand and held it. 'Oh, I knew you'd understand. That's just how I feel about the factory. If I – if we – can keep it going, if it survives, then so will Richard. I – I thought I was being silly.'

Brinsley shook his head. 'No, my dear, we're just clinging on to any kind of belief that will give us hope.'

They smiled at each other and walked on, but now Eveleen had a faraway look in her eyes as a plan began to form in her mind. 'Would it have to be near Nottingham?'

'Well, not too far away. It's our own boys we want to help.'

'What about Bernby? Is it too far away?'

'Bernby?' The older man looked startled. 'Where –

where your mother lives?' There was an unmistakable look of longing in his face for a brief moment as he asked gently, 'How is she? How is Mary?'

Eveleen touched his hand in an understanding gesture. 'She's well – and happy.'

Brinsley nodded but seemed as if he could not speak for a moment. Then he cleared his throat, murmured, 'I'm glad,' and then turned back to their previous topic of conversation. 'Why do you suggest Bernby?'

'I just might know of a place that would be perfect.' Eveleen's heart beat a little faster. Fairfield House, Stephen Dunsmore's home. She could not prevent the tinge of vindictive pleasure it would give her to become the owner of that house.

'Leave it with me,' she said. 'I'll find out if it's still for sale.'

'Eveleen, my dear, what a lovely surprise.' Stephen Dunsmore staggered across the floor of the morning room at Fairfield House. Although it was only eleven in the morning, he was already obviously drunk.

'Stephen,' she said calmly, drawing off her gloves and moving to stand in front of the roaring fire. She held out her hands to its warmth before turning to face him.

He lurched towards her. 'To what do I owe the pleashure.' He grinned foolishly, standing in front of her, swaying slightly.

She regarded him steadily. The handsome young man she had once believed she loved with all her heart was now a bloated, dissolute wreck. Stephen had been her first love and he had spurned her, turned his back on her when she most needed his love and protection. When her father had died, he had been instrumental in having them turned out of their tied farmhouse, Pear Tree Farm. Now her mother, along with Josh, owned that farm. That had been a small, but sweet, vengeance. Richard had made that possible, but today Eveleen was here to wreak her own revenge in a much bigger way.

She moved to pull the bell rope to summon the butler.

'Shall we have some tea?' she said, smiling sweetly at Stephen. He looked startled for a moment, then he grinned.

'Make yourshelf at home, lovely Eveleen.'

'Oh, I will,' she said and sat, uninvited, on the sofa. Stephen dropped down heavily beside her and leant towards her, the fumes of alcohol on his breath wafting into her face. 'Thish ish very nice.'

She looked at him fully then. The once smooth face was now blotched with ugly red patches. The bright blue eyes were now bloodshot and his hands trembled.

The butler entered and Eveleen glanced coolly at him. 'Tea and scones, if you please, Tomkins.'

The man glanced at Stephen, who nodded his approval. Eveleen smiled inwardly. The manservant, who had always treated her with disdain, was shortly in for a shock. As, indeed, was the man seated beside her. Even when the butler had closed the door, Eveleen waited, not wanting to be the first to open the conversation that must begin.

'I'll be leaving here soon,' Stephen said. 'I've had to sell the estate. This blasted war . . . it's been the ruin of us.'

'The only thing that's ruined the Dunsmore estate, Stephen, is you.'

'Eh?' Her words penetrated his befuddled state and drove home deeply. He pulled himself away from her, tried to stand, but found he could not. He sagged back against the cushions and protested weakly, 'What right have you to say that?'

'I have every right because it's the truth. Your grandfather built up this estate virtually from nothing. Incidentally, with a great deal of help from my grandfather, who was granted the tenancy of Pear Tree Farm. Your father carried on the good work, again,' she added pointedly, 'with no little help from my father. It wasn't until you – the third generation – were put in charge of running the estate, when your father became involved in politics, that it began to go downhill. You've drunk and gambled away your inheritance.'

'How dare you?' He scrambled to his feet and stood over her, his fists clenched. Slowly Eveleen rose too and faced him squarely. 'Oh, I dare, Stephen. I dare because I am now the owner of Fairfield House and all the surrounding land. In fact, I own all the Dunsmore estate.' Then she added scathingly, 'What's left of it.'

'You vindictive bitch!' Veins bulged in his neck and throbbed at his temple. For a moment, Eveleen thought he might have a seizure. 'How the hell did you manage that?'

'Agents working for me spoke to your father. He was only too glad to sell up, to salvage what was left of the estate before every last penny went across the bar or the gambling tables. I now own every square of ground, every brick, every stick of furniture.' In truth, it was Brinsley's money that had bought it, but he had insisted that the names on the deeds should be Richard and Eveleen Stokes.

'When the war's over, my dear,' he had said, 'it will be a wonderful country home for you. A marvellous place to bring up my grandson.'

Eveleen turned away from Stephen and went to stand

once more in front of the fire. In clear ringing tones, she said, 'You will vacate these premises by the end of the week, *Mr Dunsmore*.'

Eveleen stood in front of the white marble fireplace watching the man who had once treated her so callously, waiting for the surge of triumph, for the sweet satisfaction of revenge.

But it did not come. Instead her victory over him was hollow and shameful. She had used the wealth of her husband's family to make the purchase. Her outward reason had been to give help and succour to wounded veteran soldiers, but Eveleen knew that, deep down, her motives had not been completely unselfish, as were her father-in-law's.

Stephen lurched across the space between them, tripped on the carpet and almost fell against her. Regaining his balance, he stood in front of her and shook his fist in her face.

'You scheming, heartless bitch,' he spluttered again.

She faced him, outwardly calm. 'And weren't you just as heartless sixteen years ago when you had Jackson throw us out of the only home we had? At least you have a home to go to. I presume that your parents have a house in London. You're not exactly out on the streets, are you, Stephen?'

'I might as well be,' he mumbled, turning away from her as the truth of his situation began to sink in. 'I can hardly face my father now I've lost the family estate.'

There was silence between them, whilst he shambled around the room, touching objects, gazing at pictures and portraits of his family. It was a pathetic gesture and if he had hoped to appeal to Eveleen's softer side he almost succeeded. The sight of this once-proud, handsome man – a man she had idolized – stripped of all his possessions and reduced almost to poverty shook her resolve. But then he reeled towards the drinks cabinet, picked up a decanter and splashed liquid into a glass. He drank it in one gulp and poured another, which quickly followed the first. The spark of sympathy Eveleen had begun to feel died in that moment.

'I shall enlisht,' he slurred the words, even though by his bold statement he was trying to salvage a vestige of dignity. Then he pointed a shaking finger at her. 'You will be sending me to my death.'

Eveleen trembled inwardly, but she lifted her chin and defended herself stoutly. 'No, I'm not. I'm buying your house, not sending you to the Front.'

But deep inside the feeling of guilt would not go away.

Forty

As a small compensation for her actions, Eveleen kept on all the staff at Fairfield House, even Tomkins, the sour-faced butler, who had always treated her with such contempt. He was too old to find other employment. Besides, having worked at Fairfield House all his adult life, he would be useful, Eveleen thought. She smiled to herself. It would be punishment enough for him to think that she, the once scruffy daughter of the estate's stockman, was now his employer.

'Life will be very different for you all here,' she told them as she explained the plans she had for the estate and the house in particular. 'The land will still be farmed and Bill Morton will be the estate bailiff. But the house is to become a convalescent home for soldiers.'

They took her news stoically enough, glad still to have employment and she heard later that the estate workers had accepted the changes with the same thankfulness.

At Pear Tree Farm Mary could hardly take in the news. 'What would your father have thought? To see you as the owner of all this.' She waved her arm to encompass all the land around them. Then she glanced ironically at her daughter. 'And all of it without having to marry Master Stephen.'

Eveleen stood in the middle of the farmyard as she had done so many times in her life. Behind the house, to the east, the fields sloped down to the beck and then rose again on the other side towards the trees of Bernby Covert lining the hilltop. The place where, as a young, wilful and oh-so-innocent girl, she had run to meet Stephen, flinging herself into his arms, her face upturned to receive his passionate kisses. But the sweetness of that time had been soured by his selfish, callous attitude.

To the left on the brow of the hill she could see the spire of Bernby church, where her beloved father was buried. What, indeed, would he think to all this? She shuddered inwardly, knowing instinctively that he would not be proud of the way she had helped to bring about Stephen Dunsmore's downfall. He would not condone spiteful revenge. She even doubted he would have approved of the greater issue of the war, which had all of them caught up in a national fervour of retaliation.

She turned and walked to the gate to lean upon it and look westwards towards the ramparts of Belvoir Castle, standing proudly on the distant hill. 'But you would approve of the role that Fairfield House is going to play in the future wouldn't you, Dad?'

So clearly, in her mind's eye, she saw his face, and he was smiling at her.

'Can I go and nurse the soldiers, Auntie Evie? Oh, can I?'

Bridie had been back home in Nottingham for a few weeks, working in the inspection room and keeping Eveleen company. But when she heard of her aunt's plans she begged to be involved.

'I like caring for people,' she said. 'I really enjoyed

looking after Great-Gran. I think I'd like to be a nurse when I'm older. Wouldn't that be a good place to start?'

Eveleen regarded the girl standing in front of her. In the last few months Bridie had grown in stature and matured in character. Before her stood no longer a child, but a girl on the threshold of womanhood. At almost fifteen she had filled out, her figure was now nicely rounded and her face was captivating. Her eyes were her best feature. Dark blue, they shone with enthusiasm and determination.

'Please say you'll let me go.'

Eveleen sighed, reluctant to lose Bridie's company again, and yet there was sense in what the girl said.

'It might mean you living back at Pear Tree Farm again. I don't think your gran will agree to you sleeping in at Fairfield House.' She smiled. 'Not with all those soldiers there.'

Bridie laughed, but saw the truth in Eveleen's statement. 'Maybe it would be best, anyway. I can help a bit at home, around the farm.' Her face sobered as she added quietly, 'And I might be glad to get away from time to time. There'll be some dreadful sights.'

They were both silent, each thinking about the wounded they had seen around the streets of the city, some even reduced to begging.

'There'll be no shortage of takers for the places,' Eveleen murmured. Briskly she went on, 'I tell you what, you can sit in with me on the interviews next week. I'm appointing a matron first and after that all the nurses we shall need. The doctor at Bernby has already agreed to help. We'll go on Sunday and stay at Pear Tree Farm.'

'Why don't we stay at Fairfield House?' Bridie asked innocently.

Turning away so that she did not have to meet the girl's questioning gaze, Eveleen said swiftly, 'No, no, I don't want to stay there.'

There was great excitement at Fairfield House. The legalities had all been completed in a surprisingly short time. The new staff had all been appointed and had been in residence for three weeks in their sleeping quarters on the second floor, where domestic staff traditionally slept. But now there were nurses to accommodate as well. Even the attics had been cleared out and made into bedrooms. Bridie, too, was to sleep in with the other nurses. The house had been cleaned from attic to cellar and had been transformed from a shabby and neglected house into a comfortable hospital cum convalescent home. Now, at the beginning of August, Fairfield House was ready to receive its first patients.

Dulcie Barton, who had been appointed matron, took Brinsley and Eveleen on a tour of inspection. 'The dining room and, of course, the kitchens will remain as such and the drawing room will be the patients' sitting room and recreation room,' she explained, throwing open the door to each one. In the corner of the newly styled recreation room stood a gramophone with a huge horn and nearby was a piano, complete with sheet music for the patriotic songs of the day.

'Do you think they'll want that sort of music?' Eveleen said doubtfully. 'I would have thought they'd want to forget all about the war.'

'You'd be surprised,' Dulcie said. 'Some of them will still want to cling on to their happier memories, the camaraderie. They'll want to remember their pals.' She turned to Brinsley. 'It was very thoughtful of you to provide the piano and especially the gramophone. It will be a blessing for those who can't make their own entertainment. So many will be confined to bath chairs or blinded.'

Brinsley nodded and cleared his throat. 'Don't mention it, my dear, and if there's anything else you can think of, let me know.'

'The library, too, will stay just as it is,' Dulcie continued with the tour. 'It will be a peaceful, quiet room for them.'

'We must make sure there are some more suitable books,' Eveleen remarked. 'I can't imagine these dusty tomes being of interest to the soldiers.'

'The morning room,' the matron went on, 'has been changed into a room for staff use, whilst the study is now my office. The small sitting room, which I expect the "lady of the house" used, has been changed into a treatment room and a surgery for when the doctors visit. No operations will be done here, but we may well receive quite severe cases. Now upstairs.' She led the way up the wide staircase. 'On the first floor the large rooms have been turned into small dormitories holding three or four beds and the smaller rooms hold two or sometimes only a single bed. We shall use these for very sick patients who need constant attention and may disturb the others.'

The whole place still reeked of fresh paint, but all the rooms seemed light and airy. The new single beds with clean white sheets, plump pillows and grey blankets awaited their patients.

'I'm very impressed,' Brinsley said. 'And the grounds are lovely. They'll find peace here, Eveleen, my dear. I'm really proud of you and so will Richard be when he hears.'

Eveleen quelled the feeling of guilt, but she suspected that her perceptive husband would see through her ulterior motive. She was regretting now, not what she had done in acquiring a beautiful rest home for soldiers, but the way she had done it.

'I've some news for you too,' Brinsley was saying, oblivious to Eveleen's guilty feelings. 'As you know, some of my contacts are connected with the War Office and various other government departments. It seems, my dear, that the authorities would be only too pleased to treat our little venture as additional accommodation for the military hospitals closest to us.' He shook his head sadly. 'It seems they are under a great deal of pressure.'

'But – but we wanted to take the wounded from the city streets. Those who are not bad enough to be hospitalized but who are not fit enough to find work.'

'I know, I know, my dear. And we will, we will. But the seriously injured must come first. Don't you agree?'

'I – suppose so, yes,'

'So,' Brinsley went on, 'the good thing is that we have already appointed properly qualified staff and the local doctor has agreed to visit daily, calling in colleagues when necessary. And now . . .' Brinsley put his hand on her arm and suddenly his tone was diffident and there was longing in his face. 'Do you think, I might be permitted to see you mother whilst I'm here?'

Bridie had found her vocation. There was only one cloud on her horizon, which was never far away from her thoughts: Andrew. She still believed fervently that he was alive somewhere and that one day he would come home to her. In the meantime she threw herself into her work at Fairfield House.

Dulcie Barton was a single woman in her forties. She had a pleasant face with calm, grey eyes, but when she smiled her whole face seemed to light up. Her wonderful smile had heartened many a desperately ill patient and given them hope. She had devoted her life to nursing and, whilst she was a strict disciplinarian and kept a necessary remoteness between herself and the nurses under her, she was nevertheless friendly and always approachable. She had taken a particular liking to Bridie, for she saw in the girl a genuine gift for caring for others and she took it upon herself to encourage her to look upon nursing as a career.

Dulcie was adept at handling the nurses with a firm yet understanding hand. So many of them were grieving privately for loved ones snatched from them by this dreadful war, but with her guidance these young women left their personal tragedies behind when they put on their nursing uniforms.

'You can wear a uniform just like the qualified nurses, Bridie,' Dulcie had explained to her. 'A long white apron with a bib, and a neat frilled cap, but your dress will have to be a different colour to show that you are a trainee. Now, I think red and white striped cotton would be most suitable. It will be different from the colours the others wear.' She smiled. 'At least here, in a private establishment, we've been able to choose our own colour scheme.'

The sisters, who had been appointed each wore a navy blue dress with a white triangular shaped headdress, starched white collar and cuffs. The nurses wore dark grey dresses and both the sisters and the nurses wore long white aprons. Only Dulcie as matron wore the navy blue dress with no apron.

'Bridie won't accept Andrew's death,' Eveleen had explained to Miss Barton in confidence. 'I don't think she will until the war is over and – and he still doesn't come home.'

She felt the matron watching her. There was such a depth of understanding in Dulcie Barton's eyes, she experienced life's tragedies every day. Her voice was low and soothing, like soft velvet. 'It's very hard for a girl to come to terms with death and to accept that it can happen to someone she loves. What is the relationship between them?'

Eveleen explained. 'I think Andrew thought of her as his daughter, but as for Bridie . . .' She sighed and smiled sadly. 'She idolized him and *not* as a father.'

'I see.' Miss Barton was thoughtful and Eveleen felt she was watching her, almost calculating. 'Mrs Stokes, may I be frank with you?'

'Of course.'

'You already speak of Andrew in the past tense.'

Eveleen nodded.

Gently the matron went on. 'You have obviously accepted the War Office's assumption that he has been killed.'

Again Eveleen agreed silently.

'But Bridie has not.'

'She just refuses to. She's adamant he's alive. She – she says she would know, would feel it . . .'

Miss Barton nodded. 'You may think this strange, Mrs Stokes, but it might be best to allow her to think that, for the present. Oh, I don't mean to encourage it, to foster false hope, but just to let her come to the truth – if indeed it is the truth – in her own time and in her own way. At the moment – and this may sound a little callous to you – it may be in her best interests to allow her to believe he is still alive.'

All her life Eveleen had always faced up to the truth of a situation and been strong enough to deal with it. Even the things she had done wrong and regretted. Now she frowned, unable to comprehend that anything but the truth, however cruel, was best.

Dulcie went on. 'Bridie is going to be caring for young men, many not much older than herself. She will be called upon to carry out very – intimate tasks for them in the course of that nursing. Many men,' Dulcie smiled, 'whatever their age, imagine themselves in love with their nurses.'

Understanding began to dawn in Eveleen. She had wondered why most of the nurses that the matron had chosen were older rather than younger.

'So,' the matron continued, 'it might be safer – for all concerned – if Bridie's heart is engaged elsewhere. I know it might sound unfeeling, calculating perhaps,' Dulcie hurried on, 'but, believe me, I'm thinking of Bridie as much as my patients.'

Eveleen nodded. 'I do see your point.'

'This is just between you and me?' Dulcie asked once more.

'Of course.'

Forty-One

Richard's letters told of a quiet time in his corner of the war.

> *The days in the trenches are more 'restful' than the designated rest days when we do such a lot of digging. The weather is lovely at the moment – the trenches dry and it's very quiet. We have even had time to clean our boots and polish our buttons. I suppose this is because we are about six hundred yards away from the enemy front line here. We patrol our frontage at night and snatch sleep in the day.*

It was not so quiet on other war fronts. On 1 July a combined British and French offensive had begun near the Somme. By the end of the first day, nearly twenty thousand British soldiers had been massacred by enemy artillery and machine guns and twice as many had been wounded. The more serious casualties were patched up in field hospitals and then sent home to Blighty. By August, when Fairfield House opened, some of the wounded from the Somme had found their way to the Midlands and a few were brought to Bernby.

It was the first time Bridie had seen raw flesh wounds, men blinded by shrapnel, their eyes swathed in bandages. Some had terrible internal injuries, others missing limbs. And then there were those who suffered the effects of the terrible gas. But Bridie kept her feelings severely in check and, taking her cue from the older nurses, greeted them all with a welcoming smile and a cheery, bantering word. There was one lad – not much older than Bridie – who was crying out in pain as he was carried up the stairs and into one of the smaller rooms with only two beds.

'Put me in wi' 'im. I'll look after 'im,' an older man with both legs broken and a wound in his thigh said to an orderly.

'You'll 'ave to go where you'm put, soldier,' the orderly said cheerfully.

'But 'ee's me mate. We've bin together from since we joined up. I look out for 'im, see'

Bridie, walking behind the two stretchers being carried, said quietly. 'It'll be all right. Put them together . . .' She hurried ahead and opened the door. 'In here. Room Number Four. If Sister Jones wants them moved, we can do it later.'

'Ta, luv.' The older man grinned at her as he was carried in through the door and deposited on the nearest bed. He grimaced but made no sound of complaint and at once looked across to where his companion was still groaning and curling himself into a ball. Bridie stood beside the boy, biting her lip. She was anxious to help, but did not know how.

'Shot in the guts, he is,' the older man told her. 'Gets terrible pain, Nurse.'

Despite the awful sight, Bridie felt a thrill run through her. It was the first time a patient had called her 'Nurse'. It made her feel important and special.

Now she was really needed.

*

By nightfall all the patients were settled and the house relatively quiet, though from Room Number Four the sound of the young soldier's sobbing echoed along the landing.

'Sister says would you like to be moved out into another room?' Bridie whispered to the older man, whose name she learned from the board at the bottom of the bed was Jabez Field. 'I told her I didn't think you would, but she said I was to ask you.'

'No, no. I want to stay with 'im. Been in the trenches together, we 'ave. I ain't leavin' him now.'

Bridie smiled. 'No, I thought not.'

'What's your name, then?' he asked as Bridie handed him a cup of hot milk.

'Singleton.'

'Nurse Singleton. I'll remember that.'

Again, she felt the thrill at the title but said, 'I'm not a real nurse, only a trainee. You'd better just call me Singleton.'

The man slurped the hot milk, leaving a white line along his upper lip. He shook his head. 'No. If you're looking after us, in my eyes you're a nurse.'

Bridie beamed at him as she picked up the other cup of milk and went across to the other bed. The poor boy was writhing and moaning, his hands trembling.

'If you can't hold the cup, I'll help you to drink it.'

She held the cup to his lips, but even then he could not keep still enough to drink and almost knocked the cup from her hand, spilling some of the liquid.

'S-sorry,' he stammered.

'Doesn't matter,' Bridie said, mopping up the spill. 'Let's try something else.' She picked up the spoon from

300

the saucer and gently spooned the milk, little by little, into his mouth. He spluttered a little at first, but then began to swallow and gradually he became a little calmer, though tears were still running down his face.

'I want me mam,' he whispered. 'I want to see me mam again. Just once, before . . .'

Bridie took hold of his hand. 'You'll see her very soon. We'll get you better and—'

'I ain't goin' to get better.'

Bridie opened her mouth to protest, but out of the corner of her eye she noticed a movement and turned to see Field shaking his head sadly and biting hard down on his lower lip. The girl swallowed. Gently she squeezed the boy's hand and murmured, 'I – I'll see what I can do.'

She settled him against his pillows and pulled the covers up to his chin. The boy was obviously exhausted, but the pain would not let him sleep. She moved to the end of the bed and looked at the name written on the board there.

Herbert Hyde. Bridie frowned. There was something familiar about the name and yet she just couldn't think what it was. 'Herbert Hyde,' she murmured aloud.

'We allus called 'im Bertie,' Field said, his voice husky with emotion.

And then she knew. This was Bertie, Mrs Hyde's son, who had volunteered aged only sixteen.

Bridie left the room and hurried down the stairs, going straight to the matron's office. Moments later she was standing in front of the desk, facing Dulcie.

'What is it, Singleton?'

'It's the young soldier in Room Four, Matron. I know him. At least, I know his mother. She works at Auntie Evie's factory. In the inspection room. He – he's asking for her. Says he wants to see her . . .' She gulped. 'One last time.'

Dulcie stared at Bridie, then asked sharply. 'Did he say that?'

Bridie nodded. 'I tried to tell him he would get better and would soon be going home, but – but he said he knew he wasn't going to get better.' She gazed at the matron with wide, solemn eyes. 'Isn't he, Matron?'

Dulcie sighed and glanced down at the papers on her desk, straightened them unnecessarily and then looked up to meet Bridie's gaze. Her voice was gentle as she said, 'No, my dear, he isn't. His internal wounds are so severe that the surgeons can do nothing. And now he has an infection.'

'Then – then can we get his mother out here to see him? Auntie Evie would bring her in the motor. I know she would. Please send word to her, Matron.'

Dulcie sighed and, in the privacy of her office, her tone softened. 'Bridie, my dear, your aunt can't transport the relatives of all the soldiers we have out here to see them.'

'But the Hyde family are special. They work for us. For the Reckitt and Stokes factory, I mean. Mrs Hyde and her daughters. Even Bertie himself worked there for a couple of weeks before he enlisted. And if he – if he's . . .' She stopped as her voice threatened to break. She did not want to shed tears in front of the matron, indeed in front of any of the staff. She was determined to show them that she could keep her feelings under strict control whilst on duty.

Dulcie was still shaking her head. 'I don't like to ask her. It puts me in rather a difficult position.'

'Then please will you give me permission to ask her?' Bridie suggested.

'As long as you make sure Mrs Stokes understands
you are asking her in a private capacity and that it is
not an official request from me, then yes.'

'Thank you, Matron.'

At that moment, Fred Martin was driving the motor car
through Nottingham's dark streets, taking Eveleen to
her home.

'I ought to walk home, Fred. It's not far. We didn't
ought to be wasting petrol.'

'It's not a waste. You're not walking the streets alone
at this time of night, Evie,' Fred said firmly. He was
always respectful towards the woman who was now his
employer, but he had known her from the time she had
first arrived in the city, homeless and looking for work.
'Poor beggars,' he muttered almost beneath his breath
as a wounded soldier, leaning heavily on a crutch, stood
beneath a gas lamp. The man cast a baleful glare at the
motor and then spat into the gutter. Eveleen knew it
was because she was riding by in a fine vehicle, when
he, who had fought for his country, was reduced to
begging in the street.

She glanced back at the man out of the rear window.
There was something familiar. Even in the half-light she
had seen something in the set of his shoulders, the way
his head thrust forward, his bald head shining in the
light from the lamp . . .

'Stop, Fred, stop!'

Almost before the motor car had drawn to a halt,
Eveleen had opened the door and was scrambling out. 'I
know who that is. I'm sure I do.'

'Wait for me, then. Don't go on yer own—'

But Eveleen was already running down the street

towards the man, who had turned and was trying to limp away as fast as he could.

'Wait! Wait!' Eveleen called, whilst behind her Fred levered himself out of the motor and hurried after her.

She caught up with the man and touched his arm. 'Please wait. Let me help you.'

The man turned away, trying to hide his face and mumbling, 'Leave me be. I don't want your help.'

Fred reached them, panting hard, as Eveleen said clearly, 'Maybe you don't want my help, Bob Porter, but you look as if you need it.'

'Porter?' Fred repeated, straining through the dimly lit street to see for himself. 'Bob Porter?'

The man whirled around suddenly, throwing off Eveleen's hand and almost losing his own balance. 'Let me be. Let me rot. It's what you wanted, ain't it?'

Eveleen gasped, almost as shocked as if he had struck her. 'No, Bob, it isn't. It was your own stubbornness. No-one asked you to leave Reckitt and Stokes and certainly no-one asked you to enlist.'

'Well, I did, and now I've lost me leg I'll never work again.'

'We'll see about that,' Eveleen said firmly. 'In the meantime, you're coming home with me and tomorrow Fred will drive you out to Fairfield House.'

'Eveleen, I don't think—' Fred began, but she interrupted, 'Take his other arm, Fred, and let's get him into the car.'

'I ain't . . .' Bob began, but then suddenly he sagged against Fred and would have fallen if Fred hadn't held him upright. 'Sorry,' he mumbled. 'I ain't eaten since yesterday.'

Above his head, Eveleen and Fred exchanged a look in the fitful gaslight, and now Fred Martin argued no more.

Forty-Two

'Let me take him to our place, Eveleen,' Fred suggested
in a low voice after they had helped Bob into the back
of the motor car. 'My Win'll look after him and
tomorrow I'll take him to Fairfield House, like you say.'

'No, he's coming home with me. Cook and Smithers
are still with me.' She smiled in the darkness and put
her hand on Fred's arm. 'I'll be quite safe,' she whispered and Fred had the grace to chuckle. 'By the look of
the poor beggar, he hasn't the strength to try owt. Well,
if you're sure?'

'I am.'

At Eveleen's home Fred helped Bob into the house,
whilst Eveleen hurried to rouse Cook and Smithers.
Only minutes later Bob was sitting at the end of the
long table in the dining room, ravenously devouring the
dinner that Cook had kept hot for Eveleen's return from
work.

'He has more need of it than me,' Eveleen had insisted
when the cook demurred. She turned to Fred. 'You go
on home now, Fred. Win will be wondering what's
happened to you. We can manage. I'm just going to
make up a bed in the spare room.'

In a low voice Fred said, 'He's been sleeping rough,
Eveleen. He's not fit to . . .'

'Fred Martin, I never thought to hear such words
from you.' Eveleen wagged her finger in his face. Whilst

she kept her tone amused and almost teasing, there was nevertheless a hint of censure in her voice.

Fred looked ashamed. 'Oh, I know he's fought for his country and all, but—'

'But nothing, Fred.'

'At least let me stay and help you get him upstairs. Smithers is getting on a bit. I doubt he'll manage him.'

'All right.'

'And I might be able to get him to wash an' all,' Fred murmured and Eveleen stifled her laughter, at once seeing right through Fred Martin's ploy.

Half an hour later there was a lot of noise, splashing and swearing, coming from the bathroom.

'Mind me bloody stump. That butcher of a doctor at the field hospital just hacked it off. Could've saved it, I reckon.'

'Well, you'll get it seen to where you're going tomorrow.'

'Where am I going?'

The sound of their voices was lowered and Eveleen only caught brief snatches of the conversation as Fred explained about Fairfield House. Then, once more, Bob Porter's voice was raised in resentment. 'Oh, trust 'er to be playing the Lady Bountiful. 'Er and 'er do-gooding.'

'Let me just tell you summat, mate, afore you go shooting yer mouth off.' Fred defended them. 'They're doing a grand job, 'er and Mr Stokes. They didn't have to bother to set up a home for soldiers and he certainly didn't have to use his own money to do it.'

'Oh aye, money earned off the backs of silly buggers like us who've sweated for him for years.'

She heard another splash and then Fred's voice. 'Well, you can stay there till the water freezes, for all I care, if that's all the gratitude you can show. I wish we'd left you on the streets. I really do.'

There was silence and Eveleen, who had been unable to resist creeping closer to the door to listen, held her breath. There was a low mumble of words, which she could not make out, before Fred said, 'Aye, well, that's better. Come on, let's get you out of there. You've fair soaked me with all your splashing. By, you're an awk'ard bugger, Bob Porter. Still, you allus were.'

Eveleen smiled as she hurried downstairs and by the time she came back up with a cup of hot milk and plate of biscuits, Bob Porter was sitting up in the bed she had made up for him, dressed in an old nightshirt of Richard's. His bald head was pink and shining and his face – and presumably the rest of his body too – was scrubbed clean.

Eveleen set the tray at the side of him and stood looking down at him. 'Is there anything else I can get you, Bob?'

The man shook his head.

'Then I'll say goodnight. Come along, Fred. Thank you for all your help, but I'm sure Bob's tired now.'

As she ushered Fred from the room and was about to close the door, she heard Bob say, 'Missis.'

She pushed the door wider again. 'Yes, Bob?'

'Thanks,' was all he said, but for Eveleen, who knew how much even that one word had cost Bob Porter, it was more than enough.

When Fred arrived the following morning to take Bob to Fairfield House Eveleen said, 'I've decided to come with you. I'm a bit worried they might not have room.

If they don't, I'll have to smile nicely at my mother and Josh again.'

'Oho, you're on a loser there. Josh and Bob Porter never did see eye to eye when they worked together.'

'Things are a little different now,' Eveleen said quietly. 'Josh isn't the sort to harbour grudges, especially when he sees him in this state.'

Fred smiled at her. 'Neither are you, Evie, are you? Here you are, trying to help the man who almost brought your factory to its knees single-handed.'

She sighed. 'Trouble was, Fred, even then I could see his side of the argument, although I couldn't agree with it.'

'Aye well, that's as maybe.' He thought for a moment and then added, 'I must say this for him, he did always seem to have the interests of the workers at heart. I mean, what he did wasn't just for his own ends.'

'No, it wasn't. He resigned on a point of principle, didn't he?'

'Aye, an' look where he's ended up because of it. On the streets, begging for a living.'

'Not any more. He could still do the job of factory manager with only one leg. So, when he's well enough, I intend to offer him his old job back.'

'You do?'

Eveleen nodded but then smiled ruefully. 'But whether he'll take it is another matter.'

They laughed together.

As the motor came to a halt outside the front door of Fairfield House, Bridie came running down the steps.

'Oh, Auntie Evie? Have you brought Mrs Hyde? How did you know? Oh!' The hope on her face died as she saw the man sitting on the back seat. Then her eyes widened as she recognized him.

Eveleen was climbing down. 'I've brought Mr Porter here as a patient. That is, if you've a bed. If not—'

'You'll have to see Matron,' Bridie said promptly and then grasped Eveleen's hands. 'Oh, Auntie Evie, Bertie Hyde's here. You know, Mrs Hyde's son. Does she know he's here? She must come to see him. He's – he's . . .' She swallowed painfully, controlled her excited outburst and added, 'Very, very ill.'

Eveleen at once realized the situation. 'I'll bring her back myself this afternoon, Bridie.'

Bridie hugged her aunt. 'I knew you would. Thank you.'

There was one bed spare in the house. Sadly a patient had died in the night and it had been Bridie's job to strip the bed and put fresh sheets on it. It was not her place to tell her aunt that there might well be a place for Bob Porter, but as soon as the matron had given permission, Bridie helped him up the stairs and into the room he was to share with three others.

'Could I have a word with you, Mrs Stokes?' Dulcie asked.

'I'll wait in the motor, Eveleen,' Fred murmured.

Dulcie smiled at him. 'They're serving elevenses in the recreation room, if you'd like to join the patients. I'm sure they'd love to see a new face.'

'Right you are, Matron.'

As Fred left them, Dulcie drew Eveleen into her office and motioned for her to take a seat.

'Is everything all right? It's not about Bridie, is it?'

Dulcie smiled. 'No, no, she's doing really well. And on the whole all is well here. It's just that we're running awfully short of bandages. It sounds silly, I know, but I hadn't realized we would get so many post-operative cases and patients with such dreadful wounds that won't heal. Do you think Mr Stokes might be able to help, with all his contacts?'

Immediately into Eveleen mind's eye came the picture of the rolls and rolls of three-inch-wide lace stored at the factory, orders that had been cancelled at the beginning of the war.

She smiled. 'I might have the very thing for you.' Swiftly she explained to Dulcie. 'Would it be useful?'

'It'd be wonderful. We've plenty of dressings to go on the wounds themselves, you see. It's just the bandages to hold the dressings in place that we're short of.'

'I'll bring them this afternoon.'

'Oh, there's no need—' Dulcie began and then she saw the look on Eveleen's face and understood. 'Ah, Bridie has told you. You're bringing Mrs Hyde.'

Wordlessly Eveleen nodded.

'Luke, could we make bandages on our curtain-making machines?'

'Bandages?' For a moment, Luke Manning appeared nonplussed, but even as she watched him, Eveleen could see the idea begin to take shape in his mind. 'Bandages,' he murmured again and then added, 'I don't see why not, if we had the right yarn to do it. You'd get the homeworkers to cut the fabric into strips and finish them off, would you?'

Eveleen nodded. 'Or the women in the inspection room. I mean to talk the idea over with Mr Stokes, of course, but I needed to know from you if we could do it first.'

'I'll give it a try myself, Eveleen, and show you.' She felt him watching her, shaking his head.

'What? What's the matter?'

'Nothing, lass. It's just you. You're a little marvel, you are. Always coming up with new ideas, to say nothing of helping Bob Porter – and after all he tried to do to you.'

Solemnly Eveleen said, 'He's hurt, Luke. You could say destroyed. I mean to help him more, if I can.'

'You mean you'd have him back here?'

She nodded. 'I know it would mean you stepping down again, but . . .' She was interrupted by Luke letting out a loud guffaw of laughter.

'Don't you worry about that. I'd be only too glad to hand back the reins to Bob. He's welcome to 'em. I don't reckon too much to being a manager. It's a lot of aggravation, if you ask me.'

'Of course, I don't know if he'd want to come back. He's lost his leg, you know.'

Shocked, Luke stared at her. 'Oh, poor bugger.'

The fact that he forgot himself enough to swear in front of her spoke volumes to Eveleen.

Forty-Three

'You know, I'm so very proud of you, my dear,' Brinsley said, as they sat together in Eveleen's office at the factory. 'Everything you've achieved. Finding new work for the factory and warehouse and even sending workers out to your uncle to keep his little place going. How are things at Flawford, by the way?'

'Fine.' Eveleen smiled. 'I visit as often as I can, which I have to admit isn't as often as I'd like. The women we sent have fitted in very well and my grandmother and my uncle are well cared for now by Mrs Turner, who lives in the village. Bridie arranged all that before she left.'

'Ah yes, Bridie.' Brinsley smiled at the thought of the girl. 'She's a born nurse. You see, my dear, what I mean. Not only did you set up the home for the care of all those soldiers, but you found little Bridie her life's work.'

'That was your idea too. The home, I mean. You made all the financial outlay.'

Brinsley shrugged off her praise. 'It's the very least I could do. Besides, it helps me to feel I'm doing my bit towards the war.' His voice shook a little as he added, 'Helping to keep Richard safe.' He cleared his throat and said more strongly, 'But it was you who made it all happen. He will be so proud of you too, when he comes home.'

Eveleen echoed the words in her mind like a fervent prayer. When he comes home.

At Fairfield House Mrs Hyde sat by her son's bed, holding his hand. She had spoken to Dulcie and had been told the sad truth. Her son had only days, possibly hours, to live. In the bed opposite Field wiped his eyes and could find no words of comfort to say to the mother of his wartime companion.

Bridie's help was more practical. She brought cups of tea, even a meal, but the woman hardly touched anything. The nurses did their best to keep the boy comfortable, but at three o'clock in the morning, with his mother at his side and Bridie wiping his brow, Bertie died. Briefly Mrs Hyde closed her eyes and wept silent tears. Her grief, so dignified and controlled, was more heart-rending than if she had ranted and raved. She kissed her son's forehead and stroked his cheek and then allowed Bridie to lead her up the attic stairs to Bridie's own bed.

'You lie down and rest now,' the girl told her gently but firmly. 'I'm on duty all night, so my bed's not needed.'

Without arguing, Mrs Hyde lay back against the pillows and closed her eyes. 'I shan't sleep. I'll just rest awhile, but I shan't . . .' Her voice faded and already the woman had fallen into an exhausted sleep. Gently Bridie stroked the grey hair back from Mrs Hyde's face and covered her with a blanket.

Downstairs, Bridie went in search of the sister on night duty to tell her of Bertie's death. Only much, much later when she went to her now empty room to sleep during the following day, did Bridie allow herself to shed tears for the poor young boy.

Relentlessly the war continued abroad. At times Richard's letters to Bridie were quite jovial.

> *We decided that everything was too quiet and we ought to liven things up a little by annoying the enemy. The artillery began by strafing his billets, but of course he wasn't going to stand for this and he soon let us know it. Then one of our companies carried out a raid. While this was going on, I was on duty in the support line and the enemy started to strafe the line sending over 5.9s three at a time. We could even see the flash of his guns and he was sending them over about every half minute. It's the waiting for them to arrive that's the worst. It seems ages, though it can only be seconds. Then there's an explosion and you wait again and each explosion seems to get nearer and nearer as he traverses from left to right and back again. It played havoc with the support line, but somehow he missed our little spot.*
>
> *By the way, you'll never guess what we call the sixty-pounders – toffee apples!!*

At home the war had its effect too. More and more women were employed in what were traditionally classed as men's jobs. They were now a familiar sight behind shop counters, working as railway porters, as bus and tram conductresses, postwomen and even policewomen. But most of all they nursed the sick and wounded coming home from the carnage of the Front.

Just before Christmas Richard wrote,

It's raining every day. The trenches are knee-deep in water and caving in, so consequently there is very little shelter and we're wet through all the time. Luckily we can all swim!

From his letters, it seemed as if his life consisted of digging, carrying rations, and spending a few days in the trenches only to return to fatigues once more. Now he gave even Bridie very little news of the shelling and the machine-gun fire. He seemed to concentrate only on the conditions rather than the fighting, the constant noise when under bombardment and the ever-present fear that even the bravest must surely feel.

In late January and early February, he told them,

The cold is dreadful. Eggs and tins of milk are frozen solid and even the tea, brought up in large Thermos-type flasks and hot when poured, has ice on the surface within three or four minutes. Today, as I was cutting up a loaf of bread, each slice sparkled like diamonds . . .

'He never asks about what's going on here, does he?' Eveleen remarked, as once again she and Bridie exchanged their most recent letters, sitting together in the library at Fairfield House to read them. 'I send him long, newsy letters about everything that's happening here. About the factory and – oh, everything. But all he seems to want to talk about is how his feet are.'

'It's understandable,' Bridie murmured. 'We've got patients here with trench foot. It's horrible.'

Towards the end of March, Richard came home again on leave. He had changed again. This time he did not sit, lost in thought. The apathetic look in his eyes had been replaced by a cold and heartless attitude. He visited the factory, striding through the machine shop and then the warehouse, climbing to each floor. He found fault with everything. The girls working in the inspection room were too young. They were idle and their work was not up to standard. The women working in the machine shops were spending too much time chattering and not helping the twisthands properly.

'The place is untidy, too. Get someone to clean it up,' he barked at Eveleen.

'How could you?' she demanded when they returned home. 'You humiliated me in front of the workers. How do you expect me to earn their respect if they hear you talking to me like that?'

Richard, his eyes steely, shrugged his shoulders. 'I only spoke the truth. If you don't keep a tight rein on the running of things, it'll get out of hand. The youngsters will take advantage of leniency. It's human nature. They're not to blame – you are. You should never have antagonized Bob Porter. At least he knew how to run the factory.'

Eveleen bit her lip, unsure how to handle this man, who seemed to have changed from the loving, caring husband she knew into an unfeeling stranger. She went to him, put her hands on his chest and, standing on tiptoe, kissed his mouth.

'I'm sorry. I'll try to do better. Your father's much better these days. Perhaps I can persuade him to come to the factory more often.'

'It shouldn't be necessary. You should be able to handle it. We've given you the authority,' he reminded her harshly. 'You're a director now.'

Later, as they sat together after dinner, she tried to

confide in him about buying Fairfield House. 'Your father agreed. He thought it was an excellent idea.'

'It is,' Richard said. He gave her a tight smile. 'And you got your revenge at last on young Dunsmore, I take it.' There was sarcasm in his tone, something she had never heard from her husband before.

Eveleen felt the colour rising in her face. He had seen straight through her motives, as she had feared he would. 'I feel badly about that now. Especially since he said I was forcing him to enlist.'

'I shouldn't let that worry you,' Richard said with callous nonchalance. 'It was high time he did his bit. He'd have been called up sooner or later anyway.'

His words, which should have brought her some measure of comfort, did not.

Later, in bed, there was no problem of impotency this time, but he took her roughly, selfishly, with no tenderness, leaving Eveleen sleepless far into the night and shedding silent tears into her pillow.

On 6 April, just after Richard had returned to France, the news came that America had entered the war.

'Now we'll show 'em,' Josh beamed. 'Now we've got them on our side, we can't lose. It'll all be over soon now, mi duck.'

But it was not until June that the first American troops stepped onto French soil to be given a heroes' welcome.

At the end of July came Passchendaele and the newspapers were once more full of daily reports of the carnage and loss of life.

And now there were no more letters from Richard.

'I don't think he's there,' Eveleen told Bridie. 'But unless he writes I've no idea where he is. He – he could have been moved,' she whispered. 'He could be there.'

They stared at each other, neither knowing what to say to give comfort to the other.

There was nothing they could say.

Towards the end of August the matron sent for Bridie. Fearing the worst, the girl hurried to her office and only relaxed when she realized the news was not about her uncle.

'We have a new patient arriving tomorrow and I want you to take special care of him. He's a bit of a mystery.' Dulcie looked down at the sheet of paper in front of her. 'He's lost his memory and no-one else seems to know who he is. The authorities have tried to piece together what might have happened. He was picked up off the south coast and at first it was thought he could be a spy. He's been in hospital: under guard, I might add. But now they seem fairly satisfied that he must be a survivor from a British ship that was sunk in the Channel about the time he was found. His uniform – if he'd had one – was ruined by sea water and there was no identification on him.' She smiled up at Bridie. 'But his accent, they say, is pure Lincolnshire. A very difficult one for a foreign spy to impersonate.'

Bridie grinned at the matron. 'Ya right there, missis,' she quipped, deliberately accentuating her own dialect.

'However,' Dulcie went on, 'they're sending him here, hoping that in familiar surroundings his memory might improve. And this is where you come in. They want a careful watch kept on him. They want someone to monitor him closely, to see if he writes letters, sends messages, receives visitors, and so on. At the same time that person must try to draw him out, try – very subtly – to prod his memory. The doctors think that, with rest and care, there is no reason why he shouldn't recover fully.' Dulcie looked up at her. 'I would like you to undertake this, Bridie. You're not only becoming a very good nurse, but you're bright and intelligent. And you'll be able to talk to him – as none of us can – in his own language. Use all the Lincolnshire sayings. You know?'

Bridie's eyes shone and she nodded, unable to speak for excitement. She was thrilled to be trusted with such an undertaking.

'Is he injured in any other way?' she asked.

Dulcie consulted the patient's notes again and shook her head. 'No, no other physical injury apart from the effects of being in the sea for some hours.' She looked up again. 'There is another way of looking at it, of course, and the authorities are fully aware of that too.'

'What's that?'

'That he's swinging the lead to get out of being sent back to the war when he's physically fit again. If that is the case, then it is your duty to catch him out, Bridie. That's the hard part. Can you do it?'

Bridie was silent for a moment, pondering now the full extent of what was expected of her. Slowly she said, 'I didn't agree with the war from the very first. I didn't want Andrew, or Uncle Richard, to volunteer but they did and now I feel as if I'm doing my bit too.' She stared straight into Dulcie's kind and knowledgeable eyes. 'It – it might sound silly, but I feel that if I do everything I can that's asked of me then – then I'm helping to bring them safely home. I've always believed that Andrew is still alive. That – like this sailor – he's lost his memory or – or been taken prisoner.'

Dulcie reached out and touched her in a rare moment of an outward show of emotion. 'My dear girl, I do understand. And, yes, you *could* be right.' She laid great emphasis on the word 'could'. 'And I hope fervently that you are. It does happen. We are going to see that for ourselves. But, my dear,' her tone was soft and gentle, 'it is a rare occurrence.'

'I know.' Bridie nodded. 'But until someone can give me proof that Andrew is dead, I will go on believing – and hoping – that he is alive.'

'And if he isn't? If he really isn't? What then?'

The girl raised her chin defiantly. 'Then I'll cope with it.'

Dulcie patted her hand. 'Good girl,' she said briskly and turned the conversation back to plans for their expected patient. 'We'll put him in that smaller bedroom over the hallway. There's only room for two beds in there and we'll have to pick his roommate very carefully.'

'There's Joe Horton. He's from Grantham.'

The home, though originally for Nottingham soldiers, also took in a few whose homes were in the neighbourhood. Grantham was only a few miles away and Fairfield House was an ideal location for their families to visit. As for the soldiers' families from Nottingham, Brinsley Stokes had organized omnibus outings on Saturdays and Sundays to the home.

'We can't have folks like poor Mrs Hyde not being able to visit their boys,' he said.

Dulcie nodded now in answer to Bridie's suggestion. 'That's a good idea. Ask Joe if he minds being moved. Tell him only that we think he could help this poor man who has lost his memory.'

'We can't tell him everything, can we?'

'No, we can't. There's only you and I who know the full story.'

The mysterious patient arrived the following day. He had been given a new sailor's uniform – his own had been spoilt by sea water. His cap – which might have borne the name of his ship – had been missing, so there had been no clue there.

He was of medium height and thin. He had brown eyes and close-cropped brown hair. A full beard hid the lower part of his face and the visible skin was weather-beaten to a deep tan. And, Bridie suffered a pang at the realization, he was about Andrew's age.

'This is your room,' she announced, flinging open the door and trying hard to put all thoughts of Andrew out of her mind and to concentrate on helping the new-comer. 'And this is Joe. He'll be sharing the room with you.' She turned towards the man already sitting in a chair by the window. 'Joe, this is . . .' She turned back, as if innocently, to say, 'I'm sorry, I don't know your name.'

'Neither do I, lass,' the man said, sitting on the edge of the single bed and bouncing on it a little as if to test its comfort. Then he tapped the side of his head with his forefinger. 'Can't remember owt.'

'So,' Bridie asked, 'what would you like us to call you?'

The man shrugged and said morosely, 'Dunno. Some bright spark christened me "Nelson" at the last hospital. Clever devil.'

Bridie could see from his expression that the nick-name hadn't pleased him.

'Well, how about you think of a name and that's what we'll call you here,' she suggested.

321

'Surname an' all?'

Bridie spread her hands. 'Whatever you like. Doesn't matter. Just one name will do. Just so we have something to call you.'

'Bloody nuisance, more than likely.'

'Oi.' Joe spoke up from his chair by the window for the first time. 'None o' that sort o' language in 'ere, mate. Not in front of this lass any road, else you an' me is going to fall out afore we've even got to know each other.'

The newcomer seemed to take no notice of Joe. He was staring at Bridie now, his glance taking in her young, lithe body, then coming back to rest on her face. He frowned slightly. 'What's your name?'

'Bridie. Bridie Singleton.'

The frown deepened and he repeated her name. Then he shrugged. 'No, it dun't mean owt to me. Pity. I thought for a minute you looked familiar.'

He closed his eyes and lay back, swinging his feet up to stretch out full length on the bed. Bridie stood a moment, watching him. His breathing became regular and she could see that he had immediately fallen asleep. She turned, smiled at Joe and put her fingers to her lips. 'He's had a long journey,' she whispered. 'Let him rest.'

Joe nodded and turned back to looking out of the window.

The newcomer did not mix easily with the rest of the patients, not even with Joe, his room mate. It was not that he was unfriendly or snobbish, merely that he had little to talk about. No memories of his previous life, of his family, of his home, not even of his recent experiences.

'Maybe that's a blessing in disguise,' Dulcie remarked in one of their private conversations when Bridie reported on the progress of her special patient – or rather the lack of it, 'if he's lost all his shipmates. Does he talk at all?'

'He asks a lot of questions, but the others just get sick of answering him all the time. They don't want to be reminded of what happened to them at the Front. And they don't want to talk too much about their families. It just reminds them that they're still separated from them, even those that have regular visitors.'

'Is he asking anything that the authorities might regard as suspicious?'

'I'm not sure I know what that is,' Bridie admitted.

'Well, if he wants details of what regiment, battalion, company the men belonged to. If he wants detailed information of where they were on the front line. The name of their commanding officer. That sort of detail.'

Bridie shook her head. 'I don't think so. Yes, he asks how they got wounded and I suppose he might ask where it happened, but as far as I can tell he doesn't do anything with the information.' She ticked off the points on her fingers. 'He doesn't have any visitors. He doesn't write letters or receive any. How can he? He doesn't know who he is. Or at least he's not supposed to know.'

'Have you any doubts about his loss of memory.'

Bridie frowned. 'I've never known anyone before who'd lost their memory, so it's difficult.'

'Well, I have to admit that, in all my nursing life, neither have I,' Dulcie was quick to say too.

'But if he is having us on,' Bridie said slowly, 'then all I can say is he's a very good actor.'

Forty-Four

'I've had enough of him,' Joe Horton said after only two weeks of sharing a room with Walter, as the mysterious patient had decided he wanted to be called. 'He dun't give a damn about owt. He's forever flirting with the nurses.' He cast a shrewd glance at Bridie. 'Dun't you be teken in by him, lass, will ya?'

Bridie laughed as she plumped Joe's pillows. 'I won't.'

'There's a few here,' the man said gently, 'who'd like you to be their girl. And there's one or two ya'd be safe wi', but not him.'

'I'm quite safe. I'm waiting for someone to come back, you see.'

Joe glanced at her but said nothing. He'd heard the rumour that this poor lass's feller had been posted missing but that she refused to believe it.

'Anyway,' Joe went on, 'this Walter, or whatever his name is, he's a devil with the girls, if you ask me.'

'Now how would you know that, Corporal Horton?' Bridie asked him archly. 'And you a married man.'

Joe chuckled. 'I've 'ad me moments in me time, lass, I've 'ad me moments. Afore I met the wife, that is,' he added comically. 'I'd sooner be back in the trenches than face my Milly if she found out I'd been flirting with you nurses.'

'What do you make of him then?' She couldn't tell

Joe her real reason for asking, but perhaps, unwittingly, he could help her in the task she had been given. 'Do you think he still remembers nothing?'

Joe shrugged. 'Far as I can tell, though there was something the other day.'

'What?'

'Well, we went for a walk. Him not being hurt – physically, that is – and me with only me shoulder.'

Only his shoulder! Bridie thought. Poor Joe's shoulder had been badly wounded. There was still a piece of shrapnel embedded somewhere in it, yet here he was making light of his injury.

'And?' Bridie prompted.

Joe's forehead furrowed. 'It was funny. He seemed to know his way about the place. "We'll go up the hill to the village," he said. Now how did he know there was a village up the hill?'

'You can see the church at the top. Perhaps he just realized that where there's a church there must be a village.'

'Aye, I suppose so. But then, coming back, he brought me back through the fields, through the covert and down to the beck. He seemed to know his way about, if you know what I mean. Mind you, then he stood near the water gazing down at it for so long I got a bit worried.'

'Why?'

'I thought – well, I thought he might be thinking of doing summat. You know?'

For a moment Bridie stared at him, then understanding dawned. 'You – you don't mean you thought he might try to – to drown himself?'

'It crossed me mind, lass. I've heard of some of the lads who've come back from the war, maimed for life, haven't been able to face up to the future. Sad, ain't it, to think they survived the trenches and then are driven to doing that?'

Bridie nodded. 'But you don't think Walter's like that, do you?'

'No,' Joe said firmly now. 'Know why lass?' When Bridie shook her head, he said drily, 'Cos he thinks too much of hissen, that's why.'

In the September of 1917 Bridie was sixteen. She thought that the most that might be done to celebrate her birthday would be tea at Pear Tree Farm or perhaps a day in Nottingham with her aunt – if Eveleen could spare the time. So she was disappointed that by the time she awoke on the morning of the birthday, no invitation from anyone had been forthcoming.

There were no cards or letters in the morning post for her either, but she plastered a cheery smile on her face and went about her work, trying to forget what day it was.

At three-thirty in the afternoon she was surprised to see all the patients disappearing into the sitting room that had been turned into the patients' recreation room. Those who could walk were helping those who could not.

'What's going on?' Bridie asked Nurse Collier.

'Oh, I don't know,' the nurse said vaguely. 'I expect they're having a meeting or something. Look, could you do me a huge favour? There's some sheets need mangling in the wash-house in the yard. The girl who comes from the village didn't show up this morning. Be an angel and do them for us.'

Bridie sighed inwardly, but replied, 'Of course. Do you want them hanging out on the line?'

'Er – well, yes, whatever you like. It's a bit late in the day, but they might dry.'

'I'll ask Jack to put the line up.' Jack Morton, Micky's younger brother, now worked at Fairfield House.

'I don't think he's here,' came the swift reply. 'Just mangle them for now, Bridie. We'll hang 'em out in the morning.'

Bridie shrugged and went down the stone passages towards the back door. As she passed the kitchen, the door slammed shut and beyond it she heard the two young kitchenmaids giggling.

She was tempted to open it and poke her head round to see what they were doing, but then she heard the cook's sharp voice. 'Behave, you two. She'll hear you.'

Bridie smiled. Matron's authority even extended into the cook's domain.

She had finished mangling the sheets and, with little else that needed her immediate attention, she slipped out of the gate from the yard leading into the field and walked down the slope towards the beck, rippling and gurgling in the warm September sunshine. She sat down on a boulder at the edge of the water and slipped off her boots and stockings. Pulling her skirts up to her knees, she dangled her feet in the rushing water. It was cold, but the feel of it soothed her aching feet. She had been rushing around since early morning without a moment to herself. It was such a lovely, peaceful place, she thought, her gaze drifting over the fields. She should bring Walter to this spot. Perhaps its tranquillity would help him. Then she remembered what Joe had told her.

Perhaps it would be safer to keep poor Walter away. It was a strange coincidence, she thought, that the name the man had chosen to be called was the same as Bridie's grandfather, who had died here in the beck. She didn't want to risk something similar happening to him.

She sighed. Here, in the stillness, there was nothing now to keep her mind off what day it was.

Tears filled her eyes. Every year until he had volunteered Andrew had visited her on the Saturday nearest to her birthday. He had taken her on a trip into Grantham, treating her to cream cakes in a fancy restaurant, before taking her to the photographic studio to have her birthday picture taken. True to her promise to him, on her half-day off the previous week, Bridie had gone into Grantham to have her photograph taken. It lay now in the chest of drawers in her bedroom, along with the other two taken in the years since he had gone away. It was almost three years since she had last seen Andrew. Three years in which she had grown up and three photographs that he hadn't even seen.

The view before her blurred as she remembered what he had done with all the earlier photographs. When she could, Bridie promised herself, she would take the new ones to Flawford and stand them on the mantelpiece in Andrew's cottage for him to find when he came home from the war. At the thought, her heart overflowed with love for him. She lifted her face to the sky and closed her eyes, praying as fervently as if she were kneeling in her uncle's chapel.

'Bring him home safely. Oh, please let him be alive.'

'So, this is where you're hiding.'

The voice behind her startled her so that she gave a little cry and turned to see Micky Morton grinning down at her.

'What are you doing here? Shouldn't you be at work?'

He squatted on his haunches beside her. 'I got the afternoon off, seeing as what day it is.'

She gaped at him. 'What day it is?' she repeated stupidly.

'Yeah. Don't tell me you've forgotten your own birthday?'

She glanced away and looked down, tearing at the grass growing out of the cracks in the rock where she was sitting. 'No, I hadn't. But I thought everyone else had.' She smiled up at him. 'But at least you remembered. Thanks, Micky.'

He stood up and held out his hand. 'Come on, then.'

'Why?'

'You'll see.'

She shrugged, but did as he asked. Pulling on her stockings and her boots, she gave him her hand and he hauled her to her feet.

'Race you back,' he said and began to run.

'Hey, that's not fair. You can run faster than me anyway . . .'

Panting, they arrived back in the yard. He turned to look at her. 'The matron wants to see you. You'd better go and tidy your hair.' His glance took in the dishevelled uniform that she had worn since early morning. 'And put your Sunday best dress on.'

'Whatever for?' she asked again.

'Don't argue. Just do it.' He gave her a gentle push. 'Go on. Just for me.'

Muttering to herself, she went up the backstairs to the tiny bedroom she shared with one of the other younger nurses. As she splashed her face in the bowl on the washstand and smoothed back her hair – she hadn't time to replait it – she wondered why Micky wanted her to put on her Sunday frock. Then a thought suddenly occurred to her. Perhaps word had come from Pear Tree Farm. Perhaps she was going out to tea after all.

But as she went down to the hall, Micky was waiting for her and he led her towards the patients' sitting room. He flung open the door and the singing that erupted caused Bridie's mouth to drop open.

'Happy birthday to you, Happy birthday to you . . .' the whole gathering trilled.

All the patients, all the staff and her gran and Josh were there. And standing in front of them all with her arms stretched wide and a broad smile on her face, was her aunt Eveleen.

'Happy birthday, darling. Come and open all your cards and presents and then we'll have tea. The kitchen staff have been so busy. Cook has even made you a cake.' She laughed. 'But they had such a job to keep it secret.'

Cook, large and round and rosy-cheeked, waddled forward. 'She's all over the place, this one. You never know where she's going to pop up next. We had a fright earlier when she went past the kitchen. I was putting the finishing touches to the cake. The girls only just managed to shut the door in time. And then I thought she'd hear them giggling.'

Bridie laughed. 'Oh, so that was what it was all about.' It had not been the matron they had been afraid of catching them. It had been her.

A veritable feast was laid out on a table set at the side of the room. A buffet so that everyone could help themselves. In the centre stood a huge iced cake decorated with pink sugar roses and the words 'Happy 16th Birthday, Bridie' inscribed upon it.

Tears came to Bridie's eyes and she clasped her hands. 'Oh, Cook, it's beautiful.'

The cook beamed happily as everyone murmured their agreement with Bridie's praise. Then Bridie opened her cards and presents, and there seemed to be something from everyone. Little gifts, some handmade, from every member of the staff. But what touched her most were the presents from the patients. There was even a lace-edged handkerchief from Walter.

'You must come and meet him, Auntie Evie,' she whispered, explaining swiftly that they still didn't know who the man was.

She led Eveleen across the room to where Walter was sitting in front of the window, gazing out down the garden. 'He doesn't mix a lot with the other patients. I think it's because he can't hold a proper conversation with anyone. You know, he can't talk about his family, where he comes from and that, like everyone else does. Isn't it sad? He seems so lonely.'

They fell silent as they reached him and Bridie touched him on the shoulder. 'Walter? Thank you so much for the lovely handkerchief.'

He turned, his brown eyes smiling up at her. 'S'all right,' he said in his usual offhand manner. 'One of the nurses said I had to give you something. She bought it.'

'Oh.' Her disappointment was acute. She wondered how many other patients had been coerced into giving her presents. Eveleen moved and put her arm about her shoulders. She must have realized what the girl was feeling because she whispered in her ear. 'He's the only one they had to do that for. Matron told me. He couldn't seem to take in what was happening.'

Bridie nodded, but the lump in her throat refused to go away.

They stood in front of the man looking down at him. He looked up again, glancing from one to the other and then his gaze came to rest on Eveleen. She stared back at him and her heart seemed to miss a beat.

Dark brown eyes, so like her own, stared back at her. The rich, chestnut hair, cut very short, was now flecked with tiny strands of white. His beard hid his wide, generous mouth, yet she would have known him any-where. Her eyes widened and her hand fluttered to her mouth as a startled gasp escaped her lips. She knew Bridie was glancing from one to the other, looking puzzled.

Deep in the man's eyes, the vacant look began to dispel. Memory forced its way into his damaged mind and fought for recognition.

His lips moved and, as he stretched out his hand towards her, they heard his tortured whisper. 'Evie?'

Forty-Five

Behind them the room had fallen strangely silent as everyone became aware of the unfolding drama.

'Jimmy, oh, Jimmy!' Eveleen cried.

Bridie glanced up and saw Mary weaving her way around the furniture towards them. Realization came swiftly to her. This was Mary's long-lost son. This was Jimmy Hardcastle. And this, then, was her father. Deep inside her she felt a trembling, yet, as she saw the look on Mary's face, Bridie pushed aside her own feelings and moved at once to meet her grandmother, suddenly afraid of what the shock might do to the older woman. 'Gran, wait a minute.'

'Leave me be, girl,' Mary snapped, pushing her away. 'I want to know what's going on.'

Bridie watched as Mary stood before the man whom everyone present knew only as Walter. Then she too cried out, 'Jimmy. Oh, my boy. My baby! Oh, Jimmy.' She fell to her knees beside his chair, clasping his hand and kissing it fervently, tears coursing down her cheek. A look of distaste came into the man's eyes and he tried to pull himself free.

'Gerroff.'

Then Evie began to laugh and cry, almost with a tinge of hysteria. 'Oh, it is you, Jimmy Hardcastle. Now I know it really is.'

Helplessly Bridie looked round for the matron. She

felt suddenly very much out of her depth, worried for her aunt, her grandmother, but most of all for the patient.

Dulcie was hurrying towards them. 'Now, now,' came her soothing voice. 'What's happened?'

'My – my aunt,' Bridie stammered, 'seems to know him.' Could it really be true? she was thinking now.

Eveleen turned, wiping the tears from her eyes, but her voice was steadier now as she said, 'Oh, I know him all right. It's the prodigal son. This is my brother and, Bridie, your father.'

The room erupted then into noise, the news spreading like a stubble fire out of control, whilst Bridie stared down at the man she had longed to meet the whole of her young life. And yet at this very moment, if the good Lord had given her the choice, she would far rather it had been Andrew Burns who had come back into her life than this stranger. He was looking her up and down, appraising her. But there was no warmth in the look, no fatherly interest. She felt suddenly nauseous and took a step back, sick at heart. She felt Josh's comforting arm around her shoulders.

'It's all right, mi duck. Bit of a shock for you an' all. But it'll be all right.'

Bridie, not trusting herself to speak, nodded, yet she could not drag her gaze away from Walter. Jimmy, as she and everyone else must now think of him. Dad or Father, she supposed that was what she should call him, but that would take some getting used to after a lifetime of absence.

Mary was still fussing over him, stroking his hair, kissing his hand and repeating over and over again, 'Oh, Jimmy, my Jimmy.'

Eveleen and Bridie were forgotten, even Josh. Mary

had her son home again and for the moment no-one else in the world existed.

Standing up at last, Mary said, 'He's coming home with me. Back to Pear Tree Farm. I'll look after him now. There's nothing like a mother's love.'

'I'm afraid that won't be possible, Mrs Carpenter,' Dulcie said at once, still hovering nearby. 'Walter . . .' she glanced at the patient. 'I'm sorry, Jimmy, is still under our authority. I cannot possibly release him into your care without the express permission of . . .'

'Nonsense,' Mary said briskly. 'He's coming home with me.'

'No, Mam. Matron is right. He has to stay here . . .' As Mary opened her mouth to protest, Eveleen added swiftly, 'At least until we see what the doctor thinks.'

Now Josh moved to his wife's side and took her arm. 'Mary, love, we'll get a room ready for him at home. I'm sure they'll let him come home very soon, but we must do it properly.'

'This had nothing to do with you, Josh Carpenter,' Mary snapped, shaking off his touch. 'He's not your son.'

She could not have hurt the big, kindly man more if she had struck him across the face.

'Mam!' 'Gran!' Shocked, Eveleen and Bridie spoke out together.

Mutinously Mary glared at them. 'Well, he isn't. He hasn't any children of his own.'

'Not now,' Josh said quietly, his eyes full of ill-concealed pain. 'I had a son once though, didn't I?'

Mary had the grace to look ashamed as she muttered, 'I forgot.'

Years before, Eveleen remembered, Josh had told her he had been married briefly as a young man, but his wife had died in childbirth and their child along with her. She glanced at her own mother in disgust, yet Mary's behaviour was no surprise – at least not to Eveleen. Jimmy had always been their mother's favourite and the years between had made no difference, it seemed.

'And besides . . .' Josh was smiling again now, brushing aside Mary's tactless remark with his usual forgiving nature, 'Bridie has been like my own.' Now he turned to Mary again and, despite his gentleness towards her, there was a note of firmness in his tone. 'Of course, Jimmy must come home to us but only when proper approval has been given.'

'But—' Mary opened her mouth to protest, but Josh had his answer ready. 'We don't want to get Jimmy in trouble with the authorities, now do we, love? They can be very severe if they think there's even a hint of desertion.'

'Desertion? How could they possibly think that? He's sick. Injured. He couldn't remember who he was, not until he saw Evie.'

'He's physically quite fit again now, Mrs Carpenter,' Dulcie put in. 'It was only because of his amnesia that he could not be sent back on active service.' She looked down at Jimmy. 'But if his memory is returning . . .' She left the rest of the sentence unspoken, but her meaning was clear to them all.

Eveleen watched her brother as he pulled his hand away from his mother's clinging grasp. 'I'm staying here. I don't know you,' he said. 'I know Evie. She's me sister. But I don't know anyone else.' He looked up at Dulcie a hangdog expression in his eyes. 'Honest, Matron. I can't remember her . . .' He jabbed a finger at Mary then towards Josh. 'Or him.' Then he glared accusingly at Bridie. 'And I certainly don't remember having a daughter.'

'How could you?' Eveleen said, deliberately making no effort to keep her voice low. No-one had left the room; they were all far too interested in the revelations about the unknown sailor. And now it seemed family quarrels from years ago were surfacing. This was real life drama, far better than the pictures. 'Seeing as you ran away to sea before she was even born,' Eveleen went on, with more than a hint of sarcasm in her tone. 'And since then you've made no effort to find out how Rebecca was or whether you had a son or a daughter.'

Jimmy shook his head. 'Rebecca? I dun't remember no Rebecca.'

'You remember me, lad, don't you? Mr Carpenter from the Reckitt and Stokes factory in Nottingham?'

Jimmy shrugged. 'I've never been to Nottingham.'

Eveleen watched him, her eyebrow arched in disbelief. Then suddenly she leant close to her brother so that only those standing nearby heard her words.

'You might be able to fool everyone at the home here. Even your own daughter. But I know you too well, Jimmy. You're going to have to be very careful you don't get caught out. Very careful indeed.'

Forty-Six

'How could you be so cruel, Eveleen? But, then, I should have known. You and Jimmy never got on, did you?'

Having driven Josh and Mary down the lane back to Pear Tree Farm, Eveleen was obliged to listen to her mother's tirade. They had almost had to drag Mary away from Jimmy.

'I'll make you a cup of tea, mi duck, before you go back,' Josh said to Eveleen and disappeared into the scullery, whilst mother and daughter faced each other across the hearth. Eveleen sighed inwardly, but decided that honesty was the best policy.

'Mam, I've always loved my brother, but he was never the easiest person to deal with. You spoilt him.'

'Well, your dad spoilt you,' Mary countered. 'Jimmy couldn't do anything right for him and you couldn't do anything wrong.'

Eveleen felt the familiar stab of loss as she thought of her kindly, easy-going father.

'If you hadn't been deceiving us in meeting Stephen Dunsmore, your father might still be with us. And all our troubles that followed his death can be laid at your door, Eveleen.'

The old feelings of guilt she thought long buried came flooding back. Whilst she would never quite forgive herself, it came as a shock that her mother still harboured bitterness against her. She had thought, when her mother had found new happiness with Josh, that Mary had forgiven her. Now, it seemed, she had not.

'Mind you . . .' Mary glanced at her. 'You've got your revenge on Master Dunsmore now, haven't you? Good and proper.'

Eveleen swallowed. 'I only bought his house—'

'Oh, you did more than that,' Mary rounded on her. 'You disgraced him in his parents' eyes. He couldn't face them, so he went to enlist. And now he's dead.'

Eveleen felt as if her heart stopped and then began to thud loudly and painfully. Her voice was a strangled whisper. 'What?'

'Oh, aye. Word came last week.'

Eveleen closed her eyes. More guilt was being heaped upon her head. And this was a burden she would carry for ever.

But now Mary was dragging her back to think of Jimmy. 'We had to go to Flawford when your precious Stephen Dunsmore turned us out of our home, didn't we? We had nowhere else to go.'

That Eveleen could not deny. She sighed and sank into a chair beside the table. Heavily she said, 'So it's my fault that Jimmy got Rebecca pregnant and then refused to marry her?'

'They'd never even have met if it hadn't been for you.'

'But they did and he seduced a young and innocent girl. That was hardly my doing. And he had no need to run away. I couldn't have *made* him marry her.'

'Huh! You always got your own way, Eveleen.' Her mother glared at her and Eveleen realized Mary was now referring to the day's events. 'You still do. Jimmy should be at home here. With me.'

Eveleen was thoughtful and then she played her

trump card. 'He's safer there, Mam. If he leaves the home, the authorities will come looking for him. They wouldn't believe his amnesia story. He'd be back aboard ship in a trice.'

Josh, carrying a tea tray into the room, caught Eveleen's remarks.

'She's right, mi duck. He's best where he is.' He glanced at Eveleen and murmured in a low voice so that only she could hear, 'For several reasons.'

Eveleen understood. The last thing Josh would want would be Jimmy living at Pear Tree Farm.

Mary began to weep, sobbing into her handkerchief. 'You're all against me. I want my Jimmy home. Nobody knows how I've missed him all these years. You don't want me to be happy.'

Josh hurried to her side and put his arms around her. 'Mary, love, that's not true and you know it. But Eveleen's right, Jimmy is safer there. And you can visit him every day.'

Mary looked up, her tears drying. 'Can I?'

'Of course you can. Every afternoon between two and three. I asked the matron.'

'An hour? Is that all? One hour a day? Well, she can forget that. I'll go whenever I want to and stay as long as I want. So there.'

Eveleen and Josh glanced helplessly at each other, but said no more.

'What do you think you're staring at?' Jimmy challenged Bridie as she stood in front of him.

'You,' she said simply. 'I've dreamed about meeting my father all my life. Imagined how it would be . . .'

There was a catch in her voice, for her dream had been nothing like the disappointing reality. 'And now I have.'

'Huh! You don't want to believe everything Evie tells you.'

Bridie regarded him, her head on one side. 'How is it you can remember your sister, but not your mother?'

His eyes were suddenly wary. 'Dunno. I suppose me memory's coming back a bit patchy.'

'Do you remember my mother, Rebecca?'

Jimmy glanced away and shook his head, then he laughed. 'But I've had so many girls from here to Timbuktu. Mebbe I've got bastards all round the world.'

Bridie bit her lip, but raised her head defiantly. 'Well, I expect you'll soon be getting to know your mother all over again.'

He eyed her suspiciously. 'What do you mean?'

Bridie grinned. 'If I know my gran, she'll be here every minute of the day visiting you.'

He frowned and stared out of the window. 'Reckon I'd be better off back at sea,' he murmured.

He was not the sort of father Bridie had longed for. However, as the days passed she could began to understand how a young, impressionable girl, starved of affection as she now guessed her mother had been in the strict regime of Harry Singleton's home, could have succumbed to Jimmy Hardcastle's saucy charm. He still flirted with the younger nurses, though now never with her. He avoided his mother's daily visits as often as he could, pleading headaches, sickness – anything to evade her. All the staff had been briefed by the matron that Mary was not allowed to go upstairs to his room.

'We have to afford our patients the right of privacy. If there is someone they don't wish to see, then we must respect that. Whilst I have every sympathy with Mrs Carpenter,' Dulcie went on, speaking now in confidence to her trusted staff, 'I have to admit that she is visiting a little too often. One can also see his side.'

When just the two of them remained in the office, Bridie asked Dulcie, 'Do you believe that he really has lost his memory?'

Dulcie considered before answering. 'I think he did, initially, yes. But how much it's coming back now, I don't think he's telling us. I think he's playing a very clever game.' Then she smiled. 'I'm glad I don't have to be responsible for deciding whether he's fit to return to active service. That's Dr Roper's job, thank goodness.'

'Supposing you were, would you say he was fit?'

'Not yet, no. But I do think he's recovering much quicker than he's letting us know. But there's one thing, Bridie. At least we can be pretty sure now that he's not a spy.'

They laughed together, but then the merriment left the girl's face as sadness clouded her eyes. 'No, I'm sure he isn't. But he's not quite what I dreamed my father would be, either.'

Forty-Seven

The weeks passed towards another Christmas and still there was no word from Richard. Eveleen veered between crippling fear that he was dead and determined optimism that, because she had heard nothing from the War Office, he must be still alive.

'It'll just be that his letters aren't getting through.' Bridie tried to comfort her aunt. 'You'll see. There'll be some simple explanation.'

Their news of the war now came only from newspaper reports. In October the Italian army had suffered a crushing defeat, the enemy gaining many miles of ground. The Allies feared that Russia, with its own terrible internal problems, would pull out of the war when talks began in December between the Bolshevik government and Germany. By March 1918 an uneasy peace existed between the two and, as the Allies had predicted, a great number of the enemy troops that had been deployed in the east were now released to join the war on the Western Front. By the end of that month these reinforcements had helped to deliver a catastrophic blow to the Allied lines in France.

'It must be chaos out there,' Bridie said, scanning the newspaper that Eveleen had brought on her weekly visit to Fairfield House. 'No wonder letters aren't getting through. Let's just hope that he's getting ours.'

They both still wrote each week, but had no way of

knowing whether their letters ever reached their destination.

'How's Jimmy?' Eveleen asked, bravely trying to change the subject.

Bridie pulled a comical expression. 'Much the same. He's not giving much away.' She shrugged. 'I can't guess what he remembers and what he doesn't. You're still the only person he'll admit to recognizing.'

'Not Mam?'

Bridie shook her head. 'Much to Gran's disappointment.'

'What about him going home? To Pear Tree Farm?'

'The doctor thought that it might be a good idea. He thinks that the familiar surroundings might help his memory, but my father flatly refused to go. Gran's tried everything. Wheedling, crying – everything, but the more she pleads, the more he resists.'

Normally what Bridie was telling her would have made Eveleen chuckle, but laughter was difficult when her heart was so heavy with dread. But she tried to hide her fears and summoned a weak smile. 'Poor Mam,' she murmured.

In April Sir Douglas Haig, the British Commander-in-Chief, sent a personal message to the army: *'Every position must be held to the last man: there must be no retirement. With our backs to the wall and believing in the justice of our cause each one of us must fight on to the end.'*

Reading this, Eveleen gave way to tears. It was her darkest time, for now all hope seemed lost for both the war and her beloved husband. Her feeling of hopelessness was reflected by everyone around her. The veterans at Fairfield House were sombre, their cheerful banter silenced. Some of the nurses with relatives at the Front were red-eyed and even Josh shook his head in sadness at the futility of almost four years of carnage, which now threatened to end in defeat. In the city more and more wounded flooded into the hospitals and Brinsley was once more grey-faced and anxious.

Only Bridie, the youngest amongst them, held onto her faith. 'They'll come home. Both of them,' she said, confidently. 'You'll see.'

'Oh, Bridie,' Eveleen mourned, 'if only I could believe you.'

It wasn't until July that news came that the tide of war had begun to turn in favour of the Allies. Suddenly there was cause for renewed hope.

Then came the day when Eveleen received news. She drove recklessly to Fairfield House and ran up the steps. 'Bridie, Bridie, where are you? He's coming home. He's safe. Richard's coming home.'

He had been wounded in the leg and the injury was too severe for him to recover in a field hospital. It was a 'Blighty' wound.

Bridie hugged Eveleen, tears streaming down both their faces. 'Oh, Auntie Evie. He's safe. With a bit of luck, he'll never have to go back. When will he be home?'

Eveleen wiped her eyes, laughing and crying at the same time. 'Next week.'

They both met the train that brought him to Nottingham station and watched as he was carried off on a stretcher, along with other wounded, and put straight into an ambulance. Eveleen and Bridie were not even allowed near enough to him to say 'Hello'.

Bridie grasped the arm of one of the attendants. 'Where are you taking him?'

'The hospital. He's still in the army, you know. He

can't just come home when he decides. Besides . . .' The man glanced over his shoulder towards where Richard lay, silently staring up at nothing in particular. He had not even raised his head to look around for them, though surely he must have known they would come to meet him, Bridie thought.

The attendant was speaking again. 'Poor feller's shell-shocked, I reckon, as well as his injury.'

'Shell-shocked?' Eveleen frowned. 'What do you mean?'

'Putting it bluntly, ma'am, he's not sure whether he's on this earth or the next. I've got to go now, but go to the hospital later. They'll tell you more.'

'Can't he come to Fairfield House?' Bridie asked. 'We're as good as a hospital.'

'Dunno about that, miss. We've got our orders.'

The man turned away, leaving a mesmerized Eveleen staring after him with Bridie standing beside her. Young though she was, she knew better than Eveleen what being shell-shocked really meant. She had seen so many cases of it already at Fairfield House.

Much later they were allowed to see him. They sat on either side of the bed, speaking to him but getting no response. Eveleen kissed his forehead, but he did not look at her, did not even seem to notice.

'Be careful what you say in front of him,' Bridie had warned her earlier. 'Matron at the home says we can't be sure they don't understand everything that's going on around them even though they can't, or don't want to, take part.'

Eveleen had nodded, biting her lip to hold back the tears. 'What are we going to do?'

Bridie considered. 'If they'll let us, I think he should go home or at least to Fairfield House.'

'Oh no, if he's going anywhere, then it's home with me.'

'Will you be able to manage?' Bridie asked her candidly.

'Of course,' Eveleen almost snapped and stood up. Now she kissed her husband's forehead tenderly and turned away.

Bridie too kissed his cheek and whispered, 'You'll soon be well again, Uncle Richard. You're home now. You're safe.'

His eyes flickered and he turned his head to look at her, a ghost of a smile on his mouth, but he did not speak.

Watching, Eveleen was surprised at the shaft of jealousy that seared through her. Richard had responded to Bridie, but not to her, his own wife.

Two weeks later Richard was brought home. Eveleen had everything ready and had even engaged a girl to sit with him during the day whilst she had to be at the factory. Brinsley visited his son daily, though Richard's mother's visits were spasmodic.

'I can't bear to see him like that.' Sophia shuddered. 'When will he be better?'

'We don't know,' Eveleen said and added harshly, 'but his family can all help by being with him and talking to him.'

It was a deliberate reproach to her mother-in-law and Eveleen could see that Sophia recognized it as such, but still she was not prepared to let her sick son interfere with her comfortable existence. She stood up. 'Keep me informed,' she said curtly and swept out.

Brinsley, however, was very different. He could not do enough to help his son. 'Do you think this is the right place for him, Eveleen? I mean, he doesn't seem to be making much progress. He just lies there all day, staring at the ceiling. I haven't heard him speak yet. Have you?'

Eveleen shook her head. They were sitting together in the dining room over a dinner that neither of them felt like eating.

Brinsley reached out and covered her hand with his own. 'My dear, do you think he should go into a nursing home where he could be cared for properly?'

Eveleen's voice was high-pitched. 'You think I'm not spending enough time with him. That I'm concentrating too much on work and not on him.' She felt guilty enough about the fact already, but to have her father-in-law point it out hurt indescribably.

'No, no, my dear girl, I'm not criticizing you. You've done a wonderful job at the factory. But for you the whole business might have gone under. You've kept it going, kept people in jobs. Even kept jobs open for the men to come back to, but—'

'But I'm still neglecting my husband now,' Eveleen finished, her voice flat. She gripped his hand and whispered hoarsely, 'You don't need to tell me. I know.'

'I didn't say that,' Brinsley insisted gently. 'To be honest . . .' He paused, as if knowing what he was going to say would hurt her even more. 'I think he needs expert help that neither you nor I can give him. With the best will in the world we're not medically trained, my dear.'

'No.' Eveleen was forced to agree. Her thoughts turned to Bridie. The girl was not yet a fully fledged nurse, but even she had known how to reach Richard far better than Eveleen had. Eveleen knew it was the sensible thing to do, the right thing to do, but she had always been in charge of her family. It had been Eveleen who had taken the reins after the death of her father, she who had moved the family to Flawford and then later to Nottingham, with the extra burden of an unmarried mother-to-be and coming baby too. Whether everything she had done had been right, she could not say. All she knew now was that she was not ready to relinquish control yet.

'A little longer,' she pleaded with Brinsley. 'Let's try a little longer.'

A week later Bridie came to Nottingham to visit.

'You go to work,' she urged her aunt. 'And you can give the girl a day off. I'll look after him.'

Eveleen eyed her doubtfully. It was not that she questioned Bridie's capability. Far from it. She was being unreasonable, she knew, but she could not help feeling jealous that her niece was far more knowledgeable and efficient at dealing with Richard than she was. She tried, weakly, to protest. 'But it's your day off from nursing. Don't you want to go into the city? See the shops?'

Bridie shook her head. 'I'd sooner stay here with Uncle Richard.'

Eveleen sighed inwardly, knowing herself defeated. 'I'll see you this evening, then. I'll drive you back.'

'No need.' Bridie smiled. 'I've got tomorrow off too. I can stay overnight.' Her smiled broadened. 'If you'll have me.'

Eveleen felt a sudden rush of affection for the girl and guilty for her irrational jealousy. She hugged her. 'Of course. It'll be lovely to have you here.'

When Eveleen returned home that evening, Bridie had wrought a miracle. Richard was out of bed, fully dressed and sitting near the window overlooking the street.

'Go and sit with him, Auntie Eveleen. I must change for dinner,' Bridie urged. 'Just talk to him. Tell him about your day.'

Eveleen felt strangely tense as she sat beside him. This was her beloved husband, the man she had lived with, had been so close to and yet he was a stranger to her now. As Bridie had suggested, Eveleen began to talk to him, haltingly at first, but then the words began to spill out and she was chattering maybe too much in her nervousness. Suddenly she stopped mid-sentence. He wasn't listening. He was staring out of the window, yet he didn't seem to be seeing the street below and the people. As she fell silent, he turned his head slowly to look at her.

His mouth worked as if he wanted to speak, but had forgotten how. 'Where's – ' he mumbled at last – 'B-b-bridie?'

Forty-Eight

'It seems to be you he wants,' Eveleen said resentfully, when she went to find her niece in the bedroom that was always called 'Bridie's' now, even when she wasn't staying there.

Bridie stared at her aunt for a moment and caught some of the tension in her, the acute disappointment that her husband, though physically safely back home with her, was asking for someone else. She crossed the room swiftly to where Eveleen stood in the doorway, her hand still gripping the doorknob. Bridie held out her arms and tried to embrace her aunt, but Eveleen stood stiffly unresponsive.

'It's only that at the moment he looks upon me as his nurse.' Bridie laughed, trying to make light of the situation, but at the same time trying to make her aunt understand. 'We have the same trouble at the home. Sometimes when a patient's family visits, they'll hardly speak to them. Their little world is the home and the nursing staff.'

Some of the resentment left Eveleen's face, but she said flatly, 'Then you'd better go to him.'

'Let's have dinner first. Come on, we'll go down.' She took her aunt's hand. 'Just you and me. Then I'll help him into bed. You can be with me and see what to do.'

Eveleen felt like shouting back, I know what to do.

Haven't I been caring for my family for years? Didn't I care for you from the time you were born?

But for once she bit her tongue to stop the words being spoken as she realized the truth. Eveleen had to admit that she had no idea how to cope with the injured and emotionally damaged man who had returned from the hell of the trenches.

Bridie had to leave the following afternoon, and after she had gone Richard sank back into his silent, lethargic world. Eveleen could not even coax him to get out of bed, other than to visit the bathroom, never mind get dressed. Once more he just lay, staring vacantly at the ceiling.

'Please, Richard . . .' Eveleen took his hand. 'Won't you get up and sit by the window like you did yesterday?' Though the words nearly choked her, she added, 'Like you did for Bridie?'

He did not look at her as he mumbled, 'Bridie. I want Bridie.'

Eveleen sighed, straightened up and turned away. 'I can't cope with this,' she muttered as she left the room. The man who had cared for her and looked after her was now lost to her. Downstairs she pulled on her coat and put on her hat, ramming the hatpin viciously into place, anxious to be gone from the house. At least at the factory I know how to cope with all the problems, she thought. Though there had been difficult times, Eveleen had faced and dealt with them all and now the factory, though vastly changed for the time being, was running comparatively smoothly. She had earned the respect of all those who worked for her.

Eveleen decided to walk to the factory to work off some of the anger boiling up inside her. As she marched along with long, almost manly strides, her head held high, she was unaware of the striking figure she made and the admiring glances she attracted.

Why can't I cope with it? she castigated herself. Is it because I'm so used to him being the strong one? Or is it, she pondered, trying to be completely honest with herself, because after years of coping with my mother's weathervane moods I've just reached breaking point?

She had reached the factory gates and as she stepped through them she sighed. She was no nearer solving her problem, but at least, for a few hours, she could bury herself in a different set of problems, but ones that she was now fully capable of dealing with.

'I want to see my son. You've no right to stop me.'

Mary Carpenter stood in the hallway at Fairfield House, her voice raised in petulant anger, and faced the matron.

'I'll ask Jimmy if he's feeling well enough,' Dulcie said calmly. She turned and addressed Bridie, who was hovering in the shadows near the staircase. 'Singleton, will you inform Mr Hardcastle that his mother is here and wishes to see him?'

Bridie turned and began to run up the stairs, but as she did so her grandmother elbowed the matron out of the way and pushed past her. 'All this nonsense. I've a right to see my son. I don't see why he can't come home with me.'

'The authorities—' Dulcie began primly.

'Damnation to the authorities. What do they care

about my boy?' Mary was climbing the stairs now, almost up to where Bridie stood looking down at the matron, uncertain what she should do.

Dulcie nodded to her, capitulating to the determined woman with a sigh.

'This way, Gran.'

'I know where his room is, girl,' Mary snapped, but Bridie insisted on leading the way along the landing and opening the door of Jimmy's room.

She smiled as she entered and announced, 'A visitor for you.'

As Jimmy, in his chair by the window, turned and saw his mother, Bridie almost laughed aloud at the look of horror on his face. As Mary hurried towards him, her arms outstretched, he cringed back into the chair. But there was no escaping the woman's tender caress, her kiss. As she sat down beside him, she took his hand and though he tried to pull away, she held it firmly in her grasp.

Quietly chuckling to herself, Bridie closed the door.

'So,' Bridie asked Jimmy later, trying to keep her impish smile in check, 'did you have a pleasant afternoon with your mother?'

Jimmy glowered up at her. 'Who ses she's me mam? *I* can't remember.'

'Well, she's positive she is. Besides, you recognized your sister. So, if Eveleen is your sister and Mary's your mother, then I'm your daughter.'

He was suddenly angry. His hands gripped the arms of his chair until the knuckles showed white. He thrust his head towards her, his eyes glittering. 'You can't prove that. No-one can. It could have been anyone. It could have been Andrew Burns. He was like a lovesick puppy, always hanging round her.'

She stood staring down at him as he glared back at her. She brushed aside the implied insult to her dead mother as a slow smile spread across her face. 'So,' she said quietly, 'you do remember, after all?'

Appalled, Jimmy glared up at her. 'You little bastard!' he muttered through gritted teeth. 'You tricked me.'

'Oh, I'm that all right,' she said airily. The horrible name he had called her was nothing new to her. She had grown up with it being called after her in the schoolyard and along the lanes near her home. Bridie the bastard, they had called cruelly after her. Only Micky Morton had ever stuck up for her, earning himself a bloody nose more than once in her defence. 'You saw to that, didn't you? Running away to sea instead of marrying my mother.'

'I told you, you can't prove I fathered you.'

'No, I can't, but from what Auntie Evie has told me about my mother and what I've seen now I've met her father and my great-grandmother I don't reckon my mother would have been the sort to have had a string of fellers.'

His head came up sharply. 'You know them?'

His guard was down now. He was talking to her – really talking to her – for the first time. And now he was making no pretence that he had lost his memory.

Bridie nodded. 'I went to help out. I got quite close to the old lady, but . . .' Her eyes clouded. 'He won't have anything to do with me.' Then suddenly she grinned broadly. 'But I haven't given up yet.'

Jimmy snorted. 'I wouldn't count on him ever coming round. If he can cast his own daughter out, aye and his sister 'afore that, then you've no chance.'

She regarded him steadily, her head on one side. 'I grant you Andrew was in love with Rebecca.' Her voice faltered for a moment. So much in love with her, she was thinking, that he still sees her in me. Pushing aside her own sadness, she concentrated on the man before her now. 'But when you came along, she had eyes for no-one else. So I'm told.'

Jimmy shifted awkwardly in his chair.

'So,' she persisted, 'why, exactly, won't you at least acknowledge that you *could* be my father?'

He raised his eyebrows. 'Oh, I admit I could be your father, but I'm just not saying that I am.'

'Why?'

His lip curled. 'I didn't want to be saddled with a misery for a wife and a howling kid.'

'If she was such a misery as you call her, why did you – want her?'

He shrugged. 'She was there,' he said callously. 'And she was – available.' He smiled maliciously. 'And it was fun to take her away from poor old Burns.'

Bride felt the urge to slap his face really hard. Instead, she controlled her anger to say with icy calm, 'Do you know something? I think it's you that's the bastard, not me.'

Sick with disappointment at finding out just what sort of a man her father was, Bridie turned away. She was halfway across the room before he said, 'I suppose you're going to report all this to your precious matron and have me sent back to sea. Back to the war.'

She stood a moment, her heart beating fast. Then she turned and walked slowly back to him. She bent over

him, her hands resting on the arms of his chair. She
thrust her face close to his. 'I'll strike a bargain with
you. I'll not say a word about any of this.' She paused
and then added pointedly, 'At least at the moment. But
from now on you treat your own mother with a lot
more respect than you treated mine.'

He stared up at her and then there was a brief flicker
of admiration in his eyes. 'By heck, you're a hard little
bugger, aren't you?'

She stood up, her face grim. 'I can be when I need to
be. I wonder who I get it from.'

357

Forty-Nine

Midway through the afternoon an urgent message from her father-in-law was delivered to Eveleen at the factory that she must return home immediately.

She went at once, knowing that Brinsley would not panic easily. Her heart in her mouth, she hurried home, opening the front door to a cacophony of noise. Jane, the girl Eveleen had employed to watch over Richard during her absence, was standing in the hall in tears and wringing her hands helplessly. The sound of shouting and of breaking glass or pots, was coming from upstairs.

'Oh, madam.' The girl rushed towards Eveleen. 'It's the master. He's – he's gone berserk. I can't do a thing with him. Nor – nor can Mr Stokes.'

Not even pausing to remove her hat and coat, Eveleen ran up the stairs. The door to the main bedroom stood open and a scene of devastation met her eyes. Ornaments, perfume bottles, face-cream jars lay scattered in pieces on the floor, their contents spilled. Clothes had been pulled from drawers and the wardrobe and flung around, even the mattress had been upturned and rested drunkenly half on, half off the bedstead.

Richard stood in the centre of the room, his eyes wild, his arms flailing, his hands reaching for something else to throw. And he was shouting.

'I want Bridie here. Get Bridie.'

Brinsley hovered at the door, his face white with anxiety. 'Thank God you're here, Eveleen. Maybe you can calm him.'

Eveleen stood a moment and watched. 'I doubt it,' she said drily. 'It's obvious who he wants.'

She felt her father-in-law glance at her, but he said nothing. Eveleen stepped into the room and moved towards her husband. To see the loving, kindly man she had known reduced to this was breaking her heart, yet she knew she had to be strong.

'Richard, please . . .' She tried to catch hold of his arms to still them, but his hand caught the side of her face, striking her jaw and almost knocking her to the ground.

'Bridie? Where's Bridie?'

For a moment Eveleen, her hand to her cheek, stared at him. Then suddenly something seemed to snap inside her. All the emotion of the past four years: her ill-concealed anger at his volunteering, the stress of trying to take over the reins at the factory and the antagonism she had faced, and the never-ending worry for his safety. And, though buried deep, the thought too that she would never now bear a child. All of this bubbled up inside her until she felt as wild as the man before her.

With a noise in her throat like a growl, she raised her hand and slapped his face hard. There was sudden silence. Richard stood quite still staring at her. Behind her, she heard her father-in-law's muttered, 'Oh, Eveleen, you shouldn't have done that.' Immediately she was filled with remorse. After all he had suffered, all he had been through, all his loving wife could do was to strike him.

Tears filled her eyes and she held up her arms to him. 'Oh, Richard, I'm sorry. I'm so sorry.'

Richard shook his head and passed a weary hand across his eyes as if waking from a dream, or perhaps a nightmare. Drained, he sank to the floor and Eveleen knelt beside him, cradling his head against her and stroking his hair, rocking him like a child.

Brinsley stepped into the room. 'I think, my dear,' he began, but now there was a firm resolution in his tone, 'you should let him go to Fairfield House.' His eyes held deep understanding. Perhaps he guessed something of what she was feeling because he added, 'I understand how you must feel, but it seems to be what he wants and I think it would be for the best. We can't –' he waved his arm to encompass the destruction around them – 'have this and he needs proper care. Care, my dear, that neither you nor I can give him.'

It was a gentle reproach, but Brinsley was generous enough to include himself in the failure.

Eveleen closed her eyes and held Richard close to her. Then she kissed his forehead and whispered, 'You're right. It would be the best thing for him.' Though not for me, she was thinking. Aloud, she added, 'I'll take him this afternoon.'

'Will they have a place?'

As she rose to her feet, she nodded. 'I think so. Bridie said that two were discharged last week. One to go home and one to return to the Front.'

'Poor fellow,' Brinsley murmured, saddened by the thought that someone who had already suffered injury should be made to return to that living, dying hell.

There was only one place left at the home; already the other had been filled by a soldier with bandages round his eyes.

'He's been blinded,' Bridie told Eveleen. 'Isn't it sad? He was a watchmaker.'

Eveleen bit her lip. Sorry for the stranger though she was, her mind was filled with her own problems. 'Oh, Bridie, I hit him. I hit Richard. I'll never forgive myself.'

Bridie took her aunt's hands, suddenly seeming the older of the two of them. 'Don't be upset, Auntie Evie. You maybe did the right thing.'

Eveleen stared at her. 'The right thing? How can it possibly have been right to hit him?'

Bridie shrugged. 'It was a kind of hysteria, wasn't it?'

'I – I suppose so,' Eveleen responded doubtfully, still feeling the enormous guilt.

'And it worked, didn't it?'

Eveleen nodded.

'There you are then.' She patted Eveleen's hand, trying to comfort her. 'And I know how you must feel having to bring him here, but you have done the right thing. Honestly.'

Eveleen nodded again, but the tears spilled down her face and Bridie hugged her. 'There, there,' she whispered as if to a child.

Later, after Eveleen had left and Richard was asleep in his room, Bridie confided in the matron. 'She slapped his face. Was that the right thing to do?'

Dulcie pursed her lips. 'I'd sooner she had found another way. I wouldn't allow any of the nurses under my control to use such methods. The furthest I'd go is some kind of restraint.' The matron sighed. 'But I understand how difficult and frightening it must have been for her.'

'She had a bruise on her jaw,' Bridie went on. 'He caught her as she tried to calm him. He didn't mean to hit her, she said. He didn't know what he was doing.'

'He wouldn't. But he's here now and we'll keep him here until he's quite, quite well.' She smiled at the girl. 'And he can be your special patient, along,' she added, her eyes twinkling, 'with Mr Hardcastle.'

The war news was heartening. At the end of September the papers said that the Allies were sweeping all before them along the whole Western Front. On 11 November came the news that the whole country had longed to hear for more than four years. The war was over. Church bells rang out to herald the peace. In the city factories closed and a jubilant workforce rushed into the streets, cheering, dancing and waving flags. At Reckitt and Stokes Eveleen declared a day's holiday, but as Brinsley remarked sadly to Eveleen, 'The fighting may be finished, but the war will never be over for so many. They've another kind of battle to contend with now. We've lost a whole generation of our youth.'

Brinsley visited Richard regularly at Fairfield House and Eveleen came every weekend and on Wednesday afternoons. But Sophia Stokes now refused to visit her son.

Shortly after noon on Monday, the day before Christmas Eve, when Bridie was helping to usher the patients into the dining room for their midday meal and carrying trays to those who could not manage to get down the stairs, she heard the sound of a car in the driveway. Glancing out of a window, she saw her aunt climbing out of the vehicle and almost running towards the front door.

Bridie's heart skipped a beat and then began to thud. Something was wrong. Eveleen had only left the previous evening after her usual weekend visit. And Monday was one of her busiest days at the factory.

Bridie hurried into the bedroom and thrust the tray at the man in the bed. 'Sorry. I've got to go. Auntie Evie . . .' She rushed out of the room again and ran down the stairs.

'Bridie!' Dulcie's voice rang out in the hall. 'Don't run.'

'Sorry, Matron, but Auntie Evie's here.' As she spoke the urgent pealing of the front doorbell began and despite Dulcie's reprimand, Bridie scurried across the polished hall floor and pulled open the door.

Eveleen's face was wreathed in smiles and Bridie felt a sudden relief. There was nothing seriously amiss if her aunt was looking happier than she had for weeks, months – probably years – since this whole sorry war had begun. Standing on the doorstep, she flung her arms wide and cried, 'I've wonderful news, Bridie. The best Christmas present ever. Andrew's safe. He's coming home.'

Bridie smiled and nodded and gestured her aunt to step inside. 'Of course he is,' she said simply.

Eveleen entered the house, staring at Bridie. 'You don't seem surprised.' She glanced towards Dulcie. 'Oh, you've heard already?' The matron shook her head and they both turned towards the girl.

Bridie was smiling happily, but all she said was, 'I told you all along he wasn't dead. I knew he'd come back.' She shrugged. 'I just knew God wouldn't let him die.'

The two older women now glanced at each other, marvelling at the young girl's unshakeable belief. Eveleen put her arm about Bridie's shoulders and her voice shook slightly as she said, 'I wish your grandfather could see you at this moment. Your faith shames even his devotion.' She handed Bridie a letter. 'This is for you. It was enclosed in mine.'

Now the girl's hands were shaking as she took the letter and thought she recognized the handwriting. She held the letter to her bosom for a moment, then, slipping it into her pocket, she murmured, 'I'll read it later.'

'He's been in a prison camp,' Eveleen explained. 'That's why we've heard nothing. Evidently when he went on that raiding party, he was injured and lay out in the open all night. In "no man's land" they call it.' Bridie nodded. She had heard the soldiers talking about it. 'The following day,' Eveleen went on, 'he was found and taken to an enemy field hospital and then to a prison camp. He had no identification on him and he refused to tell them who he was. In fact, he wouldn't tell anyone until he knew he was back in England.'

Bridie brushed away her joyful tears and asked, 'When will he be home?'

'We're trying to arrange that. He's in a hospital in the south of England at the moment, but Mr Stokes is making enquiries – ' Eveleen laughed – 'and pulling a few strings to get him moved here.' Her face sobered and she glanced from Bridie to Dulcie and back again. 'There's just one thing. You'll have to watch both Jimmy and Andrew. There could be trouble. I've no doubt that Andrew has harboured bitterness against my brother all these years.'

'Perhaps it would be best if Andrew didn't come here,' Dulcie said.

'Oh no, please let him come,' Bridie exclaimed at once. 'I'll manage them. Besides, my father is much better . . .' Then she remembered to add hastily, 'Physically, that is. Perhaps he could go to Gran's. It's what she wants.'

Eveleen smiled wryly. 'Ah, but is it what Jimmy wants?'

In the privacy of her room, Bridie opened her letter.

My dearest Bridie . . .

His 'dearest', she thought, clasping the letter to her again. Then she read on.

How long it seems since I was able to write to you, but the worst of it is that you have no doubt been informed that I was 'presumed killed' and I couldn't send word to you that I was all right. How I long to see you again. The thought of you has kept me going all through the long years of the prison camp. We were pretty well treated, but it was no holiday. I have had your photograph with me all the time and look at it every day. I hope you've had a photograph taken on your birthday every year for me . . .

Bridie smiled gently, relieved that she had kept her promise to him.

I'll be home soon as soon as the hospital will release me. All my love, always, Andrew.

All his love, always, she thought. If only he really meant it.

'I aren't going there.' Jimmy glowered. 'I don't know them from Adam. Why should I go and live with strangers?'

Bridie could not argue, for Dulcie was standing beside her. She had no intention of breaking her promise to her father, even though he was glaring at her as if the suggestion that he was well enough to go and live at Pear Tree Farm now had come solely from her.

'Trying to get your own back, are you?' he hissed at her.

'No,' the girl said calmly. 'We thought it might be best. It might help you to regain your memory,' she added pointedly, 'if you were in familiar surroundings.'

'They won't be familiar, will they,' he countered sarcastically, 'if I can't remember them.'

'True,' the matron agreed. 'What Singleton means is that surroundings that should be familiar to you might help jog your memory.'

Jimmy's only answer was a growl.

Ignoring it, Dulcie went on with a tone of finality that suggested the decision had been made for him. 'Besides, we need the bed.'

'Don't tell him who it's for,' Bridie had warned Dulcie earlier. 'Else he'll refuse to go just out of spite, if what Auntie Evie says is anything to go by.' But it seemed that the grapevine within the home had been buzzing.

'Oh, aye. Is it for Burns?' A sly grin spread across Jimmy's face. 'Well, I'd like to be here to greet him. I'd like to see his face when he sees me here.'

Dulcie was staring down at him. Slowly she said, 'I thought you couldn't remember anything?'

'Oh – er – well, I get little flashes now and then,' he faltered and then, as his mind worked surprisingly quickly, he added, 'Besides, Eveleen was telling me. How we had a fight and all that.' He nodded towards Bridie. 'Over her mother.' He grinned broadly. 'I expect I won.'

As they moved away, Dulcie frowned thoughtfully whilst Bridie held her breath. Was she going to be questioned and found out?

'I think he knows more than he's letting on to us, Bridie, don't you?'

'It – it sounds a bit like it,' the girl said, crossing her fingers behind her back and praying for forgiveness for the little white lie. But perhaps now there was no need to keep up the pretence. The war was over and even if Jimmy went back to sea eventually he would not be going back to a war situation. Not now, thank God.

And now Andrew was coming home. Bridie skipped through her work, her heart singing.

Andrew was coming home.

Fifty

'He's here. Oh, he's here!'

Bridie ran down the wide staircase and across the hall. Dulcie appeared in the doorway of her office, but for once she did not reprimand the excited girl. Earlier she had warned her that they had not yet been informed of his injuries. Andrew might look very different from how Bridie remembered him. 'You do know, don't you, that he could have lost a leg or an arm or be blind, deaf . . .?'

Bridie had stood calmly in front of her and had nodded soberly. 'I know, Matron. I don't think there's anything we haven't seen here, is there?'

'No,' Dulcie had said quietly. 'But it's very different when it's someone you – you love.'

Bridie heard the catch in the woman's voice and wondered. But Dulcie had cleared her throat and ended the conversation by saying, 'So long as you are prepared, my dear.'

Now the moment had come and Bridie was pulling open the heavy front door and running lightly down the steps to the ambulance that had brought Andrew and another patient to Fairfield House. The two ambulance men carried off a stretcher case first and Bridie stood on tiptoe, craning to see. But it was not Andrew. This man's face was gaunt and his skin yellow, his eyes closed.

Then she saw another man climbing stiffly out of the back of the vehicle. He stooped a little and leant heavily on a stick as he moved forward. But his hair was fair, not at all like Andrew's.

She glanced again towards the stretcher that was now being carried up the steps and in through the door, which the matron was holding open.

'Private Burns, ma'am,' Bridie heard one of the men carrying the patient say. 'Where do you want him?'

Bridie picked up her long skirt and ran up the steps in time to hear Dulcie say, 'Up the stairs and it's the dormitory to the left. Ah, Bridie, perhaps you will go with them. Show them the way.'

Bridie walked beside the stretcher, gazing down at him. Tears blurred her vision momentarily; to think that she had not recognized her beloved Andrew. Impatiently she brushed away her tears, took a deep breath and led the way up to the long, sunny room on the first floor that had been turned into a dormitory for six beds.

'Please could you put him in the end bed. Has he any kit?'

One of the men shook his head. 'Not much, miss. Just this small bag.' He nodded down to a small bag that looked to contain shaving equipment.

'Nothing – nothing else?'

'Only his wallet and he won't let anyone have hold of that.' The man grinned and nodded towards the end of the stretcher. 'Keeps hold on it, tight to his chest, he does. Here we are, then, mate. Let's have you off this thing and into a nice soft bed. And here's a pretty little nurse to look after you.' He laughed. 'Some fellers get all the luck, I reckon. Ready?' He asked his partner. 'One, two, three, upsy-daisy.'

When the two men had gone, Bridie stood beside the bed. 'Andrew,' she whispered.

His eyes flickered open and for a moment he stared at the ceiling and then he turned his head slowly to look up at her. His face was so thin that the cheekbones stood out. His eyes were dark hollows yet, now she could see his hazel eyes, she knew it really was him. He was blinking at her, as if trying to focus, and for an awful moment Bridie wondered if he was blind. He had not lost a limb, that she could see now, but perhaps his injuries were the sort that were not so apparent at first.

His lips parted and he seemed to speak, but no sound came out.

She found his hand and held it close to her. 'Andrew, it's me. You're safe now. You're home and I'm going to take care of you.'

Though it was strictly against the matron's rules, Bridie leant over and kissed his forehead. 'Oh, Andrew, I do love you so.'

He closed his eyes and she heard his long, deep sigh. 'Oh, my darling,' he whispered hoarsely. 'My darling Rebecca.'

Bridie had known hurt in her young life, but all were as pinpricks beside this. Andrew's undying love for her mother stuck a knife deep into Bridie's heart. He did not even see her as herself, the girl thought. Only as her mother's daughter. Her gran had been right all along. She was determined, however, that no-one should see her torment. She plastered a brave smile on her face and kept her voice as cheerful and gently teasing to all the patients as always.

Fortunately she was now run off her feet helping to care for her three special patients; her father, Richard and Andrew. She had little time to dwell on her own disappointment. They were each demanding her time in very different ways.

Richard called for her constantly, would let no other nurse near him. Andrew lay in his bed, demanding nothing from anyone, yet her love for him brought her constantly to his bedside like a moth to a flame. As for Jimmy, he watched the goings on closely and smiled with malicious relish.

'Does Burns know I'm here?' he asked Bridie frequently.

'Just you keep away from him.' She turned on him, speaking rashly. She bit her lip as she saw Jimmy's eyebrows rise questioningly. She didn't want him guessing the extent of her feelings for Andrew. She didn't want anyone here to know. Only her family knew of her fondness for him, yet even they still believed that it was more of a father–daughter relationship. All her life Andrew had been her surrogate father, a replacement for the errant Jimmy. Sadly Bridie knew that that was how Andrew thought of her too. As the daughter he should have had with Rebecca.

She put her head on one side, her hands on her hips and met her father's gaze. 'I heard about you and Andrew fighting over me mam, so just you keep away from him.' She'd turned it neatly away from herself to the events of the past. But Jimmy was not to be so easily deceived. She felt he was watching her face intently for every fleeting expression.

'Seems to me he's more to you than just one of your mam's old boyfriends.'

With an outward calm she did not feel inside, Bridie said, 'Of course he is.' She leant towards him accusingly. 'He took your place all the time I was growing up. He was like a father to me.'

Jimmy laughed. 'Perhaps he was, young Bridie. Perhaps he really was your father. Who's to know, eh?'

His insinuations brought fresh dread to Bridie's already wounded heart.

'Seems to me,' Jimmy was still watchful, 'that it's my dear brother-in-law, Richard, who's got his eye on you. I'll have to warn poor old Evie that she'd better watch herself.' He laughed. 'She never did have much luck with the gentry.'

Despite her anger at him for his machinations, Bridie couldn't help being intrigued. 'What do you mean?'

He waved his hand and glanced around the room. 'Chap who owned this place. He was her lover.'

'Her – her lover?' Bridie's voice was a shocked squeak. Jimmy's words implied so much more than the innocent romance of a girl and a landowner's handsome son, yet Bridie could hardly believe such a thing of her aunt. She had only witnessed the strong and sure love between Eveleen and Richard, and despite their present difficulties she was convinced that, deep down, it was as steadfastly secure as ever. Once Richard was well again everything would come right for them.

They were alone in the room whilst Bridie changed the sheets on his bed, so Jimmy felt able to speak freely without compromising himself. 'Our parents tried to stop it. Me mam in particular was dead set against it. Probably because of what had happened to her when she was young.'

Bridie bit back the tumult of questions. She would learn more if she kept quiet and let him ramble.

'Anyway, when our father died suddenly Master Stephen threw our Evie over and turned us out of our home.'

'And that's when you went to Flawford and met my mother,' Bridie said pointedly.

Jimmy eyed her suspiciously, aware that she was trying to trap him into an admission. Carefully he said, 'Well, yes, I met her. Of course I did. She was our cousin.'

Bridie arched her eyebrow quizzically, but said no more.

At ease again, Jimmy looked about him once more and laughed. 'Good old Evie. She got her own back on him though, didn't she?'

Now Bridie was puzzled. 'How do you mean?'

'Bought him out, lock stock and barrel, hasn't she?' He pulled his earlobe. 'Oh, this place is a den of gossip, I don't mind telling you. The things I've been hearing. Make your hair curl, lass. It would really. There's a feller in here from Bernby. He used to work on the Dunsmore estate afore he went in the army. He's been telling me a thing or two. After the old man, Stephen's father that is – now what was his name? – Ernest, that was it. Mr Ernest. He went off to London to be an MP and left his son in charge of the estate. By all accounts, Stephen drank and gambled all the money. I bet he was only too glad to get away.' He laughed. 'I expect the Front was a better prospect than his creditors chasing him.'

'Hardly,' Bridie said wryly. 'He was killed.'

Jimmy had the grace to look startled, but it only lasted a brief moment before he said grimly. 'Good riddance.'

'That's a horrible thing to say about anyone,' she cried.

Jimmy met her gaze steadfastly and his expression

was the most serious she had ever seen it. Quietly he said, 'We're a nasty lot, us men, Bridie lass, and I'm probably worse than most. You wouldn't want me for a father, really you wouldn't. You'd best stick with Burns. He's a much better father-figure for you than ever I'd be.'

Bridie, smoothed the pillow on his bed and pulled the counterpane straight before going to stand in front of him. She looked directly into his eyes. Quietly she said, 'We can't choose our parents, can we? But you're my father. I know you are, even if you won't admit it. So it looks like we're stuck with each other, doesn't it?'

Without waiting for a reply, she turned and left the room, leaving him gazing after her. Besides, Bridie was thinking as she collected fresh laundry and hurried along to Richard's room, I've other plans for Andrew Burns, even if, at the moment, he doesn't realize it himself. The last thing I want is Andrew as my father.

Eveleen was with Richard, but the moment Bridie entered the room it was as if she no longer existed. She watched as Richard's face lit up at the sight of her niece. He even held out his arms to her, inviting a hug, but Bridie laughed gaily and said, 'Do you want to get me the sack, Uncle Richard? I'm on duty, you know that.'

She put the clean linen down on the bed and glanced from one to the other. 'Now, how about you go out into the garden or perhaps go for a drive with Auntie Evie, while I get your bed changed and Minnie comes and cleans your room.'

'Can you come with us?' He was pathetically eager and his face fell as Bridie shook her head. 'You know I can't. Now, off you go. It's a lovely morning. Far too nice to be stuck indoors. Why, don't you go to Pear Tree Farm? Gran'd love to see you.'

Eveleen stood up and smiled at her niece, though she found it difficult. She felt as if she were merely stretching her mouth and that the smile did not reach her eyes.

You're being silly, she castigated herself silently. How can you be jealous of your own niece? She's Richard's nurse and he's just leaning on her whilst he's ill. But, the insidious voice persisted, hasn't he always been fond of her? Remember the Goose Fair? The memory still hurt, but that day had been her fault. If she hadn't been so busy, so wrapped up in her own importance, trying so desperately to prove that she could run the factory, then it would not have happened. They would have had a lovely family day at the fair, the three of them.

Perhaps it was all her own fault. Eveleen was never less than honest with herself, even if the truth hurt. If she had devoted all her time to her husband when he had come home from the war, it might not have been necessary for him to have come here. She sighed, but it was too late now. He was here and there was no doubt, however painful the realization might be, that he was improving greatly under the wonderful nursing care at Fairfield House. And, if she was brutally honest with herself, it was mainly Bridie's loving care that was bringing about his recovery.

She moved to Richard's side and took his arm. Trying to make her tone playfully light, she said, 'I think she wants to get rid of us. Come along, darling. We'll go for that drive.'

For a moment, Richard looked disappointed, but then he nodded, tried to smile and said, 'Shall we go to Pear Tree Farm and take Jimmy to see his mother?'

'I don't think he'll come,' Eveleen said.

'What about Andrew then?'

'He's not well enough,' Bridie said. 'Not yet. I'm going to take him for a little walk in the garden later.'

Eveleen saw Richard look towards Bridie, who was already stripping the sheets from his bed. The look in his eyes was gentle as he murmured softly, 'Lucky Andrew.' But Eveleen knew that Bridie, concentrating on her task, had not heard.

Fifty-One

Josh lumbered forward as the car turned in at the gate.

'Oh, this is wonderful. Are you feeling better, Richard? Come in, come in. Dinner should be nearly ready and I'm sure there'll be enough for both of you. Mary, Mary love . . .' He drew them into the house, calling, 'Look who's here.'

Mary made even more fuss than Josh, but then, Eveleen reminded herself with a wry smile, Richard was a man. For Mary that was as natural as breathing.

But the man himself, though polite and smiling, seemed ill at ease, on edge all the time and perpetually glancing at the clock on the mantelpiece above the range.

'Like a walk whilst the ladies wash up?' Josh invited and though Eveleen could sense that he would rather not Richard gave in gracefully.

When they were alone in the house, Mary said, 'He's not himself yet, is he?'

Eveleen bit her lip and shook her head. 'No. I wonder if he ever will be.'

'All he needs is a lot of love and care, Eveleen.' Mary spoke harshly, accusingly. 'A bit of, of – ' she sought for the elusive word – 'tenderness. You've no tenderness in you, Eveleen. You're always too busy doing what *you* want to do. Organizing things, running things. Trying to take the place of a man.'

'We've had to these last few years,' Eveleen was sharply defensive.

'I know all about that.' Mary waved her hands dismissively. 'But they're home now and you should be concentrating on looking after your husband. You've got a good man there, Eveleen.' There was a hint of surprise in Mary's voice as if she still couldn't quite believe how her daughter had captured such a prize. 'If you don't devote yourself to him now, then you'll soon find someone else will.'

Unbidden, an image of Bridie pushed its way into Eveleen's mind's eye.

'Yes, Mam, perhaps you're right,' she murmured.

'Oh, I know I'm right,' Mary said with the conviction of a woman who had always known her lot in life. In her eyes, it was a woman's duty to pander to the man in her life.

They heard the back door open and changed their conversation swiftly, only to have it interrupted by Richard saying, 'Isn't it time we were getting back?'

As they pulled into the driveway of Fairfield House and the noise of the engine died, Eveleen reached across and touched Richard's hand. 'Darling, I've decided. Now so many of the men are back at the factory, I'm not needed there any more. And you seem so much better. You wound is healing nicely. Isn't it time you came home?'

His eyes clouded and he looked about him, almost as if the answer he wanted would come out of the air to him. He stumbled over the words. 'You – ought to – I mean, there's no one to run the place.'

Eveleen laughed. 'Oh, didn't you know? I've persuaded Bob Porter to come back. He's fit enough now. Losing a leg won't stop him managing the factory just like he always did. Besides, now he has men back, he'll be much happier. He can get rid of all the troublesome women. Several have left already of their own accord. Those whose husbands have come back.' Her voice was low as she added, counting herself amongst them. 'The lucky ones.'

'What about the widows?' Richard blurted out, a strange desperation in his tone. Eveleen could sense that he was casting about for an excuse not to come home. 'They'll need jobs. You should keep on as many as you can, Eveleen. It's the least we can do.'

She squeezed his hand. 'Why don't you come home and help me?' she said. 'I – I need you, Richard. I want you to come home.'

He shook his head. 'No, no. I'm not ready. Not yet.'

He climbed out of the motor and hurried up the steps as if he couldn't return to Fairfield House quickly enough.

Eveleen watched him go, her hands gripping the steering wheel and tears blinding her eyes.

In the yard behind Fairfield House, Bridie said, 'Now lean on me, Andrew. We'll walk down the field towards the beck. Cook has packed us a picnic so we don't need to get back for tea and I don't need to be back on duty until six. We've three whole hours.' She hugged his arm to her side, blissfully happy to be alone with him.

'You don't want to be spending your time off with me,' he said, looking at her so fondly that her heart turned over.

'Can't think of anything I'd rather be doing,' she said simply.

He was watching her, as if drinking in the sight of

her, every detail of her face, her hair – everything about her. Since that first day, he had never again called her 'Rebecca' yet she had the uncomfortable feeling that every time he looked at her she felt that it was not her he was seeing but her mother.

'I can't believe how you've grown up. When I went away you were a little girl and now, just look at you. A young woman.' His voice was hoarse. 'A very beautiful young woman.'

Now Bridie laughed, the sound echoing across the fields. 'Thank you, kind sir.'

'Have you – have you got a young man? I bet they're queuing up.'

She didn't answer him at once. They had reached the beck and she found a suitable spot to spread the rug on the grassy bank. When they were sitting side by side, she looked into his eyes, her face deadly serious, and said quietly, 'All my life I've told you that I was going to marry you when I grew up.'

He smiled and touched her cheek. 'All little girls want to marry their father—'

She interrupted swiftly, 'You're not my father.'

'No, no, I know that. But how I wish I had been. And I've always tried to be there for you, haven't I? I did my best to take his place.'

Now was the time to tell him about Jimmy, for the staff had all contrived to keep them apart and to keep the knowledge of Jimmy's presence in the home from Andrew Burns. But they were bound to meet sooner or later. Whilst Andrew had been confined to bed, it had been comparatively easy, but now he was up and about it was impossible to keep them apart much longer.

But for the moment, Bridie had another, far more important issue to discuss.

'Andrew, I've loved you all my life, but not as my father. I want to spend the rest of my life with you, as your wife.'

He was gazing at her but shaking his head slowly. 'I'm far too old for you. I'm almost twenty years older than you.'

'So? What does that matter?'

'It – it wouldn't be right. What would people think?'

'I don't care what other people think,' she cried passionately. 'Hasn't this awful war proved that we have to take our happiness when and where we find it?'

He was silent, avoiding her intense gaze now.

His glance roamed the landscape before them: the beck, the field beyond, where cows grazed placidly, and in the distance the buildings of Pear Tree Farm.

Softly, but with a catch in her voice, Bridie said, 'The truth is that you don't love me in that way do you? You're still in love with my mother.'

Andrew did not answer her.

Fifty-Two

It was as they returned to Fairfield House that they came face to face with Jimmy in the hall.

'Well, well, well! If it isn't Andrew Burns himself,' was Jimmy's greeting.

Luckily Bridie had forewarned Andrew only moments earlier as they walked back across the fields. 'He's here, by the way,' she said casually, trying to make light of it.

'Who is?'

'My father. Jimmy Hardcastle. His ship went down somewhere in the Channel. He wasn't physically hurt, but he suffered amnesia.'

Now the two men were standing face to face for the first time in more than seventeen years.

'Your memory seems to be coming back quite nicely,' Andrew said bitterly. 'Remember Rebecca, do you? And what you did to her?'

Jimmy put his fingers to his forehead and frowned. 'Do you know, I can't remember much about her at all. But then, there have been so many since then.' He laughed. 'A girl in every port, you know.'

'Why, you . . . I'll smash your face in.' Andrew clenched his fists and took a step towards him, but Bridie clung onto him, pulling him away. Andrew was obliged to content himself with shaking his fist in Jimmy's face. 'One day, Jimmy Hardcastle. One day, I'll have you.'

The tension was broken by a voice behind them and Richard came hurrying towards them. 'There you are, Bridie. I've been looking everywhere for you. Where've you been?'

Jimmy turned and, shoving his hands into his pockets, walked away, whistling nonchalantly. Andrew, his face like thunder, stared after him.

'We went for a picnic, down by the beck, didn't we, Andrew.' Bridie sought to divert his attention. 'It's the first time he's been out.'

'I wish I'd known. I'd have come with you.'

'That'd have been nice,' Bridie said evenly. She had wanted to be alone with Andrew, so desperately wanted to declare her love for him. She had even dared to hope that now she was grown up there might be a chance he would return her love in the same way. But those hopes had been dashed.

But at least now she knew the mountain she had to climb and Bridie was never going to give up. Her hope refused to die. Now she said brightly, 'Andrew's tired. I must see him to bed. I'll see you later, Uncle Richard.'

'Don't be long. I want to talk to you.'

As she helped Andrew prepare for bed, he was still smarting from the meeting with his old rival. 'I could quite cheerfully kill him, you know, Bridie, for what he did to Rebecca. And to you, of course,' he added as an afterthought.

Bridie managed to smile. 'He's denying that he's my father.' She paused, wondering if she should continue, but decided that the best course was to bring everything out into the open. She was sure Andrew was strong enough now to cope with it. 'He says it's more likely that you are my father.'

Andrew snorted contemptuously. 'Does he indeed? Well, I can assure you I'm not.' His voice softened, 'Although I have wished all my life that I was.'

She believed him implicitly and, in one way, his words gave her fresh hope. Andrew, though he might have longed for it to be otherwise, was not her blood relative.

'So,' she asked slowly, 'do you believe that he is my father?'

Andrew looked at her keenly. 'I could almost wish it had been anybody else *but* him, but, yes, he is your father.'

He got into bed and lay back against the pillows with a sigh. On the bedside table the last photograph that had been taken of Bridie, crumpled and stained from being carried everywhere through four years of war, now stood in a frame. But Andrew was not looking at her photograph now. He lay staring up at the ceiling, seeing pictures from the past. 'They came to Flawford, your gran, Eveleen and Jimmy, when they had to leave the farm. You know all about that, of course.'

'Well, bits,' she said guardedly, wanting him to tell her all that he knew. She sat down on the edge of the bed, breaking yet another of matron's rules.

'She'd never known other lads, apart from those of us who worked in her dad's workshops. And Harry kept her away from them all as best he could. I don't reckon he ever intended to let her get married. He'd lost his wife and he wanted to keep Rebecca to look after him. Before Jimmy came I thought she loved me and I was going to do it all proper. Keep in her dad's good books, court her, like, but all with his permission.'

'Perhaps,' Bridie suggested gently, 'her father would never have given permission. Not even to you.'

'Mebbe not. But I'd have waited. I'd have waited all me life for her, if I'd known that she really loved me. But then *he* came and it was as if I didn't exist any more.'

Bridie took his hand and held it to her cheek and at last, his gaze came back to rest on her face. 'You remind me of her so much. You look a lot like her, but you're very different in your – your nature. She was quiet and gentle and easily led. I can see that now. Not her fault,' he added swiftly, as if regretting even the slightest implied criticism of his beloved. 'But you're feisty. You're a fighter. I get the feeling you'll get what you want.'

She smiled broadly at him. 'You're right there, Andrew Burns. I never give in until I get what I want.'

It was not a threat, but a promise.

Richard was still hovering in the hallway when she came down the stairs. He hurried towards her. 'Is something wrong? You've been so long.'

'We were talking. About my mother – and my father. He needed to talk.'

'I need to talk to you too.' There was a plaintive, selfish note in his voice. Bridie looked up at him in surprise. This war had changed so many things in so many lives, but she would never have believed that her lovely uncle Richard could be so different. But, smiling up at him, she tucked her arm through his and led him to the patients' sitting room. 'Come along then. It should be quiet in here now. What is it you want to tell me?'

'Eveleen wants me to go home,' he blurted out when

they were seated side be side on a sofa. 'But I don't want to. I want to stay here. With you.'

'Why?' she asked candidly.

'Because – because I feel safe here. I can't – can't cope at home.'

'Why not?' Bridie asked again gently. Instinctively she was drawing him out, getting him to face whatever it was that was troubling him.

'I'll be expected to go back to work. To the factory. She's said as much. She needs me to help her, she says.'

'I'm sure she's only suggesting that because she thinks it's what would help you.'

'Mm.' He sounded doubtful.

'So tell her. Be honest with her. Tell her that you don't feel ready – yet – to go back to work.'

'I don't think she'd understand.'

'Yes, she would. She loves you so much, Uncle Richard. She'll do anything – anything at all that will make you well again.'

'I know,' he said dully. 'That's why it's so difficult.'

There was silence as Bridie almost dreaded to ask yet again, 'Why? Don't – don't you love her any more?'

'I . . .' He stopped and in his eyes she could see that he was appalled at himself at what he was obliged to say. 'She frightens me.'

'Frightens you?' Bridie repeated in amazement.

'I know I shouldn't be talking to you this way. You're only a young girl, yet – yet you seem so wise, so mature.'

'Don't worry about that,' Bridie said softly. 'I don't think there's much I haven't heard, working here.'

Although she was still only seventeen, Bridie felt years older. Was it really only a year since her sixteenth birthday, the day she had met her father for the first time? She had witnessed all manner of suffering during her time as a trainee nurse here at Fairfield House. She had heard all kinds of confessions, listened to so many sad tales, that, whilst never immune to their emotions or unfeeling for their anguish, she had grown strong enough to be a good listener. And in many cases that was all that was needed.

But her uncle was a different matter. She couldn't help but be closely involved. She took his hand. 'Tell me,' she urged gently.

'I can't – make love to her any more. I can't – feel anything. When I was at home she was so loving, so – so giving. I knew I ought to, but I – I couldn't.'

'It happens to an awful lot of you.'

'Really? You're not just saying that?'

Bridie shook her head. 'If I had a pound for every time I've heard a soldier tell me that, I'd be rich.' She leant closer to him. 'You've all been through a dreadful time. How can you possibly expect to step back into the life you had before the war as if nothing had happened? It's changed us all, Uncle Richard. Even though we haven't suffered like you have, it's altered our lives, in some ways probably for ever. But as for you – your problem – well, time will heal that, I promise.'

'How do you know?' he asked gloomily. 'What if I can never . . .'

'You will. When you're fit and strong again. What you've got to do whilst you're here is to work at getting physically well. Plenty of good food, fresh air and walks each day. The rest will come right. Honestly it will.'

He picked up her hand and held it to his cheek. 'Oh, Bridie,' he murmured, 'what would I do without you?'

Beyond him, out of the corner of her eye, Bridie caught a movement in the doorway. She glanced up to look straight into her father's grinning face.

387

Fifty-Three

'I can see I shall have to warn my sister about that husband of hers,' was Jimmy's greeting the next morning. 'Mind you, it's her own fault. She never could keep a feller for long.'

'Don't talk such nonsense,' Bridie snapped, for once her patience at an end.

He laughed. 'I expect, when all this is over, she plans to come and live here. Play the lady of the manor like she always wanted. Maybe it's all she'll have left.' He winked at her and tapped the side of his nose. 'If her dear husband's got his eye on you.'

To her dismay, Bridie could not stop the colour flooding her face. She was angry, yet knew he would see it as embarrassment.

'Oho,' Jimmy said at once. 'I see I'm right.'

'Nothing of the sort,' she answered hotly. There was only one way she could nip this in the bud. 'Besides,' she added, 'I've got my sights elsewhere.'

But Jimmy only laughed. 'Trying to put me off the scent, eh? Well, I know what I saw last night and I'm sure my sister would be interested to hear all about it. Very interested.'

'You . . .' Bridie began taking a step towards him.

'Is he bothering you, Bridie?' Andrew was coming slowly down the stairs, holding tightly onto the banister. He had not yet fully recovered his strength and the wound in his side, even after years in the prison camp, still refused to heal properly. ''Cos if he is . . .'

'No, no.' Bridie hurried towards him to help him down the last few steps. He stood at the foot of the stairs, panting from the exertion, yet his eyes glittered with hatred as he glanced at Jimmy. The latter, however, just stood smiling superciliously at them both.

'Oh aye, and what do you reckon you could do about it? You couldn't beat me last time, so what do you think you could do now, eh?'

'Will you two just stop it?' Bridie began, but already Andrew was pulling himself free of her hold and stepping towards his adversary.

'I'll swing for you, Jimmy Hardcastle. I'll—'

'Come on, then.' Jimmy adopted a fighting pose, fists raised. 'Let's be having you. Let's see what you're really made of, Burns.'

'Stop this. Please—' Bridie pleaded, but Andrew pulled himself free and lunged towards Jimmy, who landed a punch on his jaw with his right hand and then swiftly followed it up with a heavy blow to Andrew's side. Then he stood back as Andrew groaned and doubled over in agony, crumpling to the floor.

'Whatever is going on?' Dulcie was hurrying across the hall. Bridie turned to her in relief. 'I couldn't stop them. I—'

'Go to your room, Singleton. I'll deal with you later. And you too, Mr Hardcastle.' She glared at him and added sarcastically, 'It seems to me that your memory is returning very quickly now. I shall be calling the authorities to have you assessed with a view to you returning to duty.'

'And as for you.' She looked down at Andrew, writhing on the floor. 'How are we to get that wound to heal if you get involved in fights?' She tutted disapprovingly and beckoned to two other nurses to help her take Andrew back to his room so that she could examine the damage.

'Please, Matron—' Bridie began, but Dulcie only said sharply, 'I told you to go to your room. I'll send for you when I'm ready to listen to you.'

'I can't have that sort of behaviour, Bridie.'

She was standing in front of the matron's desk, whilst Dulcie sat in the chair behind it. The fight had reopened Andrew's old wound and the doctor had had to be called.

Bridie stood silently, her head bowed, taking the blame. She felt Dulcie's gaze on her and heard her soft sigh. 'I know it wasn't really your fault, but it's a mistake to have them all here. I thought it would be helpful to them, Mr Stokes as well, for them to be near you, but it seems I was wrong. I'm sorry, Bridie, but I will have to take steps to alter the situation. I intend to ask Dr Roper, when he calls to see Mr Burns, to send Mr Hardcastle to his mother's.' Dulcie smiled wryly. 'It's what she wants anyway, even if he doesn't. But he seems to be the centre of the trouble. Mr Stokes and Mr Burns have no quarrel with each other, have they?'

Bridie shook her head, but bit her lip. There hadn't been actual trouble yet, but if Jimmy carried out his threat then there very well could be.

'Very well, then. You may go now, but do try to keep them apart as much as you can.'

'Thank you, Matron,' she said in a small voice.

*

That evening, after dinner, Richard was once more hovering in the hall, waiting to waylay her. 'You're right, Bridie. I should talk to Eveleen,' Richard said. 'Perhaps she will understand.'

'Of course she will.'

'But would you – would you talk to her first? Maybe she'd understand better if you explain to her that it – it happens to a lot of men.'

Bridie nodded. 'If you really want me to.'

'I do.' He was pathetically grateful.

But when Bridie broached the delicate subject with her aunt the following Sunday, Eveleen felt humiliated. 'How could he? How could he do that to me? Discuss such a personal matter with anyone else.' Eveleen paced up and down Dulcie's office. The matron had given permission for Bridie to talk to her aunt in private and they were alone in the room. Eveleen whirled around now and faced her niece. 'And to you, of all people. You're only a child.'

'I'm seventeen, Auntie Evie,' Bridie said quietly. 'And believe me, after what I've witnessed here, I feel much older.'

'He should have talked to me.' Eveleen's face crumpled and tears threatened.

Bridie stepped towards her, her arms outstretched. 'Oh, Auntie Evie, don't. It'll be all right—'

But Eveleen pushed her away, beside herself with resentment and jealousy. Richard had talked to Bridie, had discussed an intimate problem with a young girl when he should have talked to her, his wife, about it.

'He's coming home with me. Today. I won't have him stay here another minute.'

'Please, Auntie Evie, listen to me. You mustn't be angry with him. You must treat him kindly – gently—'

'Don't you tell me how to treat my husband,' Eveleen flashed back and Bridie could see that her efforts were hopeless.

Eveleen brushed past her and marched out of the room, slamming the door behind her. Alone, Bridie closed her eyes and groaned aloud. She had tried her best, yet now she feared she had only made matters worse.

Eveleen had enough common sense to see that she must not show her anger to Richard. Though it pained her to admit it, she knew Bridie had been right in all that she had said. Many men returning from the war had great difficulty in adjusting to their home life once more, even to a loving relationship with their wives. Win, ever grateful for Eveleen's help with her son-in-law, Sid, had confided, 'Things are much better between them. He's that sorry, he can't do enough for our Elsie.' She had sighed. 'The only thing he can't do is be a proper husband to her, if you know what I mean.' Win had gone on to tell her that several of the homeworkers, whose husbands had returned from the war, were experiencing similar problems. But knowing this still didn't make it any easier for Eveleen to deal with and to have had it confirmed by Bridie had been more than she could bear. To think that Richard had preferred to confide in the girl rather than in his wife hurt her deeply.

But to Richard she presented a smiling face, a gentle tone and understanding. Only when he asked her, 'Has Bridie talked to you? Has she told you?' did it take a supreme effort to keep the smile on her face and the anger from her voice.

'Yes, yes. We've talked. But everything will be fine, darling. Matron says you must see the doctor first, but she sees no reason why you won't be able to come home next Sunday. And once you're home and we're together again everything will be fine.'

She saw him glance at her, saw his wan smile and knew he was not convinced.

After her conversation with Richard, Eveleen talked to Dulcie and then she went alone to Pear Tree Farm.

'I've got a feeling Fairfield House won't be needed as a home much longer. Several of the patients are well enough to go home now. Even some of the staff have left. And Richard's coming home next week.'

'What about Jimmy?' Mary asked at once.

Eveleen placed her cup and saucer carefully on the table. 'That's partly why I'm here. There's been a bit of trouble between him and Andrew and Dulcie feels that Jimmy is well enough to leave. Once she's had the doctor's approval and possibly that of the naval authorities too, he can be released.'

'He must come here. He must come home,' Mary said, clasping her hands in glee, her eyes shining.

Eveleen glanced towards Josh sitting quietly in the chair near the range. They exchanged a long look of understanding and she heard the big man sigh with resignation. He loved her mother dearly and Eveleen knew he could refuse her nothing, but the prospect of having Jimmy to live with them obviously did not appeal. Mary, however, was too wrapped up in her own anticipated pleasure to notice.

For very different reasons, Eveleen warned them, 'He probably won't stay long, you know. As soon as he's really fit again, he'll want to be off.'

She had a job to stop the laughter bubbling up as she

saw the acute disappointment on her mother's face, but the relief on Josh's. But then Mary smiled. 'We'll see. Once he's tasted my home cooking again, he'll not want to go back.'

'He may have to, Mary, love.'

She spun round on Josh. 'Why? The war's over.'

'But Jimmy didn't join the navy just for the war. He's been a regular for years.'

'So, he can still leave, can't he?'

'It depends how many years he's signed on for.'

Mary thought for a moment and then said confidently, 'Well, they won't want him back if he's lost his memory, will they?'

Eveleen and Josh exchanged another glance as Josh said heavily, 'No, I don't expect they will.'

'Lost his memory? My foot!'

The following Sunday, when Eveleen came to Fairfield House to take Richard home to Nottingham, she was once again in the matron's office. She had never seen the calm, usually unruffled Dulcie so incensed.

'I'm sorry, Eveleen.' The two women had become friends and had been on first name terms in private for some time. 'But that brother of yours!'

Eveleen smiled. 'You don't need to tell me.'

'He's hoodwinked the doctor and the naval people who came to assess him this week. D'you know, he should have been an actor. I wouldn't believe a word he says. He's caused nothing but trouble here since he came. Flirting with the nurses, upsetting Bridie. He won't even acknowledge that the poor child is his daughter. And then that fight with Andrew last week, well, that was the last straw.'

She marched up and down her office. Then she stopped and faced Eveleen. 'There's one good thing, though. The doctor and naval people have agreed that he can be allowed to go home to Pear Tree Farm. The only thing is . . .' She smiled slightly and there was a conspiratorial twist to her mouth. 'He's refusing to go and whilst the home is still open, I can't insist that he should leave. I was wondering—'

Eveleen smiled. 'You want me to tell him that the home is closing and that everyone must leave.'

'Would you?'

'What about the other patients?'

'There's only Andrew, who's not really quite fit to go home without someone to care for him. And *that's* Jimmy's fault, anyway.' She sat down and leant her forearms on her desk, clasping her fingers together. 'The thing is, Eveleen, Bridie is willing to go home with Andrew to care for him. In fact, she's desperate to go with him. But I wondered how you'd feel about it? Would you mind?'

'Me? Why should I mind?' Mind, Eveleen was thinking, I'd be delighted.

'Well, I understand you are her legal guardian. Or is that your mother?'

Eveleen shrugged and laughed. 'It wouldn't make a deal of difference. If Bridie wants to do something, she will, no matter what we say. Besides, I haven't any objection.'

On the contrary, Eveleen thought, it couldn't be a better solution. If Bridie were safely in Flawford, caring for Andrew, perhaps Richard would begin to forget about her.

Her smile widened. 'I think it's a grand idea.'

*

395

'I'm coming home with you and that's final,' Bridie declared, packing Andrew's possessions into a small trunk. There were pathetically few of them. He was sitting holding the photograph of her. She held out her hand. 'Let's put that on the top and close the lid.'

'Wrap it in something. I don't want it to get broken. It's the last photograph I have of you.'

She smiled at him. 'I've four more upstairs in my chest of drawers just waiting for you to come home. I even went into Grantham this September and got one done.'

'You remembered?' he said softly. 'You got a photograph done each year?'

'Of course,' she answered gently. 'How could I forget a promise to you?'

'Will you have another one done for me on your next birthday?'

'You don't need any more photographs. You've got the real thing now.'

His face clouded. 'Your grandfather won't like you being alone with me in my cottage.'

She grinned at him. 'We'll have to get married then, won't we?'

He shifted uncomfortably in his chair. 'I've told you, I'm too old for you, Bridie.'

She closed the lid of the trunk and straightened up, her face sober now. 'It's nothing to do with age, is it? You don't love me the way I love you.'

'I do love you, my dearest girl. I always have. You know that. You're the most important person in my life. You're the reason I survived the war and then the prison camp for all that time.'

'But . . .' she prompted.

He sighed, but could not answer her. She moved and

stood beside him, resting her hand on his shoulder. Her voice was shaky, but the words had to be spoken. 'You still think of me as a little girl. As Rebecca's daughter. As the daughter that you and she might have had. Don't you?'

He took her hand and held it against his cheek. 'I'm sorry,' he said hoarsely.

Bridie laid her cheek against his hair, the lump in her throat growing so that she felt as if it would choke her. And though her voice trembled as she spoke, her words were full of bravery. 'Never mind. I'm still going to take care of you. At least until you're quite well again. You're – you're not going to get rid of me that easily.'

Fifty-Four

Eveleen had arranged for Fred Martin to take Bridie and
Andrew home to Flawford.

'I must stay with Richard,' had been her excuse for
not taking them herself.

The yard was strangely quiet as they opened the gate.

'Funny,' Andrew murmured, pausing to listen. 'There's
no sound from the workshops.' He glanced at Bridie. 'I
thought you said Evie had found him some workers. And
some of the fellers should be back home now anyway.
Those,' he added soberly, 'that are coming back. Something must be wrong.'

Andrew pushed open the door to his cottage and
stepped inside, Bridie close behind him. The whole place
felt cold and damp. Thick dust covered every piece of
furniture.

'Oh, Andrew, I'm so sorry. When I left here, the
whole place shone. I cleaned everything myself.'

'Never mind, love. We'll soon have it warmed up and
spick and span.' He put his arm about her waist, trying
to chase away the look of disappointment on her face.
'Mrs Turner must have been too busy looking after the
old lady and your grandfather to worry about my place.
It doesn't matter.'

She bit her lip and nodded. She had imagined bringing him home to a glowing fire and a meal ready on the
table. That's why she had written to Gracie Turner last

week to warn her of their arrival. Surely she could have done something?

'I'll have to go to the village shop and buy a few things.' She moved to the chair by the range and dusted it. 'You sit down. I'll light a fire first.'

'No, you go and do the shopping. I can manage a fire. I expect there's still kindling in the wash-house and the coalhouse is usually kept well stocked.'

'Are you sure you can manage?'

'Yes. Off you go.'

Bridie hurried out of Singleton's Yard and along the village street towards the shop near the green. On her way she passed Gracie Turner's cottage and paused outside the gate. Then, deciding suddenly, she marched up the pathway and knocked on the door. No-one answered and the cottage had the feeling of emptiness about it. She was turning away to walk back down the path, when the woman in the neighbouring house opened her door to shake a doormat.

'Hello. Looking for Gracie, are yer?'

'Yes.'

'Didn't you know? She's in hospital again.'

Bridie's eyes widened. 'Again? What's been the matter with her?'

''Pendicitis. Rushed in two month ago. All sudden, like. It went wrong and she got – now what do they call it?'

'Peritonitis?' Bridie supplied the word.

'Yes, that's it.' The woman looked at her, marvelling. 'Fancy you knowing that. Anyway, poor Gracie was real bad. She almost died. It were touch and go.'

'Oh no!' Bridie was genuinely concerned now for the kindly woman. 'And you say she's still in hospital after all this time?'

'No. She's in *again*. She came home for a few weeks, but the scar wouldn't heal and they've taken her back in. Last week, it were. Nottingham, she's in.'

Expressing her sympathy and concern for Gracie, Bridie hurried away towards the shop desperately anxious now to make her purchases and get back home. What, she was thinking, had been happening to the old lady and her grandfather if Gracie had not been caring for them for the last two months? She couldn't blame the woman for not letting her know. Obviously she had been taken ill so quickly and so severely.

And Harry Singleton would sooner starve to death, she thought grimly, than ask her, his granddaughter, for help.

'What do you want to do today, darling?'

Eveleen was doing her best, but the days since she had brought Richard home from Fairfield House had been difficult. He was unsettled, ill at ease in his own home. Adamant that he was not yet ready to return to work – he didn't even want to set foot in the factory – he nevertheless seemed to need something to occupy him. Drives into the countryside, visits to his parents' home or sitting at home reading, still did not seem enough.

'I don't know,' he answered her listlessly.

They were sitting together in the morning room, Richard making a pretence of reading the morning paper, whilst Eveleen tried to concentrate on making a list for their cook of meals for the week. They heard the distant peal of the front doorbell and heard Smithers's footsteps crossing the hall to answer it.

'You were lucky not to lose all the staff,' Richard remarked.

'The young ones went. Emily went to work in munitions, but Cook and Smithers were too old.'

The footsteps were approaching the door of the morning room. It opened and Smithers appeared. 'It's a Mr Porter, ma'am, for the master or you. There's trouble at the factory, he ses.'

'Right.' Richard got to his feet and flung the crumpled newspaper to the floor. Eveleen held her breath. For a moment, she thought he was going to take up the reins once more, but his next words dashed her hopes. 'You'd better deal with this, Eveleen. Seems they can't manage without you after all.'

He marched from the room, leaving Eveleen staring after him.

The matter was nothing serious and, in one visit to the factory, Eveleen sorted out the problem. But the incident had shown her two things: that Richard was unshakeable in his resolve about not returning to work, and that Bob Porter could not now cope alone with any kind of crisis, even a minor one.

Eveleen pondered her dilemma. She was determined not to break her promise to stay at home with Richard and yet she could not stand by and see all her work over the past four years slip away because of the incompetence of one man. It was hardly fair to blame Bob. He had been through enough already. And it was no use asking Brinsley. Whilst he was willing, she knew his health would not now stand the rigours of running the factory and warehouse.

But there was one man who could help her, she thought. If only he would.

'Richard, Richard,' she called, running up the stairs to find him when she returned from her brief visit to the factory. 'How would you like a drive out to Pear Tree Farm? It's such a lovely day.'

Fifty-Five

Eveleen had not been inside the farmhouse many minutes before she felt the tension in the air. Jimmy sat idly by the range in the chair that had always belonged to the master of the house. In her earliest memories it had been Walter Hardcastle, their father, who had sat there. When Josh had married Mary it had become his chair. But now Mary's spoilt son had returned and had taken up occupation and, Eveleen suspected grimly, had usurped the place of the rightful head of the house.

'He's so much better. Aren't you, dear?' Mary fussed around Jimmy, stroking his hair as she passed his chair between the kitchen range and the table.

Jimmy smiled at his sister with a look that resembled a cat licking his lips after a saucer of cream.

'And his memory's coming back so well now,' Mary went on. 'I said it would if only he'd come home to familiar surroundings. He should have come home to me instead of going to that place.' She glanced resentfully at Eveleen, as if it had all been her fault.

Josh rose from the table and lumbered outside, slamming the back door behind him. Mary appeared not to notice, but Eveleen saw that Jimmy's smile widened.

'And how are you feeling now, Richard?' Mary now turned her attention to her son-in-law. 'You're looking much better. Is Eveleen looking after you properly?'

After a few moments, whilst Mary chattered happily,

not even requiring answers from anyone, Eveleen
slipped quietly from the room and followed Josh outside. He was leaning on the five-barred gate at the end
of the yard, watching the sun sink in the west, silhouet-
ting the ramparts of Belvoir Castle in the distance.

'This has always been one of my favourite views,'
Eveleen said softly. She forbore to say that it had been
her father's too. Standing beside this man, who had in
so many ways taken Walter's place, she did not want to
cause him further hurt by referring to the past. Mary
was already pushing him out of her life. Her days now,
Eveleen could see without being told, revolved around
her selfish son.

'Josh,' she said quietly, 'I need a huge favour. Would
you come back to Nottingham – just for a while – and
manage the factory?' Swiftly she explained her problem.
'Mr Stokes's health is not up to it now and Richard is
not ready to go back yet. I must give him time and I – I
need to be with him. And, to put it frankly, Bob Porter's
not quite up to it yet. He's doing his best, but with the
men coming back from the war and wanting their old
jobs back, it's causing nearly as much trouble as when
they went.'

Josh regarded her steadily for a few moments, then
he asked, 'Are you sure it's *you* who needs the favour?'

Eveleen smiled and put her hand on his arm. 'I can
see how things are. You don't have to tell me. I've lived
with it all my life. But he'll go, Josh; sooner or later he'll
be off. He's enjoying her fussing over him now, but he'll
soon get fed up with it and he'll be gone. Then – ' she
nodded – 'she'll be distraught. It'll be Mam who'll need
the cosseting then.'

The big man let out a long, deep sigh. 'I hope you're
right, Evie, mi duck. Don't get me wrong,' he added

hastily. 'I don't like to think of your mam being upset, but . . .'

'I know,' Eveleen murmured. 'I know, Josh.'

They stood in silence for several minutes before Josh said slowly, 'Yes, I'll come. There's plenty of folk who'll give a hand with the work here now. Ted Morton's brood are looking for more work now they're growing up, though we all miss Micky. Still, he's happy at his work in Grantham.'

'How is Ted? I heard he'd come home safely.'

'You know Ted. He's fine. Hardly a scratch and quite his old self.'

Eveleen smiled, thinking of her childhood friend. 'I'm glad he came back, but is there a job for him on the estate?'

'Oh, aye. His dad, Bill Morton, is a fine bailiff for you.'

'I know,' she agreed. 'He should have been bailiff years ago. I hope Ted will take it on when Bill wants to retire.'

'I expect he will.'

There was silence between them as they watched the sun sink lower.

'You know,' Eveleen began haltingly, 'I can't stop feeling guilty about Stephen.'

Josh looked at her in surprise. 'Whatever for, mi duck?'

'Well, I bought his house. I was the cause of him enlisting and then – and then he was killed at the Front . . .'

To her amazement, Josh gave a bellow of laughter. 'Him? Dying a hero? Oh, you've got it all wrong, Evie love.'

'But – but Mam told me he'd died.'

Josh nodded and his laughter faded. 'He was killed all right, but it was in a drunken brawl in the back streets of London.' He cleared his throat, obviously embarrassed. 'Over some woman, we heard. He never got anywhere near a recruiting office, believe you me.'

Though sad to hear that Stephen had sunk so low, Eveleen felt as if the burden of guilt, at least over Stephen Dunsmore, had been lifted away. She leant her head against the big man's comforting shoulder. 'Oh, Josh,' was all she said and knew he understood.

They stood together for some time before he said, 'I'll get everything sorted out here and be with you by the end of the week. Can you sort me some lodgings out in Nottingham . . .?'

'Don't be silly. You'll stay with us.' As he opened his mouth to protest, she raised her hand. 'And I won't take no for an answer.'

Josh smiled. 'I never was any good at refusing you anything, was I, mi duck?'

Eveleen smiled and linked her arm through his as they turned to walk back to the farmhouse. 'No, Josh, you weren't.'

Bridie hurried back towards Singleton's Yard, taking little running steps every so often in her anxiety to get back as quickly as possible.

Already Andrew's cottage felt warmer; a fire now crackled in the grate and the kettle was placed on the hob. He looked up as she entered.

'I haven't seen anyone yet. The place seems deserted. I've been into the workshops. There's no-one there. No-one at all. In fact,' he added worriedly, 'it doesn't look as if the machines have been working for a while.'

They faced each other, their faces grim, whilst Bridie related what she had found out in the village.

'You go to your great-gran's. I'll see if I can find Harry.'

Bridie nodded and was out of the door and along the path towards the far end cottage.

'Great-Gran!' she called hesitantly as she pushed open the door that, as ever, was unlocked. The cold met her just as it had in Andrew's house and this time, it chilled her to the bone. What had happened to her great-grandmother? She climbed the stairs calling out, but there was no answer and, until the moment she pushed open the bedroom door, she thought the house was deserted.

Bridie let out a little cry of shock. The old lady was lying in the bed, her eyes closed, her breathing a rasping sound. The state of the bedclothes and of the whole room was far worse than the first time Bridie had found her in a neglected state. On the bedside table there was the remains of a meagre meal and half a cup of cold tea, but that was all.

There was no fire in the grate. The bedlinen and the old lady's nightgown were soiled.

'Oh, Great-Gran . . .' she began and tiptoed to the bed, but at that moment there was a noise downstairs and she heard Andrew calling, 'Bridie, Bridie, come quickly. It's Harry.'

She touched Bridget's bony hand on the coverlet and whispered, 'I'll be right back.' Then she hurried down the stairs.

Andrew was beckoning her urgently from the doorway. 'It's Harry,' he said again. 'He's in a bad way.'

'What's happened?' she asked as they hurried along

the path in front of the cottages to the one at the opposite end.

'I – I don't know. He's just sitting there in his chair by the fire.'

She stopped suddenly and stared at Andrew. 'You – you don't mean he – he's dead?'

'No, no. He spoke to me, but he – he didn't seem to recognize me. I had to tell him who it was.'

She stepped across the threshold and took a moment for her eyes to accustom themselves to the gloom.

Harry Singleton was sitting, as Andrew had said, in his chair by the range. But here again, as with her great-grandmother's home, no warming fire burnt in the grate. On the table, spread with a crumpled check cloth, was a stale loaf of bread and a butter dish with rancid butter in it. The whole place was even more dirty and neglected than the first time she had seen it.

Now her attention fastened on the man himself. Though he still had a full beard, it was ragged and unkempt and, beneath it, she could see that his face was much thinner and his clothes hung loosely on his body. She moved nearer. 'Grandfather?' she said gently. He turned his face towards her, but his eyes did not focus on her.

'Who's that?' he grunted. 'Who is it? Come over here where I can see you.'

She knew his eyesight was poor, so she said, 'It's me. Bridie. Your – your granddaughter.' She moved closer and touched his hand. 'And Andrew's here too. He's come home from the war. He's not quite fit yet, so I've come to look after him. I'll look after you and Great-Grandmother too.' She paused and then added pointedly, 'If you'll let me.'

The old man pulled his hand from beneath her touch.

'Haven't got a granddaughter and we don't need help from anyone. Specially not from a child.'

A lump grew in her throat. Still, he refused to acknowledge her. Even though he was living in squalor, he would never admit to needing help. And especially not her help.

'How long have you been like this, Grandfather?'

'Don't call me that,' he growled.

Bridie sighed. 'What happened after Mrs Turner was taken ill?'

'Lil from the cottage facing the street has looked after us. We're all right.'

Bridie gave a very unladylike snort. 'Her? Well, that explains it all. Now, Andrew's going to light a fire for you and very soon I'll bring you a meal, but I must go back to Great-Gran. She's . . .' She hesitated, not knowing if he knew that his mother looked in a very bad way. But it seemed he did for he said, 'She's not gone yet, then? I keep expecting to be told . . .' His voice petered away.

'She'll be fine,' Bridie said determinedly, 'now I'm back.' Without giving her grandfather time to protest any further, she turned to Andrew. 'Can you manage? Don't overdo it, will you?'

'I'll be fine, love.' He drew her to the door and whispered, 'Your great-gran? Is she bad?'

All Bridie needed to do was to bite her lip and to nod for him to know the serious state of her great-grandmother.

'I'll get this fire lit and I'll get the doctor. You go back to the old lady.'

Bridie hurried away.

By the time the village doctor arrived, the old lady was lying in a clean nightdress and between sweet-smelling sheets. A fire burned in the grate, but Bridie had been unable to rouse her great-grandmother.

'Is she unconscious?'

The doctor did not answer her until he had examined Bridget thoroughly.

'She's a very sick old lady,' he told her solemnly. 'I'm sorry, my dear, but she may well not last the night. Do you need any help? I can send a nurse . . .'

Bridie shook her head and explained what she had been doing for the past two years. The doctor nodded. 'Very well, then. No-one can do more than you are clearly capable of doing.' He sighed. 'But I'm sorry, my dear, you must expect the worst.'

Fifty-Six

For the rest of that day Bridie seemed to be running everywhere. She made a meal and asked Andrew to take a plateful to her grandfather. 'You'll have to sit him at the table, put the knife and fork in his hands so that he can feed himself.'

'Sit down and get yours while I take it, then,' Andrew ordered. 'You're going to need all the strength you can get over the next few days.' He reached out and took her hand. 'Oh, Bridie love, I wouldn't have brought you here if I'd thought for a moment we were coming back to all this.'

'You couldn't have stopped me,' she said, giving him an all-too-brief smile. There was little to smile about at present. 'Besides, I'm glad you did. At least, I can help grandfather, if he'll let me, even if it's too late to . . .' She said no more, but poured hot milk into a bowl of bread broken into small pieces. 'I'll have a quick bite, but I'm going to sit with my great-grandmother. Will you be all right?'

Andrew nodded. 'Course I will. I'll snooze in the chair here for tonight. We can air the beds tomorrow.'

She bent and kissed his forehead briefly and then hurried back to the old lady's bedside. As she sat down beside her, Bridget's eyes flickered and she made a tiny sound.

Gently Bridie spooned milk between the thin, parched

411

lips, very slowly and carefully so that the semi-conscious woman did not choke. It reminded her of the time she had spoonfed poor Bertie Hyde. This time, though, she vowed, she would not lose her patient. And then Bridie began to talk. Quietly, but persistently, she was trying to drag her great-grandmother back in to the world of the living. The old lady was hovering between one world and the next, but Bridie's determination would not let her go.

Through the night Bridie chattered on, scarcely knowing what she said, yet instinctively knowing that she had to keep on. She refused to let her great-grandmother die without a fight.

She kept the fire built up, keeping the room cosy throughout the long night. As the pale fingers of dawn filtered through the lace curtains, Bridget opened her eyes. Looking straight into Bridie's eyes, she said, 'Can't a body get a bit of peace? Do you ever stop for breath, girl?'

Then she closed her eyes and slept. But now it was a natural sleep.

Bridie laid her head on the coverlet and allowed the tears of relief to flow.

'How is she?' Andrew tapped on the door only minutes later and tiptoed into the bedroom.

Bridie raised her weary head, but her eyes were shining. 'She's going to be all right. She spoke to me.' She was laughing and crying at the same time as she stood up and flung her arms around Andrew. 'She told me off for talking so much. Oh, Andrew, she told me off. Isn't that wonderful? She told me off.'

Andrew chuckled. 'If you say so, love.' They stood together looking down at the old lady, now sleeping peacefully. 'But now you must come and get some breakfast. I've got it all ready.'

'Oh, you shouldn't have. You'll . . .'

'I'm quite all right. I can manage a few jobs. Though . . .' He winced slightly. 'You'll have to redo my dressing soon. It's starting to hurt.'

'When the doctor comes this morning, I'll get him to take a look at it. And at Grandfather too, if he'll let him.'

'Huh,' Andrew snorted. 'There's about as much chance of that as me learning to fly.'

'Well, my dear, you've worked a miracle. I didn't expect to see Mrs Singleton still alive,' the doctor from the village told Bridie later that morning. 'I'll call each day for a while, but I think she's turned the corner. And as for Harry, well, I think you've arrived just in time to stop him sinking into a similar state.' The kindly man shook his head. 'Dear, dear, I had no idea things had got as bad as this. Someone should have called me.' He looked at her keenly. 'I understand you only arrived here yesterday?'

Bridie nodded.

'Who had been looking after them?'

'It had been Mrs Turner . . .'

'Ah, now that explains it,' he nodded.

Bridie forbore to explain Lil's part; she planned to speak to that particular lady herself very soon. 'But now I'm back and staying, things will be very different.'

'Good, good.' The doctor picked up his case. 'See

you tomorrow. If you have any problems, be sure to let me know and I'll come at once.'

Bridie's meeting with Lil was brief but fiery.

'Well, if that's how you feel, don't ask for my 'elp again,' the slovenly woman said huffily. Her apron was dirty and her hair hung down in unwashed, lank strands. She folded her arms across her ample bosom.

'Don't worry, I won't. I'm here to stay.'

Lil's face twisted into a sneer. 'Oh, staying alone in the cottage with Andrew, are yer? Yer grandfather won't like that.'

Bridie arched her eyebrow and glared at the woman whom she blamed for the sorry state she had found on her return.

She pointed an accusing finger at Lil. 'You mind your business and I'll mind mine. If there was a court of law to put you in for what you've done, I'd do it. As it is, I'll have you thrown out of your cottage if I get any more trouble.'

'Huh!' the woman sneered. 'Harry wouldn't throw me out. I've done a lot for Harry Singleton. Looking after his cantankerous mother, for a start.'

'You call that "looking after" someone? You don't know the meaning of the word.'

'He'll not get rid of me.' The woman was smug as she delivered her final ace. 'I clean his precious chapel.'

Bridie laughed aloud, the sound echoing down the narrow street. 'Is that all? There's plenty of folk willing to do that. And they'd do it a lot better than you, I shouldn't wonder.'

For the first time a flicker of uncertainty crossed Lil's face. 'Who?'

Bridie grinned in her moment of triumph. 'Me, Lil. Me. I'd clean his chapel for him. In fact, from now on I will.' Her face sobered as she said threateningly, 'You keep your distance from me and mine from now on. And remember what I said. I'll have you thrown out on the street if you don't.'

The woman gave a snarl and slammed the door in Bridie's face, but the girl had seen the look of fear on Lil's face. She would not trouble them again.

'Now, Josh, have you got everything you need?' Eveleen asked, as the three of them sat down to dinner in their city home. 'Is your room all right for you?'

Josh cast her a comical look. 'It's fine. A bit too posh, though, for the likes of me, mi duck.'

The three of them laughed together.

'I know what you mean, Josh. I felt just the same when I first married Richard.' Laughing at herself, she added, 'But it's surprising how quickly you can get used to the easy life.'

'Oh, I wouldn't say you've had it easy. Not over the last few years, anyway.'

'We've been lucky, though.' Her voice was husky as she reached across the corner of the table to touch her husband's hand. 'At least Richard's come home safely. The rest is up to us now.'

Richard raised his head slowly and looked into her eyes. He turned his hand beneath hers and gripped it like a drowning man.

Hoarsely he said, 'You're right. It is up to us now.'

Momentarily they forgot that Josh was in the room. For a brief moment, there was no-one else in the world but the two of them. In that instant, a new understanding, a fresh determination to put matters right between them, began to blossom.

Josh cleared his throat, startling them from their mutual reverie. 'Aye, you're right. So many haven't come back or, if they have, they're so badly damaged that their lives can never be the same again.'

'I'm afraid,' Eveleen said quietly, 'that's what you're going to face at the factory. There are so many pleading for jobs and yet . . .' She sighed heavily. 'I don't know whether they're capable of the work.'

'I expected as much. But we'll cope, mi duck. I'll explain it all to Bob, an' all. Make him understand that I've only come back temporary. Just to help out a bit. You leave it to me, Evie.'

The weeks turned into months. At Flawford, Bridie's days were exhausting, yet she was happy just to be with Andrew, content, for the moment, to bide her time. His health improved rapidly and his wound began to heal, so well now that he was champing at the bit to begin some kind of work.

'I'm going to talk to Harry about the workshops. I can't understand what's happened. Why is no-one working there, even if he can't any more?'

'I don't know. Go and ask him.'

'Right, I will.' He moved to the door eagerly and then hesitated. He turned back to her and said, 'Will you come with me?'

'Coward!' she joked, but moved to his side. 'Come on, let's beard the lion in his den together.'

Once, he could have been called a lion, with a fine mane of hair and head of the pride. But now the old warrior was laid low by infirmity.

'It's only us, Grandfather,' Bridie called out cheerfully as she opened the door. 'Me and Andrew.'

'What do you want now, girl?' he asked gruffly. She was still not welcome in his home, but he did now eat the meals she prepared, though she was always careful to make sure that Andrew took them along the pathway to his cottage.

'Andrew's come to talk to you about the workshops. What happened, Grandfather? Why is no-one working there any more?'

'What's it to do with you?'

Bridie and Andrew exchanged a glance, then she shrugged helplessly, gesturing that Andrew should carry on the conversation. She certainly wasn't going to get anywhere.

'I just wondered,' he began hesitantly, 'if you'd like me to get things going again?'

'We were doing all right. The women Eveleen sent did all right. I'll give her that,' he added grudgingly. 'Three of 'em got quite good on the machines and the others did the seaming, the winding or the washing, an' that. But when the war finished, they was off back to the city life. The old feller that was here gave up and the boy went to work in the city an' all. And,' he added bitterly, unwilling to admit failure, 'my eyesight isn't what it was. So, young Burns . . .' To Harry Singleton, Andrew would always be 'young Burns'. 'What do you want to do with my workshops?'

'Get them working again, Mr Singleton. Get this yard back to what it used to be.'

'Then what are you waiting for, young Burns? What are you waiting for?'

Fifty-Seven

Eveleen had not felt so happy since before Richard volunteered. Every day he was improving and the previous night he had made love to her for the first time.

At the breakfast table she could not hide the glow of happiness on her face and she was hard pressed not to laugh aloud at Richard's somewhat sheepish expression as he said, 'It's a good job Josh leaves early for work. I'm sure he'd guess.'

Eveleen giggled deliciously, like a young bride. 'I don't care if he does. Oh, darling Richard, we're going to be all right.' She held him close and he buried his face in her neck.

'Yes, yes. I really think we are.'

Even the letter that Smithers brought in on a silver tray moments later, could not cast a shadow over her new-found confidence.

'It's from Bridie.'

Already they knew about the situation Bridie and Andrew had found at Flawford. Eveleen had visited once, going alone, guiltily persuading Richard not to go. But the atmosphere between aunt and niece had been strained and Eveleen had not been able to bring herself to go recently. She felt ashamed that she had not visited again and therefore eagerly scanned the letter for news.

'Things are much better,' she said. 'Andrew's opening up the workshops.' She looked up briefly. 'Do you know, I hadn't realized the machines were idle, but now I think about it, I didn't hear any noise the day I went.'

'Andrew will soon have things up and running again. He'll find plenty of men coming back from the war who are only too glad of a job,' Richard said.

'Mm,' Eveleen agreed and returned to reading the letter. 'Gran's asking to see my mother.' Then she gave a little gasp of surprise. 'Bridie wants to know if we can arrange it.'

Richard shrugged. 'I don't see why not. Would you like me to take her? It's high time I started driving again.'

'No,' Eveleen's reply was swift – perhaps a little too swift, but Richard did not appear to notice. 'No. I – we'll – go out to the farm this afternoon and see what they want to do. All right?'

'Anything you say, darling.'

Eveleen felt the tears spring to her eyes, but they were tears of joy. His words were simple, but they spoke volumes to Eveleen. Her husband – her husband of old – was truly back home with her.

'Jimmy will take me. There's no need for you to bother. Not that I really want to go, but I suppose I'll have to. Maybe she's dying and that's why she wants to see me.'

Eveleen was appalled at the callous tone in her mother's voice. There had been a lot of bitterness in the past, but surely Mary did not still bear resentment against a frail, sick old lady – her own mother. But Eveleen made no comment, merely asking, 'How are you going to get there?'

Mary waved her hand airily. 'Oh, Jimmy will borrow something.'

'Josh can bring the car home on Saturday. He could take you on Sunday. I don't think it would be a good idea for Jimmy to go.'

'Why ever not?' Mary snapped, defensive at once.

Eveleen sighed. 'He'll only cause trouble with Andrew if he goes.'

'No, he won't. And I want Jimmy to take me. I'll only go if Jimmy takes me. So there.'

Sometimes, Eveleen thought crossly, her mother was like a petulant child. 'Then Jimmy,' she snapped back before she had stopped to think, 'can find his own means of transport, if that's how you feel.'

'It's all right, darling,' Richard said. 'Josh can still bring the car and Jimmy can drive it.' He turned towards Jimmy. 'You can drive, I take it?'

''Course I can. Nothing to it.'

But Eveleen had the distinct feeling that his answer was based more on bravado than actual capability. She knew her brother of old.

Bridie read her aunt's letter with trepidation.

I'm afraid your gran insists that Jimmy should bring her. It's the only way she'll agree to come.

'You will keep out of his way, won't you?' Bridie begged Andrew. 'Please. I don't want any more trouble.'

Andrew's mouth was a grim line. 'I'll not start anything. I'll promise you that much, but if he starts something . . .'

Bridie sighed. It was the best she could hope for.

The following Sunday was bright and warm. *They'll be coming in the morning. Your gran won't want to risk being forced to attend chapel*, Eveleen had written.

Though Bridie still went and sat in the family pew

next to her grandfather, just as she had done before, she could not persuade Andrew to attend the services.

'I've lost me faith, Bridie,' he told her. 'After all that I've seen in the war, there is no God in heaven.'

'Oh, Andrew, it wasn't God who caused the war, but the greed of men. You can't blame him.'

He'd looked away from her, ill at ease. 'I know I shouldn't, but he let it happen, didn't he?'

For the moment there was nothing she could do or say. Andrew would have to find his way back in his own time. In the meantime, her knees became quite sore from praying for her beloved Andrew.

Bridie fussed over the Sunday dinner, acutely nervous that everything should be just perfect. But it was not so much the preparation of the food that caused her concern, but the worry of the trouble Jimmy's mere presence might cause.

They arrived at half-past ten and came to the far-end cottage.

'Where is she, then?' Mary demanded curtly, with scarcely a greeting to Bridie.

'In bed, Gran. She can't get down the stairs now, though she sometimes can manage to sit in a chair by her bedroom window.'

Mary climbed the stairs, Bridie following her closely, torn between being with her great-grandmother during the visit and keeping an eye on Jimmy.

'Here she is, Great-Gran.' Bridie forced herself to say brightly as she opened the bedroom door and ushered Mary inside. 'Here, Gran, sit in this chair by the bed.'

Mary sat down and stared at the old lady in the bed. 'You're looking well, Mother.'

'Stuff and nonsense,' the old lady retorted with asperity and Bridie hid her smile. Old and frail she might be physically, but Bridget Singleton was still quite capable of dealing with a visit from her daughter.

'I'll leave you to it,' she said, confident now of leaving them together. 'I'll call you when dinner is ready.'

Downstairs she went through to the front room to check on the joint, sizzling in the oven in the range.

The room was empty; Jimmy had disappeared.

Bridie ran out of the cottage and along the footpath, bursting into her grandfather's cottage. 'Is he here?'

She glanced round the room, but Harry was sitting alone in his usual place by the range. 'Is who here?' he grumbled and Bridie realized she had awoken him from a nap.

'Oh, never mind.' She turned and hurried out again. There was no-one in Andrew's cottage either.

'I'll be in the workshop. I don't reckon he'll come up there,' Andrew had told Bridie earlier. 'Though your grandfather won't like it if he knows I'm working on the Sabbath.'

'If it prevents trouble,' Bridie had said, 'I think the Good Lord will overlook it this once.'

Bridie ran down the path towards the workshops, tripping on an uneven brick in her haste. She climbed the stone steps and heard their voices in the workroom above her. She paused to listen.

Andrew's was raised in anger. 'How dare you say such a thing about her? It's not true. None of it. I'll smash your face in.'

Jimmy's voice came nonchalant and tormenting. 'If you don't believe me, ask Eveleen. She'll tell you.'

Oh no, Bridie groaned inwardly. Even after all these years, they're still fighting over my poor mother.

Fifty-Eight

'Andrew! What a lovely surprise. What brings you to Nottingham?' Eveleen cried, rising from the sofa and holding out her arms to greet him when Smithers showed him into the morning room. Then she saw the expression on his face. 'What is it? What's wrong?'

At once, she feared the worst. Was it her grand-mother? Had the old lady died? But Andrew's expression was not one of kindly concern at being the bearer of sad tidings. It was anger that Eveleen saw on his face.

'Sit down. I'll get Smithers to bring us tea—'

'Don't bother.' His manner was curt. 'This isn't a social call, Eveleen, and when you've heard what I've got to say you'll likely have me thrown out.'

'Thrown out?' Eveleen gave a nervous laugh. 'What-ever could you have to say that . . .?' Her voice petered away and she sank back onto the sofa, feeling suddenly queasy in the pit of her stomach. Andrew remained standing.

'Your mother came to visit last week.'

'Yes, I know about that.'

'Jimmy brought her.'

'Oh!' Realization began to dawn. Once again Jimmy had tried to make trouble. She sighed.

'I tried to keep out of his way. For Bridie's sake. She asked me to. Now I know why,' he muttered in a low voice more to himself than for Eveleen to hear. Louder, he went on. 'But he found me. Sought me out in the workshop. He couldn't wait to tell me.'

There was a pause and Eveleen prompted. 'Tell you what?'

'That your husband and my Bridie are having a love affair.'

The room seemed to spin around her and the sick feeling increased so that she almost wanted to rush to the bathroom. She covered her face with her hands.

'Evie, I'm sorry.' Andrew came to sit beside her and put his arm about her. 'But I have to know. I have to know if it's true or if it's Jimmy up to his old tricks.'

In a low, muffled voice, Eveleen said, 'I haven't any proof, but I had suspected it.'

'You had?' Andrew sounded startled, as if he had fully expected her to refute any such suggestion.

Eveleen dropped her hands and turned to face him. She could see the incredulity on his face. He had clung to the belief that it was all Jimmy's lies and now the shock that it might actually be true was plainly written on his face.

Her voice was flat with defeat as she explained. 'Perhaps it started as long ago as the Goose Fair.'

'She was only a child then.'

'Yes, yes. Oh, I don't mean that he would have – but he might have started to care for her then in a way . . .' She took a deep breath. 'In a way that was not strictly uncle and niece.'

Andrew clenched his fist. 'I'll bloody well kill him.'

'He was always very fond of her, but – but it got more – more noticeable when he came back from the war. He was in a dreadful state. Shell-shocked, they call it. Bridie was the only one who could handle him. That was why he went to Fairfield House.' There was a wealth of sadness in her tone as she added, 'I couldn't help him. In fact, if I'm honest, I seemed to make matters worse.'

'Is it still going on? Because I don't see how they can have met up since we've been at Flawford. I've been with her all the time. Unless—'

'Unless what?'

He shrugged. 'Well, I've spent a lot of time in the workshops recently. I can't say that I know what she's been doing every minute of the day. When she's gone out shopping and that.'

Eveleen shook her head. 'I don't know for sure, but we've been together most of the time since he came home from Fairfield House.' There was a catch in her voice as she thought how close they had become once more. Was all that to be torn away from her again? 'But he did suggest,' she went on, her voice trembling, 'that he should drive my mother to Flawford.' They stared at each other as she went on, 'Perhaps – perhaps that was an excuse so that he could see her.'

'Where is he? I want to see him.'

'He's – he's out for a morning walk. He shouldn't be long.'

'Then I'll wait,' Andrew said grimly.

'Where's Andrew?' Harry asked belligerently when Bridie took his dinner.

'Gone to Nottingham.'

'To the lace market?' It seemed that Harry could bring himself to speak civilly to her if it was a matter of business.

'He didn't say.'

Bridie was worried about Andrew. He had been bad-tempered ever since Jimmy's visit last week. Worse still, he had been offhand with her and several times she had found him watching her with a strange expression on his face. She couldn't think what the matter was, other than that he was beginning to believe Jimmy's lies that he, Andrew, might be her natural father. But he had always been so adamant that that was impossible. Surely that meant he had never made physical love to Rebecca.

She had tried to question him, but each time he turned away from her, tight-lipped and uncommunicative. In the end, she had given up trying to coax him to tell her what was obviously bothering him.

'He'll be back,' Bridie said, forcing herself to be cheerful. 'Maybe he wants to surprise us with some good news about the workshops.'

Her grandfather gave a grunt as if he didn't believe it. And, for once, Bridie had to agree with him.

They heard the front door open and close, heard Richard greeting Smithers as the manservant took his master's coat and hat and heard the low murmur of their voices as he was told he was wanted in the morning room. They heard his footsteps cross the hall and then Richard was in the room and coming towards Andrew, his hand outstretched in greeting.

Andrew had risen from his seat, but made no effort to shake Richard's hand. Richard paused in puzzlement and glanced from Andrew to Eveleen and back again, realizing at once that something was dreadfully amiss.

'What is it? Is it bad news from Flawford?'

He moved towards Eveleen to put his arm about her, but she could not bear him to touch her and she moved away to stand near the window, leaving Andrew to broach the subject that was uppermost in both their minds.

'Eveleen?' Richard said, but as she turned her back on him, he looked towards Andrew for an explanation.

Andrew was blunt. 'Are you having an affair with Bridie?'

For a long moment Richard stared at him incredulously, as if he couldn't believe what he was hearing. 'An affair? With Bridie?' Then he began to laugh.

From her place by the window, Eveleen turned her head to look at him, but Andrew, his fists clenched took a step nearer to him.

'It's no laughing matter—'

'Oh, Andrew, Andrew . . .' Richard was reaching out to put his hand on Andrew's shoulder, but the latter knocked his arm away. Richard's face sobered as he glanced from one to the other. 'My God! You actually think such a preposterous idea is true?' He paused and now there was anger in his tone, yet it was tinged with sadness. 'How could you even think such a thing of me? Or of Bridie? Good God!' He was shouting now, incensed at their lack of faith in him. 'And you, Eveleen? How could you ever, *ever* think that about me? She's a child, for heaven's sake!'

Andrew shook his head slowly. 'Oh no, she isn't. Not now. When we went away, she was, but not any longer.' There was sadness in his own tone now as if he mourned a personal loss. 'While we were away, she grew up.'

'You want the truth? Well, you can have it. I do love Bridie – very much.' Now they stared at him and Eveleen gave a little whimper and pressed the back of her hand to her mouth. 'But as my *niece* and, latterly, as my nurse. She was the only one who could help me when I came back from the war. She was the only one who took the time to understand...' His words were a direct, hurtful accusation aimed at Eveleen. 'She *cared*.' Now he turned to Andrew and pointed his forefinger at him. 'And you, Andrew Burns, are the biggest bloody fool around. That girl has spent her life loving you. Even as a little girl she always said she was going to marry you. And, as far as I know, now she's a grown woman she still feels the same. Though God alone knows why. And she is a grown woman, despite her tender years, because what she's seen and dealt with in the time she's been nursing is more than you, Eveleen,' he swung round once more to include her, 'have ever experienced in your life and that includes the hard times you had as a girl.'

'Richard, I'm sorry...' she began, moving towards him, reaching out to him. But he held up his hands, palms outwards, to fend her off.

He turned on his heel and went towards the door, flinging it open. He looked back over his shoulder and addressed his final words to Andrew. 'I just hope she's got the sense to find someone more worthy than you for all that love she's got in her heart.'

Then he left the room, slamming the door behind him and leaving the two of them staring after him.

'Oh, Andrew,' Eveleen whispered, the tears running down her face, 'what have we done?'

Fifty-Nine

'I'm sorry, Evie.' They were sitting on the sofa, Eveleen weeping against Andrew's shoulder. 'There I go, crashing in with my big feet and all I've done is cause trouble between you and Richard.'

Eveleen hiccuped miserably. 'We'd only just got back to something like we used to be. And now . . .' Her tears flowed afresh.

Andrew hugged her. 'Me and my big mouth. I'm so sorry. I'll go and find him. Explain that it was my fault.'

Eveleen shook her head. 'It won't do any good. He could see I believed it too. Besides, I heard the front door bang. He's gone out again. Oh . . .' she cried. 'I think I'm going to be sick.' She got up and hurried from the room, holding her hand over her mouth. She only just reached the bathroom before she began to retch. When the spasm had passed she went back downstairs to find Andrew still waiting for her in the morning room.

'All right?' he asked, rather unnecessarily, for Eveleen's face was deathly white and she was shivering as if with a fever. But she nodded and sat down, gripping her hands together in her lap.

'What are you going to tell Bridie?'

He was silent for a moment before he answered. 'I'm going to ask her to marry me.' He paused and then muttered, 'If she'll still have me after this.'

She looked up, startled. 'What? But I thought you didn't think of her in – in that way. I thought you loved her, well, more as if she was your daughter.'

He smiled sheepishly. 'I did. Or at least I thought I did. But when Jimmy told me about her and Richard, well, I saw red. I was in a blind, jealous rage, Evie. The jealous rage of a man who's in love with the woman he was talking about.'

He passed his hand across his forehead, still feeling confused. 'I didn't think I could ever stop loving Rebecca. I thought that what I felt for Bridie was because she's Rebecca's daughter. But not now. Not any more. Jimmy's shown me that, even though I could have killed him for saying what he did. And when I got here this morning I could have killed Richard.' He looked Eveleen straight in the face. 'If he hadn't been so obviously telling the truth – and yes, I do believe him – I might very well have throttled him.' He shook his head as if he couldn't quite believe what he was hearing himself say. 'This war's changed us, Evie. We think nothing now of taking another man's life. Isn't that terrible?'

Staring at him, Eveleen nodded slowly.

Andrew stood up. 'If you're sure there's nothing I can do to put matters right, then I'll go.' He looked down at her once more. 'I'm so sorry, Evie,' he said hoarsely.

By dusk Richard had still not returned home and Eveleen lay on her bed, her eyes swollen but now, for the moment at least, she could cry no more. She had eaten nothing since breakfast and now her stomach rumbled with hunger and yet she still felt sick.

And yet, she began to realize, this queasy feeling had

not just occurred today. She had been feeling unwell for several days now, especially first thing in the morning.

She rubbed her stomach, gently over the place where her womb lay. Was it possible? Could she really – after all this time – be with child?

And then, as she realized what terrible damage this day's events had wrought, the tears came again.

In the moment that should have brought her the greatest happiness of her life, she was plunged into the depths of despair.

'Where have you been? I've been worried sick.'

'Oh, Bridie.' Andrew held out his arms to her. 'I've done a dreadful thing today.'

After a moment of surprised hesitation, Bridie went to him to be enfolded in his embrace. He hugged her so tightly he almost squeezed the breath from her body. 'What is it?' she whispered. 'Tell me.'

So, almost as if he were kneeling in the chapel, but instead standing with his face buried against her neck, Andrew made his confession. So, Bridie thought as she listened to him, the quarrel she had overheard between her father and Andrew had not been about Rebecca as she had supposed. It had been about her. She heard him out until the very end and then, gently, she drew back and put her fingers beneath his chin to lift his face and to look into his eyes. 'Why didn't you ask me?'

He could not meet her gaze. 'I couldn't. I was that mad, that – that jealous.'

She shook her head sadly. 'You didn't trust me, did you? You really thought it could be true?'

Shamefaced, he nodded. She uttered no word of reproach, but merely took him into her arms now and held him close for a long time. At last she said, 'Poor Auntie Evie. I must go to her.'

'Oh, Bridie, I shouldn't. I've caused enough trouble.'

'I'm not going to cause any trouble, Andrew. I'm the only one who can sort it all out. I'll go tomorrow morning. I'll leave everything ready for the old folks here. And you,' she tapped him playfully on the nose, 'will have to look after them both.'

Andrew looked askance, but – as Bridie knew full well – he was in no position to argue.

When she was shown into the morning room the following morning, Eveleen ran into her arms with a sob. Bridie held her and patted her back comfortingly. 'It'll be all right, Auntie Evie, I promise. It's not true. Not a word of it. You do know that, don't you?'

Eveleen nodded and they sat down side by side on the sofa. 'I do now, but . . .'

'You mean, you thought for a while that it was?'

'Oh, Bridie, I've been so silly. I don't know what got into me. But – but you seemed to be able to do so much more for Richard than I could. You and he seemed so – so close.'

'I told you,' Bridie said gently, but very firmly, 'it was because I'd seen so much of it at the home that I could understand. Besides, although I love Uncle Richard dearly – *as an uncle*,' she emphasized with a smile, 'I was still able to deal with it rationally. To separate myself just a little. It's very difficult, you know, for families to help their nearest and dearest.'

'Is it?' Eveleen did not sound convinced. 'I thought it should be me, more than anyone else, who could help him.'

Bridie shook her head. 'No, it's not always the case. Believe me.'

'I do,' Eveleen said simply and they both knew that she was not merely referring to Bridie's nursing knowledge.

'So,' Bridie asked, 'where is he?'

'I don't know,' Eveleen said and her voice threatened to rise again into a despairing wail. 'He didn't come home last night. I don't know where he is.'

'Didn't . . .' Bridie began incredulously, but she could see by her aunt's face that it was all too true. More practically, she asked, 'Then where do you think he might be? At his parents?'

Eveleen shook her head. 'I've already sent word to see. He's not there. Oh, Bridie . . .' she clutched at the girl. 'I'm so afraid he might have – might have done something awful. He was so angry. So hurt.'

Bridie shook her head. 'Uncle Richard wouldn't do that. He's just taken himself off somewhere to be alone.' She thought for a moment and then her expression brightened. 'Has he taken the motor?'

Eveleen nodded.

'Can you borrow another motor car from somewhere?'

'I suppose so,' Eveleen said. 'I expect his father would lend me his.'

'Right then. Send Smithers to fetch it and get your coat and hat. We're taking a trip into the countryside.'

'Why? Where do you think he's gone? Flawford?'

Bridie shook her head. 'No. Fairfield House, of course.' She knew that there was still a skeleton staff at the home. 'It's where he felt safe. Where else would he go?'

Sixty

'He wouldn't go to Pear Tree Farm, would he? To have it out with Jimmy?' Eveleen asked as she drove, a little unsteadily, out of the city.

'I hope not,' Bridie said grimly. 'Else there might be fisticuffs again.' They drove a little further and then Bridie asked suddenly, 'Does Josh know about any of this?' She was aware that Josh was staying with Richard and Eveleen.

'No. I avoided him this morning.' Eveleen smiled wryly. 'One look at me and he'd have known something was wrong. I can't hide much from Josh.'

'So, he doesn't know the trouble my dear father's been causing?'

'No. Apart from the fact that he's been the cause of Josh agreeing to run the factory for us for a while. He'd never have wanted to leave my mother if it hadn't been for Jimmy being there. Josh felt pushed out.'

The rest of the journey passed in silence, but as they drove up the driveway of Fairfield House, Bridie said, 'Now, I need to talk to Uncle Richard alone first. You go down to the beck, Auntie Evie, and wait there. If – if everything's all right, I'll send him to you.'

'Why do you need to see him alone?' Was there even yet a faint hint of mistrust in her?

Bridie eyed her, as if guessing. 'It would be awkward with you there too. You must see that. I need to give him some straight talking. I need to tell him how things have been for you while he's been away. Don't you see? These returning soldiers have no idea what we went through back here. Oh, I'm not suggesting that we've experienced anything like they've been through. But it hasn't been easy, has it, suddenly left alone to cope? Especially for us weak and feeble women.'

Bridie was laughing and even Eveleen had to smile. 'Once upon a time, I'd have said I was a strong woman,' she said, 'but not any more. I'm as weak as a kitten.' She turned to face her niece, this young girl of whom she was so proud. If only . . . She pushed the thoughts away. She must begin to trust again and what better moment to start than right here. Right now.

She nodded and climbed out of the vehicle. 'I'll go round the house and through the back yard and down to the beck. But what if he's not here?'

'He will be,' Bridie said confidently. 'But if not, I'll come to you.' She jumped down and set off towards the front steps, whilst Eveleen disappeared round the side of the house.

'He's in the gardens, miss,' the maid, who answered the door, told her.

'Thanks, I'll find him.'

She found Richard sitting on the wooden seat in the rose garden, staring straight ahead at the golden blooms in front of him, yet she knew he was seeing nothing of their beauty.

'Hello, Uncle Richard,' she called as she approached and sat down beside him.

He turned his head slowly as if waking from a dream, or rather a nightmare, to look at her. 'I'm surprised you dare be seen in my company. I'm supposed to have seduced you and we're having this passionate affair.'

435

She grinned at him, but there was no answering smile. 'Daft, isn't it?' she said.

He sighed. 'From your point of view, yes. But from mine, well . . .' He lapsed into silence.

'Why from my point of view?' she asked.

'I'm old enough to be your father, for heaven's sake,' he said testily.

'So's Andrew, but I'm going to marry him.'

'Are you?' There was a faint humour in his tone. 'Does Andrew know?'

Bridie giggled. 'Oh yes, but so far, he's refused me.'

They smiled together but then the smile faded from Richard's face. 'So what you're saying is,' he said slowly, 'that it's quite possible for other people to have thought that I – that we . . .'

She nodded. 'Of course it is. A lot of older men marry younger women. Now, just you listen to me.' She tapped him on the arm, demanding his attention. 'Look at it from Auntie Evie's point of view. You rush off to war leaving her to cope with the factory and then, when you come back, you're like a mardy child because she can't stay with you every minute of the day and hold your hand. Besides, she didn't know how to deal with you. How could she? You came back a different person from the man who went away. And then the only person you want is me! Just put yourself in her place for a minute. How must she have felt?'

'She should know I love her. That I've never loved anyone but her.'

Bridie leant forward and said gently, 'I know it's none of my business, but wasn't she hurt, years ago, by a young man she thought loved her? Didn't she trust him and he let her down?'

Richard nodded. 'Stephen Dunsmore. He lived here at Fairfield House.'

'How old was she?'

'Seventeen, I think.'

'The same age as I am now,' she said softly. 'But, you see, I'm lucky. I've never loved anyone – in that way – but Andrew. My only sadness is that he doesn't love me in return, but it doesn't – can't – stop me loving him. But don't you think that being let down like that at that age – the first big love of her life and he callously rejected her – don't you think it scars a young girl for the rest of her life? Do you think she can trust anyone completely ever again? Even you?'

He stared at her. 'Why,' he asked slowly, 'are you so very sensible?'

She laughed ruefully. 'I'm anything but sensible if I spend the whole of my life hankering after someone who doesn't love me.'

Richard made a sound deep in his throat – a sound that was suspiciously like a chuckle. 'If I'm not mistaken, Andrew is finding out that he does indeed love you – in that way, as you put it. Why else would he come looking to kill me? There was murder in his eyes yesterday, Bridie. And don't think I haven't seen that look far too often in the last few years not to be able to recognize it.'

'Then maybe I have something to thank my father for, after all. Only don't let his lies come between you and Auntie Evie. She's desperately unhappy. Every bit,' she added, 'as miserable as you look.'

'Where is she?'

'Down by the beck.'

He rose from the seat. 'I'll go to her.' He looked

down at her, then suddenly he bent and kissed her cheek. 'You're a great girl, Bridie. I just hope Andrew comes to his senses and realizes what a lucky chap, he is.'

Bridie giggled and blushed. 'So do I, Uncle Richard. So do I.'

'Are you coming with me?'

'No, no, you must talk to her on your own now. Besides . . .' She too rose. 'There's something else I have to do. I'm going to Pear Tree Farm, but I'll go round by the road.'

She stood on tiptoe and returned his kiss.

Eveleen waited by the beck, scarcely able to sit still on the rock by the flowing stream. Every few seconds she glanced back towards the yard of Fairfield House, praying that Richard would appear. But the minutes ticked by so slowly and she had begun to give up hope, tears welling in her eyes so that the sun glinting on the water blurred her vision. Impatiently she brushed her tears away and glanced up the field once more. This time she saw him coming towards her.

She was motionless, just staring at him, holding her breath. Then, halfway down the field, he held out his arms wide to her. Her heart began to thud and, with a little sob, she rose and began to run up the slope towards him.

Sixty-One

The yard at Pear Tree Farm seemed deserted. Only hens scratched about the place and the noise of pigs scuffling in the sty.

As Bridie pushed open the gate and stepped through it, the back door of the farmhouse opened and Mary came into the yard.

She flung her arms wide and gave a heartrending wail. 'Oh, Bridie, he's gone. My Jimmy. My Jimmy's gone away and left me again.'

Here we go again, Bridie thought, as she steered the weeping woman back into the house, pushed her gently into a chair and scurried between scullery and hearth, making her grandmother a strong, sweet cup of tea.

'There,' she said, placing it on the table at her side. 'Drink this and tell me what happened.'

She poured herself a cup and sat down to listen.

Mary took the cup in both hands and drank thirstily. She placed the cup down with shaking hands and leant back in her chair, closing her eyes and sighing deeply. 'When we got back from Flawford that day, he just disappeared upstairs. I was busy down here, getting his tea, but then he appeared with his kitbag and dressed in his naval uniform and announced that he was off. Back to sea. He said he was fully fit now and that if he didn't report back, the authorities were bound to come looking for him sooner or later, specially now that Fairfield

House had closed as a home. I tried to argue with him . . .' Her tears welled again, but she continued, 'I told him there was no need to go that very minute. I begged him to stay a little longer, but he was adamant. He said he had to go. "They'll come looking for me," he said. "I have to go."'

'Gran,' Bridie said gently, taking hold of her hands. 'I don't think it was the authorities he was worried about. Not really.'

Mary stared at her. 'Why? What do you mean?'

Bridie sighed. 'Whilst you were at Flawford talking to Great-Gran, he went looking for Andrew. He went looking to cause trouble. Again!'

'What sort of trouble?'

'He told Andrew that he thought Uncle Richard and me were having a love affair.'

Mary blinked and stared at her. 'How – why did he think that?'

'When Uncle Richard came home from the war, I seemed to be the only one who could help him. But there was nothing more than that between us. I promise you.'

To the girl's surprise, her grandmother snorted and said, 'Well, I know that, girl. I could have told him that. Richard's only ever loved Eveleen. Everyone knows that.' She thought a moment before saying slowly, 'So you think he believed Andrew would come looking for him?'

'Not only Andrew,' Bridie said wryly. 'Andrew went straight to Eveleen and, sadly, she believed him.'

'Eveleen did? The silly girl.'

'Then Richard came home and Andrew tackled him about it. He was dreadfully angry – and hurt. When Andrew came home yesterday and told me what had happened, I went to Nottingham this morning. Richard didn't go home last night and poor Auntie Evie was frantic. But I guessed he'd have come back to Fairfield House and he had. I've had a talk with him and they're together now.' She squeezed Mary's hands. 'Let's hope everything's getting sorted out between them right this minute.'

Mary nodded. 'Why on earth did Eveleen believe it? She must know how much Richard cares for her.'

'She was hurt years ago, wasn't she? I expect there's still a tiny part of her that is unsure. Always will be, probably. You've been very lucky, Gran. You've been loved by two wonderful men. You've never know what it is to be rejected by the man you love, have you?'

There was a silence in the room that seemed to go on and on until Mary said softly, 'Yes, I have, love. Oh yes, I have. At least, I thought so at the time. Now – well – now, I'm not so sure.'

Bridie had the sense to remain silent. She waited, willing her grandmother to tell her more, yet not wanting to press her. Doing so might have the opposite effect.

As dusk crept into the room and their faces were illuminated by the firelight, Mary began to talk.

'I fell in love with a young man when I was about your age. Desperately in love and, I thought, for ever. But his parents – and mine too, for that matter – did not approve. Then he went away and I found I was pregnant and that, to my family – my father and my brother, Harry – was the worst sin a woman could possibly commit. I thought that my young man had gone away deliberately, that he had deserted me when I needed him most. My family made my life hell and so I ran away. I worked wherever I could and I ended up here, working on the Dunsmore estate.' Her voice was flat and unemotional in the telling of her sorry tale, yet Bridie could feel the tragedy behind her words. 'I gave birth to my child in a ditch at the side of a field with only a gypsy woman to hold my hand. There in the dark and the cold, my baby died. I would have done too, if it hadn't been for your grandfather, Walter Hardcastle, who took me in and cared for me and eventually married me. Walter was a good man, a kind man. If it hadn't been for him, I don't know what would have become of me.'

She fell silent and now Bridie could not help asking, 'And your young man, your first love? Did you ever meet him again?'

Mary nodded and smiled, though the smile was tinged with sadness for her lost love. 'Oh yes, and according to him, he was deceived by his parents. He vows he never knew of my plight. They knew, of course, but he was only nineteen and when they sent him away to complete his education he obeyed, thinking that when he came back he would be of age and no-one could stop us marrying. But when he did return home, I had disappeared and he couldn't find me.'

'Do you believe him?'

Slowly Mary nodded. 'Yes, I do believe him. He's a good man, too. A fine man. Don't you think so?'

'Me?' Bridie was startled. 'How should I know?' She thought for a moment and then realization began to dawn. 'You mean – you mean, I *know* him?'

Mary nodded.

Then Bridie's face cleared. 'Oh, it's Josh. You found each other after all and . . .'

But her grandmother was shaking her head. 'No, no,

it wasn't Josh. Though he's a wonderful man and I'm a very lucky woman. No, my first love was the man who is now Eveleen's father-in-law. It was Brinsley Stokes.'

Bridie walked back to Fairfield House, her mind in a whirl at her grandmother's revelations. She had guessed something of the sort, though only part of it. She couldn't, of course, have guessed about the baby. Her mind reeled at the thought that Mary, of all people, should have had a child out of wedlock. And that Brinsley Stokes should have been the father. She tried to imagine them as young people, innocent and so in love. And the strands of their lives were still entwined all these years later, yet a lifetime of happiness together had been denied them.

She found Eveleen and Richard sitting on the sofa in what had been the patients' recreation room, their arms around each other. They looked up and smiled at her as she entered the room, but they did not move apart.

'Gran's in an awful state, Auntie Evie. My father's upped and gone again.'

'Oh no!' Evie buried her face against Richard's shoulder and then she looked up and sighed heavily. 'I'd better go to her.'

Bridie shook her head. 'I think the best thing you could do, Auntie Evie, is to get back to Nottingham as quickly as possible and tell Josh.'

Eveleen nodded. 'You're right.' She smiled and added pointedly, 'As always.'

As they rose from the sofa, Richard reminded them, 'We've two cars to drive back, you know. And we've to take Bridie back to Flawford.'

Flawford lay to the south of Nottingham and was a little out of the way of their direct route back to the city.

Eveleen thought for a moment and then said, 'You take Bridie and I'll go straight home to Josh.'

She noticed that Richard and Bridie glanced at each other and then they both stared at her.

'What? What's the matter?'

'Are you sure about that?' Richard asked, hardly able to keep the smile from twitching at the corner of his mouth, whilst Bridie grinned openly.

'Oh, you!' Eveleen said and held her arms wide to embrace both of them. The three of them stood together, their arms about each other, laughing and crying together. But now their tears were tears of joy.

It was late when Eveleen reached home, but Josh was still waiting up for her.

'I've been worried all evening. Smithers said you went off this morning very upset. Oh, Evie, it's not Mary, is it? Is she all right?'

'Sit down, Josh, and I'll tell you, but first let me ring for a cup of tea. I'm parched.'

She told him briefly that she and Richard had had a misunderstanding but that everything was fine now. Then gently she took his hands into hers. 'Josh, Jimmy's left and Mam's in a dreadful state.'

He pulled his hands from hers and levered himself up. 'Then I must go to her at once. Poor Mary. My poor, poor Mary. What a thoughtless lad that son of hers is.' He glanced down apologetically. 'Sorry, mi duck. I know he's your brother, but . . .'

'Don't apologize to me, Josh,' Eveleen said, with

feeling and hearing the tone of her voice, Josh looked puzzled.

Eveleen sighed. 'It was Jimmy who caused the trouble between me and Richard. He – he told Andrew that Richard was having an affair with Bridie. And, of course, Andrew came straight here.'

'He – said – what?' For a moment, Josh's face was like thunder. 'It's a good job he has gone, then 'cos at this moment I could break his bloody neck. How could he say a thing like that about our Bridie – or Richard, for that matter?'

'He's always liked causing trouble,' Eveleen said bitterly. 'Even as a young boy. It was like throwing a stone into a pond and watching the ripples, only Jimmy liked to do it with people's lives.'

'But his own daughter? How could he treat his own daughter like that?'

'I know, Josh. I know,' Eveleen said sadly. 'But he won't acknowledge that she is his.'

'Poor child,' Josh murmured but then added tartly. 'Mind you, I reckon she's better off without him, but mebbe she doesn't see it that way.'

'I'm not so sure now,' Eveleen said thoughtfully. 'If anything good has come out of all his lies and trouble-making, it's made Andrew see sense where Bridie's concerned. I don't think we need to worry about her any more. She's going to get what she's always wanted.' Her smiled broadened. 'Andrew.'

Josh smiled. 'That's all right, then.' Then his face sobered. 'But now I must get home to my Mary.'

'Tonight? But it's late, Josh. Won't you . . .' She did not finish the sentence for Josh was shaking his head emphatically. 'No, I must go to her now. Can you get Fred Martin to drive me back? I know it's late, but I'm not much of a driver at the best of times, Evie. I'll pay him, but I must get back to her. She'll need me now.' He needed to say no more. He was in such a state of anxiety himself that he was not safe to attempt to drive.

Eveleen stood up too. 'I'm sure he will. I'll send Smithers to Fred's straight away.' She stepped closer and put her arms as far round the big man's girth as she could. 'Do you know something, Josh Carpenter? I think you're one of the kindest men I know. It was my lucky day when I met you.'

Josh patted her shoulder and his voice shook a little as he said, 'And mine too, mi duck, and mine too.'

As Richard drew the motor car to a halt in the narrow street outside Singleton's Yard, he said, 'I won't come in, Bridie. It's late and I want to get home. But whilst we're alone I want to thank you for all you've done for me and I'm only sorry that my – my dependence on you has caused trouble for you.'

In the dusk, she smiled up at him. 'As long as you're well again and everything is all right between you and Auntie Evie, that's all that matters.'

'Not all, my dear. We want your happiness too, you know. You're very dear to both of us.'

'Well, I'm hoping I might have some good news for you soon. Wedding bells, you know.'

He clasped her hand and leant across the space between them to kiss her cheek. 'Good luck then, my dear little Bridie.'

Bridie climbed down and stood watching whilst he turned the motor around and drove off down the street. And if I'm not much mistaken, she was thinking as she waved him off, Auntie Evie might be giving you a bit of good news too very soon.

Smiling to herself, she opened the gate and stepped into the yard.

Sixty-Two

'I've been a bloody fool. Can you forgive me?'

Bridie wound her arms around Andrew's neck and smiled impishly up at him. 'I'll think about it.'

'So, when are we going to be married?'

'Well!' she exclaimed and stood back. 'If that isn't the most unromantic proposal a girl ever had.'

'Oh, Bridie, I'm sorry.' He ran his hand nervously through his hair.

Bridie chuckled and hugged him. 'I'm only teasing you. Of course, we'll be married as soon as possible. If only to stop the gossips,' she joked.

'Who do I ask for permission? Your grandfather?'

Her smile faded and she straightened up. Sadly she said, 'I wish it was. Oh, how I wish it was. But he still doesn't want anything to do with me, does he?' She sighed. 'My own father won't acknowledge me and nor will my grandfather.'

Andrew touched her cheek and said softly, 'I'll make it up to you, darling Bridie.'

She held his hand to her cheek. 'I know you will . . .' she hesitated.

'But it's not the same for you, is it, love?'

Tears were close as she shook her head and whispered. 'I'm sorry, but no, it isn't. It isn't my father so much. Now I've met him and see him for what he really is, well, he's smashed those particular dreams, but – but – it's grandfather I really care about now. If only . . .'

'Maybe in time, he'll come around.'

'Maybe,' she said, but the doubt was evident in her tone.

'I tried,' Andrew told her later the following day.

'What did he say?'

Andrew bit his lip, reluctant to tell her but Bridie was insistent.

'He – he said the same old thing. That he has no granddaughter.'

There was a lump in her throat as she whispered, 'I expected as much.' But still, deep inside her, there was a little spark of hope that refused to die completely.

Over the weeks that followed she planned her wedding.

'I shall come,' her great-grandmother said. 'Ne'er mind what Harry ses, I'll be there, Bridie. Someone'll have to take me across to the chapel in a bath chair, but I'll be there.'

'I'm counting on it, Great-Gran.'

'Who are you asking to give you away?'

'I – I haven't asked anyone yet. But I suppose it'll have to be Josh, because Uncle Richard is to be Andrew's best man.'

'You're still hoping that old fool will come round, aren't you? Well, don't waste yer life wishing, love.'

Bridie turned away. She knew her great-grandmother was right. They were all right. And yet . . .

*

It was three weeks before the day of her wedding, when Bridie was passing the door of her grandfather's cottage as she returned from the village shop, that she heard a huge crash from inside and the smashing of crockery. At once she dumped her bags on the ground and opened the door to find Harry struggling to get up from the floor. She hurried to his side to help him.

'Grandfather, what happened? Are you hurt?'

His trembling hands reached out in front of him to grasp hold of something – anything.

'Sit down in the chair,' she ordered.

He shuffled backwards, allowing her to guide him now. Then, fumbling, he found her arms and grasped them so strongly that she almost cried out in pain. 'Bridie . . .' he gasped, clinging to her like a drowning man. 'Bridie – I can't see. I can't see anything.'

She stared at him for a moment, but already she could see that his eyes, though wide open, were seeing nothing. He was staring ahead, but he was unable to focus. He could not see her. He could not see anything.

She wriggled from his grasp and then took hold of his hands in hers. 'It's all right, Grandfather. I'll get the doctor. Maybe it's only temporary. You'll be all right . . .'

He shook his head. 'No, no, I won't. My sight's been getting worse and now it's gone altogether.' Tears were now pouring from his sightless eyes, down his wrinkled cheeks and into his beard. 'I'm blind, Bridie, I'm blind.'

She put her arms around the big man and held him close, whilst he laid his head against her breast and wept.

*

Three weeks later Bridie stood in the spare bedroom of her great-grandmother's cottage before the speckled mirror and stared at the stranger reflected there.

Behind her, Eveleen, her voice choked with emotion, said, 'You look beautiful, Bridie. The most beautiful bride I've ever seen.'

'I wish Grandfather could see me today,' Bridie murmured.

Eveleen smiled, determined not to let her brood. Not today of all days. 'Come along. It's time you were going. Andrew's waiting for you. And Richard's with him. They've all gone across to the chapel. Even your great-grandmother, riding like a queen in her bath chair. They're all waiting for you – Gran, Josh, Mrs Turner, even Mr Stokes. They're all there, all except . . .' They exchanged a look and then Eveleen added, 'But I'll be there to help you. I'll be just behind you.'

Bridie nodded, unable to speak for the lump in her throat, willing herself not to cry as she carefully descended the stairs.

As she stepped out of the cottage, she stopped and gave a little gasp of surprise when she saw the man waiting at the end of the pathway; a tall, broad-shouldered man, resplendent in a morning suit, his face turned towards them.

Bridie glanced at her aunt, the question she dare not voice aloud written in her wide eyes. Eveleen was smiling, tears in her own eyes as she said, 'Yes, my darling, he's waiting for you, too.'

Bridie, her knees trembling, walked towards him, the beautiful white lace train of her wedding dress trailing behind her, her trembling fingers clutching the bouquet she carried. As she reached him, she put her hand on his arm and whispered softly, 'Here I am.' And in a voice that was a little unsteady from the joy in her heart she asked, 'Are you ready to give me away?'

'I'm ready,' Harry Singleton said, his voice husky with emotion. 'I'm ready – Granddaughter.'